AT THE POINT OF A SWORD!

Bronwyn had limped only a dozen yards up the path when a Guard stepped from within a crevice. His dull black captain's uniform had hidden him well. Now he looked like a scorpion blocking her path, brandishing his saber like a stinger. She evaded his quick lunge but in stepping back, Bronwyn missed her footing and fell. Instantly the Guard was on her.

He put both hands around the hilt of his weapon. The point pressed deeply into the soft depression at the base of her throat. "All right, Princess. Give me the package," he demanded, "or die . . ."

PALACES AND PRISONS

R. MILNIKOV, del.

BRONWYN

PALACES AND PRISONS

RON MILLER

ACE BOOKS, NEW YORK

This book is an Ace original edition,
and has never been previously published.

PALACES AND PRISONS

An Ace Book / published by arrangement with
the author

PRINTING HISTORY
Ace Edition / August 1991

ISBN: 0-441-64687-5

Ace Books are published by The Berkley Publishing Group,
200 Madison Avenue, New York, New York 10016.
The name "ACE" and the "A" logo
are trademarks belonging to Charter Communications, Inc.

PRINTED IN THE UNITED STATES OF AMERICA

10 9 8 7 6 5 4 3 2 1

THIS BOOK IS FOR PATRICIA—
A Perfect Princess
—With Love

. . . on the Bridge of Sighs,
A palace and a prison on each hand.
—LORD BYRON
Childe Harold's Pilgrimage

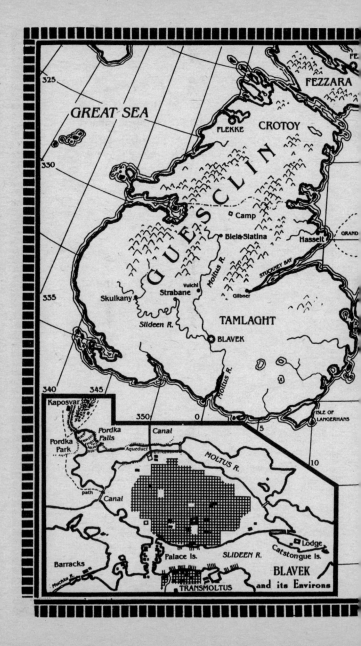

THE RESCUE

IF IT HAD NOT BEEN for the strong arm of Thud Mollockle, the Princess Bronwyn would today be languishing in some unknown and mossy dungeon, had she been allowed to remain alive at all.

Thud was a sarcophagus-maker for a stonecutting firm in the Transmoltus district of Blavek. He worked without assistance in a large, low-ceilinged ground-floor room. Directly above him were the studios of the more skilled stonecarvers, who worked on Church and private commissions. They provided more than a third of the city's architectural decorations: caryatids, capitals, friezes, pediments, cherubim, urns, bas-reliefs and portrait busts, among many other standard and commissioned items. Dust—fine, white and talclike—filtered through the wide spaces between the boards that formed the stonecarvers' floor and Thud's ceiling. When the afternoon or morning sun beamed in through either the southeast or southwest windows this ever-present lithic miasma was illuminated with a milky glow that made it almost impossible to see one end of the shop from the other. Thud was probably doomed to a lingering death from silicosis since he had begun working at the age of six and was now thirty-two. Still, he just as certainly would have thought it unnatural to breathe an atmosphere composed of anything other than ten percent oxygen, fifty percent nitrogen and forty percent marble. All day long Thud could hear above his head the ceaseless, fussy *tink*, *tink*, *tink* of sharp steel chisels.

Thud's workroom was occupied by Thud and perhaps a dozen rectangular blocks of stone, the color of oxidized potatoes. These averaged about four feet thick, about the same in width, and five or six feet in length. It was Thud's job to hollow them out. When finished, each solid mass of stone was transformed into something resembling a deep, uncomfortable-looking bathtub. These were sent upstairs to the stonecarving departments where it became the job of, normally, junior stonecarvers to decorate the four sides of the sarcophagi with appropriately funereal decorations. Meanwhile, the great slabs of the lids were being prepared else-where—a small subdepartment of the firm being devoted to just this one product. There was a known and steady demand. Even-tually some merchant or politician would have his mortal remains sealed within one of these stone cocoons, where it could safely moulder away, decomposing decently out of sight and memory.

What became of his vast stone basins is a question that very seldom troubled Thud, whose skull resembled his raw material to a striking degree; in density, at least, if not in form.

The stoneworking firm of Groontocker and Peen was never, during working hours, a particularly quiet place. An ancient frame building that filled an entire irregularly shaped city block, it was divided into five floors or, rather, for the most part, vast open lofts. More than one hundred and twenty artisans worked in them, and not one of them worked at anything that did not make noise. Mallets struck chisels, chisels struck stone, stone struck floor, rasps abraded marble and granite, winches and pul-leys screeched under their massive loads, drills bored holes into resisting stone with a sound that made teeth whimper in empathy. To all of this the old building vibrated sympathetically like the sounding-box of a guitar; all day long it hummed and throbbed and groaned. Nevertheless, as the Transmoltus is a district of industry, Groontocker and Peen was a comparative island of serenity; try as it may, its contribution to the general din was almost negligible. The building of the stoneworking firm was crowded by its neighbors, vast and ancient piles of frame or brick or stone all stained alike by the oleaginous soot that made the atmosphere of the Transmoltus unique. Only lightless cobbled paths snaked among the buildings. These were filled with a chaos of carts and vans; trolleys and trucks; people with baskets, boxes and bundles. The sound had nowhere to go: the squealing of axles, the rumble of iron tires on stone, and the shouting of peddlers, merchants and angry drivers who should have known better than to have been in a hurry in the Transmoltus in the first place. From the surrounding buildings came unearthly noises, few of them identifiable except by the very knowledgeable or excessively imaginative, but all of them unpleasant. High, sustained shrieks that made one's head feel as though it were being threaded on an endless steel wire; bass moans that made the lower intestine shudder weirdly; and resonating *bongs* that sounded as though boilers were being dropped a full story onto hard ground—which, in this instance, was just what was happening. Directly opposite the one large open window in Thud's workshop that faced the main thoroughfare were the open windows of a vitally active, mechanized factory: the belts that ran the great heckling machines within screamed and buzzed and occasionally cracked like whips; the machines themselves clattered, smacked, knocked, clicked, clacked, thumped, plumped, popped, whirred, banged, rustled, droned, drummed, hummed, trilled, rang, jingled, and hissed. Thud had no idea what heckling machines actually made, other than noise. In fact, Thud did not even know that there were such things as heckling machines. However, all of this unholy, brain-numbing, bone-rattling din was only a background murmur to anyone who had grown up among it. Thud was no more consciously aware of the stormy sea of vibration that washed over him, like a tsunami over an innocent tropical islet, than any one of us might be of the ticking of a clock, the song of the cricket or bird, or the beating of our own hearts.

Which all goes to show why it was not surprising that Thud heard the princess.

Or, rather, he heard the armed men who were close behind her. Shouting and a single pistol shot drew Thud away from his work and to the open window. Just as he thrust his head into the full sonic fury of the heckling machines, he saw a girl turn the corner and pause just below him. She looked like one of the rats that Thud occasionally cornered in his shop: completely out of wind, head twitching side to side, looking for an escape that didn't exist. The girl was cornered just as effectively as one of the rats, too. On her right was the vast, unbroken wall of Groontocker and Peen; ahead she was faced by the equally unbroken wall of the factory that housed the mysterious heckling machines. Unbroken at least

so far as the girl's immediate needs required, since the only
windows were far above her head. To her left was the entrance
to the alleyway from which she had just appeared. The streets in
both directions were plugged by a nearly impassable logjam of
human bodies and vehicles. Once caught in that writhing mass
she would have been ground to dust, like a stone in a lapidary's
tumbler.

Thud would have been hard put to explain his next action,
as he would have been hard put to explain anything he did.
Thud was a creature of action, if absolutely necessary; not one
of introspection, which was never necessary. He certainly wasn't
moved by the girl's appearance, since all he could see of her was
the top of her head. He always felt sorry once he had trapped
the rats in his shop: he hated the way they looked at him just
before he hit them with his mallet. He was always tempted to
let them go, though he didn't dare or they would bite his ankles
and steal his already meager lunches. He felt much the same way
about the creature he saw beneath his window—and here was a
chance to make amends to hundreds of mashed rats. "Hey! Girl!"
he shouted down at her. She looked up, twitching like a startled
cat, and saw dangling before her a knotted, brown, ropy, hairy,
scarred thing: something like a tree root and something like a big
sausage: Thud's arm. "Come on, grab hold!" The girl, without
a moment's hesitation, did so and was whisked into the window
as though she had been a handkerchief Thud had been waving at
some departing acquaintance.

Thud now saw what lay below the thatch of hair he had
been staring down upon only a moment before. It was indeed
a girl, as he had suspected. Immediately below the hair, which
was just shoulder length and colored a dark auburn, like oiled
mahogany, was a face lean from fright and exhaustion. Very large
bottle-green eyes, slightly and unusually slanted, were dilated
from fright and the sudden darkness. These were framed by
rather thick peaked eyebrows, each as elegant and eloquent as
a Chinaman's brushstroke. Her face, initially red from exertion,
was now taking on an equally unnatural parchmentlike tint. It was
roundish, with prominent cheekbones slanting toward the corners
of her wide mouth. The face looked to Thud like one of the cold
alabaster busts from the third floor. Her nose was long, rather
thin and ever so slightly convex. She looked older than she was,
though there was no way then Thud could have known that. In
fact, she was young: seventeen or perhaps eighteen. She was tall,

though Thud would never have described her that way; from his mountainous viewpoint, *everyone* was short. Her legs were long, comprising more than half of her not inconsiderable height. She was slim-hipped, small-breasted and rather snakily lithe-looking. She clutched a battered leather satchel to her chest, held in place there by a stout strap that crossed her breast diagonally. She wore a long-sleeved, ankle-length dress of a fine cloth that, though torn and bedraggled, still looked more elegant than anything else Thud had ever seen.

What had suddenly appeared before the girl she did not recognize immediately as something human. Something more like a bull, perhaps; it was very bull-like, though it had something bearlike about it, too. As well as oxlike, or even like a walrus a bit, but a lot more like a gorilla. With a sudden inspiration she thought of an enormous loaf of bread with clothes on. She imagined such a loaf nearly seven feet high, with four additional loaves for arms and legs; she thought that, in color, texture, shape and general overall impression, the simile was fairly accurate. A muffin was balanced somewhere near the top: a currant muffin, since a pair of black dots were staring at her.

The baked-goods-man image was so perfect she almost couldn't believe it when the muffin spoke to her. "Somebody chasing you?" it asked, and the girl could only nod. "Somebody real bad? You scared?" She nodded again and jumped away from the window with a gasp, as the voices of her pursuers reached her. They were rough, supercilious voices and they were commanding the street people to tell them where the girl had gone. But in the few seconds that had passed, the people in the alleyways had been completely replaced: they weren't the same ones who had been there when a girl was lifted through the window by an arm like a tree root (or loaf of braided bread).

"They're coming!" she cried, and there followed the sounds of crashing doors, stamping feet and muffled shouts of command and protest, vindicating the accuracy of her observation.

"All right, then," Thud said, pointing to a spot on the floor. "Curl up there, like a ball."

"What?" said the girl curtly, not understanding and, even in the throes of a precarious situation, finding herself bristling at being given such a peremptory order. "Hurry! Sit down there— curl up, like a ball." Puzzled, the girl sat on the snowy floor and hugged her knees. She did as she was told, in spite of her lack of practice and inclination in doing that, though she would not have understood why. Since the big man was not shouting "Here she is!" or trying to arrest her, which he could have done with one hand, he couldn't be up to anything much worse. She watched with amazement as the huge creature picked up one of the massive sarcophagi, seemingly without effort, and lumbered over to where she sat. "Be real quiet, now!" he said, and upturned the stone coffin on her.

The girl was plunged into profound darkness before she even realized what the big man's intention was. She felt trapped, as one of Thud's rats might have felt if a bowl had been dropped over it. Panic reared up in her, its waxen, sweaty face urging her to please become hysterical. Only a second ago she had been out in the bright, noisy street, running for her life. Now she was caught in a trap as dark and silent as a nightmare. The transition was bewildering and disorienting. Had she been offered the two as options, she would have considered them fairly well-matched choices. What if he left her here? She could never lift the block of stone, and there must only be a few minutes' worth of air within its cavity. What if he forgot about her? He hadn't looked very bright. What if they arrested him, and took him away before he could tell them where she was? What if they shot him, and he died with her hiding place bubbling on his bloody lips? How many months or years would it be before someone decided to move the big block of marble, discovering to their horror and mystification her decomposed or even mummified body? She could visualize herself transformed into a kind of monkeylike caricature sculpted in jerky. Perhaps it would be a fate better than the one that awaited her otherwise. Her head pressed against the bottom of the sarcophagus, which was barely wide enough for her shoulders. Her prison was roomy enough longitudinally, however, so that she could stretch out her legs, and she leaned against the back wall. The stone was cool and moist, and she gratefully pressed her face against it. It smelled cool and earthy, like fresh mushrooms. She rolled her head and when her ear came into contact with the stone, she could hear voices. Simultaneously, she felt the floorboards vibrating with heavy footsteps.

The voices are muffled, but they are those of the Guards, for sure. They are demanding the girl. The big man asks, *What girl?* (*Good man!* she thinks, immediately following this generosity with a less kind thought: *What if he really* has *forgotten that I'm here? Maybe this isn't an act!*)

There's a girl hiding in this building, the Guard replies.

Who? the giant asks.

That's none of your business! replies the Guard.

It isn't?

No, it's not!

That's fine. She could hear the big man starting to chisel on a stone.

Stop that!

All right.

Look, have you seen anyone?

Where? asks the big man.

We *don't know*, replies the Guard. *We're asking you*.

What? rejoinders the big man, anxious to help. The Guard calls him an idiot and orders his men to search the room. There is a great deal of noise, which ceases presently. The floor vibrates again from the weight of the armed men, followed by a long silence. Long enough that the girl begins to have renewed fears about suffocation and entombment—and imagination though it might be, it was becoming extremely difficult to breathe.

The sarcophagus gave a groan and a line of bright light suddenly appeared where it had met the floor. It was dazzling to the girl's eyes and she squeezed them shut against the pain of rapidly constricting irises. When she opened them a second later, the great block of stone was gone from around her. It was in the arms of Thud, who was setting it down a few feet away, with a thud of its own. It was only at that moment that the girl realized what the big man had done: overturned, the hollowed-out block looked exactly like the solid, unworked cubes that ponderously littered the room. It would have strained anyone's imagination to have suspected that a girl was *inside* one of them. And the Guards were notorious for lacking that useful mental faculty. It did not occur to her (and least of all to Thud) that the ploy had been a pretty astute one for someone of Thud's obvious limitations.

The big man turned to her with his forefinger upraised to his lips in the sign for silence. He crouched down near her, folding up on invisible joints like a collapsing blimp (or a failed soufflé, to maintain the earlier culinary similes). Seen from a distance of only three feet or so, Thud's face was a marvel to the girl. She had never seen anything even vaguely similar to it; what gradually amazed her was that she *liked* it. The head was as smooth, round and featureless as a mushroom; the mouth was a slit so wide that the entire top of the head threatened to hinge over backwards whenever he grinned—an action that served to expose a pink cavern full of gnarled yellow stalactites and stalagmites, behind which lurked a restless, scarlet tongue, like a fretful blindworm. His eyes, socketless like a mole's, were bright black beads nearly a hand's-span apart. Roughly between them was a kind of lump that might have been a nose or might have been a wart. Thud by all rights ought to have been monumentally ugly, though he wasn't. It is difficult to explain why, and, in all the time to come that she was to know him, the girl certainly never even considered trying; but perhaps it was because the face radiated an uncomplicated *kindness* the way a burning coal fills a hearth with warmth.

"Please," whispered Thud, "be very quiet. Those men were looking for you, weren't they?"

"Yes."

"What did you do that made them so mad?"

"I *haven't* done anything!" She lied, but Thud did not know that, yet.

"That's good."

"I can't stay here!"

"Oh, sure, they might be back, all right."

"But I can't leave, either."

"They'd spot you in a minute," agreed Thud.

"I have to get out of the city! I must!"

"I bet," agreed Thud.

There was a silence between them, since there wasn't much that could be said after that; the conversation was going nowhere. The girl's sadness lacerated Thud's heart because he had no idea what he could do to relieve it. His great hands wrestled with one another, like a pair of small dogs roughhousing. The girl looked up at him with eyes that were like the peal of bronze bells. An idea squirmed its way to the forefront of Thud's consciousness, where his mind's eye blinked at it in unexpected and unfamiliar realization of his genius.

"I can get you out of the city," he said.

"You can? How? When?"

"I can't tell you. I'll have to show you how."

"Thank Musrum!"

"It's a way I used when I was a kid"—a mental image that the girl found impossible to create—"but you've got to get out of here first." Thud rose to his feet and went over to the big window with the kind of ponderous grace a cow affects, and occasionally achieves. He leaned out over the sill and gave a good, long, hard look in both directions and then returned to the girl, still with the unhurried deliberateness of the truly bovine.

"There're Guards in the street. They're likely all around the place. If I can get you out of the shop, I can get you home. It'll be easy from there."

From his workbench, Thud selected a large chisel, nearly as long as the girl's arm, with a blade as sharp as a razor. It winked at her conspiratorially in the windowlight. Thud jammed its cutting edge into a chink between two of the wide floorboards and bore down upon the opposite end. The board lifted with a protesting screech. Moving down its length, he repeated the action two or three times until an entire ten-foot-long slab of thick lumber had been pried from its moorings. Rusty spikes hung down from the moldy underside. A hundred annoyed spiders dropped from it and scurried for cover. Thud got down on his hands and knees and dropped his head into the rectangular hole. He looked up and said, "Come on, this way!" as spiderwebs floated from his face, and a small insect, panicked, disappeared over the curve of his head like an arthropodal Magellan.

The girl looked into the hole with extreme distaste. She imagined a thousand unwinking little eyes looking back at her. "In there?" she asked, unnecessarily.

"Please," the giant begged. She reminded herself that there were worse alternatives. She had seen some of them. In fact, it was just because she knew that there were worse things than a damp hole, slimy with grey fungus and alive with invertebrate *things*, that she had been forced to flee, and that was why she climbed down into the darkness after only that single moment's hesitation. She left shreds of her rumpled dress festooning the splintery edges of the narrow slot, which was perhaps just an inch less wide than it should have been. Whether or not she thought of it, the girl ought to have been grateful for her boyish silhouette. The earth was only about three feet below the floor. It was covered with a kind of grey-green gruel of mud, decomposing wood and the dust of limestone and marble. Her feet sank into it until her ankles were buried. It sucked at her feet when she tried to lift them. She looked up at the gargoyle face that hovered over her head, round and pale and grinning, like a moon. "Turn around and crawl," it said. "You'll see a little bit of light. Head for that. When you get to it, stay there. Wait for me."

"But . . ." she began.

"Please hurry!" he said, and she had to duck as he replaced the plank over her head. A dozen sharp blows rained dust and crawling things down upon her as Thud reset the nails. It was absolutely dark, with the exception of the thin lines of light between the floorboards. They receded from her in either direction like an elementary exercise in perspective. They striped her body so that she looked like a topographic map of an adolescent girl. She turned around and saw the patch of grimy-looking daylight that Thud mentioned. It looked about a mile away where the endless lines of light met. She made certain that her leather bag was strapped tightly across her chest and began crawling toward the glimmer. On all fours her legs were covered with the glutinous slime halfway up her thighs and, worse, up to her elbows. Each time her hands sank into the sediment she could feel it writhe. Her dress, already ragged, clung to her like papier-mâché. Half sliding, half crawling, accompanied by sounds very much like a cow sucking on its cud, she made her way toward her goal, such as it was. The squarish satchel on her chest acted like an anchor, dragging in the slime, dredging up malodorous bubbles that burst flatulently beneath her nose.

She discovered that the light was an opening between the floor level of the building and the cobbled alleyway. The opening had been created to act as an outlet for the drainage of moisture from beneath the building. It was working as intended and a stream of tepid, mucus-streaked fluid leaked from the opening; it then flowed over the cobbles into the central channel that drained the alley. She tried to straddle the flow, but it ran over one ankle and a hand, and within inches of her nose, which, not for the first time in her life, she wished was not so long. She tried not to think of any of the several possible sources of the liquid.

Keeping her head within the shadow of the hole, she peered as far into the street as she dared. One black-armored Guard stood at the entrance to the main thoroughfare to her right (the street Thud's large window overlooked), and another Guard had just turned the corner to her left, walking in her direction. She withdrew further into the darkness. The Guard, attracted perhaps by a hint of her movement, a shadow within a shadow, or noticing a possible hiding place previously overlooked, came toward her. She had no place to go where she wouldn't be able to see her if he bent down and looked into the opening. The Guard came within a few feet, drew his saber, and began to squat down on his haunches, turning his head so that he would be able to see into the hole, trying to minimize his proximity to the fetid drool issuing from it. The girl felt her stomach wrench with the expectation of immediate capture when something warm and furry scuttled over her legs with icy little feet. A rat the size of a pampered housecat brushed under her nose, its cold, naked tail giving her lips a snide fillip as it headed for the street. It ran out between the Guard's legs, who leaped erect with a cry of disgust. He struck at the rat with his blade, drawing a spatter of sparks from the pavement, but the animal disappeared into the jungle of crates, ashcans, and garbage with a supercilious chuckle.

The Guard flung a curse at the vanished animal and continued on his way. The girl thanked Musrum for rats. A shadow fell over the opening once again, and again she shrank from it. This time a familiar voice husked, "Girl? Are you there?"

She cautiously poked her head into the open air. Thud stood there, towering over her like a captive balloon. He held a large, stained canvas bag in such a way that it shielded the girl's hiding place from the two Guards at the end of the alley. He was busily picking up bits of broken wood and tossing them into the bag.

"They looked in the bag when I came in the alley and they've watched me all the way. They think I'm just getting firewood."

The girl crawled out of the hole and into the protective screen created by the bag. Thud casually bent to wrench a slat from the side of a fruit crate. As he placed his foot against the box to brace it, he let the near edge of the bag drop free. It fell to the cobbles, making a yard-wide circular opening. From the point of view of the Guards, the bag remained unchanged. The girl needed no prompting to catch onto the idea and scuttled into the bag instantly. Thud tossed the broken wood on top of her and moved on down the street. The entire act had taken but a moment and there had not been even a second's suspicious hesitation in Thud's movements. He stopped twice more, piling more scrap into his sack for realism's sake, waved to the Guards, who good-humoredly waved back at the enormous half-wit, and disappeared around the corner.

The next ten minutes were not the most unpleasant the girl had ever experienced—little, she suspected, could have been nastier than the crawl through the darkness under the stonecutters'. However, they were more painful. Thud had been overzealously conscientious in his attempt at appearing casual and had tossed in the firewood with an abandon that had left the girl with more than one bruise and abrasion. Now as he strode along with the bag hanging against his back the girl wondered if it was ever going to be possible to sort herself out from the scrap. The contents of the bag were being stirred into a kind of aggregate girl-lumber. She was almost upside down, knees pressed to her nose; the bag, none too roomy, squeezed her like a large bunny being digested by a small but ambitious boa constrictor. Soon enough, the character of the bouncing changed and she guessed that they were ascending a flight of stairs. Several flights, from the time that passed. The bag slammed against a wall, first on the right and then on the left, and the girl hazarded a protesting kick into the small of Thud's back. The jouncing stopped, there was a rasping squeal, another jostle, a blow against the back of her head, and the bag was set onto a floor. She looked out of its opening in time to see the big man closing the door through which they had just passed. When he turned he saw her climbing from the sack, all akimbo.

"Are you all right?" he asked. She immediately thought of replying *no*, an answer that her bruises, scratches and imbedded splinters argued for persuasively. But she saw that the ugly man was in earnest; he hadn't asked casually: he was truly concerned. To have replied in the negative would have been cruel; petty as well, since she was alive and *that* certainly was all right. What were bruises compared to what she knew could have happened to her?

"Yes, I'm fine!" she answered, gladly, pleased when she saw the worry wiped from his face by one of his amazing grins.

The room she found herself in was obviously the big man's home. It was no larger than a big closet, perhaps ten feet by twelve or so. Which left little enough room to spare when the big man was at home. There was not a right angle in it; the ceiling and walls sloped together into compound angles that made the girl guess, correctly as it happened, that the room was tucked into the attic of a building. Thick wooden beams criss-crossed through it, emerging from the walls, disappearing into the ceiling. The walls had once been plastered; that had mostly fallen off, leaving leprous, lath-boned holes. Thud had attempted to improve on the dreary appearance this gave his home by pasting over the holes with woodcuts and chromolithographs torn from the illustrated papers. He was pleased, but this really only succeeded in making the room look shabbier, possibly because the woodcuts were never quite the right size or shape to entirely cover the plasterless craters. Instead, the walls looked like they had been partially made of papier-mâché. No matter. The floor was of bare planks, but very clean. In one corner was Thud's bed: a pair of large canvas bags, like the one he had carried the girl in, sewn mouth to mouth and filled with straw. A plain little table and a chair to match (which seemed altogether incapable of dealing with Thud's immense behind) completed the major furnishings. What little else there was is quickly listed: a curtain over the single window, washed and scrubbed to colorlessness and near-transparency; a small wood-burning stove made from a discarded iron keg (in which Thud was now starting a fire); a wooden crate nailed to a wall that acted as both cupboard and pantry; a little oil stove on the table, next to a cracked, handleless cup filled with dirt from which sprang a twiglike plant with a single leaf; and, centered on one of the trapezoidal walls, a lone tintype photograph, surrounded by pictures of flowers, some of them gaudy chromolithographs cut from the papers, others laboriously hand-colored. The silvery picture was a portrait of a pretty, thin-faced girl who looked not very much older than Thud's foundling—except for the sad eyes; those looked very old.

This made the girl think of her own appearance, and she looked down at herself. Her dress was plastered to her body by mud and filth; it was as heavy and clammy as if it were made of clay. It was ragged, one sleeve gone altogether, and huge rents were torn down either side. The petticoats beneath made a solid, sodden mass. She had only one shoe. She touched her hair and could have cried: it felt like cold, boiled spinach.

Thud was busy at the little table. He had pumped up the pressure in the oil stove, and it was now topped with a hissing blue flame. He was filling a battered tin pot with water from an unglazed ceramic jug. He had opened some cans and small packets.

"Would you like something to eat? I'm making some hot tea, if you'd like that."

"Yes! And I want some of that water. I've got to wash my face."

"Sure, here. You want more hot water so you can clean up?"

"That'd be wonderful! I'll be able to think clearly once I've gotten some of this filth off me," she said, scrubbing at her face with the offered cup of plain water and a piece of coarse cloth that came with it. "What's your name?"

"Me? Oh. My name's Thud. Mollockle. Thud Mollockle."

"It's a pleasure to have met you, Thud. My name is . . . Bronwyn."

"I am pleased to know you, too, Bronwyn."

The room was quickly warming up, for which she was grateful; she wrapped herself in a threadbare blanket Thud handed her.

"I'm afraid that I have gotten you into a lot of trouble, Thud. Small enough thanks for saving my life, I suppose."

"Me?" He seemed to have continuous difficulty believing that anyone was addressing him personally. "No, no trouble. You needed help. And I hate the Guards."

Bronwyn looked at him sharply, surprised and interested in the sudden bitterness with which the otherwise placid man had spoken those last five words. He seemed to sense the alteration in the girl's attention. It embarrassed him.

"I'll get you that water for your bath—you must feel terrible. There's hot tea, now, and some food here. Please, help yourself. I'll be right back." And before Bronwyn could say another word, he was gone. The door opened and shut so quickly it was barely able to utter a surprised "Eek!" She stepped over to the table and suddenly realized how weak she was. Her legs nearly collapsed under her like a stringectomied marionette's and a wave of vertigo swept over her, leaving her eyes momentarily unfocussed. She fell gratefully into the chair. She picked up the thick mug of steaming tea; it was like cupping a kitten in her hands, it felt so wonderfully soothing. She held it up to her face and let the fragrant vapors caress her cheeks, nose and eyes. The heat made her nose start to run.

When Thud returned, she was eating one of his fat, stale soda crackers and a slice of potted meat. He was carrying a pair of enormous buckets, each holding at least ten or fifteen gallons of steaming water. He set them on the floor heavily and said, "I'll be right back." A moment later, there came sounds like the bonging of a giant cowbell from beyond the door, which burst open revealing the vast dorsal view of Thud. He backed into the room, pulling in after him a battered tin tub. Dropping it with an unresonant clang in the middle of the room, he circled it to close the door. There was now not a square inch of floor left unaccounted for. Still without a word, he poured the contents of the buckets into the tub. The water was still so hot it fizzed as it splashed onto the metal.

"You had better take your bath while the water's hot," Thud said. "It'll get cold real quick."

Bronwyn was taken aback for a moment, as she realized that Thud meant for her to take her bath right there and then. A word of chiding protest came to her lips but died there aborning, when she looked into the ridiculous round face and saw nothing but kindness and a concern so earnest and gentle. It was an unkind but natural thought that taking a bath in front of Thud would be not unlike taking a bath in front of a pet dog. Natural and probably quite accurate. She was suddenly overbrimming with fatigue and every bruise and muscle in her body gave a single throb in unison. She stood up from the chair and took but one step toward the tub before she started to topple.

Thud was beside her in an instant and supporting her by one hand with the firm gentleness that always seemed so impossible for him. With the other he peeled the nearly disintegrating dress from her like the skin from a scalded tomato. Finished, he slipped his free hand behind her knees and lifted her into the tub. The water felt boiling at first and she cried out weakly. Thud ignored her; soon she felt as though she were dissolving into the steam that boiled up around her. She could feel herself turning bright red as blood that had withdrawn deep within her rushed back into her skin.

A hand, rough as leather, touched her on the shoulder and carefully leaned her forward, until her nose nearly touched the water. Using handfuls of crude soap, scooped from a wooden tub, Thud began scrubbing her body. In her previous life Bronwyn would rather have died than put anything on her skin like this corrosive, abrasive, raw substance. Now it felt like cream. Anything would have felt better than the unspeakable filth and slime that covered her. Thud's soap was pungent and clean-smelling. A day's worth of dirt washed from her, a day's worth of pain, and many weeks of fear and anger. She felt herself drifting; the firm massaging was hypnotic. She felt safe and, for the first time in months, as though she might have some hope in carrying out her mission.

"Hold your nose," Thud said; he pushed her face under the surface of the water. The heat pressed against the lids of her sore eyes and it stung wonderfully. She lifted her head from the water, streamlets pouring in a circle around her downturned face. Thud worked a handful of the raw soap into her hair. His thick fingers kneaded her scalp as though it were a ball of dough.

Bronwyn had long since passed into a kind of reverie. She had no recollection of Thud lifting her from the bath, holding her by passing an arm behind her back while he rubbed her dry with a coarse, brown cloth until she was as pink as a shrimp. He wrapped her in ragged, patched blankets until she looked like a fat, hand-rolled cigar, then laid her so gently onto his straw pallet that it scarcely rustled. She had long since fallen asleep.

Night had meanwhile fallen over the city of Blavek, and Thud had had to finish his work on Bronwyn by the light of a single tallow candle. When he was done, he picked this up, not minding the molten pearls of wax that ran over his fingers. Carrying the candle over to the tintype portrait, surrounded by its field of gaudy flowers, he looked for a long moment at the silvery face that seemed so alive in the flickering candlelight. Leaning forward slightly, he kissed it, just once, just so.

Blowing out the candle, he crossed the lightless room. Only the grey square of the window relieved the darkness. He sat in the small wooden chair under the window, beside the table, and stared into the room for a long time before he, too, fell asleep.

2

THE ESCAPE

THE CITY OF BLAVEK WAS more than the seat of Tamlaghtan government, it was the largest city of the island kingdom. It straddled the confluence of two rivers, the Moltus, which ran down from the springs and melting snows of the rugged northwestern mountains, and its tributary the Slideen, which meandered from the lowlands, forests and farms in the west. It was the Moltus that continued on to the small estuary that opened into the sea about one hundred miles in a straight line to the south; one hundred and fifty miles if you followed the river.

Blavek lay at the fall line; the Moltus was navigable by ships of considerable draft as far as the city, but beyond, either to the north or the west, the two rivers were shallow, rocky or interrupted by waterfalls and rapids. This was particularly true of the larger Moltus, whose first major fall was on the outskirts of the city itself. A park had been established around the falls, named for an ancient hero, and they were a considerable attraction for tourists.

The city, to be truthful, had little else to recommend it, other than its size. It had been a commercial center long before it had become the home of the ruling families. Unlike the capitals of many other nations, which had been more or less built around the governmental cores and were consciously meant to be showcases,

17

Blavek seemed a little drab, functional and uninviting. There were larger and more beautiful churches in other cities of Tamlaght, as there were more beautiful homes, larger and more attractively landscaped parks, broader boulevards, better restaurants, more exclusive shops, friendlier people.

The main city was on the long, triangular peninsula between the converging rivers. It was virtually, if not literally, built on an island, since the peninsula was nearly cut off from the mainland by a broad pool in the Moltus directly below the falls. As a short canal cut this narrow isthmus, the city had been, in fact, turned into an island artificially.

The city proper was very old, a settlement of some sort having been established on the peninsula as long ago as the twenty-eighth century, and it has been continuously inhabited ever since. It became a major port for maritime commerce about four hundred and fifty years ago, and grew rapidly in size and importance after that.

As a result of its haphazard and rapid growth in a period when most of the traffic within the city was either on foot or horseback, wagon or cart, its streets are a labyrinth of meandering ways, some barely wide enough to accommodate two people abreast. In the older parts of town, the second floors of the buildings jut beyond the lower, and sometimes the third floors as well, like inverted ziggurats. The streets are so narrow that the outside walls of the upper floors of facing buildings almost meet—it would be easy to step casually from the window of one through the window of the other. This had no doubt been done often enough, and perhaps not always very casually. The streets below were converted to meandering, dark tunnels.

The city's buildings are unprepossessing. They reflect the sober, business-minded Blavek citizen. Vast blocks of severe brick office buildings, massive stone banks and commercial institutions, rows of anonymous warehouses, long ranks of mansions, squat and grey, as undecorative and forbidding as bank vaults. All broken only by the occasional small, uninviting park or one of the many churches built in the uninspired Musrumesque style.

If the city of Blavek and its citizens seem bleak, colorless and without humor, it is perhaps because the city goes further back into the history of Tamlaght than any other (although it might be begging the question to suggest that Tamlaght actually had any other *cities*—small towns and large villages accounted for its few other urban areas). It represents more than any other place the true heart of Tamlaght. The name of the city comes from a pair of ancient words, *blavis* and *vekken*, meaning "root" and "soul," reflecting accurately how the Tamlaghtans think of their venerable capital. And if the root and soul of Tamlaght is best expressed by a bleak, grey city, what else need be said?

The nation had never recovered from the intense xenophobia that had been inbred into its people from the earliest days of the island's habitation. Mostly inspired by their Church, jealous and self-confident, Tamlaghtans never joined in the great renaissance of learning, science and art that had swept the Continent barely two centuries earlier. They viewed such advances with distrust and considered them decadent. They clung to their True Faith and the simple ways of a thousand years earlier.

As the power of the Church waned, eroded by the glamour radiating from the enlightened and ever more powerful nations across the Straits, progress was allowed—reluctantly—to seep into Tamlaght's Society. Businessmen, still fearful and mistrusting of anything foreign, had seen themselves bypassed—and growing poorer; there was no longer any market for the crude goods, unrefined and artless, of their country. Only the banking houses had been thriving—the dour honesty, and canniness, of Blavek's bankers had attracted the rich merchants and investors of the Continent.

So the ancient hermit-city of Blavek, as the country's only seaport, found itself in the position of also being Tamlaght's most cosmopolitan city. Its cheap labor—uneducated, unskilled peasants lured by Blavek's siren-song—made it attractive to those businesses whose factories turned imported materials into exported goods. Thus was created the industrial quarter of the capital city, an island of modernity in a stubborn mediaeval sea. An island regarded with suspicion and contempt.

Across the Slideen to the south had grown the sprawling Transmoltus district. Here, spreading from the seed provided by the docks and shipyards, was the most modern addition to Blavek. Made possible by the invention of mechanization on the Continent and the importation of the steam engine barely a century ago, the Transmoltus was the industrial quarter of the whole nation. Hundreds of factories produced every conceivable product, from steel to cheap jewelry, from leather goods to clothing, from glass to furniture, from patent medicines to dairy products, from the products of slaughterhouses to coalyards. And sarcophagi, of course. Almost none of which—except the latter—were intended for domestic consumption. Virtually all of the materials were imported—though Tamlaght was certainly rich in untapped natural resources of its own—and virtually all of the products were for export.

Blavek treated the Transmoltus like a cancer—a thing to be contained. It was not about to be allowed to spread beyond its strict confines. While raw materials came in and finished products went out, the Transmoltus had no outlets for any of its other produce: incredibly noxious factory wastes; criminals; hungry, ignorant, jobless people; the envy and loathing of the outside world.

Dreary roads, black with cinders and coke, wind around the sides of the monolithic factories. Heaps of variegated trash, which the scanty vegetation fails to cover, glance and glare like the eyes of a basilisk. The air is heavy with smoke, and hangs like a pall over the ground. Not a bird nor an insect is to be found. From this rise dark masses, huge and strange, an agglomeration of regular buildings, symmetrically pierced by tall windows, and surmounted by a forest of cylindrical chimneys, which continually vomit clouds of oily smoke. Through the black curtain which veils the sky dart red lightninglike flames, while a distant roaring is heard, resembling thunder or the beating of surf on a rocky shore.

The Transmoltus was dirty, smoky, loud, busy, odorous, rough, ugly and squalid. While it had made them immensely wealthy, no one from the City liked to think that it existed. Not one of them would have been caught dead on the south side of the Slideen, which, naturally, would have been their fate had they gone there. Even the police did not patrol the district's streets except in pairs, and not at all at night.

The simple people of the country considered the Transmoltus an abomination, a literal outcropping of their Hell, the Kingdom of the Weedking, and treated it as anathema, avoiding looking in its direction, passing too closely to its borders, or speaking its name aloud.

Between the City and the Transmoltus, in the broad, shallow Slideen, was the island on which the royal palace, the houses of the Privy Council and the various chambers of the government had been established. The island spanned the river nearly from bank to bank. Over the years so many bridges and buildings had been built across the narrow streams separating the island from the land on either side that the river now ran in tunnels beneath broad causeways.

* * *

Thud was still in the chair, which after all really did hold him, when Bronwyn woke the next morning. A slender needle of light lanced through a hole in the window's gauzelike curtain, hitting her squarely in the left eye. She shielded that eye from the glare and could then see the mountainous silhouette of her rescuer bulking opposite. *Rescuer and protector*, she thought, suddenly remembering the events of the previous night. That immediately led to a recollection of the events that had preceded those, and she shuddered. Nevertheless, she had escaped with her life, had found a haven safe and warm, and now had some real hope of carrying through with her plans. She listened to the low rumbling of Thud's breathing, like that of a dreaming tiger. *With the help of a man like him*, she thought, *I could do it*. But how to go about recruiting a man who seems to be so content? His power seemed limitless but so did his inertia; he was more like an ox than a bull: placid and imperturbable. *Then why did he risk his life to rescue me?* He did it as though there had been nothing unusual about it at all; not once did he show any particular emotion, other than concern for her safety. *Would he do it again?*

Her eyes roamed the room. It looked worse in the morning. Her first thought was of her precious satchel. She discovered it lying next to her, against the wall. It appeared to have been left scrupulously untouched, but who could tell about such things? She felt a little guilty about it, but nevertheless unbuckled the straps holding the flap closed. Beneath was a seam, tightly laced shut. Unthreading this, and opening the mouth of the bag, she pulled out one of the bundles it contained. It was tightly wrapped in oilcloth and tied with waxed string. Her wax seal over the knot seemed intact. Leaving the others uninspected, she reinserted the first and continued her visual tour of the room. Her gaze stopped at the tintype surrounded by its paper flowers. *It's like an altar*, she realized. She then recalled Thud's one admission the night before, when she had realized that there might be more motivating the big man than whim: *he hated the Guards*.

Bronwyn wriggled out of the cocoon in which she had been wrapped. The wood stove had long since gone out, but the early morning sun on the slates of the roof had warmed the little room. She stretched like a cat, up on the balls of her feet, her hands nearly reaching the ceiling, arching her back until all her joints and seams cracked, one after the other. She then looked around

the room to see if she could find anything to wear. She noticed
that the tin tub and the buckets were gone.

Padding softly on bare feet, she searched the room's several
corners until she found a pile of rough cloth. It turned out, when
she held it up, to be one of Thud's tunics. It looked like a tent. She
slipped it over her head and it promptly fell to the floor around her
feet. Suppressing a laugh, she went back to the bed and the blankets and found one that was about five feet square. It was riddled
with moth holes. Feeling only a little guilty about destroying a
possession of someone who had so few, she worked her fingers
into a hole near the middle of the blanket and carefully began
tearing the cloth. In only a minute or two she had enlarged the
hole enough so that she could pass her head through it. Wrapping a cord around her waist, she succeeded in creating a kind
of poncho.

Now what? she wondered. Did she dare try to wake the sleeping
giant? *Why not?* She touched his arm and said softly, "Thud?"

His bright little eyes opened immediately and he said, "Good
morning. How are you feeling?"

"I'm fine."

Thud reached for the oil stove and began pumping its lever, to
build up the pressure needed to light it.

"Would you like some breakfast?" he asked.

"Yes!"

It was amazing! The man was instantly awake; there was no
transition between sleep and wakefulness with him, whereas it
had taken her several minutes to work the sleep out of her eyes
and the kinks from her bones. *Oh, Musrum,* she thought, *if only
I can get this man to help me!*

In a few minutes, Thud had the fire lit and a pan full of fat
canned sausages frying. After they had browned for a bit, he added
a can of small, sliced potatoes, and an onion he had minced. The
smell was wonderful and Bronwyn hoped that he couldn't hear
her stomach growling in response. He had already heated water
for tea, in a squat tin pot, and a pair of heaping spoonfuls of
black leaves were brewing in it. He produced a half-loaf of bread,
full of bubbles, yeasty and crusty, and the meal was complete.
Bronwyn was handed a stoneware plate, its surface crazed with
brown cracks. Thud divided the food exactly in half, scooping the
sausages and potatoes onto her plate. He poured her tea into the
same mug she had used the night before; she took it and squatted
on the floor to eat. Thud had not moved yet from his place in

the little chair. Everything he had done, he had done from that place.

He tore a chunk from the loaf and passed it on to the girl. She tore off a smaller bit and used it to mop up some of the savory juices puddled in her plate.

"Thud?" she asked, around a mouthful of food. "Aren't you curious about yesterday?"

"Yesterday?" He spoke the word as though it were a concept new to him.

"Yes. Don't you want to know why the Guards were after me?"

"I knew that I didn't want them to get you—I don't want them to get anyone. Why, did you get them mad?"

"Oh, Thud! Did I get them *mad*? You have no idea!"

"No . . . I guess not."

"Do you know how many Guards there are?"

"No. A lot?"

"A lot indeed. There are ten thousand, Thud."

"Ten thousand . . . I see. I thought there were about a . . . hundred. Is that right? That's a lot more, isn't it?"

"Thud, they're *all* mad at me."

"All of them? You mean all *ten thousand*? Why? I don't understand."

"Give me some more tea. It's a long story." And it was, indeed. Even though Thud interrupted very seldom, it was a long time before she finished. This pleased Thud, since he hated to talk while he was eating, even more than he hated to talk at any time. He also began to think it might be the last meal he would ever have in his little home; and when she had finished he was sure of it.

This is what Bronwyn told him:

"Thud, my brother is Ferenc, the Prince of Morvane-Silenne. Do you understand what that means? I'm the *Princess* Bronwyn. When our father, the king, died last winter—what? eight months ago?—Ferenc was the heir to the throne of Tamlaght. When the coronation takes place in a few weeks, he will be the new king, Ferenc III. You remember when the king died? Well, maybe it really didn't matter much to you. It probably isn't very important to anyone below the aristocracy; I suppose your lives go on pretty much the same no matter who is on the throne. But believe me, it will be different if my brother is crowned. He will sit on the throne with the orb in one hand and the wand in the other, but it will not be Ferenc who will be ruling Tamlaght. It will be something truly evil.

"I suppose I had better explain from the beginning. From the time we were children, Ferenc was the weakling. Weak in body and weak in mind. He was clumsy and slow to learn. He was forever getting hurt doing the simplest things; most of my earliest memories are of him being coddled in the arms of a nurse. I often suspected him of deliberate injury just for the luxury of the attention and fawning he received. When he wasn't hurt, he was sick, and I *know* that was mostly lies.

"I couldn't believe that anyone could be so taken in by such patent fabrications—but our nurses and governesses and especially my father acted as though they thought the fate of the nation hung on every runny nose, bruise or bellyache. Although I outstripped Ferenc in every sport and study, our father treated him as if he *could* have been the country's greatest soldier, sportsman or statesman—if only his development weren't being delayed by these pesky illnesses and accidents. Just give the boy time, he seemed to think, and Ferenc would come into his own. Not a chance!"

"Your brother's not very smart, huh?" asked Thud.

"No, he's not," replied the princess.

"Maybe he's too dumb to find you?"

"He is, but he's not the problem. There are other people who want to find me who are a lot smarter than my brother."

"Why?"

"That's what I'm trying to explain. You see, I would do almost anything to prevent my brother from becoming king . . . in fact, I *have* done something. If I'm not prevented, I can not only keep my brother off the throne, but I can also rid this country of some evil people."

"Bad?"

"The worst. *They're* the ones who are after me, trying to stop me from exposing them."

"Not your brother?"

"No, no, not my brother. He's too stupid. But the people who control him are very smart. They're not going to leave a stone in this city unturned until they find me and get back the incriminating letters I've taken. I have to get out of here."

"Where do you want to go?"

"My cousin, Baron Piers Monzon, can help me if I can get to him."

"Where is he?"

"Camped out at the northern border with his army, five hundred miles from here!"

One of the problems facing Bronwyn and Thud was that two rivers and the City separated them from the way north. And the only way into the City on foot was across Palace Island. That was clearly impossible. The island was crossed by a wide boulevard, but this passed through four gates at either end. They would surely be heavily and warily guarded.

Thud's plan was to cross the south river by boat, simply drifting with the slow current until they reached the easternmost point of the peninsula, called Catstongue. This would bring them within a few hundred yards of the bridge that connected the easternmost part of the City with the north bank of the Moltus. It was the least direct passage between the Transmoltus and the roads north, and might be less watchfully guarded. At night, with absolutely no motion of oars or sculls to attract attention, a small boat ought to be completely invisible. With only the feeble light of the smaller moon, the river would be as black as a sheet of cast iron.

The first real difficulty they needed to face was getting from Thud's room to the docks, which were about a half-mile away. Thud had no workable suggestions.

"Time is critical," said Bronwyn. "The coronation is only three weeks away. I must get the letters to Piers before that, and with enough time for him to show them to the other barons and plan a course of action. We must be on our way tonight. We have to be on the north bank of the Moltus and on our way by tomorrow morning, at the latest."

"It's after noon now. It will be dark in about five hours. I've got to find some clothes for you before we leave."

"Can you do that safely?"

"Sure. I can go anywhere: the Guards have no reason to stop me."

"Well, all right then, but don't be gone too long."

"I can probably get some clothes from one of the women who lives here."

"How can you do that without making them suspicious? What will you tell them you need girls' clothes for?"

"Don't worry. We'll be ready to go as soon as it's dark." The giant turned to leave and Bronwyn caught his arm.

"Thud, I don't know why you're doing this . . ."

"Don't worry about that either," he answered as he closed the door after himself. Bronwyn heard his heavy footsteps descending the groaning stairs.

Alone, she tried to carry the details of her plans further ahead than the next morning, but her imagination failed. There were a dozen ways to get to the north country, and she had no idea which might be most practical. She had seldom traveled within Tamlaght by other than first-class means. Her usual official transport was naturally out of the question. She wasn't altogether certain what her alternatives might be. Frustrated, she paced the room furiously.

The blanket-tunic, created only for modesty's sake (in spite of the previous night's intimacy), began to irritate her and she pulled it over her head and tossed it aside. With great satisfaction she scratched every place the bristly cloth had touched her body, until she was covered with red welts. Pouring some water from the stoneware jug into a bowl, she washed herself with Thud's thick, alkaline soap and the itching passed. Finding a comb, and feeling a little mean about rinsing it first, she combed out her mahogany hair. Thud had not bothered to do this after he had washed it for her, and it had macraméd itself into a complex, solid mass. Thus passed a pain-filled hour or so.

She then discovered that Thud, unfortunately, possessed no mirrors. She tried to use the glass in the window, but as long as it was darker in the room than outside, the window wouldn't reflect her image. She tried the small, reflective surface of the palm-sized tintype hanging on the wall, surrounded by its paper garden. She could see, mirrored in the dark, shiny surface, that her face was framed by its usual waves of dark metallic copper. It floated in the midst of the rusty billows like a pale moon rising through a sunset sky. Of her features she could only clearly see the full lips of a broad, mobile mouth and the jade spheres of her eyes. An errant ray of light from the setting sun caught them and they shimmered at her like two drops of dew on a mint leaf, cold, green and liquid. By a trick of focus, she saw her face blend into the face in the photograph, then disappear, absorbed; her minty eyes, cinnamon lips and rusty hair were transformed into eyes like drops of black oil, hair like obsidian, lips of pewter and a face of silver. It was a fairy-face, of a beauty as fragile as blown glass; the eyes were full of painful sadness. Bronwyn couldn't look into them. She couldn't understand the question they seemed to be asking her. And she didn't like things she couldn't understand.

The room was getting chilly, and she hoped that Thud would be getting back soon. She squirmed at the idea of wrapping herself in the blanket again. The lowering sun, passing through filtering billows of steam and coal smoke, lit the room with a sanguineous light. Bronwyn thought it almost unbearably depressing. She sat in Thud's little chair and leaned her chin on her arms, crossed on the window sill. Twenty yards away was the vertical brick wall of the building opposite. All of the buildings opposite Thud's were nearly windowless; probably big, uninhabited warehouses. They were persimmon orange against the iron sky. She seemed to be on a level with the warehouse's roof, which would put Thud's room, it appeared, about seven or eight stories above the street.

She glanced downward. The lower two-thirds of the buildings were in darkness. This was broken only by a very few sullen rectangular glows from oil lamp-lit windows, further up and down the street. The street itself was visible only as a meandering purple thread. Street? There was no street below Thud's window, she realized. The purple thread was the twilight sky reflected in a stream of water. It was as though she were on the rim of a deep, narrow, winding canyon of brick. She opened the window and leaned as far out as she dared. The canyon curved away from her in either direction, so she couldn't see very far to the right or left. Looking down she saw that a dozen windows in her own building were brightly lit. Moving shadows occasionally dimmed them. They cast wavering patterns on the opposite wall, like candle flames.

It was a sheer drop into the darkness below. She closed the window and sat back in the chair, wondering what to make of the brick canyon and its purple thread of a stream.

Bronwyn was not given to introspection. She had probably not once in her life ever examined her reasons for doing anything. Considering her position, there had never been any need: to examine motives would have been to try to justify them, and she required no justification; and if not from herself, then certainly from no one else. Now, it was occurring to her, she was in a unique situation. She had entered into this adventure with all of the self-assurance with which she had always approached any game, and now she was beginning to realize how little control she had over the events around her—not at all as her life had been before.

She was now in a world that she had not been required to admit the existence of . . . certainly not a world she had been prepared to deal with. The world beyond the palace walls, beyond proper, genteel, civilized Society, was as foreign and unreal as the Fairy-land of her childhood. She was as unprepared to live in it as a newborn infant. If she had been successful in her old world, it was because that world had been biased in her favor. Now she real-ized—though perhaps the realization was only just aborning—that she had always been as aware of the play-acting as she supposed her playmates had always been. While she had become physically and morally strong, self-assured and intelligent, the artificial basis of these qualities had also made her grow up vain, selfish and arrogant, overconfident in her ability to take care of herself, to determine her own fate—and, she thought a little sadly, without a real friend in the world. She appreciated Thud's help, but no one did anything for nothing. There would eventually be a price, she was certain. She was almost sorry she had told him that she was the Princess Bronwyn. It would have been interesting to have seen what he would have done with some ordinary homeless, wretched urchin.

Soon she heard the heavy footsteps again. They were unmistak-able, but her heart began racing nevertheless. There was no place to hide in the tiny room. She felt as vulnerable as a naked slug that was dimly aware of a giant hand approaching with a salt cellar. The door opened and the comforting bulk of her giant savior was momentarily silhouetted in the dim glow before the door closed behind him. She hadn't realized how dark the room had become until Thud asked quietly, "Princess?"

"By the window," she answered, and the big shadow moved toward her.

"I've got clothes and some more food." A bundle thudded onto the table. There was a scratching sound and a flame spluttered and hissed in the middle of the darkness, like a skyrocket. She saw Thud's face briefly illuminated by the winking match. It was sus-pended in the midst of the darkness like a smooth, expressionless moon, only the twitching shadows cast by the nervous flame giving it any life. He turned from her and lit a candle, placing it on a tin plate on the table. Lit now from below, his head disappeared into shadow, a moon eclipsed by the vast planet of his body. Bronwyn untied the bundle and a heap of tangled, multicolored cloth fell into her lap.

"I got mostly dried things, fruit and jerked meat, and some boxes of biscuits and candy. Cans're awful heavy. And some oth-er things. That stuff all right? I couldn't remember how big you were."

Bronwyn discovered how simply Thud had solved the problem of procuring women's clothing: he had instead brought her a wide selection of *boys'* clothes to choose from. And to take care of the question of size, he had at least a dozen different ones represented. Some of the garments seemed intended for an infant, while others might have fit Thud himself. But it all seemed a rather haphazard collection; all of the stockings, she saw, were of a single size, and that for someone half her age. On the other hand, all of the shirts seemed too large. She hoped that she would be able to piece together a complete costume fit to wear.

Discarding everything too small, she spread the remaining garments over the floor. All of it looked hopelessly tawdry and of questionable cleanliness. Musrum! Being chased by armed Guards was one thing, but all of this dirtiness . . . she hated dirt . . . And even if the clothes were clean there was no doubt in her mind that they had been worn in the not too distant past by people who were unclean and possibly even . . . but here her mind veered away from the approach of the awful word *diseased*.

"Thud," she asked, "is that a stream below this building?"

"That? It's really a sewer. Oh, I heard that a long time ago, when this was still country, that used to be a real nice little river. I don't know if that's true. It's always looked like this, so far as I know."

"This stuff looks awful!" she cried, spreading the clothing across the floor. "I can't wear these!"

"Why not?"

"Look at these! It's all . . . ugly!"

"It looks all right to me."

"Well, it would," she said, unkindly.

"What can I do?" he asked. "It's all I could find."

"I suppose I haven't any choice. Musrum! I won't wear this stuff in the daylight. I won't do it, that's all."

Thud didn't say anything for several long seconds. Then Bronwyn asked, "Do you know where the stream goes?" She had found an undervest that seemed the right size, as well as clean and soft. She slipped into it.

"I'm not sure. I guess it goes to the river, wouldn't it?"

"I'd think so." She had tossed aside three pairs of pants until she found a pair of patched knickers with black pot-metal buckles at the knees. She stood, pulled them on and buttoned up the fly. Not bad, but pretty loose around the waist. Well, one more use for the cord.

"Is there any way down to the stream?" she asked, as she found a dark red shirt with a faded blue check. Perfect fit! Perhaps too perfect; fortunately there was a short, belted jacket baggy enough to hide her distinctive shape.

"I don't know. Wait a second; yes, I used to play down there, when I was little." (Was *that* possible?) "I just don't know if I can remember how I got there."

He continued shoving supplies into the same big sack he had carried Bronwyn in the day before. His face bore its usual lack of expression.

"Did you find any shoes or boots?" Bronwyn asked, holding her bare feet up and wriggling her toes at him.

"Oh, yeah . . . someplace." He burrowed into the remaining pile of goods and held up a pair of lumpy-looking short boots, tied together by their laces and looking like two freshly caught yet elderly catfish. "I hope these fit. They're all I could get."

Bronwyn took them, gingerly, as dubious about their freshness as though they *had* been elderly fish. She pulled them on and the fit wasn't too bad, with an extra pair of socks to make up the difference. She buttoned them up.

"I think," said Thud, "that we could get down to the stream through the basement."

"All right, then; I'll be ready in a second." Which she actually needed several minutes' worth of, to braid her hair into two plaits, then to coil those tightly against the back of her head. A floppy, billed cap covered her head to the ears. She would pass for a boy—more or less—at least in the dark. Thud waited for her patiently, the bag lying at his feet like a sleeping hound. She picked up her leather satchel, unbuckled it and checked its precious contents. She felt a little silly doing that; where would they have gone? She tucked the oilcloth bundles in firmly and rebelted the bag tightly. Ducking her head under its strap, she made sure it was held snugly under her left armpit. As most people do when they know they are leaving a place forever, she gave the room an automatic, semiconscious scan; what could she have forgotten? She hadn't brought much in with her. In fact, she was taking out more than she had brought in. And another weird thought passed in review before her surprised brain: for all of her vaunted independence and competence, whenever had she been anything other than a dependant?

Her eyes rested briefly on the wall opposite the stove; the paper garden—grey, brown, umber, indigo and black in the darkness—

now surrounded a rectangular patch of bare plaster, about the size of a playing card; the only thing Thud had taken from the room was his tintype.

"All ready, then?" she asked. At a nod from Thud, she opened the door as quietly as she could and started down the stairs. From here the building was new to her; she had yet to see anything of it other than Thud's room. The stairs were narrow, with high risers and short steps. She had to be careful not to miss her footing, or topple forward, off balance. The stairs coiled down through the building in an irregular helix. They passed half a dozen landings, each surrounded by numerous narrow doors. Some had been painted a bright color; most were bare wood, stained black in semi-circles around their latches and unhinged edges from the touch of ten thousand unwashed hands. A few had a square of cardboard or a piece of torn paper pinned to their center panels, or to their frames, with a clumsily and painfully scrawled name proclaiming *person here* in block letters of crayon or charcoal. Most occupants, however, preferred or accepted anonymity.

Finally reaching the ground floor, she found herself in a broad hall, flanked by psoriatic stucco walls, with a large door at one end, its glass criss-crossed with wandering sutures of tape without which it would have fallen into pieces. In the other direction the hall vanished abruptly into darkness. Thud touched her arm and led her into the ammonia-reeking shadow, plaster fragments crunching under their feet. At the end of the hall, set into a corner, was a small door. Bronwyn tried its latch and found it was locked. She stepped aside for Thud. He took the latch in his fingers and bore down on it steadily, like a hydraulic press. There was a sudden, sharp *crack* and the latch and its lockbox popped neatly out of the door. It swung open easily, sweeping a fan of floor clean as it did. Wooden steps, set into a stone wall, led down.

Using the shelter of the open door as a shield, Thud took a lantern from his bag. It had been homemade from an empty soup can. He had soaked off the label and polished the metal, inside and out. Holes punched around its bottom seam allowed air to reach the candle inside. A square hole cut in the side let the light out in a single direction, reflected from the shiny, curved inner surface. He had fashioned a conical cap out of another piece of tin, a can he had unrolled into a flat sheet, and had finally attached a curved handle made of bailing wire. It was really a very neat job. He lit the candle and replaced the little metal duncecap. A shaft of steady yellow light beamed from the lantern's square cyclopean eye.

Still without a word, Thud proceeded down the steps, Bronwyn
close behind. It was a short flight, leading to a small, brick-floored
room. The walls were stone all around. An arched passage led
to the top of another flight of steps. These were of stone and
descended much further. There was no railing, and the steps
were mossy, wet, and rounded with use. Bronwyn hugged the
damp wall, certain she was going to shoot off into the darkness
with her next step onto the slimy stone, which was as slick as wet
ice. She reached the bottom dizzy from holding her breath.

She found herself in the foundation of the building. Fat columns of roughly cut stone supported a low, vaulted roof. The
floor was dirt: grey and compacted to the hardness of cement. In
the darkness beyond the glow of Thud's little lantern she could
hear scuttling, scampering, and a squeaking like someone twisting
a wet cork in a wine bottle. She was reminded all too vividly of
the cat-sized rat that had run past her face the afternoon before;
she could still see a malevolent red eye, like a drop of blood, and
wet yellow tusks.

Following as closely behind Thud as she could while still avoiding being stepped on—which would have been disastrous—she
accompanied him to one of the walls. It was pierced, she discovered, by a row of deep, square windows. She could feel air
drifting in through them and could hear a faint trickling from the
stream outside. The bottom edges of the holes were on a level
with her chin.

"Are there bars?" she asked. "Can we get out?"

"Well, you can, but they look awfully little for me."

"You mean you think you won't be able to squeeze through?"

"Come around here in front of me. I'll lift you up. Slide through
on your stomach and see if you can tell how far down the ground
is." Thud lifted Bronwyn onto the stone shelf. The window was
about half her height in depth. She wriggled and found her head in
the open air. The black earth was scarcely a foot below her chin.
By its sound, the water was only a few feet away. She pushed
herself backwards and dropped into the basement.

"The ground's almost level with the window," she reported.

"Good," said Thud, as he ran his hand all around the perimeter
of the square opening. Suddenly, with a grunt, he hoisted himself
into the hole. His broad, flat feet waggled in front of Bronwyn's
nose for a moment; then he dropped back to the ground, with
an appropriate thud. "It's gonna be awful tight. Stay here for a
minute."

He vanished into the dark before Bronwyn could utter a word. *Where did he think I'd go?* she wondered. She could follow him by the lance of flickering light that ducked and shot around and through the black columns like a little comet. When it turned back toward her, with the looming black bulk of Thud behind it, she was reminded of the great steam locomotives she had seen in pictures. Thud, she saw, had a big ball of black slime mounded in his hand, thick drools of it dangling from between his fingers.

"There's a big oil pipe that leaks," he said by way of explanation. "Hold the light, please?" She took the tin cylinder and held its beam on him as he smeared the gelatinous substance over his equatorial circumference.

"All right, then," he said, apparently satisfied with the mess. Once again he climbed into the window. He jammed himself in tightly, his enormous spherical rear suspended above the floor like a balloon. "Princess!" She heard his voice float in from one of the adjoining windows. She ran to it and lifted herself onto its slippery shelf, just barely avoiding cracking her head on the stone above. Slithering as quickly as she could, she popped her head out into the open on the other side. There was Thud's head just a couple of yards to her left. It looked like a jack-o'-lantern sitting in a window. He called her name again. "Stop doing that!" she ordered. "Someone's going to hear you!"

"Put out the light, and come over here, please," he whispered. Bronwyn crawled out onto the moist, gravelly soil, which was so close to the edge of the window that she was able to emerge on her hands and knees. She stood erect and hurried over to Thud. His little round head was at knee level. His arms and hands protruded on either side. "Take my hands, please," he asked, "and pull as hard as you can. I'm just stuck a little, but I don't have anything to get a grip on." Bronwyn took one of his wrists in each of her hands, and Thud in turn gripped hers. His were so thick that her fingers failed to circle them. She pulled. She pulled again, so hard she could feel her face turning deep red. She released his arms with a gasp of exhaled breath. "I moved, I think," he said. "I just got to get my knees into the hole." She gripped him again, bracing her feet against the stone at either side of the opening. She pulled until her body was as taut as a bowstring and almost parallel with the ground. Thud's body came free suddenly and Bronwyn shot from the wall like a quarrel from a crossbow. She landed squarely on her rear ten feet away with a jolt that clacked her teeth like a nutcracker. She slid backwards on the smooth, small pebbles until she came to a stop in a few inches of cold water. Her jaw ached, her coccyx felt inches shorter—she was afraid to bite down, certain that at least three inches of her spine must be protruding from her mouth—and the water was making her feel exceedingly uncomfortable. Thud emerged from the window like a fat pupa wriggling from its eggcase. He waddled over to where she sat and helped her up. "Are you all right?"

"Yes, I think so," she answered, waggling her jaw. Her spine felt as though its vertebrae were rattling like beads on a string.

"All right, then. All we have to do is follow the water." He started off ahead of her and she had to hop and skip a few steps to catch up. Bronwyn decided then that she would speak to Thud at the first opportunity about his continual habit of giving her orders. She did not take orders, and he was making her angry.

They kept to the scanty strip of gravel as often as they could, not wishing to make any noise by splashing water or to take the risk of a fall. The narrow ravine they were in was absolutely lightless at the bottom. Only the upper stories of the buildings, which loomed above them dizzily in vertical walls, were silvery phosphorescent. Directly overhead was a ribbon of indigo sky, like a bandsaw blade of blued steel. The buildings between which they were passing seemed for the most part uninhabited; only an occasional ruddy light shone through the midnight walls, like a nova in a starless sky. They passed under several footbridges, which spanned the stream at various heights. They passed by the openings of numerous drains, pouring or dribbling their effluvia into the community sewer that the stream had become.

They had just detoured around a fat iron conduit that protruded from the wall beside them, when Thud suddenly stopped and, with a low hiss signalling for quiet, pushed Bronwyn back behind the big pipe. With an almost inaudible whisper, he said into her ear, "There's someone up ahead." Her heart quivered, curling into a little ball like a hedgehog. She bent down and looked under the pipe, where it cleared the bank by half a foot. She could see nothing; then, suddenly, she heard the faint, crisp sound of paper being crumpled. She looked in the direction of the sound, avoiding using her direct vision, bringing the more sensitive peripheral part of her retina into play. Under the shadow of a footbridge . . . yes, now! The sudden flare of a match and the bearded face of one of Payne's Guards appeared and was gone again. She blinked and could see the negative image of the face. Thud touched her shoulder, and his breath tickled her ear. "Wait here, and don't move, please."

She reached to touch him, but he was already gone. She ducked down and peered from under the rough, wet pipe. Thud had melted into the darkness. An agonizingly long moment passed; then she heard a muffled grunt and the clatter of something metallic dropping onto the stones. Quiet again for a heartbeat and then a sharp *crack*, like a broomstick broken over a knee. She could guess what that sound represented, and felt ill. The agonizingly long moment of before seemed like nothing compared to the time it took Thud to return to her. When she heard his soft voice ask, "Princess?" she could have laughed with relief. But she was too smart and too frightened to do that.

"I was sure surprised to find a Guard down here!" he hissed. "They must want you real bad. It was a good thing they don't know anyone's with you."

It certainly is! she thought, *and certainly nothing like the champion I have in you, Mr. Mollockle.*

The passage of only a few hundred additional yards brought them around a sharp bend and the harbor opened before them. The stream ran directly into the Slideen, and the parallel walls that had been flanking the two fugitives went right up to the water's edge. The river water lapped against the buildings' foundations around either corner. The gravel bank had disappeared, the stream widening to fill the space from wall to wall. Thud and Bronwyn were forced to wade in it to get beyond the limit of the brick and stone canyon. The water only covered their ankles when they first stepped into it, but it quickly deepened. It was above Bronwyn's knees when they reached the point where the stream actually joined the river, and above her waist when they entered the harbor. The water only came up to the top of Thud's elephantine thighs. Turning to the right, they saw that a broad ledge ran along the front of the building; steep stairs rose from it to doors at different levels in the facade. Steps also led down into the water, apparently to allow access to boats of assorted sizes.

The anchorage beyond was a confused mass of ships and boats of every imaginable size and shape: hulls, some like massive, square, black mountains, others low-slung and rakish; a jungle of masts and spars, festooned with cobwebs of rigging; smokestacks—some squat and barrellike, others like slender pipes; the enormous striding spider-shapes of cranes and derricks. Pale clouds of steam and opaque clouds of smoke drifted and shifted among the tangle like ponderous and incurious cetaceans cruising through the lightless forests of the deep.

Wharves and piers protruded into the river like the teeth on a comb, adding to the general and disorienting confusion.

From the palace on the island upstream—the lights of which were visible, twinkling and merry, giving Bronwyn's heart a painful jab as if it were emphasizing some secret joke—Bronwyn had often watched the coming and going of the busy Slideen shipping. She remembered how she had spent hours on sunny afternoons or crimson evenings watching the elegant craft. She would wonder where they had been, what kinds of cargos they were delivering into the warehouses, what might be in those mysteriously anonymous crates, cartons, bales, hogsheads and barrels she saw the cranes lifting from the deep wells of the holds, like their feathered namesakes dipping into a pond to spear some surprised frog.

True to their national distrust of anything foreign, few monarchs of Tamlaght, and fewer of its citizens, had ever wished to leave its borders, or ever had. In recent history only the western portion of Londeac, where it bulged toward the island of Guesclin (the island of which Tamlaght occupied the greater part), separated by the few miles of the Strait, had been visited by a Tamlaghtan ruler. And then only because until just two generations earlier it had been a territorial possession, since ceded to Londeac, thereby saving future monarchs the trauma of ever again needing to leave the island proper.

Bronwyn had never in her life been farther from Blavek than the mouth of the Moltus, scarcely one hundred miles to the south. Those visits to what seemed to be the edge of the world haunted her. The great ships that came and went in the estuary—where did they come from? Where did they go when they disappeared over the horizon?

The poles of the planet were as alluring to her as they were to the needle of a compass. She devoured geographies and never went to sleep at night without having explored the enormous globe that swelled luminously in her room. She orbited it, trapped within its irresistible gravitation like a helpless satellite. It had been created by a master cartographer and illuminated lovingly by four monks, one of whom died before his masterpiece was complete—but much of the lovingly applied gilt and colored paint had been eroded by her traveling fingers. She had traced onto it the routes of the great adventurers, explorers, traders and caravans. With her fingertips she had tried to imagine what the painted deserts might really feel like, what the green tempera patches of jungle might sound like at night, what the people who lived on the banks of the mighty rivers, drawn on the globe like the blue veins on a great, milky breast, looked like, how their strange tongues might sound. She tried to conjure the smells and tastes and textures that the cartographer's symbols represented. But her imagination was never as sufficient as it was provocative.

All of the ships that came and went in the Slideen, and the Moltus beyond, she thought were beautiful. She loved the functional-looking freighters: they looked boxy and gruff, with no nonsense about them, like the moustachioed, red-cheeked sergeants in the Royal Army. Some carried three or four masts, but more and more were converting to steam . . . and she realized that she had never in her life actually *seen* a steam engine, those wonderful symbols of the Conqueror Engineer. A stumpy funnel protruded behind their wheelhouses, pouring out boiling clouds of black coal smoke that made the sun look rusty brown when it shone through them. Even then they kept their masts, though they might be as rudimentary and functionless as an ostrich's wings. Outsiders—other than merchants—seldom came to Blavek, but on rare occasions an elegant yacht would pull into the harbor. Its hull would be as white as an iceberg, its long, low superstructure glinting with polished wood and brass. Its masts would be raked back at a slight angle—its funnels, too, if it had them—giving it an impression of speed even as it sat motionless in the midst of the river's more mundane traffic, like a greyhound in a dog pound.

Pilot-boats and steam-launches would crawl across the grey water, leaving behind them pale wakes, like fat snails sliding over a sheet of glass.

She remembered how at night she would watch the twinkling yellow lights from portholes and the bright beacons of red and green running lights that looked like stars against the dark water, shifting and changing as though Musrum had stirred the very constellations with His great forefinger.

Bronwyn looked upstream and could see the lights of the palace, and the hazy, bright glow of the lamps that illuminated the boulevard that spanned the river. She hadn't realized that the harbor would lose so much of its romance when seen close at hand, at night. She felt as though she were standing at the brink of a deep and primeval forest.

"We need to find as small a boat as we can," whispered Thud. Which they did, shortly; a shell that looked scarcely large enough for Thud alone. It was tied to the end of the platform by a long painter, which they used to maneuver the boat near one of the sets of steps that ran down to the water. They found themselves adrift moments later.

"When I was a kid," whispered Thud, leaning toward Bronwyn and rocking the little boat distressingly. Bronwyn had never been a great one for swimming, let alone in the chilly, black waters of the Slideen on a starless night, and Thud's movement shifted the center of gravity toward her; cold water slopped distressingly over the gunwale behind her. "When I was a kid, I made myself a raft from some barrels and stuff. I couldn't steer it with paddles for nothing; that just made it spin in circles. But if I just let her alone, the current would take me right across the river, right to Catstongue. Anything drifting in the river ends up in a big eddy there. We'd never be able to find our way in the dark, but if we just let her go, we'll be all right."

"I can't believe this is your big plan," Bronwyn answered testily, forgetting that it seemed fine to her only a few hours earlier. "And I wish you'd sit still!" At that moment, a large steampilot passed them in the channel, its paddles thrashing the water. Their little boat was spun by the wake as though it were caught in a whirlpool. Bronwyn gripped the sides until her fingers ached, and she squeezed her eyes shut, flinching at every splash of icy water that hit her. The shell was sucked out into the middle of the river. The moving lights of ships were all around them, ghostly bulks, hissing steam or creaking with cables; their engines and chains clanking. Voices came over the water from all directions. Bronwyn felt like a rabbit in a herd of cattle.

"I don't remember it being this busy," apologized Thud.

"You were a kid thirty years ago, that's why."

"Yes, I guess so."

"I don't know why we couldn't at least have taken some oars, just in case."

"I don't know."

"Why aren't we moving anymore?" asked Bronwyn. The city, to their left as they faced downstream, should have been moving to the left as the current carried them. It was not just motionless, as Bronwyn thought at first; it was moving in the wrong direction.

"The river's going backwards!" Thud whispered in surprise.

"That's impossible," hissed the princess.

"Well, look, then," answered Thud, and when she looked, sure enough, they were unquestionably moving upstream. This wasn't possible! The river came from the mountains, it was headed to

the sea; how could it be going the wrong way? The answer came
to her immediately, and she felt as stupid as she ever cared to—
which generally was not at all: *the tide*!

Blavek was at the fall line of the river, at the northernmost
limit of the tidewater country. The city was virtually at sea level,
and when the tide came up the estuary, it backed the water of the
river up as far as Blavek. *Damn*! How could she have known? She
was no sailor. She desperately wanted to blame Thud—it had to
be someone's fault, so why not his? This was his idea, after all;
why had she ever gone along with it? It was stupid on the face of
it. Now look at what was happening: they were drifting directly
toward Palace Island. Merciful Musrum, it was the very place
from which she had been trying to escape! For all she knew, Payne
and Ferenc were in one of the towers watching her inexorably drift
toward them. They would be vastly amused.

Soon enough, the vertical stone embankment of Palace Island
loomed above them. It was a peculiar sensation, looking at a
place as though it were a prison that for eighteen years had been
a home. She could see the towers and turrets of the palace proper
and the government buildings that surrounded it. They glowed
in the buttery light of the boulevard's gaslamps. She could see
figures moving regularly along the parapet's edge, not fifty feet
over their heads: Guards on patrol. The little boat rounded the
northeast corner of the island. Ahead of them yawned four vast,
black mouths—the openings to the tunnels that allowed the Slideen
to pass beneath the causeway. Above the tunnel mouths were the
bright lights lining the roadway, and the dimmer, golden lights in
the windows of the official mansions and palaces built over the
river. She could see the busy shadows of people and vehicles.
When will someone finally see them and raise the alarm?

They were in a narrow channel, only a hundred yards across; the
clifflike stone wall supporting Palace Island was now on their left,
and the embankments of Blavek were on their right. They were
almost within one of the cavernous tunnels; Bronwyn could see
the parapet of the causeway only by bending her head completely
back and looking straight up. To her horror, she saw the pale blob
of a face looking back down at her. It was topped by the distinctive
plumed shako of one of Payne's Guards. Just before the face was
cut off by the edge of the tunnel, as they passed within it, she heard
a rasping sound and something plopped wetly onto the floor of the
boat alongside her foot. Then the darkness of the tunnel swallowed
them. *He spat at me*! Bronwyn realized with disgust. *He was just*

using some drifting debris for target practice. The Guards were animals.

The tunnel was roughly a half-cylinder over them, the roof perhaps twenty feet above. Chandeliers of lime and calcium hung down toward them, dissolved and redeposited by the constantly dripping water that drizzled from fissures, cracks and seams in the vault, and which had them drenched within minutes.

It took perhaps ten minutes for the boat to pass from one end of the tunnel to the other, though it seemed hours to Bronwyn. Finally, they emerged from the western mouth, Palace Island behind them. The boat stopped drifting, rotating idly in a slow eddy. They were only a few yards from a weedy bank on the City side of the river. Thud climbed out of the boat, sinking nearly to his waist, and pulled it and Bronwyn to the shore.

Bronwyn could have cried with fury and frustration. After all she had been through, she was back exactly where she had started from, her deadly enemies not five hundred yards away.

3

GYPSIES AND HISTORY

THERE IS some good in everything, if one only troubles to look for it. Bronwyn was willing to try if only because the effort involved was no greater than that required for becoming hysterical. And she normally wasn't that latter sort of person. She had always disliked making a spectacle of herself and felt that tears, wails, recriminations and self-pity usually drew the kind of attention normally reserved for people who have sidewalk fits. Being practical, she also thought that the energy would be better spent on finding a way out of their predicament, a task she feared would not be easy.

Thud, however, was in a paroxysm of remorse. When he had set the princess onto the bank she had shot him a look that had pierced him like an icicle nailed through his heart. In his efforts to help the girl, he had only succeeded in making her troubles worse. Would this happen every time he tried to be kind to someone? Bronwyn had been one of the rare people in his life who had not looked at him with automatic repugnance, nor had she treated him like an idiot, as nearly everyone else did. Now look how she had been repaid!

In actual fact, though Thud would never have known this, Bronwyn had been treating him not like an idiot but like a servant, accepting his services with gratitude, but under the assumption that

Thud could scarcely be doing otherwise. This is what people like Thud were for, from Bronwyn's viewpoint—Still, the princess's attitude had not made much difference to Thud; he realized that he was not her equal on any count, except perhaps size and physical strength, and in those categories he vastly surpassed her; her treatment implied that he possessed an equality with that vast number of human beings who occupied the social classes beneath the princess's, and that was good enough for him. He had never been anyone's equal before. And now he was equal to millions!

Bronwyn was all too aware of how the ramparts of Palace Island were glowering at her; she was certain that it would be only minutes before a Guard would see them. At the top of the bank was a road; across the road were buildings, and the sooner they were among them, the better she'd feel. While things weren't going according to plan at all, they could have been a lot worse. They were at least on the right side of the river. All they needed to do was get across the city undiscovered. Unfortunately, they were nearly two miles from the bridge they had originally planned to use. The one now nearest would surely be heavily guarded. The Guards would be stopping everyone, suspicious or not. And there was no way in the world that she would consider crossing the Moltus by boat; there had been enough of that. *Well,* she thought, then laughed silently; she had been about to say to herself, *we'll cross that bridge when we come to it.*

She started up the bank, then looked back when she realized that Thud wasn't behind her. He was still sitting on the grass, watching her with his usual lack of expression. "Come on!" she hissed. "We've got to hurry—we can rest once we're in the city."

He seemed to be surprised, but got to his feet and followed her; they quickly crossed the road and were in the shadows of an alley between a pair of dark storefronts. Bronwyn mentally oriented herself. They were on the north bank of the Slideen, on the south side of the city, at the point where the peninsula was broadest (naturally). There would be at least a mile and a quarter to travel to reach the Moltus bridge. In a straight line, that is: a direction not possible to travel in Blavek. The West Side was the oldest part of the city. Its narrow streets were a maze, meandering in all directions, like an ant nest, and each one was seldom more than a few hundred yards long. The buildings were for the most part still made of wood, and their overhanging upper stories made gloomy tunnels of the passages even during the day.

In all her life, Bronwyn had never been on foot within the laby-
rinths of Old Blavek.

"Thud," she asked, "do you know your way around the city?"

"No," he answered.

"Well, that's no help. I suppose we ought to keep going north
as best we can. Try to keep track of our turns."

She started up the alley, but it ended after a few score yards
when it ran into a cross street. This didn't appear to cross exactly
at a right angle. She chose the turn that seemed to go into the
City, the one to the right. Thud followed silently. Once again the
street she was on ended in an intersection. The right branch, she
thought, looked as though it would take her back in the direction
of the river. She turned to the left. The narrow lane curved in
a quarter circle before crossing another street. This time a right
turn seemed correct, their footsteps clop-clopping in the quiet.
Street after street they traversed in this supposedly methodical but
actually completely haphazard way. So far they had seen no one
else: the district they were passing through was mercantile, but
all of the businesses were closed for the night and were dark. Gas
street lighting had not yet been introduced into the shop districts,
and only an occasional oil lamp on a corner relieved the gloom.
This worried Bronwyn. Should the police see them, they would
surely be stopped.

Bronwyn, who had never been in the city when the streets had
not been teeming with people, found the lifeless dark frightening. Thud, who had lived his life within the confines of the
Transmoltus, thought it fascinating. He had never before felt
so safe while virtually alone on a street at night. It was pleasant
but disconcerting. He had never seen buildings so beautiful, nor
windows with so many wonderful things in them—though he
couldn't tell what most of those things were, swimming behind
glass panes like ghostly fish of gold and silver.

Again the street they were on ended when it ran into another. There seemed, as usual, to be equal choices between which
way to go. Bronwyn headed to the left. This way made a long
curve between the overhanging buildings. The silence and solitude
was complete and concrete; around them rose, black and dumb,
an imposing mass of architecture that glared at them each time
lanternlight glinted from one of its thousand windows.

At the end of the curve, the street made a sharp turn to the left
and, to Bronwyn's horror, revealed not a hundred yards away the
broad causeway to Palace Island, alive with traffic. She quick-

ly about-faced, bumping into Thud's broad chest. "Quick! Back around the corner!"

She leaned against the grimy building and pounded her fists together. "Damn it! We've just gone around in a big circle. We've been wandering for an hour and we're practically back where we started. How are we going to get out of here? I don't know my way; we could wander all night and just keep going around in circles. Damn!"

Thud was surprised; the princess had made practically the same mistake he had.

"Well, what now?" said Bronwyn, more to herself than her companion. "Let's try up this parallel street. At least it heads away from the palace."

"What are you two doing there?" came a strange voice. Bronwyn jumped, turned, and saw that it issued from a Guard, who had approached unseen from the other arm of the intersection. The black-uniformed patrolman was crossing the broad street, lowering his rifle as he came. His black cuirass shone dully, like a beetle's carapace . . . or a cockroach's, to be truthfully specific. Bronwyn felt her huge companion stiffen, and she laid a restraining hand on his arm. "Don't," she said. "It's dark. Maybe we can bluff it out."

Thud grunted doubtfully. The Guard stopped a few paces away. "What are you two doing on these streets?"

"We're lost, officer," answered Bronwyn. "We can't find our hotel."

"And which hotel would that be?"

"The, uh, Excelsior," answered Bronwyn, thinking too quickly, giving the name of the most exclusive hotel in the city—the only one she had ever heard of.

The Guard looked at the pair that faced him: an ugly giant, probably an imbecile by his looks, dressed in a brown suit that was a crazy quilt of mismatched patches and carrying a suspiciously rattling bundle over his shoulder; and a lanky, effeminate kid in ill-fitting hand-me-downs. The Excelsior Hotel, by the warts of Musrum! They must think him an idiot.

"I think you two'd better come along with me," he said.

"Well, officer, I don't think that you have to go to all that trouble," replied Bronwyn. "If you'd just point us the right way?"

"The only way you are going is to the district office."

"What for?"

"Never you mind. Just do what I say, if you'd rather not be

carried there." A ridiculous threat, considering Thud, that was overlooked by all three.

"We weren't doing anything except walking, officer; why don't you just let us go on our way?"

"Just keep quiet and do what I tell you," answered the Guard, raising the muzzle of his rifle.

"Well, I don't think so," said Bronwyn. Thud dropped his bag with a clattering crash. The Guard swiveled his gun toward the big man. Bronwyn pounced on the black-sleeved arm like a terrier, biting into the wrist as hard as she could. The Guard growled in surprised pain and struck at her head with his free hand. Bronwyn's hat went flying. The Guard goggled at her exposed face and then cried, "Holy Musrum, it's . . ." His exclamation was cut short by Thud's fist bursting his nose like a ripe tomato. The gun fell to the street with a rattle, followed by the Guard, clutching his squashed and squirting nose with both hands.

"Run!" urged Bronwyn, and the two bolted down the street. Behind them, the wounded Guard had gotten to his knees and was creating piercing shrieks with his whistle.

"We've had it now," panted the princess. "The place will be swarming with Guards any minute. Musrum damn it, can't anything go right?" As she spoke, something like a hornet buzzed past her ear, at the same moment a sharp crack sounded behind them.

"They're shooting at us!" said Thud, unnecessarily. Bronwyn made a right-angle turn into a narrow gap separating two buildings. Peering back around the corner, she could see a confused mass at the far end of the street. "There must be at least a dozen of them, coming this way."

"Which way do we go?" asked Thud.

"How am I supposed to know? We can't go back out to the street, so let's see where this takes us."

The alleyway was barely wide enough for Thud's broad body, and he brushed the walls as they hurried through. Bronwyn was praying that the passage didn't end in a cul-de-sac. It did and it didn't: their way was blocked by a fence, about midway in height between Thud's head and Bronwyn's. Behind them they could hear the noise of the soldiers as the passageway was discovered. Bronwyn was panting, and a stitch in her left side threatened to fold her like a jackknife. "Come on, quick!" said Thud, making a stirrup of his hands. Bronwyn stepped into it, balancing herself with a hand on Thud's shoulder, and was effortlessly launched over the fence. She went over with all the grace of a rag doll, landing, fortunately, in a mass of refuse excelsior. She clambered to her feet, covered completely with curly little shavings that made her resemble even more completely the terrier she had recently impersonated. "Thud?" she called through the slats. "How are you going to get over?"

A good question, since he would never be able to hoist his own enormous bulk over the barrier. She heard the banging and crashing of ashcans and boxes. She peered through the fence, but could see nothing but movement. The sounds of their pursuers were getting far too close. Bullets began to whistle over their heads, the reports of the guns echoing thunderously in the tunnellike alley. Two or three times there were little bursts of splintered wood as a bullet smacked into the opposite side of the fence.

"Thud?" she called again.

"Watch out!" came the answer, from over her head. Looking up, she saw the big man hovering directly above her. She nearly fell over backwards scuttling out of his way as he dropped to the ground, with all of the grace of a walrus completing a *grand jeté*. He picked the girl up and set her on her feet while running. "I made a stairs," he puffed, "and climbed up them."

"That was dumb! The Guards will just use them, too!"

"I don't think so," he answered. "Look." Bronwyn stopped and turned. A glow was flickering through the gaps in the fence. Suddenly a pennant of orange flame licked up from its far side.

"That'll give them pause, all right," she observed with a kind of awe. "But you'll set the whole city on fire!"

"I never thought of that," said Thud, surprised and a little hurt. He felt stupid again.

"Well, who cares? We've got ourselves to worry about. And you're right, you have stopped them for now."

The lurid light from the blazing barrier lit the two fugitives until they disappeared into a branching alleyway. They zigzagged at every opportunity. They had long since lost any sense of where they were within the city and only hoped now to confuse pursuit as much as possible. They were at least certainly confusing themselves.

Finally, the labyrinthine passages opened into a broader street and that in turn led into a small plaza. The grassy rectangle in the center was occupied by a circle of rustic wagons. The scrawny trees amongst them were festooned with garlands of paper lanterns. Bronwyn recognized the set-up as belonging to gypsies.

They, or ones just like them, had often been invited to perform on the lawns of the palace, or in the parks surrounding any one of the several royal country houses. She had always loved their sad music. There were eight or nine of the boxy caravans, their sides bright with gaudy and imaginative designs and figures. A little corral had been created with rope and stakes in one corner of the plaza, and a dozen ponies stood sleepily within it. All but one or two of the lanterns were dark, and no light shone from within any of the wagons. It was well past midnight and the music, games and fortune-telling were over for the night.

Bronwyn and Thud by unspoken agreement decided to circle the camp, keeping as far away from the caravans as they could. They had completed half of their circuit when an amused voice from nowhere asked, "Running from someone?" The voice seemed, to Bronwyn, to have been whispered into her ear and she jumped convulsively. The voice chuckled, "I might have guessed so."

Bronwyn would have run if she could, but she was exhausted. Her legs simply refused to answer to her orders any longer and her brain had simply coasted to a standstill, like an engine whose fire had gone out. "Where are you?" she asked.

"Right here!" came the jovial answer. But still she could see no one.

"Please, I'm too tired to play games. Either show yourself or let us go on our way."

"Who is stopping you?" Bronwyn had to admit that was a fair question. "Do not worry, I am a friend." A figure stepped out of a shadow that Bronwyn would have sworn was cast on a flat wall. It was a large man, something like a scaled-down Thud. He wore high, wrinkled leather boots into the tops of which were tucked the baggy legs of his striped trousers. His broad chest was covered, barely, by an elaborately embroidered vest over a dark shirt with balloonlike sleeves. Teeth, alternately white and gold, glinted in the midst of a face as broad and hairy as a buffalo's. Even in the darkness Bronwyn could see the twinkle in at least one eye.

"You do not have to tell me what you have done. I am friend to anyone the Guards are looking for."

"How do you know that?"

"They have been here already. Half a dozen were here an hour ago. Rousted us all out of our honest slumber. Went through every inch of the wagons while we stood outside shivering."

"I'm sorry."

"No matter. Happens everywhere we go anyway, but I appreciate your concern."

"Are they coming back?"

"Oh, I doubt that they will be back before morning, though there is no telling—they seemed to want you very badly, I think."

"They tell you why?"

"They would never tell us anything. Just a description. I was waiting for you. Did not expect your friend here, though. I do not think they know about it, do you not think so? Is it human?"

"Of course! I think they do know about him now, but I don't think they know who he is. He saved my life."

"Well, well," he said to Thud, "good for you! That is all the recommendation you need." Then he said to the girl, "Does it have a name?"

"My name is Thud and I have a temper, too."

"No offense meant!"

"You must tell us how to get out of the city! We've been trying all night," begged Bronwyn, who was too tired not to beg.

"I could, but I doubt it would do you any good. It is more of what you have already been through; I would have to draw you a map, practically, and, besides, the district is as crawling with the damned Guards as a whore is with crabs." Bronwyn winced at the crude simile.

"I guess we'll have to chance that," she said.

"Why? No need to even worry about it. Hungry?" he added, irrelevantly.

"We brought some things with us . . ."

"Pooh! I can guess what you have in that bag, and the thought makes me ill and my eyes to water. You need some honest food and a rest, for sure. Come along, then."

The man turned and crossed the street into the plaza. Bronwyn looked at Thud, who shrugged. The gypsy had a point: with all the places the Guards would be at this very moment, this was one place they were certain the Guards were *not*. And they *were* hungry and tired (or at least Bronwyn knew she was; Thud looked like he had been out on a bracing stroll). So they followed the gypsy.

He led them to the door of one of the dark wagons. He tapped at it lightly and a light came on instantly. "Open up," he whispered. "It is them." After the sounds of a latch unlocking, the door swung open an inch and a face peered out at them above a lantern shielded by a hand. "Come on!" said the man. "Let us in! Do I look like a damn Guard?" The face answered with a sniff, but stood back and the door opened. The gypsy let Bronwyn and Thud precede him up the short steps into the wagon.

It was as cozy a little room as Bronwyn had ever found herself in. A miniature cast iron stove warmed it like a big fat black cat. On its flat top rested a covered kettle from which savory vapors puffed. Everything was so cozy, friendly and safe that it actually seemed weird. The gypsy gestured for them to sit. Bronwyn feared for the elaborately carved and painted chair that Thud lowered himself onto, but it was made of stern stuff.

"You are welcome here," said the gypsy; his grin shone through his grizzled beard like a crescent moon seen through treetops. Every other tooth was gold, a decoratively checkerboard effect from which Bronwyn found it difficult to take her eyes. "You are quite safe. Henda! Give these poor travelers some food! Can not you see they are tired and hungry?"

The creature Henda, a shapeless mass of colorful rags from which a pair of birdlike eyes peered, the rest of the face being swathed in scarves, gave another sniff and began ladling the contents of the kettle into deep bowls. It set them before Bronwyn and Thud; the girl thought she had never smelled anything quite so good. Thud began shovelling it in without preamble. His head had hinged back from his enormous mouth and it was as though the food were being dropped into the top of an open pipe.

"Go ahead and eat, Princess, we can talk after," said the gypsy; he laughed at the surprise on her face. "Don't worry about how I know; a word here, a word there, the news traveled faster than you did. The mystery is why a princess would be chased by the Guards like a criminal. No one can understand that. I cannot, that is for sure!"

Bronwyn told the gypsy what she had a day earlier told Thud, and then elaborated:

"As my brother got older, he just became lazier and more stupid. Once he realized they were activities reserved for his rank, and not chores being forced on him, he became an enthusiastic hunter, rider and yachtsman. He has surrounded himself with a gang of unemployed, aristocratic parasites who term themselves 'sports.' He discovered that he did have one talent, for being entertaining. So he never engages in any activity that requires him to be more than a charming half-wit.

"Ferenc is a year and a half older than I am. He's tall and slim and exceedingly good-looking. He has an ingratiating smile and laughs at everyone's jokes, whether he understands them or not, and in a silly giggle that makes me want to vomit. He's invited to every party and ball, where the petty nobility force their inbred daughters on him—and it makes me laugh to think what a child by him and one of those glassy-eyed sluts might be like. They're all over him, the simpering idiots, like flies on a dead squirrel.

"Ferenc has never had an original idea in his life. Everything he says is simply repeated from what he has heard—there's no more intelligence behind his words than a parrot's. His toadies and sycophants think he's a clever wit. Compared to them, I suppose he may be.

"He does have certain beliefs: he believes that his right to rule is granted by Musrum; that the king is not simply the representative of the ruling class, but is absolute monarch. These two things, his lack of imagination and originality, and his wholly mistaken conception of the throne, are what make him so dangerous.

"Ferenc's fatal weakness is that he cannot stand on his own: he must have someone stronger to lean on, someone who will provide the words he speaks, the thoughts he will believe are his own, the reasons and justifications for his actions; who will tell him—as though he were only being reminded of something that has slipped his mind—the things that he must do, when he should do them . . . and to whom."

"My brother found his alter ego in Lord Payne Roelt. He was the only son of the elder Payne Roelt, the Earl of Swynborn, a powerful baron. Payne had been a playmate of my brother's since childhood; he is only a year younger, I think. Even in my earliest memories I can recall how Payne controlled Ferenc's every thought and action, as though my brother were a hound and he the master. Payne had—*has*—a way of *suggesting* things to Ferenc in such a way as to make Ferenc think they came out of his own head. And when Ferenc finally gets the idea that has been planted and speaks it aloud, or carries it out, Payne laughs and says, 'Good boy!' as though he were delighted with a puppy that has just learned a new trick! And when Ferenc smiles at him in that simpering way, I know that nothing in the world has pleased him more than the thought that he has won the approval of someone like Payne Roelt.

"Payne is everything my brother is not. His intelligence is diabolically reptilian; he is ingratiating, suave, and urbane. He is a clever and plausible diplomat: he creates intensely loyal friends and can win the support of his enemies before they even realize what has happened to them. Afterwards they cannot think what could have caused them to ever dislike such a clever, courteous fellow—until they unwittingly cross him.

"He is a smallish man, perhaps an inch or so shorter than I am, slightly built and very pale. Nevertheless, he has great strength. His physical power and stamina is probably not rivalled by anyone outside the Guards; I've seen him outride the best of them. He not only has great psychical power, but a scheming intelligence to go with it. He can convince anyone of anything. Yet Payne has only one motive for everything he does: his passion for wealth is overwhelming. His interest in gaining power over the throne is only in the wealth it will ultimately gain him. He has no real desire for power in itself. He needs power only to wring every poenig possible out of the throne and the country. He is absolutely blind to everything else.

"My brother is so enamored of his 'protégé' that, since our father died, he has lavished enormous wealth and property on him. The drain on the state treasury has been a scandal. Ferenc has taken every possible step to prevent the Privy Council from meeting since my father's death, from fear that they will discover exactly how much he has been spending on Payne. He doesn't realize that this has probably cost him money in taxes they might have been convinced to vote for his use. He has made Payne the household chamberlain, and Payne has used this position to loot the palaces and to juggle the housekeeping accounts so that most of the money goes into his own pockets.

"Payne has created a wall around Ferenc that is virtually impenetrable without Payne's knowledge and permission. No one sees Ferenc unless Payne knows about it. No one speaks to Ferenc without Payne being present. Since it wearied and bored my brother, he was glad to let his aide gradually take over his correspondence. Now neither letter nor proclamation is issued over my brother's signature that has not been written or dictated by Payne. My brother sees no letters that have not first passed through Payne's hands. If they contain anything he feels Ferenc ought not to see, they are destroyed—or even rewritten. Payne has a veritable army of spies and informers throughout the city, who keep him apprised of even a single word that might be spoken against him.

"Ferenc is absolutely unaware that any of this is taking place. He is so happy in his dreamy world of dances and parties and yachts and hunts that he isn't aware of the cage that Payne has

built around him. Payne doesn't begrudge my brother his mind-
less, simpering 'friends'—he knows that they are utterly harmless. They are the toys that he uses to keep a child happy and
uncomplaining.

"The barons—the landowners—are intensely jealous and afraid
of Payne's influence and power. Half of them would like to see
him disposed of, by force if necessary. The others advise waiting, thinking perhaps that some of our father's belligerence would
eventually manifest itself in the prince and he would banish the
interloper himself. I think that Payne enjoys seeing the baronage
split, something I wouldn't doubt he planned all along.

"What has made all of this so dangerous is the constant threat of
war from the north. Crotoy is perfectly aware that the heartblood
is being drained from this country. What Payne has been doing
has been no secret from Crotoy's barons. It is not an alien nation;
we have a common language, and a common heritage, since three
hundred years ago we were a single people. Bloodlines cross the
border at every social level, but especially among the nobility.

"Once Payne made an enemy of our barons, the barons of Crotoy
knew all about it as well. They are all too aware of what has most
angered our baronage: that Payne has effectively disarmed the
army. With no money for weapons, uniforms, food or pay, the
army has gradually disintegrated. What is left has nothing to fight
with. I know that Payne has created the Guards—ten thousand of
them—and they are well fed, well paid, well armed and powerful.
But they are Payne's personal army, loyal to and answerable only
to him. They are the only thing that has kept him alive to this day.
The barons fear and despise Payne and would like nothing better
than to see him dead. This is something he is well aware of.

"Anyway, Crotoy knows that our army is ineffective, and that
the nobility is busy fighting amongst itself: the barons against a
vapid, useless monarch, or monarch-to-be, that is. Can you imagine Ferenc leading an army into battle? Already, Crotoy has made
exploratory incursions onto Tamlaghtan soil. It has armed camps
on our side of the border, and not a soul has tried to stop them.

"My cousin, Piers Monzon, is on his way to the border now,
with a small army the barons have raised, to see if it is not too late
to do something. Piers is my first cousin. He is a powerful man,
probably the most powerful of all the barons. He is hereditary High
Steward of the court, which would make him regent in Ferenc's
absence or incapacity, and holds half a dozen earldoms. He is
a big, charismatic, physical man. We always liked one another

quite a lot; when I was a young girl, I spent more time with Piers than with my own father. It was Piers who taught me to ride and shoot, for example. It's my greatest pride that he once told me that he thought that I was the best swordsman he had ever trained. Unfortunately, Cousin Piers has nowhere near Payne's cunning and intelligence. Payne can outthink him easily; Piers's brain is just too honest.

"Be that as it may, Cousin Piers has the undiluted respect of the other barons. Not one of them has a greater hatred for the leech that has attached itself to Tamlaght than has Piers. He is the leader of a formidable opposition.

"Well, that more or less brings you up to date; there is only one more incident to tell you, and you'll understand why I was in need of Thud's rescue yesterday.

"Three weeks ago, a group of the barons decided that they had had enough of Payne. Without the knowledge of Piers or the other barons, they invaded Payne's estates. The barons had pooled their private militia into a small army of about five hundred men. All of them changed their distinctive uniforms for civilian clothing. If it weren't for their orderliness and economy of action, anyone would have taken them for a mob of countryfolk.

"In two nights of deliberate, organized pillaging they destroyed hundreds of thousands of crowns' worth of Payne's property. Fifteen manors were burnt to the ground; tens of thousands of sheep, cattle, oxen and horses disappeared or were slaughtered; yachts were burnt to their waterlines. Art, jewelry, silver, clothing—all vanished or were destroyed.

"Payne was in a paroxysm of fury; the barons—and he knew perfectly well who had been behind the raids—had knowingly or inadvertently hit him where it hurt the most. He made the error of taking his complaint to the Privy Council, I suppose because he believed that he owned it and controlled it. He might have been right, except for one thing: he found the barons waiting for him there. With the strength of the nobles behind them, the chancellors of the Privy Council found the courage to confront Payne. The barons read a list of their grievances, enough to have sent any other man to the gallows a dozen times over.

"Unfortunately, my brother by this time heard what was happening to his friend and hurried to the chambers. Confronted by the man who was soon to be their monarch, the chancellors began to waver. They thought they were caught between the baronage and loyalty to their country, in the person of the prince, who begged with surprising eloquence (coached, I suspect!) for the life of his chamberlain. You must remember that the one man, Piers Monzon, who could have possibly swayed the Council against Ferenc was miles away in the north. They opted for merely exiling Payne.

"The barons were furious, of course; they wanted Payne's blood. But there was little they could do. Payne had not pursued his complaints against them, and I think that they were afraid he might. What they had done had been absolutely illegal, of course; and quite a large number of people had died, too. I think that even at the moment of Payne's sentencing, the barons realized that the victory was more their enemy's than their own. He was blackmailing them as he stood there listening to the chancellors exiling him from Tamlaght.

"Payne's exile has taken him only as far as one of the islands in the Gulf. He's not more than two hundred miles from Blavek at this moment. And he is coming back. I discovered that more or less by accident just a few days ago. I make no apologies for going through my brother's papers and despatches—they mean more to me than they ever would to him, anyway, even if he cared to look, or could understand them. I found that he has been in constant communication with Payne since the day Payne left. Some days half a dozen letters would arrive from the coast. These were delivered directly into my brother's hands, but once I discovered that they existed, it was easy enough to get hold of them. Although each one exhorted Ferenc to destroy the communications, he was too stupid or careless to do so. Maybe he felt too sentimental about them; I wouldn't doubt it. Anyway, I found them.

"At Payne's direction, Ferenc has started to plot Payne's return.

"There has been a victory in the north. Maybe you heard about it. It was small enough; Piers only overwhelmed an undermanned, out-of-the-way post that had no particular military importance, but it's a victory nevertheless and the papers are full of it. It's the first good news in a long time and the people are crazy over it. Do you know about all of this nonsense? Well, following Payne's directions, Ferenc is using this victory to gain a lot of public support—who else do you credit for a great victory but the man who is the corporeal representation of your country?

"Using this new popularity, he has gone to the Church and—Musrum forgive them!—has convinced the priests that Payne's exile was illegal. They will now pressure the Privy Council to overturn their decision and allow Payne to return. What's worse, he is trying to force the chancellors, as compensation, to have the barons make full restitution for Payne's damages. This, of course, would bankrupt most of them, as well as increase Payne's power a hundredfold over what it had been before. And that is assuming that the barons wouldn't simply opt for civil war, which would be the most likely turn of events. What is worse is that while he is using the Church, through the prince, to further his own ends, Payne is plotting its destruction. He is covetous of the Church's wealth, and I know he has devised some plan to loot it after the coronation.

"There is just one thing that might prevent all of this from happening: letting the Privy Council and the barons see the contents of the letters Payne sent to Ferenc.

"I have them. Payne knows I have them. His island is not far enough away to prevent him from maintaining full control of his Guards and spies—and he has agents everywhere. He knows everything that goes on. As soon as he learned that I had the letters, he sent the Guards orders to prevent me from reaching the chancellors and to recover the letters—at any cost. I barely got out of the palace with my life.

"That's why I was being chased. There is no way that Payne is going to allow me to get those letters to the Council."

4

SMILES AND BEARS

THE GYPSY POKED at the embers in the little stove, stirring the slumbering coals into a few fitful flames. "I can see that you have had some difficulties," he said, finally.

"I'm glad that you can appreciate that," the princess replied.

"But they are not difficulties I have not dealt with before, except perhaps on a matter of scale: I have not before had an army after me. Perhaps there is something I could do. We shall see."

"I'd appreciate all the help that I could get . . . if it's a question of a reward . . ."

"No! no!" he answered with some heat. "That is not something to mention. I will help you, that is all, it is enough."

"I must get to my cousin Piers as soon as possible."

"And your friend?"

"Thud? What about him?"

"There is something about him I find very strange."

"I can't imagine what," she answered sarcastically. "But don't judge him by his looks; he's a good man."

"Please do not misunderstand me! I can see that he is. Honored guest," he said to Thud, without a trace of mockery, "where do you come from?"

"Groontocker and Peen."

"This is another planet?"

"I don't know; I just cut stone there."

"I see! An artisan! And before that?"

"I always cut stone there."

"You were a child once, were you not? Although I find that very hard to imagine." Bronwyn almost protested this slur, but then she recalled that the very same doubt once ran through her own mind.

"Sure I was, I was a kid like anyone else. Just a little big, that's all. I've always been big."

"Please! No offense meant! Believe me when I say that you are a very admirable man. Who else could have brought the princess here safely? Eh?"

"Well . . ." Thud was embarrassed by the compliment, and thought of mentioning his failure in getting Bronwyn to the destination he had promised her, but thought better of it. Why spoil things?

"But look here, I am serious—believe me, I have good reason for asking. What do you recall of your boyhood? Do you remember your parents?"

"No, not exactly. I kind of grew up mostly around the streets." He fidgeted, not sure how far to open himself to a stranger. He looked to Bronwyn.

"I'd like to know, too, Thud, so go ahead." Thud pulled his bag over to his chair and rummaged in it for a moment. He pulled a cloth bundle from it and began unwrapping it. Bronwyn was not surprised when Thud laid the hard rubber case of the tintype on the table. He opened it as reverently as he would an icon— or perhaps it was an icon. The sad, silvery face shimmered up at them.

"Holy Sister of Musrum!" whispered the gypsy. "And this . . . ?"

"I always liked to think she was my mother, but I really don't remember too good; it was long ago. I've just always had this picture."

"What is it?" asked the mystified Bronwyn.

"Nothing, nothing. She . . . just reminded me of someone. It is of no matter."

"Thud is my man; I'll not have anyone laughing at him!"

"Oh ho! The *princess* speaks, eh? No, I would not mock your friend. I will show you why not. Henda, come here."

The strange little creature came waddling and sniffling to its master. The eyes were very much like a bird's. Bronwyn had seen their like once in a bird her cousin Piers had caught in a net, its wings hopelessly broken.

"Henda, these are very good people; they are friends of mine and so they are friends of yours, too. Understand me?" Henda's bright black beads sparkled first at Bronwyn, then at Thud. The raggedy head nodded, uncertainly. "All right, then, you can take those things off your head."

The sniffing came more violently and Henda shied back from the gypsy, eyes jumping twitchily from girl to giant to gypsy, like fleas. Then a hand appeared from the midst of the rags. It was small, smooth and pink. Bronwyn realized with a jolt that it was a child's hand. It began unwinding the long scarf that was wrapped around its face. Then Henda turned and smiled at Bronwyn. And smiled and smiled and *smiled*.

"Do you see why I do not laugh at your big friend, my Princess?"

"What happened to him?" asked the girl, in a hushed voice.

"There is a band of wicked people—not true gypsies, I thank Musrum—who wander through the villages of Mostaza. They are only beggars; thieves, pickpockets and cutthroats, and worse. They have no *art*, do you understand? They call themselves *Verstummellin*. They say that it means 'the misshapen,' as though they were describing themselves, their own appearance. But the word really means 'misshapers.' It is difficult to translate the difference. 'Mutilators'? That is better. They are the Mutilators.

"It is not what they *look* like, it is what they *do*. They do not wish to give in return for the money that they beg: you will not receive from them music, a good medicine, your fortune; no. They are too lazy for that. They sell *pity*. They do things to their poor children, and to children they steal. They set them to wander through the villages, if they *can* wander, you understand? People see these babes and say, 'Oh! What has happened to you, unfortunate one? What has happened to your eyes? What has become of your leg, your arm? Look how the poor thing must walk hunched over, look how it must drag itself through the dirt, look what it must accept my money with instead of hands!' "

The gypsy was quite red and he realized that he had raised his voice. "Forgive me, please. It is just when I think . . . Well. Henda here, the *Verstummellin* thought it would be amusing to make *smile*. They had tried many other things before, with other children, but never this. Henda had a long career before I found him. It is why it is best that the rest of him remain so bundled, you understand? The face is really not so bad. Not like the rest. I do not think that he is more than eight years old yet. So they thought they would make him smile. And now poor Henda smiles and smiles, no matter what he may feel inside. My poor little Henda." He cradled the child's head in his lap.

"Now you two," he continued, allowing the child to replace its raggedy mask, "you are welcome to sleep here. In just a few hours we will be preparing to leave the city and things will be very busy. You will be coming with us."

"With you? But how? The Guards will be searching everywhere. There's no place here we could hide from them. You said yourself they didn't miss a thing."

"They did not *think* they had missed anything, which is not quite the same thing. You must trust me. We gypsies have much experience at this. I believe that the Guards will abandon the idea of searching the city for you. All that is really necessary for them is to prevent you from *leaving*, is that not so? Yes. I thought as much. Well, I do not think, then, that they will waste very much more time chasing you through the streets. I think you have only made them angry this night. They will realize this. They will be very wary at the bridges and other places, instead of searching the streets. As long as you are trapped here, your brother and his friend have little to worry about, no? And after the coronation, what do they care?"

"Then you have a way . . . ?" Bronwyn began.

"Do not have a mind about it. I will send Henda to wake you. My home is yours tonight." And without another word the gypsy left the wagon, Henda following closely behind. The thick wooden slab of a door closed gently behind them.

"Did you see the kid's face?" asked Thud. "How could somebody do that to a kid? Gave me the creeps."

Bronwyn lowered the iron bar across the door. She returned to where Thud lounged on the built-in bed, and sat beside him, drawing her legs up onto the cushion.

"Thud, my worthy friend, I think that we are both learning that there is a lot more about the world than we ever thought possible."

"What do you think the gypsy meant about my picture? Do you think he knew what my fortune was? I've never seen a gypsy before, but I heard that they can tell people's fortunes. How do you think they do that?" He got no answer from the girl, other than the soft purring of her breath. She was fast asleep, her head against

Thud's broad hip, her hair spilling over his lap. Thud sighed.
He leaned his own head into the corner of the nook; his hand lay
gently over Bronwyn's head, a hand so large it seemed to engulf
it like a pink starfish devouring a clam. The big fingers gently
stroked the hair above her ear, and soon he, too, was asleep.

It was still dark when a rap came at the door. Thud, as usual,
was instantly awake. He was slumped in the bed nook. Bronwyn
was asleep still; her head looked like a cat that had curled into a
lap for a nap. He shook her shoulder, "Princess? Princess? It's
time to wake up." Another light tap sounded. Bronwyn sat up,
blinking and rubbing the sleep from her eyes, as Thud went to
the door. "Yes?" he asked it.

"It is me," came the voice of the gypsy, "and Henda. It is time
to leave. May we come in?"

Thud threw back the bar and the door swung open. The gypsy
and his boy entered, shutting the door quickly behind them.

"Good morning, my friends. I hope that your sleep was pleasant, if brief."

"Was I even asleep?" asked Bronwyn, who ached in every bone
and whose eyes seemed filled with powdered glass.

"It will be dawn in an hour. We are late in leaving, but none
of the others wished to disturb you so soon. Now, however, we
must hasten."

"What do we have to do?"

"Trust us." The four exited the caravan. The sky blushed with
the suggestive promise of dawn, and the air was crisp and damp. A
dozen people were busy in the plaza, puffing white vapor into the
cold air; the paper lanterns were gone, the grass had been combed
of every scrap of litter, the cooking and campfires had vanished.
The iron tripod, its kettle, the folding stools and benches were all
gone as though they had never existed; the striped pavilions of
the fortuneteller and sideshow had collapsed upon themselves and
disappeared like a magician's card trick. The other gypsies, male,
female and young, barely spared Thud and Bronwyn a glance.

"You are lucky, my friends, that the dancing bear died. I did
not know about you, Thud Mollockle; you might have presented
me with a difficulty, no?"

He led the two to a wagon that had large barred openings in
its sides. These were normally hidden by a pair of hinged panels that were now swung up like wings. It was an animal cage,
though presently unoccupied. The frame of the wagon was as flor-
idly decorated as the others. As they approached a gypsy was

harnessing a brace of small, shaggy horses to the wagon tongue. They looked at the strangers with sleepy, doleful eyes.

"This was the home of poor Gretl. Ah, the children loved her, she was so gentle and such a fine dancer. But she was an old bear and three days ago, in the night, she died, just like that. We loved her, old Gretl, but what could we do with a dead bear? She was as big as you, friend Thud. Could we bury her in the plaza? No! How could we do that to such a loyal friend? It was out of the question. So, being a practical people, we sold her. I like to think that Gretl will be feeding many hungry children, and keeping them warm with her fine, thick pelt. Too, the money we were paid will be keeping a company of excellent gypsies honest and fat. Would Gretl have asked for more? I see you agree!"

They had circled the empty wagon. The horses had in the meantime been harnessed, as similar animals had been to all of the other wagons. And these were beginning to be pulled into a rough line, guided by gentle flicks from the drivers' whips and lilting words in the gypsies' musical language. It was apparent that the band was anxious to depart. "Hottl!" cried their gypsy friend to the driver of the empty bear wagon. "These are our new companions; do you have the coat?"

Hottl gave Thud and Bronwyn a curt look, turned, reached behind his seat and pulled out what at first the girl thought was some sort of large, limp animal. It was the biggest fur coat she had ever seen. The driver handed it down to the gypsy leader, who in turn handed it to Thud. "Put that on," he ordered. Thud slipped his arms into the sleeves. Bronwyn was amazed: the coat was actually a size too large! What kind of person had it been made for? It was shaggy, moth-eaten, balding, mangy and so long its hem brushed the ground. Bronwyn giggled.

"What's so funny?" Thud asked.

"Nothing! I'm sorry, but you really do look like a bear!" Hottl tossed a furry ball to the gypsy, who handed it to Thud. It was a hat, with long flaps that hung down on either side, like the ears of a spaniel. They hugged his head when Thud tied them under his chin.

"Wonderful!" cried the gypsy. "How I wish Gretl were still here to see you!"

"You think it looks good?" asked Thud, straining his neck to see himself.

"Inexpressibly handsome! Now quickly, into the wagon." The gypsy unlatched a padlock as large as Thud's fist and swung open the rear gate of the wagon. Thud clambered in, his broad hips just scraping through in a shower of brown hair. The wagon's springs groaned.

"Stay in the corner, keep your back to the gate; if anyone looks in, growl. Can you growl?"

"Grrr," growled Thud.

"I knew you could! Now," said the gypsy, closing and relocking the gate, "we will tend to the princess." He untied the cords that held the winglike side panels up. He let the cords run through their pulleys and the panels slammed shut.

"Thud?" he called to the interior as he fastened the wings down.

"Grrr!"

"Good! Do not do anything until you hear from me or the princess again; understand?"

"Grrr!"

"Quickly now," he said as he turned to the girl, "come with me."

"What are you going to do?" she asked, trotting a step behind. She really hated the way the gypsy insisted on ordering her to do things; he was worse than Thud, who at least tacked a "please" at the end. She didn't take orders; it was a matter she wanted very much to call to his attention, since it was gradually making her angry. But he was making everything happen so fast!

"You I shall make invisible!" The gypsy and the princess entered the rear of another wagon. It was obviously used to carry all the paraphernalia the gypsies used for their shows and daily life; it was packed with baskets, boxes, bags, coils of rope, lanterns, sacks of feed, meal and flour, canned foods, clothing and so forth.

"Wait right here," commanded the gypsy, and he disappeared back into the daylight. Bronwyn could hear his deep voice giving orders to his band. He sounded like an iron bell when he spoke in his liquid native tongue. He had apparently given the command to start the procession. She could hear whips snapping, the ponies nickering, and suddenly her own wagon gave a jolt and began moving, its iron-shod wheels rumbling on the cobbles. The door flashed daylight at her again, and the gypsy climbed back inside. He shut the door and the interior was once again plunged into twilight. Only thin blades of light sliced through the dark, from around the shutters that ineffectually sealed the windows.

"Pardon me, please," begged the gypsy, as he moved around behind the princess. There was little room. He pulled a cloth away from a large object and Bronwyn gave a little gasp of surprise and delight. Revealed was a splended Peigambarese sultan, a pudgy little man with a hooked nose and black eyes. Above the grinning mouth was a pair of long, pointed moustachios, like the antennae of an insect. A dart-shaped goatee hung from his pendulous chin. The head was topped with a jeweled turban, the body wrapped in a silken robe. The figure sat with its legs crossed in front, the toes of its silk slippers curled in full circles. Its hands, the fingers buried beneath an encrustation of jewelry, lay idly on the chess board that was balanced on its lap. One held the long, curved stem of a clay pipe.

He had been artfully carved entirely from wood, painted and decorated with real clothing and paraphernalia.

The figure sat cross-legged on top of an ornately decorated box. This was about three feet high, four wide and three deep. In the front were two panels. The gypsy opened these, which comprised almost the entire façade of the box, by sliding one over the other. The inside, in the half Bronwyn could see, was filled with machinery. The gypsy opened another sliding door in the rear of the box. Now she could see entirely through the mass of gears, cams and springs to the grinning face of the gypsy.

"It's beautiful," said Bronwyn, with genuine admiration, though failing to see the point. "But why are you showing me this?"

"Ah! It is the most wonderful thing! He is really a star, this Peigambar sultan. Everyone wants to see him, and everyone who does must pay their ten poenigs. But does he want much? Does he eat like poor Gretl did, bless her soul, if bears have souls, and why should they not? No! Does he demand more than his share of the profit, because the people love him the most? No! In fact, he asks for nothing at all! Except perhaps a drop of oil now and then. Ah, I love my gypsies, but I also love my fat little Peigambar sultan!"

"But what does it . . . he . . . it do? What's the point of this?"

"He plays chess, my Princess! He plays like a master! Anyone is welcome to try and see if he does not, but they must pay for the privilege!"

"It's a mechanical chess-player?" asked the girl, interested in spite of herself, if still mystified.

"Ah, now I must be sad because I must tell you a great secret." While he spoke the gypsy had been turning a handle on the side of the box. A whirring sound, like beating wings, came from inside. He pulled a lever beside the sultan's knee and the inside of the box came to life. The machinery began turning with a pleasantly soft metallic purring. Bronwyn bent to get a better look at the spinning works; it looked immensely complicated.

"Make it work!" she demanded.

"Come around to this side," invited the gypsy. Bronwyn sidled between the figure and the piles of stores that crowded it, until she could see the back of the figure. "Watch!" He shut the sliding panels, then touched some hidden lever or button, and the back of the sultan hinged open. The interior of the figure was hollow.

"This is Henda's job," explained the gypsy. "It gives him great pleasure. He is a very intelligent boy, but, as you might understand, very shy with strangers. It pleases him to be shut up inside the sultan, where he can see others while they cannot know he is watching. I think that it gives him pleasure, too, to know that he is tricking the very people who once laughed at his face or turned away in disgust. I will not ask him and you should not either. You noticed that I had to shut the sliding panels before I could open the sultan? Good! That is one of the secrets. I can open either one side of the box or the other, but not both at the same time. I can open the back of the sultan, but not when the front panels are open. You are looking bewildered, Princess! Let me tell you what our villager sees once he has paid his ten poenigs admission.

"When I bring the sultan before him, Henda is inside. I open one side of the box. I go to the back and open it, too. I hold a candle behind so that the villager can see the light through the machinery. Henda, he has swung his legs to one side, into the closed half of the box. I then slide the panels and do the same for the other side. Henda, he does as before. I close these and open a big door in the chest of the sultan, I open his back. The villager, he can see that the sultan has nothing in him but a few wires, rods and springs. Henda, he has dropped into the box below, bent over as much as he can. I close everything up and invite the villager to a game. Henda raises his head just far enough into the sultan to see the board. Do you see that big jewel in his chest? Look closely, see? It is just mesh. Henda can see through it like a window. He stretches a hand into the arm of the sultan—it only needs to move from the elbow, you see?—and can move the pieces on the board with ease. It is so simple!"

"I think that I know what you have in mind," said Bronwyn, sorry that she had laughed at Thud, "but my chess-playing is not very good."

"It is not necessary! We will not be putting on a show for the Guards, we only need a place to hide you. You are much taller than Henda; it will not be easy for you. But you are young and can bend like a sapling. You *must!*" he finished with sudden intentness.

"I can try. But I'll die in there! How long will it take us to get away from the city?"

"I do not think that you will need to stay inside the sultan all the time. I will show you how to get in, and we will practice the movements and timing. It is very easy. Then all I will need to do is to signal you if we are to be stopped. I will be riding beside the driver. We will be taking the canal north from the city. I think that we will only be searched at the barge pool, but it will be a good search, they will try to miss nothing."

In the northwest of Blavek's island, on the bank of the Moltus, was the reservoir that fed the canal that ran due north out of the city. It was on a high bluff overlooking the water, just downstream from the Pordka Falls. An aqueduct carried the canal from the reservoir, over the churning river, to the top of the vertical granite cliffs opposite. A full troop of Guards were waiting for the gypsies.

The caravan joined the milling throng of passengers and freight wagons that were waiting to be inspected before they could board the canal barges. The Guards were being as thorough as the gypsy had warned Bronwyn they would be. It was slow work and tempers were short. Few, however, dared to speak out too harshly against the inspection. The mood of the soldiers was too obvious, and already several people had been beaten and arrested for obstructing the work—or for just simply being annoying. The message was too blatant for those remaining to miss. The people mumbled, but they wisely kept it *sotto voce*. Slowly, one barge after another moved through the lock and onto the aqueduct.

Finally, the gypsy wagons came under the scrutiny of the Guards. The fugitives' gypsy friend accompanied the inspection—which was thorough indeed. Half a dozen men combed through each wagon down the line, one at a time. They sounded the walls, they looked beneath the vans and on the roofs, they checked every box, basket, pot, baggage, sack and bundle; even things it would have been impossible for either the girl or the big man to have fitted into. They were thorough, but, as has been said already, they had no imagination.

When they reached the wagon containing Thud—the wagon immediately preceding Bronwyn's—the Guard in charge asked,

"What's in here?" Which was an entirely unnecessary question, since the closed panels were covered with colorful paintings of a giant, snarling, slavering, sharp-fanged and dagger-taloned animal. Surrounding these were words in gold-outlined red (and altogether belying the ferocious images): *Gretl the Dancing Bear*.

"It is a dancing bear," answered the gypsy.

"A dancing bear?"

"Yes, a bear; very dangerous animal, I do not know why I keep it, it will kill someone some day, I know it. And it dances."

"Well, open up, let's see it."

"As you wish." And the gypsy pulled on one of the dangling cords, raising a side panel a few feet, so that it angled out like an awning, shading the inside. The Guard peered into the dim interior. He could see that there was nothing in the cage but a great black shape sitting huddled on the bare wooden floor.

"That's it, huh?" the Guard captain asked. He rattled the bars with the butt of his rifle. "Hoo! Hoo!" he cried. The black mass shook itself.

"Grrr!" it said.

"Ugly brute, ain't it?" said the Guard, stepping back a pace involuntarily. "All right, close it up."

As the gang of soldiers approached the next wagon, the driver gave the wall behind his seat a surreptitious tap, tap, taptap.

"What's in here?"

"It is the supply wagon. A little bit of everything: clothes, props, I do not know. A catch-all."

"Open it up."

Inside, the Guards faced the almost solid mass of baggage with an air of dejection. "Go through every piece!" ordered the captain. Only two of the men could fit into the interior at one time. They began passing the larger boxes and trunks to the men outside. In only minutes, the ground surrounding the wagon was buried under the contents of the wagon. There was a surprised shout from inside the van. "Captain!" called one of the two Guards.

"What is it?" asked that officer, putting his head into the doorway. Then: "Holy Musrum!" Then: "Get that thing out of there; it scared the shit out of me!"

The sultan was wrestled out of the wagon. "Please be careful," worried the gypsy. "That is a valuable work of art!"

"You," said the captain to the gypsy, "can get your people to load this other junk back onto the wagon. What is this thing?"

"It is the Peigambar sultan!" To which information the captain merely looked blank. "It is a chess-player! You wind it up, it plays chess."

"Open it up, I want to see what's inside." The gypsy opened the first sliding panel, and then the matching one in the back. The captain bent to look inside and could see one of his other men peering back at him through the maze of gears, pinions and cams. Before he could say anything, the gypsy slid the panels to the other side of the box, revealing the remaining half of its contents. The captain and the soldier repeated their performance. The gypsy was easily able to keep his face sober: he had seen bumpkins in every village in Tamlaght do what he was watching the Guards do now. Once again anticipating the captain's orders, the gypsy slipped the panels shut and opened the sultan's chest and the door in its back. It was hollow but for a few rods, springs and cables coming from the machinery below.

"Make it work," ordered the Guard.

"What?"

"Make it work. I want to see it play this game."

"Yes, sir," the gypsy said as he felt around in his pockets. "Do you have a crown on you, sir? I need to put a crown in it before it will work. I do not seem to have anything less than an eagle."

"Yes, yes." The captain fumbled for a second in his uniform, finally pulling forth a golden coin, with the pride of a magician producing an egg. The gypsy took it and inserted it in the machine. Stepping to its side, he cranked the handle for a turn or two. The machinery began its mysterious writhings. The captain was fascinated by the spinning works.

"You must make the first move," said the gypsy.

"Eh?"

"The game. The sultan cannot play until you make the first move."

"Oh. Well, ah . . ." The captain reached out a tentative hand and moved one of the pawns. The sultan whirred like a cat; its free arm vibrated, raised itself above the game board, moved until it was above one of its pieces, dropped, grasped the pawn between a pincerlike thumb and forefinger, and moved it one square ahead.

"Fascinating!" exclaimed the captain. "Well, we must move on . . ."

"You will not finish the game?" asked the gypsy. "You are doing so well!"

"Yes? Ah. Well . . ." He moved another piece. So did the sultan. He moved another, and so did the sultan. "Ha! Ha!" cried the captain, and jumped four of the automaton's men, sweeping them off the board into his hand. "Your machine is not so clever as a captain of the Guards, is it, gypsy?"

"I should have known it was futile! My machine has been outwitted! My congratulations, sir!"

"All right," said the captain, "get that thing back in your wagon and move on. Damnedest thing I've ever seen!" he confided to the man next to him. "Scared the shit out of me when I saw it sitting in there. Can't play, though! Ha!"

"If I were you, sir, I'd check to make sure I still had my watch," suggested the lieutenant, who did know how to play chess and had always thought his superior officer an idiot. He watched superciliously as the captain checked his watch pocket, meanly deciding not to remind him that he *had* lost a gold crown in the demonstration.

The dozen wagons were loaded onto one of the long, flat, very narrow wooden barges. The animals were penned closely together amidships. The bargemasters with their fifteen-foot wood poles lined either side of the boat. They pushed against the bottom of the shallow reservoir; guided by shoremen hauling on cables attached to the bows, the heavily laden barge moved into the rectangular stone lock, within which it was just small enough to fit with a foot or two clearance all around. The entrance was sealed by thick timber gates. The water began churning and there was a distant throbbing sound of draining liquid. The water level dropped quickly until the tops of the wagons were well below the rim of the lock. The gates at the opposite end opened and the barge was pushed out into the canal solely by the efforts of the bargemasters, their poles straining against the mossy sides of the lock. It glided between grassy banks for a few yards, then entered the aqueduct. Here the canal was carried nearly a hundred feet above the turbulent Moltus by the ancient stone structure, its piers planted firmly in the boiling waters of the river. It was a vertiginous five minutes; the sides of the aqueduct were low, barely above the level of the water, and scarcely further apart than the width of the barge. It was possible, by grasping some firmly attached object, to lean out away from the barge and look straight down to the river below. There was no way Bronwyn would be convinced to try this—in fact, it was just as well for her that she was still hidden.

The barge sailed smoothly into the broad main canal beyond the cliffs. The gypsy climbed to the driver's seat of his caravan and rapped his knuckles against the wall behind it: tap, tap, taptap.

"Princess?" he whispered to the wood. "All is well, come to the door." He climbed back to the deck of the barge and circled to the rear of the wagon. He unlocked the door and swung it open. "It is safe to come out. The bargemen, they are blind and dumb. Do not concern yourself with them."

Bronwyn stepped down from the wagon, shielding her eyes from the glare that squeezed tears from them. The gypsy lent her a hand until her vision repaired.

"Ah, you were wonderful," said the gypsy. "Perhaps you were not meant to be a princess; you are intelligent and brave enough to be one of us!"

"I may never walk erect again," she answered, bending her back and stretching her knees, up and down. "I feel like a used paper clip."

"Let us go and fetch your friend; I do not think he is any more comfortable than you."

The late Gretl's wagon was directly behind the gypsy leader's. He unlocked the rear gate. "Grrr!" came a throaty snarl from inside. Bronwyn almost forgot that there was not a wild animal in there. "Thud!" she cried into the dark interior. "It's me, Princess Bronwyn. You can come out now, everything's all right."

She stepped back as the enormous, black, furry creature emerged. The wagon looked like a square egg giving birth to a gorilla. The creature shrugged and molted its skin as neatly as a snake. Thud's clothing clung to him wetly: he was drenched to the skin with sweat. Now, however, he began to shiver in the brisk wind that whisked across the open deck.

"Are you all right, Thud?"

"Sure. Fooled them, didn't we? That was a lot of fun. Grrr! That Guard almost made me laugh!"

"Well," said the gypsy, "it is a good thing you did not; even a Guard would not be stupid enough to believe in a laughing bear."

"I think Thud should find something warm to put on. Look at him, he's freezing!"

"Come, my friend, I think that we can accommodate you!"

The gypsy took Thud by the arm and led him to the baggage wagon. Bronwyn balanced along the narrow catwalk that ran the perimeter of the boat. It took her to the bow, a blunt, triangular point. The clean air from the north tumbled her hair, shaking it like a terrier worrying a fox. It brushed her cheeks until they stung, and she knew they were bright red. The air was as clear as a vacuum and she could see the multicolored leaves on distant trees with

the clarity of the dots in a halftone engraving. They had entered
the rolling, open countryside north of Blavek, the foothills that
promised ragged mountains that were still beyond the horizon.
The grassy undulations were dun from the frosts of approaching
winter. There were bleak times ahead.

5

A JACKAL, A FOX AND
A HOUND

MEANWHILE, back at the palace, Prince Ferenc was in a frenzy of despair. Lord Roelt would be returning to Blavek in a matter of days—he was probably on the road now—yet Bronwyn was still missing, and with her the damning letters. Why hadn't he listened to Payne? Why hadn't he destroyed them? Payne was always right in matters like these: if he needed proof of that, this affair was certainly sufficient. He expected that Payne would be furious when he discovered how badly these simple tasks had been botched. And Prince Ferenc hated making Payne angry.

The prince and his sister had grown up all in a golden afternoon; the handsome boy and the handsome girl. They knew only parks and green forests, broad lawns and small, clear lakes with fountains and beautifully carved and painted boats. They each had stables full of lean and muscular horses, with steaming breath and rolling eyes. There were carriages, carts, and buggies for whatever degree of comfort or occasion of state might be required. When they were taken on afternoon drives, it was in a carriage with a coachman, two footmen and a groom. A vanguard of household militia made certain that the way was without hazard. Every day, at exactly the same time, on a lawn during the brief summer or indoors when the weather turned frosty, the children gathered for

71

tea, accompanied by their governesses and tutors. At small tables covered with embroidered linens and set with silver and translucent china, they drank their spicy tea from crystal glasses in silver holders. Their birthdays were as lavish as a coronation. For toys they had real armies and real houses full of living dolls that would do whatever they were asked. The children's companions were chosen from the highest-ranking families, and were intelligent, active and obedient. Neither the boy nor the girl wanted for anything. However, there was one great inequality: one was a prince and the other a princess.

Their father, the king, had left the rearing and education of his children to professionals. There was always a proper method of doing anything, and the best way to approach a problem was to find the people who are expert at solving it and let them alone to do their job. This was his philosophy and, as applied to the rule of his nation, was admirable on the whole. So perhaps he had no reason to imagine it would be any different with his children.

Bronwyn discovered that even a king is entitled to his mistakes. By right and precedent, the boy as both the elder child and, incidentally, the male child was heir to the throne. Had the girl been the elder, the king would have treated her more as the boy had been treated—they were elements of tradition, not the fruit of his loins, flesh of his flesh, his son, his daughter. If Fate had chosen one to be the elder, rather than the other, so be it. Tradition dictated that that child would eventually be the monarch. So be it. Suitability for the role was a consideration that never entered into the matter.

The children's lives were in the hands of a succession of nurses, nannies, governesses and tutors. Loving hands, no question about that; caring and capable ones, there was never any doubt. But they were still hands controlled by the Great Puppeteer of tradition.

The prince was destined to be the king someday, and all of his education and training must be toward making him prepared for this career. Long days were spent in lessons on military matters: strategies of historic victories, the lives of the great generals and admirals, the rudiments of weapon construction and the theories of ballistics, chemistry and metallurgy; he was taught sailing, naval architecture and navigation.

Nor did his education neglect the intellectual and artistic, for a king needed to be wise and cultured; or at least be able to maintain the appearance of being such, if he was not to be considered a bumpkin by his fellow heads of state. The prince was instructed in philosophy, the classics, languages ancient and modern, astronomy and geography, music and art.

For a child of even modest intelligence, curiosity and ambition, this education would have been a joy, since its teachers were all expert, enthusiastic and sympathetic—an ideal composition—and would have, even at the worst, turned out a passably usable product. Unfortunately the prince was sullen, lazy, unambitious and if not intelligent, had made up the difference with craftiness. He had taken all that his privileged life had allowed him and considered it as nothing less than what he was due. He was spoiled. His attitude toward his training was that it was an unnecessary and nearly unbearable burden he was forced to tolerate, if only to avoid his father's wrath; there was an image of the future king that his father was adamant that the prince be made to fit. He escaped it as often as possible, having also measured his father's indulgence to a fineness.

The younger child's life was very different, though she did all she could to improve it according to her own ambitions. Her official education was limited to those subjects that would best suit her for making intelligent conversation, as a suitable ornament for the court of her brother the king, and toward developing into a respectable and desirable bride who would contribute her part in making the international ruling class even more interrelated and inbred. This did not place any great demands on her time. It was supposed that she would devote her free periods to riding, playing croquet or tennis, being taken sailing or for carriage trips through the city parks, or whatever other gentle pursuits were appropriate for a young royal princess.

Her free time was her own, however, and she quickly discovered that there was nothing preventing her from accompanying her brother in his lessons. The prince's tutors just as quickly discovered that while they were ostensibly instructing a patently dull-witted boy, they were in fact educating another child, one who was officially invisible to them, but whose intelligence was as brightly keen as a kitten's.

She loved to run and climb and fight with the children of the servants. She had to be more circumspect here. Her father must never be allowed to see her in a tree or wrestling in the dirty furrows of the kitchen herb gardens. More than once a sniffling servant child was sent to its room by angered and frightened parents, after they had caught him or her pounding the royal princess's face with a pulped tomato. The fact that the princess had given their child a black eye was of no account in the matter.

Still, it must be admitted that the punishments were only token. The princess never seemed aware of differences in rank—at least she seldom made an issue of it, and the servants loved her like one of their own. Perhaps she benefitted, in their affection, from a kind of rebound, since her brother enjoyed a perverse pleasure in creating situations where he would be able to bring grief to the defenseless palace staff.

Thus the two children each became the opposite of what the king intended to create, though he was to his dying day unaware of this. The prince was unpleasant, condescending, physically weak, vain, dull, supercilious, sarcastic and lazy. The princess was intelligent—though not particularly intellectual (she enjoyed learning but had not yet learned to enjoy thinking), curious, too pragmatic to be romantic, a little too ambitious, a little too serious, reckless, selfish, physically strong; self-important, perhaps, more naïve than she believed and quick-tempered, but not altogether an unpleasant person.

If there was any error in the princess's education, though perhaps miscalculation is a better word, even if it implies that what was done was done consciously, it was that of artificiality. If her playmates and their parents treated her as an equal, it was not because they actually believed that to be so. Certainly not. The children were always aware that the princess was of another, and superior, species than they. She had dozens of fond playmates, but not a single friend. The parents were all too aware of the power that lay behind the girl. While they were not obsequious, neither were they stupid: they still pulled their punches. If the children's play was rough-and-tumble, the princess was never hurt beyond a bruise or a scuff. If she occasionally lost at the games they played, she never lost very badly, and never as often as she won. If she thought she had grown tough and self-assured, it was in large measure because her opposition was resilient; she believed that her world was an accurate replica of the larger world beyond the palace. It was not: it was a fictional simulacrum. Within the palace it made a difference that she was Bronwyn Tedeschiy, no matter how much it was pretended it didn't; no one told her that the world outside didn't care.

There was more than the obvious differences in the manners with which the two treated their inferiors. And it is difficult to truly tell which was the worst: while the prince considered people of common birth with contempt, the princess never considered them at all.

As part of the prince's training, his friends were carefully chosen from among the leaders of the ruling class. Sons of the most powerful barons, dukes and earls were selected for his companions. He was expected to play, exercise and study with those who would eventually support his throne. These boys would come and go, as circumstances, politics and personalities dictated.

One only was a constant. He arrived at the palace when the prince was only seven years old. The newcomer was an elfin child, preternaturally thin, with black eyes sunken deep within their sockets and hair as black and glossy as oil against his pale, dry skin. He had hands like spiders, but they were not fragile: the princess once saw him break walnuts in them. He had not been in the prince's company for more than a few days before it was clear who possessed the dominant personality.

While always obsequious and demonstrably aware of his rank in relation to his royal companion, he was no toady like the others. Instead, the princess saw that the other boys were treating him with the same fawning respect they dealt the prince. Eventually, in games and conversation, he became the acknowledged leader. It was he who suggested the sports, the day's activities, the rules by which they played, and the topics they discussed. It was his opinions that settled any debate, his rulings that squared any dispute on the field.

The prince seemed relieved to be able to delegate his authority to his friend, who in turn merely acted in the prince's name. The prince was pleased at how accurately his lieutenant was able to translate his desires into such intelligent commands, and was amazed at how often his thoughts were anticipated. His friend was able to come up with the most impressive ideas just minutes before the prince himself was about to think them.

And did the new boy ever for a moment consider taking credit away from the prince? Not at all! What honesty! What loyalty! His teachers took pleasure in making him feel stupid, and his sister treated him like a simpleton. Here at last was someone who appreciated his intelligence.

Less than a year after his arrival, the father of the new boy died. It was easy, then, for him to gradually become a permanent fixture of the royal household.

The princess and the lieutenant quickly developed a loathing and fear for one another. He recognized in her an intelligence as vital as his own, if of a different variety. She saw in him a power that her brother lacked, and that he was exercising this power in the prince's name and with the prince's authority. The tall, lean girl and the slight, reptilian boy were, in fact, more equally matched than either would care to have realized. Both were dedicated individualists, powerful both physically and intellectually, imaginative, ambitious, heedless, and with great courage, single-mindedness and boldness. But the energies they possessed were of very different sorts, and manifested themselves in very different ways. It was like comparing the relative deadlinesses of a wildcat and an electric current.

The princess knew what the boy was doing to her brother within weeks of his arrival, and the boy just as quickly was aware of her knowledge. Even though he recognized the girl as an enemy, he never treated her with anything other than his usual faultlessly polite respect. There was little or nothing that the princess could do about him, or to him, and he knew this. But he also realized that she was an implacable foe, and possessed of a mind so alien to his own that to attempt to predict what she could or could not, or would or would not, do would be impossible for him. So he was polite to her, always watched her and tried never to underestimate her.

The princess found herself being gradually forced out of the palace. More and more often she discovered rooms locked where they had once stood open; unfamiliar faces among the servants: faces surly, evil and sneering; strangers coming and going on business of which she had no knowledge; banquets, balls and receptions held from which she was excluded by never being told of them. The number of occasions where her official presence might have been employed—christenings, openings, concerts, operas and that sort of thing—declined. These, which her brother had once shunned like the plague, were now attended by him, always with his amanuensis at his side, to provide the witty remark, the pithy epigram that would soon be quoted throughout the city as having been spoken by the prince. Occasionally, the intriguing pale young man who always accompanied the prince—someone of undoubted importance, everyone was certain—would appear in the prince's place, if the heir to the throne were indisposed or demanded elsewhere. Fewer people all the time asked themselves where the princess was; eventually few people even missed her.

*   *   *

The tall young man in the tight-fitting, dove-grey and entirely honorary uniform of a major in the Royal Slottenen Fusiliers paced the ornately parqueted floor of his apartment. The handsome, babyish face was twisted into a pink knot with the effort of puzzling out his dilemma. Ferenc's features were a kind of boneless version of his sister's: where her hair was copper, his was rust; where her eyes were like jade, his were like green gelatin; where her full lips were sensuous, his were sensual. Since his discovery that the letters were missing—can it only have been a day?—he had spent most of the subsequent time worrying about the consequences. He hadn't yet thought much beyond the immediate wrath of Lord Roelt, but it was gradually coming to him what exposure of the letters to the barons would mean.

As soon as he had realized that his secretary had been rifled, and that the incriminating packets had been stolen, he knew who must have taken them. He had immediately stormed Bronwyn's apartment, but she had not been there. Reluctant to raise an alarm, if there was yet a chance to regain his property quietly, he searched the palace. There had been no sign of his sister in any of her usual haunts. There had been no point in trying to look any further: the palace was labyrinthine, having grown like a kind of architectural coral reef with, he had no doubt, literally thousands of rooms and passages. He would not have been surprised to learn that in his lifetime he had not visited more than a small fraction of them—which was true. In the time that he would waste searching for Bronwyn, she would be at the doors of the Privy Council. And he would certainly rather see his sister dead before that.

So, acting with atypical astuteness, he had called in the Commandant of the Guards, Major-General Jaeger Praxx. It was something that he loathed doing, and it was only because he feared the general slightly less than the wrath of the Privy Council—who could deprive him of the throne—that he was able to summon the man. And once he had done so, he awaited the general's coming by curling into one of the luxuriously upholstered chairs that decorated the chamber, tucking patent-leather boots under his soft hams—and if he was not actually sucking his thumb, he gave every impression of doing so.

In his fear of the major-general, Ferenc had some reasonable justification. The man wielded power exceeded only by that of Lord Roelt and, ideally and supposedly, the prince himself. Although Praxx was mightily ambitious, an emotion

that drove him like a hundred atmospheres of live steam
drives a locomotive, that ambition gave Lord Roelt little
to concern himself about. Praxx was no rival. Unlike most
mortals, Praxx was one of those exceedingly rare individuals who had been fortunate enough to have realized their
fondest ambition; in Praxx's example, this required serving
the one man in the world he admired: Payne Roelt. He
recognized that his only opportunities to acquire the power he craved were tied to his association with the young
man.

Wealth and property interested him not; domination of human
beings did. He desired only power and the opportunity to exercise it on his fellow creatures. The fact that out of the billion
or so inhabitants of the planet there would always remain one
undominated human bothered him not; he was a realist, and there
was no need to be selfish. He was honest enough to admit to
himself that while he had the genius to devise schemes of dia-
bolical complexity—his Guards had infiltrated the body of Society
like the invisible tendrils of a cancer and the survival of even
the smallest organ depended upon his lightest word—he simply
hadn't the sort of personality that inspired loyalty, confidence or
trust. It was no good having the ability to create great events without the means to carry them out, and have them remain carried.
Lord Roelt provided that instrumentality. There was the sole consolation for falling one short of the potential of dominating the
entire human race: if that last human was not exactly under Praxx's
thumb, he was at least being *used*, and that was the next best
thing.

Praxx entered the prince's chamber as he normally did, without
announcement. Ferenc hated that; it denoted a lack of respect,
which, of course, was Praxx's intent.

To the prince, the genius of the Guards seemed to material-
ize. Praxx had the peculiar and disconcerting ability to seem to
move from place to place without traversing the intervening space.
When caught in actual motion, he always seemed to be *gliding*,
feet motionless, like an ice skater.

Praxx was totally bald. Not by choice, as were many of his subordinates, for the demoralizing effect it had on *their* subordinates,
and possibly in fawning imitation of their leader, but because he
was in fact genuinely hairless. He had a head shaped precisely
like a light bulb (though he might not have known this himself
since that invention had not yet made its way from the Continent).

He hated his hairlessness, which was the aftermath of a childhood illness, but being utterly without vanity never considered the possible use of a wig. Which was just as well, as he would have looked ridiculous.

However, he was not a person one laughed at; being humorless, he did not tolerate humor in others. His eyes were unblessed by lashes or brows and resembled a pair of chrome-plated ball bearings. His nose was like a cold chisel and his lipless mouth contained two stainless steel teeth, one to each side, perfectly symmetrical, and no others. The cumulative effect was like the spare, hard-edged attempt of a draftsman—more used to steam engines, industrial machinery and organizational charts—to draw a human face using only compass, straightedge and ruling pen.

However, if Praxx was machinelike, it was a cheaply made machine; like a gold-plated watch with tin gears, pot-metal parts and a rusty mainspring, he was a frail man with an inordinate number of ill-made things going wrong inside.

"Yes, your Highness?" he said, in the kind of voice a dentist's drill would have.

"Praxx," answered the prince, "do I have to demote you to some provincial station to teach you a little courtesy?"

"I came the moment I received your Highness's summons," Praxx replied irrelevantly.

"You know exactly what I'm talking about! I want to know when you arrive . . ."

"I'm here."

" . . . and not have you suddenly appear in my room, unbidden!"

"The prince no longer requires my presence?"

"Yes! I mean no! Damn it! Stop doing that!"

"Yes, your Highness."

"Yes, well. Praxx, a serious problem has arisen."

"Your sister, your Highness?"

"How do you know that? I mean, what about her?"

"She's been missing from the palace for half a day."

"She could be anywhere; how can you say she's missing?"

"I know exactly where everyone in the palace is at all times. Pardon me, your Highness. With the present temporary exception of the Princess Bronwyn."

"What do you mean, 'everyone'? You had better not have any of your damned spies following *me* about! I won't have it!"

"Of course not, your Highness."

"Well, good then. About Bronwyn . . ."

"She managed to elude the man assigned to her. It is a great surprise to me to learn that she even knew of him. I am embarrassed." He didn't look it.

"The hell with your damned embarrassment! Where is Bronwyn?"

"That I am ascertaining to discover, your Highness. And when I find her?"

"Just bring her to me."

"Yes?"

"Yes! And, and . . . ah . . . anythingshemighthavewithher," he finished in a rush.

"Your Highness will pardon me, but I do not understand."

"She's got something of mine and I want it back."

"Something of value, your Highness?"

"Never mind what it is!"

"But how will I know what to return?"

"It doesn't make any difference! *Whatever* she has with her! That's all! Bring her back to the palace. She'll have a box or a package; that is, she might; make sure that you bring that, too. Whatever it is, that is. If she has anything. Unopened! Tell your men that. I mean, if it's a package. I'll have the head of anyone who looks at what she is carrying! I mean, if she's carrying anything, it's probably not important and it's no one's business anyway."

"Yes, your Highness." Nothing more would have been needed to guarantee the examination of anything found with the princess than what her brother had just babbled. The prince's threats, Praxx knew, were meaningless. As it was, however, the general knew exactly what the prince was after, and had known before he even entered the prince's chamber. He had seen Lord Roelt's letters long before Ferenc or Bronwyn, knew that Lord Roelt had requested that they be destroyed and knew where the prince had disobediently cached them. Out of simple loyalty to the prince, he could have easily stolen and destroyed the incriminating papers himself. But he felt no loyalty toward the Crown (why be petty and limit him: he felt no loyalty toward anything).

He had quietly observed, through his argus-eyed organization, the theft committed by the princess. He was pleased at having gained knowledge of such increasingly convoluted events: knowledge was power, and he was watching his increase like a flywheel gaining speed. Or like a dynamo; it was throwing off sparks, already overflowing with potential energy.

"Your Highness," Praxx asked, "has no idea where the Princess may be at this moment?"

"No, I do not! That's supposed to be your job!"

"Or what she intends to do with your, ah, property?"

"That is of no concern to you!"

"If I cannot find where she *is*, I might be able to discover where she *will* be."

"Hm. I suppose I see what you mean, I think. Well. If I were you, I'd keep an eye on the Privy Council."

"The Privy Council, your Highness?"

"That's all I'm going to say about the matter. Except this: if she even steps foot into their chambers, you're a dead man, Praxx!"

"I understand, your Highness." Had Praxx possessed a sense of humor, he might have let slip a supercilious smirk at Ferenc's toothless threat. As it was, his face maintained its usual machine-like expressionlessness; as lacking in overt emotion as a pencil sharpener.

Once outside the prince's apartments, Praxx allowed his formidable brain to work freely on the assorted ramifications of the problem. It wasn't too difficult, in the abstract. Until now, he had operated more or less according to the theory that what was good for Roelt was good for Praxx, that what was bad for the prince only made things better for the chamberlain, which in turn was once again good for Praxx.

Was this problem of the stolen letters good or bad for Ferenc and/or Payne? And, ultimately, good or bad for Jaeger Praxx? Lord Roelt had explicitly ordered his communications destroyed, and with good reason. They contained his plans for the immediate future in altogether too much detail. Lord Roelt did not have the craftsmanship that came from a true distrust of human beings, such as Praxx possessed. The general would never have written such letters in the first place; such revelations should only be carried in the memories of couriers—who can be much more easily silenced, if need be, than pieces of paper, whose apparent ephemerality belies an aggravating longevity. But what has been done has been done.

There was no question but that if the Privy Council got their hands on the letters, they would be quick to act. There was no love lost between them and Payne. The barons would be informed immediately, of course, as they wielded martial power and would be quick to move to protect their own interests. And if the barons openly denounced Lord Roelt, the lesser nobility would follow and then eventually the citizenry.

The latter especially would be aroused by the Church. He musn't forget the Church. It was only waiting to pounce upon Lord Roelt like a cat hovering over a mousehole. There would be no stopping the wave that would wash the palace clean of the chamberlain and his retinue, like a wet mop erasing a flyspeck. And that would include the Guards and their general. That was the important part to consider.

Once he had gotten possession of the letters, all would be well. But was it really necessary to destroy them? Possibly not. In his hands, they were as good as nonexistent, so far as the intent of Lord Roelt's order went. It was not in Praxx's nature to wantonly destroy anything potentially useful—a quality the letters possessed to an unprecedented degree. Power over Payne Roelt was a possibility Praxx found unexpected, heady and not a little frightening. He enjoyed the exercise of power, but he was no acrobat. These events could bring him considerably closer to the point of the pyramid than he perhaps cared to find himself. It is too easy to topple off that apex. It is far safer and surer to control power than to possess it. Great care would need to be taken in the next two weeks.

By this time, Praxx found himself in one of the great halls of the palace. He summoned to his side one of the tall soldiers who waited there, so rigidly at attention that he was almost indistinguishable from one of the marble columns. The man was a captain of the Guards, in the distinctive fur shako, fur-trimmed short cape, and elaborately frogged black tunic. A thick black moustache drooped on his upper lip, like a rodent pinned there by the knifelike nose.

"Captain," said Praxx, drawing the man well away from the others, "a matter of the utmost urgency has occurred. It is vital that not a word of what I am to tell you leaves the walls of this palace. Do you understand?"

"Yes, General," answered the soldier, who had not only seen with his own eyes what happened to people who did not understand Praxx, but had carried out many of these chastenings himself.

"Good. Be certain that no one knows what I am to tell you who does not need to know. Use only your most trusted men."

"Yes, General."

"The Princess Bronwyn has disappeared. A cursory search has

not found her anywhere within the palace. I want you to conduct a thorough investigation. I don't want a single room overlooked, however unlikely it may seem that she may be there. Start in one location and make a sweep through the buildings. Comb her out like a louse."

"The general knows how many rooms and corridors the palace has? It will take a great many of my men."

"All right then, you're right. But tell them as little as possible. Tell them, if you have to tell them anything, that the princess may have been kidnapped. Tell them that you suspect that it may be a group trying to disrupt the coming coronation. That will be an excellent reason to impose strict secrecy on the search."

"Yes, General."

"Start immediately; I want the first report by this evening."

"Yes, General."

"Also, I want a Guard posted at the Privy Council. The princess may be on her way there. Surround the building if necessary. She is not to be permitted entrance. Under any circumstances," he added darkly. "Do you understand?"

"I understand, General. And when the princess is found?"

"Bring her to my chambers immediately."

"Yes, General." The captain gave a spring-loaded salute, turned and left the hall, his bootheels ringing like a clock chiming an endless midnight.

It was long before the deadline he had set that Praxx received his first report from the captain. As soon as the man requested an audience, the general knew something was wrong. The palace had literally hundreds of rooms of all kinds (though not quite the thousands that Ferenc imagined, there were more than enough all the same) and scarcely a fraction could have been visited in the time that had passed. The soldier came to attention, heels rapping together, fur shako held in the crook of one arm.

"Well?" asked Praxx.

"General, I have news of the princess."

"It is not anything that I really hoped to hear, is it?"

"I am afraid not, General. The search that you ordered had barely begun when I received a report that the princess was no longer in the palace."

"What? Why not? She could not possibly have known of the search; why would she leave the palace? She has nowhere to go but the Privy Council." These last two sentences were muttered to himself.

"General, the princess apparently tried to enter the Privy Council chambers. One of the Guards there attemped to forcibly prevent her."

"The idiot! I want that man's name!"

"I have it here, General. The building had not yet been surrounded, but extra Guards had been placed at the entrances. The princess apparently noticed this, and turned to leave. Instead of reporting this to me, the man tried to stop her. He shouted to her to halt."

"Musrum!"

"She ran across the open grounds; the Guard who had challenged her raised an alarm and was joined by two of his comrades. The princess disappeared into the construction area where the new greenhouses are being installed."

"Damn. Those are on the south side of the island, are they not?"

"Yes, sir, they are."

"Is there any chance of her escaping across the north causeway?"

"No, sir. The search was begun from the north. There is a virtually solid wall of men stretching from east to west. There has been a roadblock on the north causeway since you issued your orders to me."

"Good! Good man. Now, what will her options be?"

"I cannot hazard a guess there, sir. I do not know why she is running."

"So you don't. You don't need to know that much; not yet, at least. I will tell you this, however: the princess has taken something of great value, something of deadly danger to both the throne and to our positions, yours and mine. You don't need to know what it is, only that it exists and that the princess has it and has every reason to use it."

"What should I look for?"

"A package, I would expect, about so by so. I don't know what she would be carrying it in, but it isn't large and couldn't weigh more than a pound or so. When the princess is found, bring whatever she has with her to me, whatever it may be, anything at all. Under no circumstances is anything to be examined before I see it. Is that understood?"

"Yes, General."

Praxx paced his austere apartment for several minutes, while the obedient captain stood waiting, as still and patient as a tombstone. The general was thinking: *What harm can the princess do if she is prevented from reaching the Privy Council? The coronation is only three weeks away; after that she will be powerless. The Council will disband next week in order to allow its members to prepare for the ceremonies. Many of them have homes in distant parts of the kingdom: in seven days they will be scattered over hundreds of square miles. Reaching any one individual will do the princess no good.*

All that is necessary is to prevent her from approaching the Council while it is still in session. Afterwards, she can be arrested at leisure. That would be easy enough to do; that fool this afternoon demonstrated that. But I know the princess. She will not give up that easily. She is stubborn, loathes Payne Roelt, and would do almost anything to see her brother not ascend the throne.

So what will she do? What are her alternatives if she is prevented from reaching the Privy Council? The barons are Lord Roelt's only other real enemies—well, so is the Church, but we will be taking care of that soon enough—his most formidable enemies, if it comes to that. Will the princess be able to do anything with them? I don't see how. They have no formal organization, no elected or official leader.

No, that's not strictly true. Baron Monzon, the prince and princess's cousin, is in fact the leader of the baronage. A powerful man who has the respect of all of the barons, though his power is certainly more physical and charismatic than it is intellectual. Nevertheless, the barons are looking for any excuse to destroy Lord Roelt. After the fiasco last month—and didn't that scare the hell out of Payne!—they would be careful to do it legally. The letters will be exactly what they need. Like the Privy Council will be in a week, the barons are presently scattered all over the country. But what if the letters were to fall into the hands of just one particular baron, namely Piers Monzon? He would have the news spread to the others within days. They would march in force on the city and that would be that. There is not a soul who would lift a finger to save Lord Roelt. Certainly not I.

Well, then. If she can't get to the Council, she'll try to reach her cousin. But he's north, on the border, some five hundred miles from here. Can she get there in time? The barons would only need a few days to organize themselves. They could probably delay the coronation by word alone, well in advance of any march. She would have two weeks, then; seventeen days at the most. It was possible.

How to keep her at bay? It isn't necessary to actually find her, though it would be reassuring to know exactly where she is. It is only necessary to block her way to the north. The same strategy as had been tried with the Council Chamber, on a larger scale. There are only a few ways to cross the Slideen River, if she is on the south side of Palace Island. The causeway is the only option for miles in either direction. Two bridges cross the Moltus on the other side of the City, one due north of the causeway and the other from the Catstongue district. If she went west she'd have both the Slideen and the Moltus to cross. If she goes to the east, she'll have only the Moltus, though it has fewer bridges because of the shipping. Blocking all of these would be simple. Of course, easiest of all would be keeping her from leaving Palace Island in the first place.

Praxx turned to the captain, who stood exactly as he had been. His eyes had a lusterless look, as though he had not even blinked while the general's back was turned, and his eyeballs had dried out.

"Captain," said Praxx, "the princess must at all costs be prevented from leaving the island. If she is indeed on the south side, keep her there. Double the Guards on the south causeway."

"Yes, sir."

"I want a report every half-hour."

"Yes, sir."

"That's all." And the captain spun on his heels as though he were on ball bearings and left the room. Praxx went to the single small window of his apartment. A pigeon rested on the sill and he chased it away.

Time passed, as it will.

The first three or four reports from the captain or one of his aides brought no news of the princess, which was only probably not good. The next report was definitely not good.

"General, sir," said the captain, "there has been an incident."

"An incident?"

"Yes, sir. There has been a fire and an explosion."

"That was that strange thump I heard?"

"I expect so, sir. It was in the heating plant for the stables."

"How many abandoned their positions in the search cordon to investigate?"

"Eight, sir."

"You have their names?"

"Yes, sir."

"Then you know what to do about them."

"They are being taken care of, sir."

"That is when she left the island."

"So I presume, sir. Do you have orders?"

"She'll avoid the roads to the west and south. Besides, to the west of the city she'd run into the Muchka River as well as having to pass the garrisons. I suspect that she will not stray far from the Slideen. That leaves the Transmoltus. So far as I know, she has never been there nor knows anyone there. She ought to be easy to pick out of the rabble. Alert your men and agents to be on the lookout. As long as she keeps moving in any direction but north, all's well; but I *would* like to get my hands on what she is carrying."

"Yes, General," replied the captain, saluting and exiting the apartment with precision.

Two more hours went by without significant news. The next time Praxx heard from the captain was by way of a handwritten note delivered by messenger. After sending the man away perfunctorily, Praxx broke the thick seals and read the letter, written in such a neat hand it might have been typewritten. It said (after the usual greetings):

The trail of our quarry was easily picked up. She had been seen passing through the Slideen Gate by the one man who had remained at his post when the others had abandoned theirs. I have recommended this soldier for a commendation (please see the attached memorandum). He did not pursue the fugitive since his orders were only to report any observation. I alerted the commandant at the garrison as a precaution, though, like you, I did not believe she would try to escape in that direction. I also established roadblocks along all roads to the south. The Guard post in the Transmoltus was notified, as were the police in that district. The police were told nothing other than that we were in pursuit of a fugitive and were given only the most superficial of descriptions. They have learned in the past not to ask questions. They were ordered not to interfere with the fugitive, but to report directly to me. It was through a police report that we got our first sighting. I sent a squad to her last reported location. By then I had received two more reports, which gave me a rough indication of the direction she was traveling. The reports were from random points: as I had suspected, she was giving every indication of being lost. I had my men circle the area in which she had been seen and it was not long before she was sighted. Unfortunately, she saw the Guards as well (they are too distinctive among the rabble) and took flight. As you know, the Transmoltus is a crowded district and pursuit was made difficult by the number of civilians on the streets. Warning shots were fired, which tended to help, but the men were never able to approach closer than a few score yards. She disappeared while hotly pursued. She had turned a corner, just ahead of my men, and apparently vanished. I am convinced that she has found succor in the factory there, a firm of stonecutters. I am presently having the building thoroughly searched.

Praxx crumpled the flimsy paper and threw it angrily into the ceramic stove that filled a corner of his room. There were no further reports until the next morning.

A Guard had been murdered (said the first report of the new day) in the main drainage canal that ran through the Transmoltus. Praxx puzzled over the significance of this for some time. There had been no other reports that seemed to mean anything, yet he could not understand the meaning of this one either. Still, it bothered him. The man had been placed in the canal as an afterthought by the captain, who in his thoroughness meant to leave no exits unaccounted for, however unlikely they might seem. And of all the Guards in the district, this man had been the only one to have experienced any difficulty—if difficulty is not too great an understatement, since the man's neck had been broken like a pencil; very much, in fact, like the broken pencils that now littered Praxx's desk. There was simply no way the princess could have been responsible for that. At least not while she was alone.

But Princess Bronwyn had no acquaintances outside of the palace and aristocratic circles, and certainly none within the Transmoltus. So far as the outside world was concerned, she had no existence.

She could have appealed to a stranger. There were, Praxx knew too well, all too many who would be glad to frustrate Prince Ferenc, Payne Roelt and himself. Could she have found help in someone like that? When and where? How? He pressed a button on his desk and almost immediately the captain entered in response. Although the man must not have slept a minute since the last time Praxx had seen him, he looked exactly as before, like a photograph cut out of a magazine.

"Yes, General?"

"What was that place, where the princess was last seen?"

"The general refers to the factory where she was lost?"

"Yes, what was it?"

"It's a firm of stonecutters, Groontocker and Peen. A highly respected firm, sir."

"Any kind of record with us?"

"None whatsoever, sir. Silvanus Peen has been dead for some years, but Groontocker, Ald geld Groontocker, is an enthusiastic friend of both the prince and Lord Roelt."

"I see. Can you check their employees? I want to know if anyone is missing this morning."

"Yes, sir. I can have that in an hour."

"All right then, see to it."

It was going to be necessary to see the prince again; summonses from Ferenc had been piling upon his desk with ever-increasing frantic urgency all morning. It was not that Praxx feared the prince, it was just that time spent with Ferenc was always time wasted. But then, there was little else to do until he heard from the captain.

The prince also had spent a sleepless night. Unfortunately it was far more obvious with him than it had been for the Guard captain. His face looked like a two-minute egg. He had not bothered to dress, but was wearing only a richly embroidered robe. Nothing seemed to have been able to divert his mind from the tragedy he found impending; even his prized collection of wax fruit had failed for the first time to offer him solace. When Praxx entered Ferenc's presence, the prince pointed an accusing finger at him. It shook with anger, exhaustion and unbridled pique.

"Well, where is she?" he demanded. He picked a wax tangerine from a silver and glass bowl and began fondling it nervously.

"I expect to learn that momentarily."

"Momentarily! Momentarily! You sound like a policeman. She was here in the palace; why couldn't you find her?"

"There were unforeseen circumstances, your Highness."

"Unforeseen, duckshit! I know exactly what happened! Do you think I'm an idiot?"

"Not at all, your Highness," Praxx lied.

"Well then, how do you explain her escape? I never heard of anything so fouled up as that vaudeville act your presumably elite corps entertained us with yesterday."

"The men responsible are being punished, your Highness."

"The *man* responsible is standing in front of me! I want Bronwyn stopped! I don't care what you have to do to accomplish that, do you understand?"

"Is the prince sanctioning the use of force?"

"I didn't say that! No! Just do whatever you have to; I want to know nothing about it. Just bring me that package, with or without my sister. I'm not interested in her."

"I'll give the orders, your Highness. Is there news from Lord Roelt?"

"News? What sort of news?" The prince had given such a violent start at the mention of his chamberlain's name that he involuntarily crushed the tangerine. "Now look what you've made me do! Damn."

"Does the prince know when Lord Roelt might happen to be returning?"

"Why? What possible difference could that make? What does Lord Roelt have to do with this?"

"Nothing, your Highness. I was only asking." Praxx in fact had received a communication that very morning from Lord Roelt, warning of his impending arrival within thirty-six hours. Contrary to what Princess Bronwyn believed, and to what she had told Thud, Lord Roelt knew nothing of her theft. So far only the prince, who thought he was the sole possessor of the knowledge, and General Praxx knew.

It is going to be extremely interesting, Praxx thought, *to observe Lord Roelt's reaction to the news, particularly if I am the one to hand over the documents—after they have been carefully copied, of course—rather than the prince. Ferenc would simply pretend that they had never been missing. Instead this is an excellent chance to place a heavy obligation upon Lord Roelt while simultaneously discrediting the prince.* He almost smiled in anticipation. For a man who enjoyed manipulating human beings, this felt like the opening moves in a grand championship chess match.

There was a discreet rapping at the door. The prince admitted the petitioner, who was a messenger asking for the general. He passed a folded slip of paper to his superior, saluted and disappeared. "Will the prince pardon me for a moment?" the general asked, receiving a peremptory nod by way of answer. He unfolded the note and read its brief message. "Your Highness," he said, refolding the paper and inserting it into an inner pocket of his tunic, "I have just received important news regarding your Highness's missing, ah, goods. If the prince will please excuse me, I will immediately attend to the matter?"

"Bronwyn's been found? She had the . . . things?"

"That is what I shall endeavor to discover, your Highness."

"All right then, endeavor. I want a report immediately!"

"At your command, my Prince," replied Praxx, backing through the door.

"And Praxx," added Ferenc.

"Yes, my Prince?"

"I won't forget this!" he answered, showing the general the sad handful of broken orange wax.

In his own chambers, Praxx found one of the captain's lieutenants waiting.

"Report," the general ordered.

"There is a man missing from the staff of Groontocker and Peen, sir. He has never until this day, in twenty years of service, failed to appear at his job."

"What is he?" interrupted Praxx.

"He is a common stonecutter, sir."

"An artisan?" Praxx asked in some surprise.

"No sir, only a laborer. He hollows out the stone blocks used for coffins—I don't know what they're called."

"Sarcophagi—plural for sarcophagus. Go on."

"Yes, sir. The man apparently left the building not long after our last search. Then he failed to come to work today. We obtained his address from his employer; it was not far from the factory. A single room partitioned off an attic in a tenement residence. There was little to search: the room was virtually bare. If he had any belongings, they had been removed. We did find this, however." Here the lieutenant reached into a bag and pulled forth a sodden lump of cloth. The general took it from him, carefully unfolding it. It was the remnants of a frock, and he recognized it as one of the princess's.

"Where is this tenement, exactly?"

"It is on the Nixnixx Road, number fifteen-oh-six."

The general pulled a large-scale map of the city down from its rollers on the wall. He checked the index on its margin and with the point of a finger traced the reference lines to where they crossed. "Ha!" he said. "And where would fifteen-oh-six be?"

"Between Deedle and Onteveronte."

"Yes! I thought so. Well. The drainage stream that the Guard was found dead in runs directly behind fifteen-oh-six. Was he found upstream or down from this location?"

"May I see the map, please? This is the block of fifteen-oh-six? Then the Guard was found murdered here, sir, downstream."

"Describe this man for me, the one who worked at the stone-cutters. What is his name?"

"Mollockle, sir, Thud Mollockle. By all accounts he is a remarkable-looking person. He is apparently nearly seven feet tall. Even allowing for exaggeration, he is larger than average. His strength is prodigious, I understand. I was told that he was able to handle stone blocks as large as he is. The company is providing us with a photograph of Mollockle from their files, but he should not be hard to identify . . ."

"I can see that," interrupted Praxx.

"Not only by way of his abnormal size and strength, but he is extraordinarily ugly—freakishly so, I am told."

"Any trouble with him before?"

"None whatsoever, sir, at least as far as the local police are aware."

"They are notoriously tolerant. Any reason that he would suddenly give aid to a fugitive girl? Would he have any reason to help the princess?"

"By all accounts, no, sir. He is not considered to be especially intelligent."

"I see. Well, he has nevertheless done so; I think we can take that as given. I see that the stream leads to the harbor. That is clearly where they were headed." Praxx stroked his burnished cheeks with a caliperlike hand.

"If they have found refuge on an outbound ship," he said, "all may be lost. A dozen ships must have left the harbor since last night. They could have been on any one of them. Damn it; well, we'll see what we can do. Will you please give your captain my compliments and ask him to come to this office as soon as possible?"

"Yes, sir."

Twenty minutes later, the Guard captain was once again in Praxx's presence. "Captain, I have every reason to believe that the princess and at least one male accomplice may be attempting to escape the city by boat . . ."

"Pardon me, sir, for interrupting, but this male accomplice . . . a large man, almost a giant, with an unnaturally small head, possibly deformed features?"

"Yes! How did you know this?"

"There was an incident in the City very early this morning, a few hours after midnight. A squad of Guards were in pursuit of a pair of suspicious persons they had found loitering in the shop district. The men described them as a tall young boy and an extremely large man. However, one of the Guards, who was assaulted and injured by the pair, swears that the boy was in fact a girl in disguise."

"Did he recognize her?"

"No. In fact, the Guards in the City were not even yet aware that the princess was wanted. I think that it is entirely possible . . ."

"So do I. Where was this confrontation?"

The captain pointed to a spot on the wall map, about a third of the way into the island from the Slideen. Then he moved his finger a little ways north.

"They were pursued some distance," he explained, "and were eventually lost somewhere near here."

"I wonder now. Was that the direction they had intended to go? Or were they simply running blind? If the princess were alone, I would assume she was lost, but this man Mollockle may know the City. If that is so, where could they have been going? For that matter, I wonder how they were able to cross the river. It seems clear that they did, in any case. And with some destination in mind. The Pordka Bridge? She must have known that would be heavily patrolled. She couldn't possibly have been after the Catstongue Bridge; otherwise why was she west of the middle of the City? Was she looking for a place to hide? I must find out if she has any acquaintances or friends living there."

"Pardon me, sir, but the general is overlooking the aqueduct."

"The what? Oh. I see! You are quite right, Captain."

"Orders were given yesterday to post Guards at the reservoir, to search outgoing barges, but it was only considered a routine precaution."

"Double the men. I want a crack squad there immediately. Search every cubic inch of every item going onto every barge; I want every person positively identified before they can leave the City. I want a copy of the cargo manifests and passenger lists of every barge that has left the city since midnight. Understood?"

"Yes sir."

Two days elapsed before Praxx had a glimmering of how he had been deceived. He had puzzled over the reports from the men at the reservoir. There had been only four barges out of the City that entire day. Winter was coming and there was little cargo going either north or south. The gypsies worried him the most. They were too exotic to suit him, but the search had been thorough, at least according to the report. And that also worried him: it had been made by the token patrol that had been placed there the day before. The gypsies had left the city before the more elite squad had taken over. Still, they seemed to have overlooked nothing. The man in charge was not intelligent but he was thorough. He had even had the sex of every one of the gypsies established beyond doubt. The princess could not have maintained her disguise as a boy. There was no question that the princess was not hiding in or among them. The bear disturbed him too, though he couldn't say why. Possibly because he hated all animals. Possibly. However, the captain gave him an even better reason late on the third day after the princess's disappearance.

"Sir," he reported, "I have been investigating the movements of the gypsies while they were in the City. They performed at three locations. The last one was in a plaza here"—he indicated a position on the map—"between the last sighting of the princess and the location of the reservoir."

"Very good. But what does that really tell us?"

"In itself, nothing, sir. But at this last location, a week ago, the bear died."

6

THE PURSUIT

THE COUNTRY NORTH OF BLAVEK and south of the ragged mountains that separate Tamlaght from Crotoy is a broad, fertile, U-shaped valley called the Zileheroum. It was scooped out of the island of Guesclin by an ancient glacier, which, half a million years earlier, had been on its way from the polar cap to the equator but had never made it much further than the middle of Guesclin, where it had given up, depositing a couple of million tons of rubble like a discouraged immigrant abandoning his baggage before returning to the homey comforts of the far north.

The valley's rocky meadows are not well suited for farming, but orchards and vineyards thrive, and cattle contentedly mow its wildflowers and emerald grass. The canal that longitudinally bisects it runs more or less due north from the City, never straying far from the wide, shallow Moltus for which it was substituting. There were only occasional farms within sight of the canal barges, and one or two small villages.

These villages were located on the main road which lay a mile or two to the east of the canal, so there was seldom any danger of observation; every hamlet had its station of Guards. It was extremely doubtful that word would have gotten to these outposts yet, but it was thought best not to take any chances. Bronwyn knew that such things as the electric telegraph had existed on the

Continent for some years past; but it was a device far too radically modern—let alone foreign—for Tamlaghtans to deal with. With the exception of a few military semaphore stations, there were no means of fast long-distance communication.

Bronwyn and Thud took care to be on the far side of the barge whenever buildings of any sort hove into view. Only once since leaving the City did the canal actually pass through the body of a village, the miniscule town of Vulchi. Bronwyn regretted missing a view of the famous Simmering Heath, but agreed with her gypsy friend that it would be wisest to make the transit hidden inside one of the wagons. There would not be another such incident until they reached the terminus of the canal in the village of Biela-Slatina, still two days ahead. Three times only had they passed another barge headed south. It was long past the time for sending any agricultural products to the city's markets; the bleak Tamlaghtan winter was near.

Tamlaght, which occupies most of the southern portion of the island of Guesclin, lies between the high northern latitudes of fifty-five and sixty-seven degrees. Its summers are warm and golden, but brief; each of those days are only a bitter reminder that for six endless months the countryside would be a wasteland of interminable snow and ice, glaringly white during the few hours of daylight with shadows blue as turquoise; at night a glowing indigo under the stars and the flickering, hissing auroras.

Only three bargemen were needed to tend to the vessel; tough and single-minded, they had interest neither in the gypsies nor their affairs. The flat, shallow boat was steered (or kept straight, rather, since there really was no place to steer *to*, since the canal was only slightly more than twice as wide as the long, narrow boat) by one man at a tiller in the square stern with the other two men on either side of the bow, using poles. A rope from the starboard side of the bow led to a pair of tandem mules that trod the towpath that paralleled the canal. A fourth man walked beside the animals, giving them an occasional switch with a flexible wooden wand. This was really unnecessary: the mules knew their job; they never slowed down, and the touch of the wand never sped them up. It was really done only to remind them that the man was there, and to give the man something to do. The mules appreciated it because it didn't hurt and it helped to keep the flies at bay.

The teamster was not part of the bargecrew, who had their own guild. He was in fact an independent contractor, who owned the mules that drew the barge. The bargemen tended to think of themselves as a variety of able-bodied seamen, and the teamsters as land-loving farmers, though the obvious truth of the matter was that their ocean was narrow enough to throw a rock across—or, in some places, for an athletic person to jump—and in the thousands of miles of travel accumulated during a year, the courses of the bargemen and the teamsters were parallel and never more than a few yards apart.

The barges were long, narrow affairs, and very shallow, only drawing a few inches of water. The one here was little wider than the gypsy wagons, which were lined up end to end, leaving only a narrow catwalk along the gunwales. With the animals taking up any remaining space, there was scarcely a cubic inch to spare. Bronwyn could have stepped ashore at almost any time; the canal only grew wider when a siding was allowed for the passing of barges going in the opposite direction.

The first three days on the canal could not have been more pleasant. The weather, while sharp as a razor, was bright and clear. The sky stretched overhead as blue and taut as the skin of a balloon. The gypsies took the opportunity of not being on the road to repair their wagons and trappings. The band swarmed over the caravan—painting, scrubbing, blacksmithing, leatherworking—like ants on an apple core. Thud had become fascinated with the gypsies' animals—he had never in his life seen anything larger than a rat (though some of these had rivalled in size the shaggy little gypsy ponies). He asked Hottl numberless questions about them, and though most were childishly naïve they all received thoughtful and serious answers. Like most people who were practiced at penetrating superficial appearances—and the gypsies' living depended a great deal on their ability to do this accurately—Hottl and his companions never took Thud any less than seriously. Like Bronwyn, they had discovered that though he was big and ugly and not extraordinarily bright, he more than made up for these deficiencies, like a sightless person compensates for his lack of vision. They had also been impressed by how good a bear he had made.

Bronwyn spent most of her time with the gypsy. Each was very curious about the other and most of one silvery day was spent in mutual questioning. The gypsy, being far more skilled than the princess at drawing information from people without their ever being aware of it (hence his great success as a palm reader), came out far ahead of the girl in this exchange of information.

Bronwyn's first question, and one of the few direct ones he ever answered, was about the man's name, and "Janos Plodsku" was the reply she received.

With few exceptions the people with him were blood relations, in varying degrees of consanguinity. Most were Plodskus or Dardles, with one each of Bridskutin and Zattlottl (this latter represented by Hottl). They sang beautiful, sad songs, together and individually, and told endless stories in their own ancient language; but there was little real conversation among the gypsies; they seldom spoke even among themselves unless it was necessary.

Although Bronwyn had been introduced to each, and had been made to feel welcome by the firm, rough handshakes of the men and the warm embraces of the women, brown cheeks pressed to rosy one, and even more so by their eyes, like deep, peaty ponds, they never, after that first welcome, said a word to her. She felt a little jealous, since Thud had been deep in conversation with Hottl about the animals since crossing the Moltus. But Thud himself did seem more like one of the gypsies—somehow; perhaps his simplicity attracted them, or his honesty or earthiness.

As much as she liked Janos and his company, and as grateful as she felt for their unsolicited and freely given help, she could not help but feel apart from them. They seemed so alien to her, so unrelated to her own life; yet she really couldn't understand why they deferred to her. She was certain that it wasn't due to any snobbishness on her part. Bronwyn liked to think that she was unaffected by class distinctions in her dealings with the common people of her nation, but, realistically, how could a princess be otherwise? Just the evidence that she thought of them as *common* at all ought to have told her that something was amiss with her egalitarianism.

Janos knew how Bronwyn thought she ought to feel about him, knew that she was uncomfortable because she *did* feel that way, knew that she was ill at ease with the general informality, knew that she had nothing whatever in common to share with him or his people—and that she knew this, even if she couldn't explain her feelings—but he also knew that the princess was trying not to let him see that she possessed this knowledge: that she thought she was doing her best. Janos was far from being mean-spirited enough to not appreciate this effort.

"Princess," said Janos, as the two sat on the bulwark of the barge, their feet dangling within inches of the icy water, "what do you know of your friend, Thud?"

"Nothing, I guess. I never saw him before the day before yesterday. There hasn't been much time since to get really acquainted. He was a stonecutter in some factory in the Transmoltus; that's about all I know."

"He is a strange man, I think. He is not as stupid as he looks, although, I am forced to admit, that still leaves a lot of room for being very stupid. Forgive me for saying this about your friend . . ."

"I know what you are going to say: he looks as dumb as a brick, doesn't he?"

"Yes, he does, but there is something inside that head, even if it does not look like there would be room in there for even a small walnut."

"He is very kind and . . . well, he is kind." She had been about to say, "knows his place."

"Yes, he is. But I think that the strangeness that I speak of is something other than how his face gives the lie to his . . . I do not have the word . . . sweetness? That sounds wrong."

"I know what you mean. I trust him, though."

"You have seen the picture he carries?"

"Yes, he used to have it hanging on a wall in his room. It was tacked in the middle of hundreds of cut-out paper flowers. Very weird. It's kind of a spooky picture, isn't it?"

"Hm. Spooky, yes. What is very strange is that I know that woman, the one in his picture."

"How is that? Who is she?"

"He believes her to be his mother and, for all that I truly know, she is. Yet . . . Look, I must tell you a little story. It is not much of a story, because it has no ending, and I do not even know what it means. Well. Many years ago, maybe thirty years, when I was still a young man and my grandfather was leader of the clan—did I not tell you what happened to my father? Another time. When I was a young man, we brought a girl into the Circle, much as we have done with you, Princess. We are very proud that we have never turned away anyone who has needed our help. Sometimes there is little we can do; sometimes we can only offer sanctuary, sometimes a little food, a place to rest, perhaps a place to leave a tiny portion of their troubles. You have noticed that we are much better listeners than talkers? No matter.

"One night we found this poor child; she was not much older than you . . . How old are you, Princess? Is that all? Then perhaps this girl was much younger. I cannot tell these things." (This was a lie, of course.) "She was wandering in a woods not far from where you are going. I am not sure whether we were on this side or the other of the border. We try not to let such political things bother us. In any case, there she was, half-naked, nearly frozen, almost starved. We gave her shelter, of course.

"It was many days before she would take any food, and then only a little. She was so weak; it must have been a long time since she had had anything much to eat, she was so skinny. I remember that her face looked like a skull, that her eyes shone like someone who has eaten too much *premsyl*, and how her ribs stuck out from her. Aie! She would at last take a little broth, so Mama mixed it with some of her roots and herbs, and that seemed to help the girl very much.

"She still would not speak; she had not said a word since the day we had found her. But she began eating a little more each day. Soon she was strong enough to walk a little, but it made her very tired. I remember the first day she smiled at me. I regret that I then asked her who she was and why she had been lost in the woods. The smile went from her face like frost in the sun. I was very sorry I had spoken.

"It was Mama, who would know such things, who told me what she had discovered about the girl: that she was with child. I believe that we all thought we knew her story then. That some villain had carried her from her home and had raped her, leaving her in the wilderness for the wolves. Or something like that. I accepted this, but I should have wondered how long she had been lost; as I said, she was very starved. Exactly what had happened, none of us ever did learn.

"The girl soon grew much stronger and even began to help with the work. We explained that it was not necessary to do this, but she was so willing and it seemed to bring her such pleasure, that we could not say no. And it did seem to help. She ate what we ate and worked hard at whatever tasks she was set to. She always remained thin, but her bones no longer stuck out; her thinness was a sleek kind, like an otter's. Her face was always a little skull-like, though her cheeks were no longer hollow and her eyes had lost that terrible metallic glaze.

"She would speak whenever she was spoken to, she would ask about our work and she would sing with us at night—I remember her voice, sweet and bitter like the tears of a pine—but we never learned anything about what had happened before the night we had found her. You understand that we could not ask?

"Soon she became great with child and she spent her days in our wagon. She became weak again and we feared for her. She gave birth very late one night in the early spring. When the child was born we thought that she would surely die. I can remember thinking: Ah! She is so pale, like a candle, I can almost see through her. In your palace, you have cups of fine porcelain like this? Yes, then, like that. But she surprised us by asking for the infant and Mama gave it to her. She held it close to her bosom and I do not think that I saw her again so happy.

"The child was exceptionally beautiful. Pink and fat and as wrinkled as a prune. When Mama and I left the girl for the night, the baby was already suckling at her tiny breast.

"I see you stealing a glance at our friend. You cannot imagine him as a beautiful child, eh? I have seen far worse come from better beginnings. But that is usually by disease or accident or inclination. When I finish, you can decide for yourself.

"The next morning, when Mama and I returned to the wagon in which we had left the mother and child, we discovered that something strange had happened during the night. Me, I am not very sensitive to things like this, but I could tell that something had happened to the infant. Its shape was somehow different, though I cannot tell you in what way. Only that it was, what? *Awry*. The hair that had been but a few fair wisps was now thick and red. And the eyes . . . I knew that there was something wrong with the eyes. The night before they had been as big and blue as a kitten's, but now they were like little black beads. The baby looked like a fat mole.

"The girl did not stay with us long after that. She never seemed to notice that there was any change in her child, or that there was anything strange about a baby that never laughed nor cried. We were camped then near a village not far from Blavek. And one day she was gone."

There was a long moment's silence before Bronwyn realized that the story was over.

"That's it, then? You think that Thud is this baby?"

"He has the picture of the girl."

"And you are certain?"

"It has been a long time, but I can remember that face. I think you know why . . . you have seen it."

"She is beautiful in her way, but it makes me very uncomfortable to look at her. But I guess I know what you mean; I don't think that I could forget her, either."

"Yes, then, I think that Thud is that child."

"I don't understand, though. Are you puzzled because Thud didn't turn out as beautiful as he was as a baby? These things happen. Look at everything that poor girl had been through; it surely would have affected a baby. And you don't know who the father was; Thud may take after him."

"I am sure you are right."

"Do you think you ought to tell him?"

"No. I do not know what he has told himself, and I really have so little to offer. No, it would be better to leave things as they are."

As they drifted north, the Zileheroum gradually narrowed. The low hills that bound it to the east and west grew closer together, and blue mountains became distantly visible in the northwest. They were not high, but looked dangerously jagged, like shattered glass. There was already snow on them. The canal no longer strayed very far from the river, which was now almost continuously broken by frothing rapids. The canal itself passed through locks more often. Where they had been ten or even twenty miles apart at the beginning, they now came every five miles, or less, as the valley floor became steeper. It took the barge upwards of fifteen minutes or more to transit one lock, and Bronwyn chafed and complained at every delay.

They no longer passed villages, only an occasional shepherd's or hunter's hut. They saw—more often than in the south—the tiny pyramidal wayside Musrumic altars, gleamingly whitewashed, deep within the thick woods that were gradually encroaching on the floodplain. They looked like a collection of eyeteeth that some dentist had spilled onto a dark green carpet. They saw fewer cows and more herds of goats, their bells clanking clearly from the hillsides.

One of the gypsy women, a sister-in-law of Janos's, gave Bronwyn an embroidered skirt and blouse to wear, with a bolero vest very much like the gypsy leader's. The princess gratefully changed into them from the now-filthy clothes that Thud had found for her. Janos was delighted with the alteration.

"Ho! You look more like a gypsy than my own sister, by the hairy knuckles of Musrum!"

"It is a beautiful dress," she answered, pleased. "I've never seen such lovely embroidery!"

"Thank you," Janos said, answering for his sister-in-law, who was blushing at the compliment. "It is all Marishka's own work."

"I have never worn anything so beautiful." Marishka beamed even more.

"Princess, may I ask you something?" spoke Marishka shyly.

"Of course."

"May I see your hand? Please?"

"My hand? I suppose so; why . . . ?"

"The palm up, please?" A slender finger with a sharply pointed nail, more like a pen than a digit, traced one of the lines that creased Bronwyn's palm. The gypsy woman frowned. "Ah, yes . . . poor girl!"

"What is it?"

"Why are you doing this?"

"Doing what?"

"You have put yourself into deadly danger, more danger than I think you know. Why have you done this? I do not wish to offend you, but I do not believe that it is for love of your country."

"That *should* be offensive!" Bronwyn said, her back stiffening huffily.

"But it is not?" Janos asked.

"No . . . no, I guess not." Then, to the woman: "You're not suggesting that I don't love Tamlaght—I do!—you're suggesting that I'm not here because of that love; that's it, isn't it?"

"Perhaps."

"Maybe it isn't love of Tamlaght, maybe it's hatred of Payne Roelt. But doesn't that amount to the same thing? He is going to destroy this country!"

"From what you have told us, that seems to be true," said Janos.

"Well, then, if I can get these letters to my cousin, it'll destroy Payne and everything he has done."

"But why you, Princess?" asked Janos.

"What do you mean, 'why me'?"

"Why are *you* doing this, Princess? There must be hundreds of people—soldiers, servants, I do not know—who could have acted as a courier for you, and would have known exactly what to do. That is why Marishka asked why you do this yourself."

"Well . . . I don't know. So what?"

"I love this life, Princess," said Janos, apparently irrelevantly. "That of my gypsy band. I would trade it for no other. But sometimes it is hard and often it is hungry. When we have set up our little carnival on the grounds of some great estate and performed for the beautifully dressed people, I admit to feeling envy. Wealth and position: accidents of birth—pfah! They cannot guarantee happiness. I am happy, I have been happy and I expect to die happy. But still . . . still . . . it can be hard; money and position, they can be like the grease on an axle. So much of what I and my people do, it is just to stay alive. Only when there is something left over can we have anything more, a little luxury that to you would be nothing.

"This trip north on the canal, it has cost us everything that we made in the City. Well, nearly; the owner of the barge line owed us a favor, but it was only a small one. We have very little more now than we had when we first entered its gates. And what is this luxury? It is that we can travel to a new city while at the same time we can do all of this work we must do.

"That is why she asked you what she did, Princess. We cannot understand why you would give up so much. You had all the freedom in the world to do and go whatever and wherever you pleased. And now you are hunted like a criminal instead of being treated like a princess. Why?"

"Janos," answered Bronwyn, turning from the gypsy toward the drifting landscape, "Janos, you don't know how many walls a palace has."

There were beautiful gardens, she thought, *dressed in rainbows, roses in velvet gowns jeweled with dew, quiet pools of pansies, irises like ribboned lances and a full breath of mignonettes. Beyond: hills of billowing blue gauze. And I—I would give the whole of it, and all my poor heart, to feel the salt wind on my face, to taste it on my lips, to look down from the bow of a ship at the foam spreading a lace coverlet over the waves.*

There was not a ship that I saw pass down the Slideen but held my heart as a stowaway. One will sail to Peigambar, another will swing around the Cape, another to the vast archipelagoes beyond Socotarra; oh! I'd have been a happy girl if I'd been common-born! I swore that one day I'd break my bonds, close my books, burn my great globe and wander free, before my eyes and mouth are stopped up with clay. There are a thousand who would take my place and no one would know the difference.

There was so little that I was doing in my life; the months and years were going by as one day went. And I wasted them, here a week, there a week, with nothing ever done. I ornamented parties and charmed hostesses and watched all of my dreams evaporate like shining bubbles. I had nothing to hope for but a miracle. I don't know, I can't even explain to myself the way I feel.

*Somehow I seemed to see tall masts and swinging stars where
I should have seen columns and chandeliers, and, if Musrum
pleased, I would sail to the rim of the world. Maybe I would
find there, and could keep, a dream or two that I could sleep
with. It would have been simple if it had only been walls that
surrounded me, but I was tied by golden strings that bound me
tighter than iron bands. Why, why did Musrum give me dreams
like these?*

"I don't know, Janos," she continued, turning back to face him.
"I guess I hadn't thought things through."

"There is one other thing, Princess," said Marishka.

"What is that?"

"Be wary," the gypsy said, tracing a line on Bronwyn's palm,
"of wide grey strangers."

Bronwyn took the opportunity given her by her new dress to
give her boy's costume a well-needed wash, which she did in
a deep wooden bucket full of cold water drawn from the canal.
While she worked, Bronwyn noticed that Henda was perched on
the wheel rim of a wagon, watching her. His face was unswathed,
as it often was when he was alone among the gypsies. She was
surprised that he was uncovered in her presence, something he
had not done before.

She nodded to him, trying to keep her expression uncommitted;
she did not feel comfortable with the idea of returning his smile.
She would hate for him to think that he was being mocked, or
reminded of his disfigurement. She continued her laundry, scrubbing the heavy, corrugated knickers on the corrugated metal wash-
board. She pushed back an errant lock of hair with a soapy fist
and stole a glance at the boy. He was watching her intently and
shyly.

The wound on his face was terrible; she couldn't imagine such
cruelty being done to a child. She wondered how old he had been,
what the pain must have been like; had it been done by his own
father? Or was he a child the *Verstummellin* had stolen? Did he
remember his real parents? She glanced at Henda again, through
strands of wet hair. Was he *really* smiling at her? Or was it just the
scar? It was impossible to tell. The wound that had been carved
into his face was too deep. He would smile if he were happy, he
would smile if his heart were broken, he smiled in his sleep, he
smiled when he ate, he smiled when he cried. The scar split his
face in a sickle-shaped curve from ear to ear and as it healed it
had stretched what was left of his mutilated mouth into the tragic

laugh that clowns try so hard to create on their faces, but without anything like Henda's success.

On the morning of the third day, Bronwyn found Janos at the stern of the barge, studying the southern horizon. She looked in the same direction, shielding her eyes against the glare of the low autumn sun. There was a dun cloud where the canal met the horizon.

"What is it?" she asked.

"I think you have been found out," he answered.

"Guards?"

"Yes, it must be. They will catch up with us long before we reach Biela-Slatina."

"They look so far off."

"No, only two hours, perhaps three at the most."

"We're still more than a day from the town!"

"Yes. We must make your preparations now. There will be another lock we must pass, one or two miles ahead. You must leave us there."

"But where will we go? It's still more than a hundred miles to Piers's camp! You can't leave us here!"

"I do not have much that I can tell you. I am sorry, Princess."

"Please . . . don't be sorry; you have helped us more than I had any right to expect," she said to her credit, and then spoiled it by adding: "I will see that you will be well repaid . . ."

"We are going to embarrass ourselves if we start thinking of obligations and debts. I, for one, *never* think of debts. You had better get your big friend, and I shall have Marishka pack some things."

"There is no other way? No place we could hide?"

"Not this time. We are not abandoning you: there is no other choice."

Bronwyn found Thud with Hottl, who was introducing the big man to the art of sleight-of-hand. The gypsy was a skilled manipulator of playing cards, and they danced and fluttered through his hands like butterflies in a bouquet of weeds. Thud was absolutely entranced; watch as he might, he was unable to follow the intricate moves or discover where the cards came from or went to, when they appeared with a snap or evaporated like snowflakes; in his life he had never seen anything to equal it.

"Thud," Bronwyn interrupted, "Janos says we are being followed by Guards and that they'll catch up with us in a couple of hours. We have to leave the barge at the next lock."

"All right," he answered, with his usual agreeability tainted for the first time by reluctance. "May I watch Hottl for a few minutes more? I can't figure this out . . ."

"Yes, I suppose so. There's nothing to do until we reach the lock. I'll come for you in half an hour." Thud replied with a nod only, already deeply reabsorbed into the whirlpool of painted pasteboard. She looked at the gaunt, morose gypsy and Hottl grinned back at her, quickly; or, grinning as best as anyone could with eight teeth. She nodded to him a thank-you for pleasing her friend. A glint of mockery sparkled in the man's eyes, and Bronwyn felt herself flush with anger.

She felt a touch on her shoulder, turned to find Marishka at her side. "I have food for you; and Janos, he wishes to speak."

Bronwyn followed the woman to her brother-in-law's wagon, where Janos was waiting. He held a large canvas rucksack in both arms. He set it at the princess's feet and opened its flap. Inside was a densely packed assortment of food and packages. "It is all that I have to give you; more than you could possibly have carried yourself, but your friend's powerful back will not notice it. You have far to go and there is no place you can stop for food or shelter with safety. You must carry all that you need. Without your friend, you could not go far."

"Without Thud, I suppose I wouldn't have gotten this far."

"I am glad that you appreciate him. Here are your clothes, and a fresh suit, and a coat—see? It is lambswool inside—because the cold will be as steel needles in the mountains, and two blankets, one for each of you. You can carry these things in this pack. That is all that I can offer."

"It's more than enough!" she said, but was distressed that it was not more.

"Do not worry yourself so—though your honor flatters you— I will be repaid. Gypsies always are. Ah! Here is your friend."

"Princess," said Thud as he joined them, "I can hear the horses!"

Bronwyn didn't want to believe it, but when she listened she too could hear a faint vibration, as though the hills were muttering among themselves. She turned to the gypsy with panic in her eyes. "They're almost here!"

"No, they are still an hour away. The valley is like a hearing trumpet. We will be at the lock in a few minutes. There is time."

Bronwyn changed from her gypsy costume, reluctantly, replacing it with the rough clothes Thud had found for her. She was wrestling into her pack when Thud returned. He wore the great, shaggy fur coat in which he had masqueraded as the late Gretl; the massive sack of supplies on his back made him look humpbacked, like a buffalo. She made certain that her precious satchel was well strapped across her shoulders. Just then, a cry from one of the boatmen announced, "Lock coming!"

Ahead was a low grey stone wall blocking the canal. In the middle was a wooden gate. On the bank was the rustic log cottage of the lockkeeper, and beyond that Bronwyn could just see the thin blue line of the pond that supplied the lock with water. The lockkeeper was standing on the wall, signalling the barge with a small red flag. The muledriver brought his animals to a halt and disconnected the cable that attached the team to the barge. One of the bargemen reeled this in, coiling it neatly on the deck.

With their poles, the bargemen centered the big boat in the canal, which was here more than three times the width of the barge, and began to push it ponderously toward the gate. Meanwhile, the lockkeeper was spinning a massive wheel and the gates began to swing inward. The water must have been at a slightly lower level in the lock, for there was a rush of water into the stone basin. This made the work of the bargemen easier, since the water carried the boat with it. There were one or two bumps as the barge squeezed through the gate. The lockkeeper immediately spun his wheel in the opposite direction and the gates began to shut behind the boat.

"Now," said Janos to Thud and Bronwyn, "is the time for you to leave us."

"I am sorry to say goodbye, Janos," said the girl.

"No more than I. I hope that Musrum speeds you. Perhaps we will someday receive an invitation to perform at one of the magnificent royal houses? Then we might meet again."

"I promise!"

"See what I told you? Now, up that ladder. Cross the dam and you will be on the west bank. Not far is the Moltus, but you will have no trouble finding a place to cross it. It is still broad but it is very shallow this far north. You will easily find a ford; follow the trails the shepherds use. However, you cannot follow the river very far: it will take you too close to Biela-Slatina. You will have to bear west. It will take you away from the most direct route to the border, but it will also take you away from the main roads. You will soon find a road that will lead you through the mountains. I cannot tell you what to do beyond that."

"I suppose we'll make our way," she answered glumly.

"Be careful, Princess, of your confidence—you are too sure of yourself; these are new things!"

The water from the reservoir had been pouring into the lock, raising the barge to the level of the canal beyond. Bronwyn stepped to the ladder, one foot on a mossy rung, straddling the gap between boat and wall. "Goodbye, Janos," she said.

"Musrum be with you, Princess," he answered. "And farewell to you, too, my big friend."

"Thank you for the coat," replied Thud. "I've never had one like it."

"You are more than welcome! Now, please, you must hurry."

Bronwyn scrambled up the slippery ladder like a monkey, Thud following like a sloth. She paused for a moment, to turn and wave to her friends, Janos, Hottl, Marishka and . . . where was Henda? There was no sign of the boy, and she felt a little saddened.

"Look," said Thud, pointing downstream. From the vantage of the high stone dam, Bronwyn could see far down the valley. She was horrified to see that the plume of dust signalling the approaching horsemen was so close. The muffled rumble of their hooves was as clear as her own heartbeat. "Quick!" she said. "We have to hurry!"

Without another look back, she raced across the top of the dam, Thud close behind. The floor of the valley was a broad, grassy meadow—crisp and brown now from the frosts that had been heralding winter. High hills walled it in on both the east and the west; a blanket of dark, shaggy pines covered them. The Moltus was less than a mile away to the west, flowing at the base of the steep slope. The forest came to the water's edge. Once across the river and into the woods, they would be relatively safe. She would certainly feel safer not being as visible as she and Thud were on the open floodplain. She felt like a bug on a wall.

It would be terribly close: under the best of conditions, Bronwyn's long legs could carry her three or four miles in an hour of brisk walking. At that rate she could cover the mile to the river in less than twenty minutes. But unlike the manicured lawns and playing fields she had grown up with, the deceptively smooth valley floor was booby-trapped with pits, crevices, hummocks, rocks, gravel, marshy pools surrounded by gluelike mud, and a nasty, cordlike, thorned vine that hugged the ground in convoluted tangles. Its loops lassoed their ankles and legs, bringing both crashing to the ground more than once.

They were forced to stop, untangling themselves when the vine snared them, or watch with care where each step was placed—either action slowing them maddeningly. Worse, the foul stuff was equipped with sharp thorns, and in minutes their pant legs were shredded and blood ran down their calves in a dozen rivulets. Their progress was little better than a casual stroll. Bronwyn tried not to pay any attention to the approaching banner of dust, or to the sound of hooves that thundered from the hills around them. It no longer seemed possible that they would be able to reach the river, and cross it, before the pursuers reached the lock and saw them.

The Moltus, when they reached it, was more or less as Janos had described it. It was perhaps three hundred feet wide and very shallow, judging by the numerous rocks that protruded from its surface. But the current was swift, the clear water cut into foaming ribbons by the jagged rocks, and while the river was not deep, it was deep enough. Even Thud would not be able to resist the force of the rapid stream, with only rocks slippery with moss and algae for footing.

"Damn it!" cursed Bronwyn, which she repeated a second later because, looking back toward the lock, she saw that the plume of dust had disappeared. Its remnants were drifting raggedly over the hilltops, dispersed by the breeze. "They're at the lock! I wish I knew how far the ford is! Or which way." She hoped that the Guards would not be too hard on the gypsies—still, and she did feel a small pang of guilt at the thought, it would serve to delay the pursuit a little.

They were standing on a narrow path, a groove cut into the bank of the river. Countless generations of shepherds and goat herders, to say nothing of countless sheep and goats, had created it while on their way from farm to mountain pasture (she supposed, having no idea what people actually did with sheep and goats). It would surely lead to a ford shallow enough for the small animals to safely cross, but in which direction was it? There was no way to tell. On the basis that the path to the right at least went north, if nothing else, she turned in that direction. The path, thankfully, was clear of stones and the triply damned vine, and it was packed almost as hard as cement. She and Thud broke into a trot.

They had covered only a few hundred yards when they heard the first shot. Looking across the plain, they could see the dark figures of the mounted riders. As they watched, there was a flash and a puff of smoke. A second later came the sharp crack of the exploding cartridge. They were either still beyond the range of the rifles, or presented too small a target for the charging riders. Or perhaps they were just warning shots. Bronwyn had no idea, nor did she care as the results were the same: they were as yet unpierced by lead; a situation, she realized, that could change for the worse within minutes.

She and Thud broke into a run, or as much of an imitation of one as their full loads—and Thud's physique—allowed. Bronwyn thought that the pain she had felt running through the alleys of Blavek was nothing compared to this. The stitch in her side had returned; the pain was bad enough, but perhaps not as bad as the frustration of trying to run upright while cramping muscles were trying to roll her into a ball.

Bullets began raising jets of dirt and splinters of rock from around them, each hard *whack!* of an impact making Bronwyn wince.

Then the trail suddenly made a right-angle turn to the left and there it was: the ford, a widening of the river where the water was so shallow the princess could see the gravel on its bottom as far out as the middle of the stream. Without hesitating, she called to Thud to hurry and plunged into the river. The icy water felt like broken glass on her bare, lacerated ankles. They ran, high-stepping, through the water, their feet pumping explosions of spray. Smaller geysers erupted around them as more of the pursuing Guards found their range. She could hear them shouting. She realized then that their intent was not necessarily to kill her or Thud, at least until the packets of letters had been retrieved. Still, she felt confident that there would be few reprimands should a stray bullet find its way into the back of her head.

They reached the west bank of the Moltus at the same time the Guards reached the ford. There were ten mounted men. Their leader lost valuable seconds in allowing his men to mill about while he shouted to the fugitives to surrender themselves.

The west bank was steep and rugged, with broken and precipitous boulders. Black, shaggy pines, with trunks as straight as a rocket and as big around as Thud, grew to the water's edge. By the time the Guard captain realized that he was being pointedly ignored, Thud and Bronwyn had scrambled to a position on the opposite bank well above his head, and were now dodging between massive trunks and lichen-mottled rocks. The captain, followed by five of his men, charged into the river. The remaining four continued to pour rifle fire into the trees.

The girl and the big man were not looking back. The steep hillside was a jumble of shattered boulders, some as large as houses, and the fallen trunks of dead or uprooted trees. They had to clamber over or crawl under these, while bullets whipped through the brush around their heads. It was painful and exhausting; their clothing was being shredded by plucking branches and knife-edged rocks, their hands and knees were bleeding, and what wasn't bleeding was abraded or bruised. Nevertheless, the further they penetrated the forest and the higher they climbed above the river, the safer they became. Rounding a boulder that protruded from the hillside like a charwoman's wart, Bronwyn risked a backward reconnoiter from its shelter. Below, the captain and his men had reached the west bank, but were foiled by its steepness. The chase could not be continued by mounted soldiers. The captain regrouped the five Guards who had accompanied him and returned to the east bank, where the other four were still firing into the trees.

"They'll be after us on foot," said Bronwyn, "but I think it's going to take them a few minutes to get organized."

"Let's keep going up, then," answered Thud.

"Right you are. I don't believe they can go any faster than we can; if we can just keep up our lead we might be all right. The leader will send at least one man back with the news, and he'll probably leave one or two with the horses. There'll be that many fewer to worry about."

They turned from the sheltering stone and continued on up the slope. Above that point, the way became a little easier. It was as steep as ever, but less rocky and with fewer fallen trees. The short late-autumn day, however, was ending. The sun was already brushing the ridge of hills above them. Darkness would come early in the shadow of the mountains. The air was growing rapidly chill.

They had gained only a few hundred feet when they heard the first crashing of the Guards behind them. The captain was shouting for them to stop. *He must think I'm an idiot*, thought Bronwyn.

The diagonal course they were forced to take in climbing the hill took them in an ascending curve around its slope. Though the Guards were close behind, they were out of the line of sight. Nevertheless, Bronwyn and Thud were only minutes from being overtaken. Their path dipped into a narrow gully or cleft; this made a sharp turn and they found themselves suddenly in daylight once more. Before their dismayed eyes was a chasm: the cleft had emitted them high up on the side of a steeply sloping cliff. Or rather, now that there was a moment to observe their situation, near the rim of a vast bowl. A boulder-strewn crater had been carved from the hill as though some monstrous hand had scooped the earth away, leaving behind a vast, canted hollow. It was perhaps half a mile or more to the opposite side.

The bowl was tilted so that the uphill rim was several hundred feet higher than the downhill rim. The bottom was covered with boulders of all sizes, which had undoubtedly broken from the sides over the centuries and tumbled to the lowest point. A large stream—some tributary of the Moltus, no doubt—poured into the crater from its upper lip, tumbling in a frothing cataract over, under, around and through the confused mass of shattered rock, finally disappearing through a gap in the lower rim, below them to the right, beyond which it was lost among the trees. It would be possible to pick one's way from boulder to boulder, making a circuit midway between the edge of the cirque and the shallow pools at its bottom, but there would be no way to do it without presenting an excellent target for anyone standing where Bronwyn and Thud were now.

"Keep on going," said Thud to the princess, slipping his bulky pack from his shoulders.

"What?"

"Just go, please," he answered, wrenching a massive oak branch from where it had wedged itself in falling from the edge of the cliff above them. It was as long as the girl and as thick as one of her thighs.

"You'll never be able to stop them with that!" she cried.

"Sure I can! They can't see me before coming around this bend. I'll surprise them."

"You can't! There're too many! And as soon as they find out what's going on, they'll pick you off from above. They might try to take *me* alive, but they don't care about you!"

"I can at least keep them busy. If I don't try, they'll catch us for sure. I know it's not much of a chance, but it's the only chance you have. Don't you see?"

Bronwyn did see. She had seen from the first that their flight was hopeless, and that Thud's ambush, while ultimately futile, was her only chance to gain a lead. But she was loathe to abandon her friend. If she left him, it would be the last time she'd see him alive. And what would she do without him? She'd be alone!

"Princess, all the things you told me, about your brother being king, and that fellow that wants to ruin everything, and those letters and all; that's a lot more important than me. I know what's worrying you: you're worried about me dying. Well, I'm going to anyway. I'd like to die *for* something. I've never done anything important."

"All right, Thud." Thud was wrong at one point: Bronwyn was not so much concerned with what his dying meant to him as by what his death would mean to her. At the moment her thoughts were not occupied with the potential reality of a very nice person being *dead*—they were occupied with the terror of having to be alone. However, if the choice was between them both dying or just Thud dying, it wasn't a difficult one to make. "Maybe you will kill them all!"

"Maybe."

"Well, good luck!" She began to turn from him, half of her mind thinking that Thud was stupid to stay behind, at the same time thinking herself incredibly lucky that he *was* so stupid. No, she suddenly contradicted herself, he is not . . . hadn't she just been telling people that he wasn't? He's being . . . *decent*, and it has nothing to do with the *Princess* Bronwyn. Impulsively, and before her normal personality could reassert itself, she pulled the surprised Thud to her, hugged him around what passed for a neck and kissed him quickly on his cheek. "Goodbye, Thud!"

Before either one could say anything further, and sparing both a great deal of embarrassment, there came a crashing from nearby. "They're here! Hurry!" said Thud, hefting his club and taking a step back toward the bend in the trail. Bronwyn hesitated only an instant, then turned and fled toward the falls.

There was no longer any path; she had to hop and scramble from stone to stone, and most were lubricated with dark green algae and moss. Behind she could hear surprised shouts and a single shot, but didn't dare turn to look. When she finally reached the cataract, she was forced to pause, daunted by the boiling water. There was the sound of another shot, and a rock by her foot exploded. She turned then, and saw that a terrific battle was taking place at the rim of the crater. Two Guards were down, one lying at Thud's feet, the other draped across a rock several yards below, trickles of blood candy-striping the green stone. Two others were wrestling to pass Thud, or trying to get an opportunity to use their sabers.

The other two had retreated and climbed higher up the rim of the cirque. They had no clear view of the fight taking place below them, but they did have an unimpeded prospect of the girl, not a hundred yards away. They tried another shot, and this one passed through the pack Bronwyn was wearing, from side to side. Thus encouraged, she leaped into the stream, bracing herself against the water crashing against her at several angles from above, trying to find footing on the slick, polished rocks. Another bullet flew past her ear like a hornet. It was rapidly getting dark and the cirque was awash in amethyst light. Very soon she would be invisible within the mosaic of darkening shadows. She had her sights set on a mass of angular boulders on the far side of the stream that would easily provide shelter against the marksmen.

If she had her sights set lower she might not have set her foot on a rock that had been carved by the rushing water into the shape of a scoop. It was as smooth as glass and lubricated by a thin coating of algae. Her foot shot out from under her and she landed back first into the rushing water, the cushioning of the clothes-filled pack preventing her spine from breaking. The stream spun her in a half-circle, rolling her down the rocks for several yards. She caught herself when her left leg jammed into a cleft, saving her from a precipitous tumble into a shallow pool twenty feet below, but wrenching her knee painfully.

She heaved herself half-sitting, sputtering and coughing a spray of water, caught at a dry rock and pulled herself onto a kind of spur between branches of the cataract. She rolled onto her stomach, turning her face toward her enemies.

Thud had one of the Guards pinned to the rock face, by the simple expedient of leaning his vast back against the man, while the other had finally gotten enough clearance to pull his saber. Thud parried the first two blows with his oak bludgeon, then jammed the end of the log into the man's face. The saber didn't have the mass to deflect such a heavy weapon, and it was sent flying over the brink, winking purply in the dim glow of twilight. The Guard stumbled backwards, his last step being into space, and he followed his weapon down to the rocks below.

Then something happened that Bronwyn couldn't believe.

There was a splitting, ripping, cracking, shattering sound, like Musrum tearing the seat of his titanic trousers. The rim of the cirque on which were Thud and the remaining Guard slipped away from the surrounding rock like a calving glacier. Bronwyn saw the two men, momentarily, stuck to the face of the collapsing wall like flies on a swatter, before an explosion of dust and earth enveloped them. The cloud rushed over her, damping the sound of the avalanche. The thundering crash threatened to pitch her into the cataract as the ground bounced in response to the landslide.

As the echoes died, the dust remained hanging in the air. The bowl-shaped cirque held it cupped and there was no breeze to carry it away. It blocked the glow from the twilit sky, and the crater was filled with obscurity. "Thud!" she cried, again and again, but there was no answer other than the careless laughter of the stream.

She continued on as best she could. The temperature had dropped rapidly, once the sun had set. She was wet through and through and shivered violently. Her knee was swollen, and each step made it throb painfully. She was no longer on a route that circumnavigated the crater, but was instead more or less descending into its depths. She was beyond the cataract, or at least its main course, since she was still splashing through icy rivulets. It was one of these that nearly finished her story right then. The darkness within the crater was treacherous; the princess had to feel her way from one smooth, slippery boulder to another. Her only consolation was that it would be equally difficult for the remaining two Guards to follow her. She would be relatively safe until morning if she could use every moment to increase the distance between herself and her pursuers.

Safe, that is, from capture or murder. Death from accident was imminent; she risked a fall with every step she took. A broken limb would immobilize her: she needed arms and hands as well as legs to navigate the wilderness of boulders that filled the bowl of the cirque. If anything like that happened, and she wasn't discovered, she'd quickly die of exposure. Still, the crater was not that large. Had it been daylight, she could have scrambled out of it in a matter of minutes. As it was, she would have to be extraordinarily lucky to reach the opposite rim by dawn.

Her luck was not extraordinary. She stepped into a rivulet that wound from between a pair of mammoth rocks. Its U-shaped channel sloped down at a steep angle, and her foot shot from under her. She landed in the stream, her breath knocked from her in a grunt, slid its length, bounced with a sickening crunch against some rocks and suddenly there was nothing beneath her. There was a split-second of vertigo; then she found herself plunged under water. It was as though she had been suddenly imbedded in a slab of black marble. She had no sense of up or down. She thrashed wildly, panicked, swallowed water. Suddenly her head broke the surface and she gasped a lungful of air, before the waterlogged pack pulled her back under. She wrestled out of it, thrusting herself back to the surface. She was in a small pond. In the starlight, she could see the ripples in its surface and above her the black silhouette of the ledge she had fallen from. A foot-wide torrent arched from its lip, splashing into the pond with a hollow gargling. The water's edge was only a few yards away and she pushed herself toward it. Her swimming abilities were limited to a kind of froglike crawl, which was severely hampered by the sodden clothing which probably doubled her weight. Grasping rocks and some gnarled driftwood caught between them, she dragged herself from the water. She lay for a few moments, legs still in the icy pond, letting her retching stomach pump the water out of her.

Now Bronwyn really was freezing. She was exhausted and the fires of her metabolism were burning low. She was wet to the skin and had no means of creating a fire. Blankets and extra clothing were at the bottom of the pond. She now realized that even wet, their woolen layers would have insulated her from the cold air that was pouring into the cirque from the mountains above it.

Against the indigo sky she could see the rim of the crater. It was only a few score feet above her, but she had neither the energy nor the courage to go any further. She crawled entirely onto the shore and stumbled, half-erect, half on her hands and knees, well away from the water. She collapsed once again. The forest groaned as its vertical masts stirred together in the breeze, and midnight stalked down from the clouds. Her eyes closed and she began to feel a warming numbness crawling up from her fingertips and toes, as though those limbs were gradually dissolving. A seductive drowsiness blanketed her and she gratefully wrapped herself in it.

Something like an alarm must have been ringing in her subconscious for a long time. She answered it like a dreamer being aroused from a deep sleep. She forced a leaden eyelid open and realized, *I'm letting myself die!* It was a disagreeable realization. Death was altogether too pleasant a sensation; it came too easily and was much too welcome.

She stirred and saw a pit only a few feet from her head, a velvet blackness against the carbon black of the boulders around her. When she forced herself to move toward it, she nearly screamed from the pain in her leg. Dragging herself into the hole, she let herself slide down its gentle slope. It was filled nearly to the brim with leaves and pine needles that had sifted down from the surrounding trees. She burrowed into them. A sweet, resiny, earthen odor filled her head. The deeper she dug into the pit, the warmer she felt. Finally, she stopped. Surrounded by the natural warmth of the mouldering vegetation, blanketed from the freezing air by its soft layers, she drifted into fragrant sleep.

It was well into the following day when she crawled from her sanctuary, like a hedgehog emerging into the spring from its winter's hibernation. She looked like a freshly exhumed potato.

Bronwyn reviewed her situation, which was a depressing thing to do. She had lost her only friend, all of the food and supplies he had been carrying, and the spare clothing in her pack; she had only a vague idea of where she was or the direction in which she had to continue; her only possessions at hand were the clothes on her back (such as they were) and the leather satchel containing the letters, which was still securely strapped to her chest. She took an anxious moment to check, and was relieved to find the packets still dry and safe. *Well*, she thought to herself, *now what?* It was at least a lovely day; the pewter light of the winter sun was filling the rocky bowl like a sweet, clear syrup. Its rays were warming, but the air was still cold. Seeing that the rim of the cirque was not far away, she decided to postpone any additional worrying until she had climbed out of at least one depression. Once on the rim, she will have raised both hopes and body.

There was a nearly vertical stone wall before her, but even before reaching it she could see that there was a narrow path that snaked up its face, reaching the parapet after a couple of tight switchbacks.

She had limped only a dozen yards up the path when a Guard stepped from within a crevice. His dull black captain's uniform had hidden him well. Now he looked like a scorpion blocking her path, brandishing his saber like a stinger. She could see that the man had suffered no better than she had. His plumed shako was gone, as were his cape and gun. One black boot had been shredded from ankle to knee. A sleeve was nearly torn free at the shoulder and its epaulet was missing. Blood trickled down the back of that hand, and his black-moustachioed face was colorful with its bruises and smears of green slime and dried blood.

"Well," he said, "Princess Bronwyn, I presume?"

"Let me pass," she ordered, mustering as much royal dignity as she could. It either wasn't much, or, more likely, the man simply wasn't impressed by the bedraggled and powerless princess.

"Make it simple, Princess: just give me the package; that's all I want. I have no orders to hurt you."

"What about my friend?"

"What about him? He killed four of my men yesterday; he was supposed to have killed another in the City. The man was a criminal, a murderer. And we didn't kill him. You must have seen what happened. The wall collapsed. He died in the landslide. Give me the package."

"No, I won't!"

"Give it to me, Princess, and I'll leave you unharmed."

"Yes, you'd leave me to die out here!"

"That's up to Musrum. But I am not going to ask you again: give me the package! I don't want to hurt you!"

"It's the only way you'll get it."

"So be it," he answered, quickly lunging for her. Bronwyn barely had time to step back beyond his reach. He missed his grab at her satchel, but in stepping backwards Bronwyn missed her footing and fell. Instantly the Guard was on her. He kneeled across her thighs, pinning her to the path. Her hurt knee protested the man's weight in waves of pain. He held the point of the saber pressed to her throat. With his free hand he began fumbling with the fastenings of the satchel. The soaking they had gotten the evening before had made the leather straps swell, and the buckles were almost impossible to unlace. He abandoned that effort, and put both hands around the hilt of his weapon. The point pressed deeply into the soft depression at the base of her throat. "All right, Princess," he said. "Unfasten the straps. This is your only chance. Do it now!"

"No," she answered.

"I have no orders to hurt you, but neither have I orders to bring anything back other than the package," he replied. "You'll simply have vanished from the face of the earth. Perhaps it will be easier for everyone this way." He raised the point of the sword, ready to skewer her like the last pea on a plate. Then Bronwyn saw something amazing happen: the Guard's head suddenly turned into a large rock, about the size of a hassock. It was like an amazing magic trick. Almost immediately she realized that the stone had fallen from above, squashing the Guard's head as though it had been a ripe eggplant. Before she noticed some of the more horrific details, the body toppled from her, slumping over the edge of the trail, tumbling disconnectedly the few yards to the floor of the bowl. Still on her back, she turned her gaze upwards and saw, mirrorlike far above her, the grinning face of Henda.

7

A FAMILY REUNION

THE BOY SCUTTLED DOWN from the rim of the crater. For a few moments Bronwyn could hear only the rattling of dislodged pebbles. She had regained her feet, if not her equilibrium, by the time Henda appeared around a curve in the path a few yards away.

"Henda!" she greeted him. "What in the world are you doing here?" His only answer, considering he was mute, was in signs frenzied and incomprehensible to the girl. "I don't know what you mean," she said. "How did you get here?"

Exasperated by her lack of comprehension, Henda took hold of one of Bronwyn's sleeves and tugged her, not up the trail toward the rim, but back down into the crater. "What do you think you're doing?" the princess asked. "I'm not going back. What do you want me to do?" But the boy only held a finger to his crescent lips and pulled her even more urgently.

She followed Henda through the maze of shattered boulders at the center of the cirque until a black pit suddenly gaped in front of her. A moist, cool breath poured from its mouth. Trickles of water from the stream drooled in clinquant threads over its polished lips. From somewhere far below she could hear the hollow clucking of the water as it struck an invisible pond or pool. In the spring, when the stream was at full flood, the hole must act like the drain in a washbasin.

The word triggered a memory. *It's a sinkhole*, she realized. *The whole crater is a sinkhole. There must be caverns under these hills and the roof of one collapsed, creating the cirque. But why should I go down there? I don't need a place to hide anymore.*

Henda was already a score of feet down a steep semiconical slope of clay that had washed into the opening. He paused, gesturing to Bronwyn insistently, then continued into the darkness. The princess followed, still hoping to stop him.

The clay slope was as smooth as glass. Bronwyn slid down it, sitting half-reclined, braking with her heels, leaving behind a pair of deep furrows like a wagon track. The bottom was reached quickly, where she found Henda waiting for her. Now that she was within the pit, she could see that it was not nearly so black as it had looked from the sunny exterior. The light that funneled down from above lit her surroundings well enough for her to see clearly. Where the opening of the pit had looked like a velvet disk from outside, now, seen from the other side as it were, it was a circle almost as dazzling as the sun itself. Pools and rivulets of water were everywhere; it rained from pores in the ceiling in a chilly drizzle, and the rocks around her were covered with thick cushions of moss.

Once again she felt the urgent tugging at her sleeve. She looked at Henda, puzzlement and grey clay covering her face in equal amounts. The boy nodded his head violently, in what was apparently meant to be positive reassurance. "All right, Henda," said the princess. "I'll see what you're after, but I'm not going into this very far. Understand?" Henda nodded even more vehemently and pulled her into the darkness.

One side of the dome-shaped room they were in had been split, like an inverted bowl broken in a fall. They exited the chamber through this wedge-shaped opening, which was barely wide enough to admit Bronwyn's shoulders. She felt a momentary panic at the cold embrace of the heavy stone that would have chilled even the most unclaustrophobic, but the passage quickly widened. At the same time, however, it took a steep turn downwards.

She suddenly realized how committed she was becoming: if she turned back now, it would mean abandoning Henda. Well, that would have to be his look-out, she reasoned; she had better things to do, and certainly better places to go. She knew for a certainty, however, that no matter what she did, the boy would refuse to follow her out. But yet—there was a strange reassurance that he seemed to know what he was doing. His urgency pricked her curiosity.

She became aware of an odd thrumming; not quite yet a full-fledged sound, rather a nearly subliminal throbbing in the air. A waterfall? The passage had widened considerably; it was still wedge-shaped, but the base of the triangle had broadened, while the apex had lowered. Soon the floor, eroded by a million years' worth of running water, began to develop a rut in its middle. This eventually became a V-shaped gully that mirrored the ceiling above it; the passage was a narrow lozenge-shape. Walking consequently became extremely difficult. They had to brace their feet on either side of the sloping floor while the stone was as sleek and white as wet chalk. Every step risked a twisted or broken ankle if a foot slipped into the narrow cleft.

The passage opened into a large chamber. Bronwyn stopped, sat on the stump of a broken stalagmite and massaged her cramping calves while her injured knee throbbed with each heartbeat. Henda plucked at her sleeve, hurrying her along, and she pushed his hand away. "Whatever it is, Henda, it can wait five more minutes." The boy, morosely, sat at her feet to wait.

As the pins and needles of her knotted muscles withdrew, Bronwyn became aware of the thrumming once more. It was truly a sound now: a regular, modulated sibilance, rather like the chanting of priests in a church. It seemed to come from the walls themselves, as though she were within a seashell listening to the susurration of her own surging blood.

The chamber was crescent-shaped in plan, but of indeterminate height. Down one convex wall poured a frozen waterfall of pearly calcium carbonate, the glistening mineral leached out of the soil above by the percolating waters and redeposited hundreds of feet underground in an ossified imitation of its watery origin. Peering up its fluted cascades, Bronwyn could not see its top. *Why can I see at all?* she suddenly wondered, standing up and looking around. She realized that she could clearly see the rock walls, and Henda, and the crystalline waterfall in a sort of grey phosphorescence, like that of a moonless night in the country. Before it could puzzle her any further, Henda seized the opportunity presented by her ambulatority, clutched her by the hand and led her in a rush around the bend of the crescent.

Here was the opening of another, larger passage. Bronwyn was well into it before she realized that it was more than broad, regular, smooth-walled and level: it was artificial. The realization did not come as an immediate shock, as it should have if suddenly noticed. Instead it had been blurred by speed, like a motion picture film that has jumped its sprockets, a painting spread out as it were by the trowel of Henda's rush. Nevertheless, Bronwyn suddenly began to no longer wonder at *where* the boy was taking her, but to *whom*.

Before this revelation could manifest itself as reservation, she reached the end of the corridor. A circular stone blocked it as neatly as a cork in a bottle. The stone face was flat and intricately worked with sinuous patterns and angular symbols.

"I don't like this," she told Henda, and began to hang back, away from what she knew was a door. Who or what needed a door nearly twelve feet high and Musrum knew how thick? Henda ignored her, picked up a rock from the floor and began to beat on the decorated stone. It rang like a drum. "Don't do that!" cried Bronwyn, grabbing at the boy's arm, wresting the stone from it. It was too late: they had knocked and someone was answering.

Grittily grinding like a giant gristmill, the stone began to withdraw into the wall, revealing a round tunnel almost twice Bronwyn's height. It was a short passage; a circular portal rather, or a kind of anteroom. When the stone had been pulled beyond its farther limit, it was rolled aside. A fluttering, silvery light poured through. Henda plunged through the opening at once. Bronwyn, stiffening her courage, followed. On the far side of the doorway stood a massively familiar figure.

"Thud!" she cried. But there was no response from the giant. She turned in confusion, and became even more confused. There were Thuds all around her. Dozens of them.

"Welcome, Princess Bronwyn!" came words in the kind of voice a ton or two of polite granite might have. One of the giants stepped forward and once again she thought it was her missing friend. But this creature would have made the Thud she knew seem like a toy balloon compared to a dirigible. It had the same pumpkinlike head, and eyes like nailheads, but while it shared Thud's general baldness a semicircular fringe of grey hair grew from ear to ear, passing beneath the nearly nonexistent chin. The hair was woven into scores of long plaits that hung down the creature's chest for at least a yard. The effect was rather like an inverted Medusa.

A robe of grey asbestos, threaded intricately with gold and silver and trimmed with knobs of uncut semiprecious stones, hung from its shoulders. Beneath the robe it wore only a kind of wide apron of some thick grey felt. In one hand it grasped a pole as large as the bowsprit of a ship. "She seems confused," said the creature. "She is worried about her friend. We should have thought of that. We will take her to him directly; and she must accept our apologies!"

Bronwyn realized that the monster was talking about Thud, and in the present tense. "Thud is alive?" she asked.

"Oh yes!" answered the giant. "He is quite all right. Does she want to see him?"

"Yes! Yes, but . . . where is this? Who are you?"

"This is impossible and so embarrassing!" the giant said to no one in particular. "Our first visitor in . . . how long? Never mind! It must be centuries. Fellow royalty at that, and how is she treated? The princess must let us beg for her forgiveness!"

"Well, certainly, of course . . . but . . ."

"No offense?"

"None! I . . ."

"What a relief that is! Please, then, will the princess do us the honor of coming this way? We must make her comfortable, and then all will be explained." The giant, with a swooping gesture, allowed the princess to precede him through a doorway excavated to his gargantuan scale. With the exception of three who followed, all of the others remained behind. She found herself in a large room, lit by the same sourceless phosphorescence. It was a pleasant, soothing light, but its shadowlessness was disconcerting and flattening. The chamber was furnished, more or less, in a kind of High Rustic style, though instead of wood, logs or branches everything had been fashioned from stalactites, stalagmites and some of the weirder formations that only caverns have the time to create. The furniture looked fluid, and was polished to a lustrous translucency. It was very artistic, but Bronwyn felt that the artfulness came from the nature of the materials and not from any skill of the giants.

Bronwyn looked from the furnishings to the giant, then to the attendants who had accompanied him. Like those who had remained behind, they wore only thick grey aprons, like those of blacksmiths. She was glad she had never seen Thud nude.

"May we make so bold as to introduce ourselves?" asked the giant.

"Please!" said the dazed princess. "You have had the advantage."

"We are the princess's humble and obedient servant, King Ooflool Slagelse, the one hundred and thirty-third."

"King? Of what? Oh, I'm sorry, I . . ."

"No, not at all! We realize perfectly well how few people from the princess's world know of our kingdom. We rather prefer it that way, so she must not blame herself. Her ignorance, in fact, is very gratifying!"

"Well, ah, thank you, ah, your Highness."

"*This* is our kingdom." He waved a hand in wide gesture. "The princess is in it now."

"I don't understand you. This is Tamlaght; I haven't left it."

"The princess left it the moment she stepped beneath the ground."

"Well, I won't argue the point now . . . But the name of this kingdom?"

"Name? We are not certain what the princess means. Our kingdom has no name."

"Please go on."

"Our kingdom is far, far older than the princess's own. It was old when the house of Slagelse was founded one hundred and thirty-three generations ago—and we must tell the princess that we are very long-lived."

"Who are you, then? I'm sorry, but I don't know any other way to put this: *What* are you?"

"We are a Kobold, these gentlemen here are Kobolds, our kingdom is of the Kobolds."

"Kobolds? I *have* heard of you . . . such things . . . but only in fairy tales, in stories."

"Really? We know that our people are known to the surface dwellers who live on the mountains above our kingdom but, between the princess and ourselves, we don't believe that they are very intelligent representatives of her race. They'd believe anything. It is very gratifying to learn that someone of relative education and breeding knew of us."

"Well, I had heard of Kobolds, but I can't honestly say that I believed all that I was told."

"No matter, no matter! Now we know that the princess is anxious to be reunited with her friend?"

"Thud? Yes, very much! I thought that he was dead."

"We are sorry about that, we really are. We had no idea that the two of you were in any way connected, not until we spoke to Thud. It was quite a surprise, the princess can believe us, to learn that one of our own had become so involved in a convoluted upper-world intrigue."

"That's something that I would like the answer to before I see Thud . . . Why do all of you look like him? And what did you mean, 'one of our own'?"

"Why, Thud's a Kobold, too, of course."

Before Bronwyn could close the mouth that had involuntarily dropped open, there was a knock at the door and the king called out, "Enter!" Flanked by two Kobolds, Thud entered the room. He still wore the long fur coat, though by now it was looking as though it were well into its last molting season. With a glad cry, Bronwyn ran to her friend. She was engulfed in his massive arms.

"I'm glad to see you, Princess," he said, but Bronwyn could say nothing.

She finally stood back a step, so that she could look up into Thud's face. She wiped away some of the wetness on her face and said, laughing, "I thought you were dead!"

"I thought I was too, Princess. I thought that the whole mountain had fallen on me."

"That was our doing," interjected the king. "The sinkhole is one of our few accesses to the surface and we guard it carefully. We knew that outside people were coming, but can the princess imagine our surprise when it was reported that one of our own was in mortal peril?"

"It must have been a shock."

"It was, indeed! Well, it was simplicity itself to arrange the landslide and rescue Thud."

"Simplicity," repeated Bronwyn.

"Everything went black," explained Thud, "and I woke up here."

"I think that everything is going black again," said Bronwyn, who suddenly sat down. Waves of nausea and dizziness were washing over her like an oily surf.

"Oh dear!" cried the Kobold king. "What is the matter?"

Thud picked the princess up gently and carried her to a variety of couch. He stretched her out at full length on it, but as soon as he stepped away, the girl turned her head over the edge and vomited. She retched violently but only a thin drool splashed onto the floor. She dropped her head limply back onto the cushion.

"What is wrong?" asked the king.

"I think that she is just hungry," answered Thud.

"Well, I am now," added the princess, weakly.

"Of course! How can we have been so remiss? No visitors in a century, and one's skills as a host vanish. How can the princess ever forgive us?" He rapidly issued orders to the two Kobolds who had accompanied Thud. In his own language, the words made him sound like a gravel crusher. The Kobolds hurried from the room.

Only a few minutes passed before they returned, one carrying a large bowl of something liquid and steaming, the other carrying a large brown bundle. "Can you take care of this?" asked the king of Thud, indicating the bowl of food. Thud nodded assent, took the bowl and squatted beside the semiconscious girl. He lifted her head a few inches and held a spoonful of thin, grey broth up to her mouth. He pressed the rim against her lips, and she took a little of the food. He waited for a minute, but the soup stayed put. He ventured another spoonful, with equal success. Emboldened, he began feeding her in earnest.

"We found this in the pool," said the king, as he directed his Kobolds to open the bundle. A mass of sodden fabric erupted from it, spilling messily to the floor. "Are these the princess's?"

"Yes," answered Thud, "those are her clothes. Can they be dried? She shouldn't put them on wet."

"Oh, certainly. Spootka, Stradool, take these to the smeltery. See that they are made dry." The two Kobolds thus directed scooped up the clothing and hurried from the room. The king turned once more to Thud. "Is it damp enough here for the princess?"

"I don't think that damp is good for her, your Majesty."

"No? Are you sure?"

"Damp makes people sick."

"How strange. Well, that is easily remedied. There are dry rooms near the furnaces that are otherwise very nice. The princess can have any one of them. We'll see that they are properly furnished; do you know what else the princess will need?"

"Well, your Majesty, she is wet, cold, tired, dirty and hungry. She ate some food, and she is sleeping, so that takes care of, uh, two things."

"Do you think that the princess can be moved?"

"Oh, yes, I'm sure."

"Good. We'll order a room made ready now. We only hope that we can make up for such a poor introduction to our kingdom. We will need her to feel friendly toward us."

When Bronwyn awoke, it seemed that little had changed. She was still in a room built to the bosnian proportions of her hosts. Hosts, indeed! The walls were a fine-grained pale stone, finished as smooth as plaster. They were innocent of any decoration. The

Kobolds seemed to be thoroughly innocent of any art. The room was equipped with the same sort of strange, half-melted-looking furniture she had seen before. The bed she lay in was large enough for a dozen humans. Though its mattress was barely resilient, she had slept comfortably enough. There were four towering cornerposts: vast stalagmites left in their natural state, like enormous pink candles, veined with rose and lavender. Lying near the edge of the bed on her right was a momentary mystery. A small beige globe—like a cantaloupe—that she finally recognized as the top of Thud's head. The big man had fallen asleep sitting in the chair next to her, and had toppled over onto the bed. Poor man! This was the second time she had caused him to sleep in a chair. *Poor man, indeed*, she thought, then: is *Thud a man? Or what?*

She reached over and touched the pink sphere, and Thud was instantly awake, sitting erect and looking at her with his customary emotionlessness. "Good morning, I think," he greeted her. "Good morning, Thud," she answered, stretching. "Ow! I think every muscle in my body is the wrong size. Rigor mortis has set in. I feel like an old carpenter's rule. And Musrum! I'm hungry!"

"You can have food brought here anytime you want. All you have to do is ask."

"Have you eaten?"

"Oh, yes. I ate plenty even before you came here. But you haven't eaten much at all. Just a little soup."

"You don't have to tell me!" She crawled to the side of the bed and swung her feet over the edge. She pushed herself upright. "Ohh!" She clutched her head. "I feel terrible. Oh, Musrum! And I'm still in the same clothes. I must smell as bad as I look. Phoo! I do!"

"I would have washed you, but you seemed too sick. I'm sorry. I thought you needed to sleep."

"Let me do my own thinking . . . I don't know what I want first: a bath or breakfast. A bath, I think, definitely."

"They found a pack, the one you must have dropped in the pool?"

"Wonderful! I can change clothes, then; where are they?"

"I don't know. They took them to dry somewhere. I can find them for you."

"I wish you would. And where am I supposed to take this bath?"

"I don't know. But I can ask someone."

"You can speak their language?"

"Sort of. It's funny. I didn't think that I knew any foreign languages." He went to the door, opened it and spoke quietly to someone standing just outside. "Someone will bring your clothes here," he reported, "and someone's coming to take you where you can have a bath."

"Where is Henda? I haven't seen him since he led me here."

"I don't know, Princess. I haven't seen him at all. I didn't know he was here. I can ask."

"Would you, please?"

At that moment, there was a discreet rapping at the door. At Bronwyn's bidding a Kobold entered. Until that moment, Bronwyn had never considered the necessary presence of female Kobolds, and she had never in her life imagined anything like the creature who stood patiently waiting for her. *Thud with teats*, she thought, inadequately. Even "udders" seemed insufficient to describe the pendulous masses that hung, like half-filled sacks of grain, to the female Kobold's vast waist. *Either one must weigh as much as I do. Amazing.* With the exception of Slagelse, all Kobolds apparently dressed exactly alike. *Unfortunately*, she thought unkindly.

"It's Sligool," said Thud.

"It's what?"

"She's your bath attendant," said Thud.

"My what?"

"She'll take you to the baths. Just follow her, Princess, I'm sure it's all right."

Bronwyn had only taken a single step beyond the threshold of her door when she froze, struck as dumb as though she were eyeball to eyeball with a furious basilisk.

In the Great Temple of Musrum, in Blavek, was a magnificent painting by the legendary artist Ludek Lach-Szyrma. It covered an entire wall of the East (or Iron Gate) Chancel and, when seen from the proper distance, filled one's vision like an overflowing cup. It was an apocalyptic re-creation of the Musrumic Hell—the Realm of the Weedking—and few could stand before it unmoved by its beauty and horror, its glamour, seduction, savoriness; its monstrousness, succulence and damnation. Flames like phosphorescent tentacles stroked and relished the roiling black clouds that poured from hissing, sparkling furnaces. The smoke greased the bilious sky with oily smears; green and violet beams of light wove through it like ribbons. A shattered city, ragged and black as the Weedking's teeth, was silhouetted against the licking ember of

His glowing tongue. Lambent coals radiating within the empty sockets of windows turned the buildings into squinting, baleful dragons. Over and through the carbonized city scuttled thousands of pale, glistening workers, their white bodies as taut and round as fish eggs. They were the furnacemen, the stokers, the smelters, without whom the fires of the Weedking's realm would dwindle to sour ashes. On their backs, in wagons and in carts they carried the endless supplies of coal and peat and dung that fed the hot-blooded, hungry Weedking.

That is what Bronwyn saw before her, more or less. Later she wondered if Lach-Szyrma had somehow stumbled into the Kobolds' world, taking back to the Church-smothered Tamlaght of three centuries ago a vision of Hell. There were some differences: where the artist had seen horror, there was industry; where he had seen chaos, there was metamorphosis; where he had seen the curse of Musrum, there was single-mindedness, bland contentment. Where Lach-Szyrma had seen Hell, Bronwyn saw the mills and forges of the Kobolds.

Seen from her vantage point, a wide ledge perhaps seventy-five or a hundred feet above the floor of the main cavern, the Kobold refinery looked like the Transmoltus at night. The naked Kobolds were not the horrifying monsters of Lach-Szyrma's nightmare, but they made Bronwyn's head spin with metaphors. The white giants looked like hairless bison; in their purposeful industry they looked like termites; splashed with livid colors from the furnaces they looked as sinister as circus clowns at midnight, or gods at their forges smelting planets, or demons pan-frying the damned. The mural in the Church had scared her into nightmares for a week when she had first seen it more than ten years before, and its frightfulness had never been forgotten—exactly as its author intended. She knew that it would never allow her to see the Kobold works without prejudice, that she would never see the beauty there without the superimposition of Lach-Szyrma's fundamentalist horrors.

She was eventually led by way of a dark and circuitous route to a large chamber, its stalactite-festooned ceiling barely visible forty feet overhead, the distant walls invisible in the thick, white vapors that rose from hundreds of bubbling, circular pools. She was led in a winding path between the thermal springs, their superheated water crackling and fizzing like champagne. Some of the springs were only navellike holes in the wet, rocky floor, hissing and sputtering like teakettles; others were fuming lakes, the centers of which would suddenly heave upwards in glassy domes as their subterranean plumbing belched.

They finally came to a halt before a vast pool, its rim raised five feet above the floor of the cavern, like a lunar crater, the glasslike water level with the edge. With gestures the Kobold (Koboldette? Koboldess?) clearly indicated that this was the spot. Bronwyn gingerly touched the wet stone, but it wasn't hot. The water trickling in a film over the rim was blood-temperature—the pool could be but only a little hotter. As the Kobold emptied a bag of soaps, towels, jars and bottles, Bronwyn stripped herself of her clothing. She had not had them off for at least three days, and it felt as though they were taking skin with them.

Then a problem presented itself. Her first effort at climbing the nearly vertical rim landed her on the floor of the cavern. The travertine wall that the spring had gradually built around itself was bulbous and slippery. There were neither crevices nor angles to give purchase to bare feet and fingers. She had tried several places, at grave risk to both limb and dignity, before her attention was caught by Sligool. The huge female locked her fingers together, palms up, and leaned over, letting her long arms dangle. Bronwyn stepped into the stirrup thus made and before she knew what had happened found herself launched into the air like a slung shot. At the descending end of her parabola, she dropped into the spring, arms and legs flailing, with a graceless splash.

The water was wonderful. It was slightly warmer than body heat and its surface was alive with curling tendrils of steam. The pool's crater was infundibular, and bubbles drifted up like fireflies from its narrow purple throat. They tickled as they rolled over the impeding island of her body, like curious minnows swarming around a whale. *Am I still in the cirque,* she wondered, *dreaming this fantasy in a hypothermic coma? Will it all go black in a moment when I die of exposure and exhaustion? Or did I die, and am I now discovering what a whimsical god Musrum is?*

The Kobold held a cylindrical bar of soap at the rim of the pool, and Bronwyn drifted over to take it along with a square of fuzzy, abrasive cloth. She soon forewent the latter; she'd let the Kobolds scrub with sandpaper if they wished. Although it was a little clumsy, bathing while floating free—especially for such an indifferent swimmer as Bronwyn—she finally finished, hair and all. She paddled to the edge of the spring, and Sligool lifted her from the water like a boiled dumpling. The princess allowed herself to be rubbed and anointed with several headily aromatic oils and salves, as amazed with Sligool as she had been at Thud for his gentleness. The firm massaging re-created muscles, untying them from complicated knots and manipulating them into their proper places. Wrapped in a tentlike towel of the Kobold's cardboardlike fabric, she padded barefoot behind the woman as the Kobold led the way back to the princess's chamber.

There she found Thud waiting with the clothes she had carried in the pack, now dried and neatly laid out on the bed. She was especially delighted to see the pair of thick woolen blankets that Janos had given her. She chose trousers and a soft flannel shirt from the collection. As she dressed, she said, "Thud, do you have any idea at all about where we are?"

"Like the king said, Princess, we're in his kingdom."

"Well, yes; but where is that?"

"What do you mean? It's right here."

"You don't find any of this strange?"

"Why should I?"

"I mean, for example, you *look* like all of these, uh, people."

"Sure. Why not?"

"Well, look, I don't know how to put this, but haven't you ever felt, well, *different*? I mean, look how big you are, for instance."

"Oh that."

"Where we came from, everyone looked like me, more or less, isn't that right?"

"Uh-huh. Little."

"But here, you're actually only medium-sized."

"I noticed that. It makes me feel kind of funny."

"I can imagine. The king makes you look like a baby. But don't you think that this *place* is strange?"

"I don't know. I've never been outside the City before. Isn't this right?"

"Only in fairy tales, Thud."

"No one ever told me any fairy tales."

"Maybe you're making up for lost time."

"Huh?"

"Do you know where we can find the king? I've got a lot of questions to ask him."

"I can ask."

"Please do. And that's another thing, Thud: just how is it that you can speak the language?"

"Why not?"

"Could you speak it before?"

"I don't know. I never had to."

She suddenly stopped the process of dressing herself. She had realized that she was still extremely hungry, more so than ever, in fact. She pulled off the trousers and climbed back onto the big bed. She explained her need to Thud, who spoke to someone at the door. Not too many minutes later there was a discreet knock and Thud admitted a Kobold who was carrying a tray loaded with covered platters. Bronwyn squatted cross-legged and allowed the tray to be placed on the bed before her. She lifted the cover from one of the dishes.

"What is this?" she asked, repelled by the objects revealed.

"Food," answered Thud.

"It looks more like something a cow coughed up."

"No, I don't think it is."

"All right, what is it then?"

"Well, those things there, the grey things, they're what-do-you-call-them? The things that grow in wet, dark places?"

"Mushrooms?"

"That's what they are, mushrooms!"

"I know what mushrooms look like. *This* is fungus." She lifted the other covers warily. There were things made from lichens, and it got much worse.

"It doesn't look so bad," offered Thud.

"You've tasted this stuff?"

"If you don't look at it, it's not so bad."

"It's too late, then. I've already seen it."

Inquiry brought an invitation to join the king in his throne room early the next day. Bronwyn awoke that morning without the sense of urgency she ought to have felt. She was not feeling any of the hurry and bustle normally attendant on an immediate departure. She was already becoming accustomed to a subterranean existence; she had almost ceased to think of the sun, the moon, the stars, trees, houses or towns—in fact, about any of the terrestrial necessities. The artless unimagination of the Kobolds was acting like an hypnotic drug. She was certainly in the midst of more adventure than she had ever hoped to attain. If that was indeed her goal, as she had once believed, why was she so anxious to move on? Why was she so keen on continuing toward her cousin's camp? She was out of the palace, beyond the influence of Payne or her brother—in fact, they probably assumed her to be dead. She was her own mistress now; an entirely new life was before her, if she wished to begin it. Why then the compulsion to plunge back into the old one?

As she dressed, she tried to puzzle it out. Perhaps Janos and Marishka had overestimated her . . . they had not reckoned on her pride, stubbornness and vindictiveness. Neither had she, if it came to that. It angered her beyond measure that her enemies were undoubtedly at this very moment gloating over her defeat and failure. And that was motivation enough.

She went alone, accompanied only by a Kobold guide. She was left to wait in what she guessed to be an antechamber. It was already occupied by a small figure.

"Henda!" she cried with gladness. The boy rose at the sound of his voice. In spite of his dolphin's smile, she knew that he was unhappy—as a blind man's hands come to replace his eyes, Henda's eyes had gained the ability to show all the emotion his mutilated, frozen face was denied expressing. "What is wrong?" He only shook his head slightly. "But something is the matter?"

Henda fumbled in his pockets for a moment, and pulled forth a stub of charcoal and a scrap of brown paper. He scribbled on it briefly, then handed the paper to the girl. "thar iz nuthen rong [said the note] i am afrade uv maken yu sad."

" 'Making me sad'?" Bronwyn quoted, puzzled. "Why should you make me sad?"

Henda retrieved the paper, but before he could form a reply the doors in the end of the room opened with the sound of a huge gong. Two Kobolds stepped forward, through the door, and turned to escort Bronwyn and Henda into the throne room. The two humans followed them.

The room beyond the door was a great chamber that Bronwyn caught herself thinking of as cavernous—but then, of course it was. It was not as large as many of the others she had been in, but it was certainly the most beautiful. She would have credited the Kobolds if she had not already known them to be incapable of such artistry. The vaulted roof was supported by buttresses of prismatic black basalt; crystals of every kind encrusted the walls like fungi on a tree stump, but of sizes, colors and shapes that took Bronwyn's breath away. She had not been a good student of geology, and could identify by name little of what she saw, but she recognized the glistening fool's gold of iron pyrite: its intersecting cubes looked uncannily artificial and the golden crystals were a foot or more on a side; wine-colored tetrahedrons of amethyst, each the size of her head, clustered like grapes; sheets of delicate

mica, like insects' wings, hung in curtains. There were encrusta-
tions of garnets, and pendants of rutilated quartz grew from the
ceiling like rock candy chandeliers.

The same sourceless, phosphorescent light that illuminated the
rest of the Kobolds' world washed in incandescent, reticulated
patterns over the surfaces, as though she were at the bottom of
a sunlit pool and the Kobolds in the room were looking at her as
dispassionately as a school of goggle-eyed groupers.

King Slagelse sat upon a raised dais at the center of the chamber, the sawed-off stump of a giant stalagmite, surrounded by a
dozen or more of his Kobolds. Their round grey bodies looked
like a collection of dinosaur eggs. *No, not quite right*, she thought.
More like spider's eggs left in a jewelry box.

"We welcome the Princess Bronwyn Tedeschiy," said the king
politely.

"Thank you, your, um, Highness. You have been very kind."

"The princess is now sufficiently rested and recreated? She has
slept well and has eaten?"

"Yes, your Highness. Physically I'm well enough, but I remain
very confused. What is this place? I don't understand where I
am."

"All in good time! The princess will please trust us? First, we
would like to introduce you to Thud."

Bronwyn blinked twice. Her friend wasn't anywhere in the
room, so the king's unexpected words simply did not make any
sense to her. Nor had she any reply that made better sense. Then
she realized that as the king was speaking, the man beside him
had taken a half-step forward. It was he to whom the king had
introduced her.

The man was a *man* in fact: he was positively human, and
almost supernaturally male. And he no more resembled the Thud
she knew than he did Omar the Wonder Fish (her favorite story
character when she had been a child). He did not appear to be tall,
though that was mostly due to the giant Kobolds who surrounded
him. In fact he was a full head taller than Bronwyn, whose scalp
was elevated to an even six feet when she wore sufficiently thick-
soled shoes. He was spectacularly muscled; his body looked like
a relief map of the mountains above them. That rugged fleshly
topography was like a sculptor's rough sketch for an unfinished
statue, carelessly hewn from an oak log by an adze. It possessed
the flinty, chiseled leanness of musculature developed through
hard daily labor, rather than conscious, deliberate exercise. His

arms and thighs were fasces of steel rods, his stomach as hard and rippled as a wave-washed beach.

Like everyone in the chamber save Bronwyn, he wore only an asbestos breechclout; Bronwyn found herself unexpectedly, and surprisingly, stirred. Never before in her life—outside of artwork—had she seen a naked male human being, and this man was within a very few, albeit significant, percent of being as nude as a human can get. When she reluctantly moved her glance to the man's face, she realized with some shock and not a little distress that the quality of incompleteness was carried through here as well: looking into his eyes was like looking into a pair of clear glass marbles—she could have sworn that she was looking right on through the back of his head. There was no more intelligence in them than if he actually had been a statue of stone or wood rather than of flesh.

"Who is this?" she asked the king.

"That is something it will take some time to explain," answered Slagelse. "Does the princess truly wish to know?"

"There are many things I would like to know, your Highness. And if I had the time . . ."

"Thud has told us something of the mission the princess has set for herself," said the king. "She has certainly gone through a lot of difficulty."

"It hasn't been as easy as I thought it would be," admitted Bronwyn.

"But what is?" offered the king. "It has been hard for us to truly appreciate the princess's adventures, or to truly comprehend what would drive anyone to such extremes. So little changes here, she must understand, that change itself is forgotten. It is always the same. Always."

"I wish I could say the same for my world, your Highness."

"Couldn't the princess? It would seem to us that the very world she came from was as changeless as this one."

"I don't think that your Highness understands."

"Don't we? We are not as ignorant of the surface world as the princess and her people are of ours. But we were not speaking of that large a scale, but only of the *princess's* world, the one she is fighting change to return to."

"No, I . . ."

"We have gotten around more than the princess would believe. Our lives are not confined to the caverns and mines, at least not entirely. The people who live in the forests and mountains, and in the littlest, most remote villages, still leave milk by their hearthsides for us, just as they have done for countless generations. And we still accept these offerings, as we have done for equally countless generations. Their food truly is nothing to us: what are a few drops of disgusting milk or indigestible crumbs of cheese to our thousands? No, it is a contract that we are faithfully fulfilling. Has the princess read much of the folklore of her land? No? A shame; and she is wrong, if we may be so bold as to say so: they are not mere fairy-stories. There is so much to explain, then. Where to begin? Does the princess know the origins of her own race? First, would she care to sit? It is not necessary for her to stand in our presence."

"Forgive *me*, your Highness," answered Bronwyn, a little coldly, "but if I stand it is because I choose to. I am not a subject of yours *and* I am the daughter of a king, as you obviously know full well—I will sit if and when I please." Then she took one of the seats at the base of the dais. It was made for the scale of the Kobolds and made her feel like a doll, rather spoiling the effect of her speech.

"Yes! Of course she can! We were very stupid; she will, of course, forgive our tactlessness?" Though the king's expression was as changeless as Thud's had always been, and as unreadable, Bronwyn now detected a subtle hardness in all of the king's speech, however pleasant and innocuous it remained. She wondered if perhaps she might not have made a mistake in her assertiveness.

"Of course. It was rude of me to correct you. Your Highness had asked me a question?"

"Yes. We were wondering what the princess knew of the origins of her own race?"

"Well, the Book of Musrum tells us that He created the first people from rocks in a field, but I don't know if I really believe that. It's not what the natural philosophers say, anyway."

"The princess must not be too quick to doubt. The story told by her people is not very far from the truth. It has only been retold from the peculiar viewpoint of the surface dwellers. Listen: in the very beginning of time, Great Musrum created a race of near-gods, for He was very lonely. The princess can imagine the loneliness of a god who has all the infinite universe to Himself? Musrum created a race of giants, the Kobolds, to keep Him company. He gave us the safekeeping of the treasures of the richest of all the worlds in His universe. That is why we live underground, where we can caretake Great Musrum's wonderful minerals, his succulent ores, graceful synclines and fluent anticlines . . ."

"Pardon me," interrupted Bronwyn, "but do you mean that you don't *do* anything with all of that refining and . . . everything you do? I mean, what are all the furnaces and things for? What do you do with all that metal and, um, stuff?"

"Oh, we certainly do something with it! We cleanse it and put it back!"

"You bury it again?"

"Of course. What else? What *would* we do with it?"

"I don't know. Sell it or something, I suppose. Or make things."

"For what? What for? But there is more to our story, if the princess will allow us. Many thousands of generations ago there was a kind of civil war among the Kobolds. There were renegades who were seduced by the sun, and other living creatures, creatures lower than the Kobolds who were the ideals of Musrum's creation. Their eyes had been blinded by *colors* and they had an unnatural craving for open space. Their distorted minds could not stand the vaults that Musrum in His wisdom had created for our protection. They wished to abandon the stewardship He had entrusted to them.

"The war went on for many years, but we will not burden the princess with its details. Suffice it to say that in the end the renegade Kobolds—the insane ones, to be completely truthful—took upon themselves a self-imposed exile. They left the bosom of Musrum. They went *outside*, into the open. There the great sun burned them like coals in a furnace, shrinking them into cinders. With each generation they shriveled, growing smaller and smaller, darker and darker. And the generations grew shorter as well, for the further they went from the true home, the less life they were able to draw from Great Musrum. They had to grow hair on their bodies, like the animals, for protection and warmth. Soon, the most distant generations forgot their origins, in the struggle for existence on the outside of the world. It is a hard world out there, as the princess must surely know, not at all what Musrum meant for His people. He meant us to be here."

"Pardon me," interrupted Bronwyn. "Is your Highness telling me that human beings *descended* from Kobolds?"

"Well, of course!"

"I have to admit that it's not the way I heard it."

"The princess interests us . . . we have never heard the story from a human's point of view."

"Well, I've heard of Kobolds, of course; I told you that. It's just that I had never thought that you were anything *real*. I mean, I heard about you in stories, in, ah, fairy tales. Until now, I had always thought that Kobolds were make-believe, like fairies and giants and things."

"Humans have forgotten their origins, then."

"Your Highness, I'm not too sure that we ever knew them; I mean, the version that you just told me. Scientists and people like that have studied things for a long time. In school I learned that human beings have been around for millions of years, at least. At first they were just like big apes; they weren't very smart, I suppose, though they painted pictures on the walls of the caves they lived in and they invented fire and discovered the wheel. We call these ancestors *cave men*."

"Well?" queried the king.

"What do you mean, 'well'?"

"Isn't that just what we were telling the princess? Allowing for the distortions to be expected by the passage of time—and probably a natural jealousy, of course."

"No, the cave men were human enough. They were just big and lived in caves . . ." She let the argument drop, realizing that, indeed, the king had a certain point.

"Well, look here," she went on. "The cave men didn't look anything like you Kobolds, not really. They were big, but not anywhere near as large as you, or even Thud for that matter. And they were all hairy and walked hunched over like this" (she demonstrated) "and they didn't know about metal or anything."

"It's not a flattering picture the princess draws, but we find it amusing. We suppose that we had expected the surface people to have remembered their origins and the True People better and perhaps with a little more reverence. Why else do the mountain dwellers leave little offerings for us, if the Kobolds are not being honored as Musrum's chosen? But if we had truly thought about it, we might have expected this. It must be with great shame that humans look back on the gifts that they abandoned; they see their withered, scrawny bodies and remember the giants they once had been. It is no wonder that they have protected themselves with a special retelling of their creation, one that allows them to pretend a little dignity, to imagine that they have risen rather than fallen."

"With all respect, your Highness . . ." began Bronwyn.

"It is disappointing. We thought that we would have been better remembered. But perhaps it has been for the best, after all. By all accounts, humans have been toughened by having to live beyond Musrum's care; they have become ambitious and powerful. It may be as well that most of them do not believe that we exist outside their children's stories."

"I am sure your Highness is right," Bronwyn agreed, not only wondering where all of this madness was leading, but what the king's intentions toward her really were. If being a little agreeable with the giant's fairy tales helped to make him look upon her a little kindly, she would accept whatever he told her as gospel. This was not much better than a nightmare and as in any dream, good or bad, you went along with its rules.

"In any case," the king continued, "her version of the story has a great deal to do with what we must tell the princess. We must tell her of our dealings with the surface people and we must ask of her a great favor—though we think that we can make the latter more in the nature of a trade in services."

"I would be more than happy to be of service to you." And even happier if it meant being safely on her way.

"We are delighted to hear that. Several generations ago—*our* generations, the princess understands—one of our ancestors decided that it was incumbent upon our race to purify the bloodline of the surface people. He was a kindly Kobold, and it pained him to see how much they suffered. And he understood that it was not the surface dwellers' fault: the terrible life they were forced to endure on the outside, their physical degeneration, all was brought upon them by the actions of a few renegade Kobolds. Why should they continue to suffer for something they had had no hand in? It was neither possible nor desirable for us to interfere with the lives of the surface people directly. But we were in no hurry: thousands of years had already passed; what would a few hundred more matter?

"The old king's plan was a simple one: to reintroduce the pure bloodline. And his solution was equally simple: merely substitute Kobold children for those of the surface dwellers. It has not been terribly difficult. There is little that occurs within or upon these mountains that we do not know about. Occasionally, when we learn of an imminent birth, we prepare ourselves. In the first night after the surface baby arrives, we make the substitution. We leave a newborn Kobold child and take the other away."

"You don't . . ." Bronwyn half cried, rising from her seat.

"Please do not look so horrified! We don't harm the poor things. We raise them as our own. They cannot help their disabilities; we pity them."

She remained on the edge of her seat. The king had misunderstood her shock; she was not concerned with what the Kobolds did with the human children. "What you are trying to tell me is that Thud is really a Kobold? He's not human?"

"Of course he's human! We would have thought the princess would have realized that by now."

"That's not what I mean. Thud's one of you? He's a baby you left with a hu . . . a surface mother?"

"Yes! Exactly!"

Well, Bronwyn thought, *what do you know*? She had no reason to doubt the king. As he was speaking, the story Janos had told her came back: the poor foundling girl whose newborn baby was so mysteriously changed overnight. It explained a lot of things about her big friend—even his choice of occupation, she suddenly realized. It was one a Kobold would naturally gravitate toward, she supposed. Thud was a born rock-pounder.

A movement beside the king attracted her attention. It was the other Thud shifting his weight to a different foot. *Oh, my dear Musrum*, she thought, reminded of the presence of the big nude human, *that's the baby Thud was meant to be*. That thought didn't make as much sense as she would have liked. *That's the baby Thud was substituted for*, she tried again. *That is a human being who was kidnapped and raised by the Kobolds, and Thud,* my Thud, *is a Kobold child, raised by a human mother. Holy Musrum, she must have known all along what her child was*! She looked again at the new Thud, with even more fascination, with even more disgust. Working with his step-people had created a magnificent body—what were light chores for a Kobold would be violent exercise for a human; living with them had destroyed his mind.

"We will take the princess to her cousin," said the king, "if she will agree to take Thud to the Continent."

"What?"

"Thud, this Thud, must get to the Continent . . ."

"Socotarra?"

"Yes, Socotarra. The nation of Londeac, specifically. There is a very important mission he must perform. If the princess will help him, we will take her to her cousin."

The king made his proposition far too casually for Bronwyn's taste. *It was what he has been leading up to all along*, she thought. *He must want more than that*. For the first time since her arrival within the underground kingdom, Bronwyn felt definitely afraid—replacing a general anxiety. She had been drifting through the past three days in a kind of reverie: halfway in a dream. Now she looked at the king and his retinue not as creatures of her imagination somehow brought to life, but as the grey, inhuman troglodytes they really were. The smallest of them was capable of crushing her within its great hands like a meatball in a hydraulic press. The emotionless faces, with eyes like glittering chips of obsidian, vast lipless mouths, and no noses to speak of, were now as frightening as they ought to have been all along.

The king had been careful to explain that he regarded her as something less than human, a degenerate Kobold in fact, physically and morally far lower than an animal. They could destroy her without compunction, they could keep her within the caverns for the rest of her life—and there had been no indication yet, she belatedly realized, that the directions to the nearest exit were forthcoming. She would grow to be like the pseudo-Thud: as white as a slug, her body wasting on a diet of lichens, moss and fungus, her eyes atrophying in the darkness, her hair vanishing, her mind slipping from her like a sugar cube dissolving in a cup of hot water. Slagelse's kingdom was one without art, without literature, without imagination, without change and without time—it existed in a perpetual, eventless, out-of-focus *now*. She would have to escape at any cost: the cost of staying was too dear.

"That won't do me any good now," she answered. "It's far too late. My brother's coronation begins about ten days from now and I still must be one hundred and fifty or two hundred miles from Piers's camp . . ."

"Yes, about two hundred as the princess reckons them."

"Then there is just no way that I could get to him in time for him to be able to do anything about my brother and Payne."

"We mean it is two hundred miles as the princess reckons them, but not as we do."

"What are you saying?"

"Distances in our world are not the same as they are in the princess's. Even though it exists within hers, our world is much larger than the princess's. We don't know if we can explain that . . ."

"Please don't try."

"But what it means is that her cousin's camp is only a few hours' journey from here."

"I don't understand how that's possible, but if it is true, why do you need me to take Thud, this Thud, to Londeac? If you can travel two hundred miles in just a few hours, Londeac would only be a day or so away. Why do you need *me*?"

Slagelse sighed, and shifted to a more comfortable position in his throne. He twirled the braided strands of his beard around his stumpy fingers. For the first time a certain reticence entered his voice.

"Our kingdom does not extend everywhere: the earth is not hollow. Much of the journey would still have to be made overland. We would not know our way on the surface, supposing one of us could survive any length of time on the outside. And even if our kingdom did underlie all of Guesclin, the Strait between this island and the Continent is a barrier that we cannot pass. Thud, here, is our answer, or at least part of it. He is a Kobold in all ways except by birth. Our interests are his. And he can travel on the surface with impunity; he can cross the Strait; he can carry out this mission where none of us would succeed. And he is the only one of a very few who are ready . . . or able. Physically, that is: Thud is as ignorant of the surface as we are. He needs the princess's help. Will she help him?"

"If I can. I'll try, at least," Bronwyn answered, realizing that all she need do to carry out her part of the bargain would be to take this Thud to the coast and put him on the first ship to Londeac. Her uncle, Felix, was king there and would surely help. But there was no need to let the king know how simple this would be. The more obligated he felt toward her, the better.

"I hope your Highness will understand and forgive my haste, but I would really like to be on my way as soon as the, uh, two Thuds and I can get ready."

"We are afraid the princess is under a slight misapprehension— only one of the Thuds, as she puts it, is going with her."

"What do you mean?" she asked warily.

"The princess's Thud, the Kobold who accompanied her here, will remain with us. This is his home."

"He's staying here?"

"Certainly; of course. What else did the princess expect?"

"I don't know, but I was counting on him going with me. I guess that I assumed he would."

"No, no. He must stay with us. How soon does the princess think she could be ready to leave?"

"I don't know," she answered, distracted by thoughts of Thud's perfidy.

"Would an hour be too soon?"

"May I ask: what *is* this mission that is so important?"

"We are helping the refugee fairies of Londeac to emigrate."

* * *

Bronwyn found Thud waiting for her when she returned to her chamber. The news that he would not be going on with her had depressed her more than she would have expected. And it had angered her as well: she felt cheated, abandoned and betrayed. Loyalty was something she expected; it was her due.

She did not say a word to the big man, but went directly to the small pile of neatly folded clothing and began stuffing it into her pack.

"Where are you going?" asked Thud, but Bronwyn refused to answer him. "Princess?" he repeated. "Are we going somewhere?"

She turned to face him. "No, *we* are not! *I'm* leaving here. You've made your decision: now stay here if you want."

"I don't understand; why can't I go too?"

"Because you would rather stay here, that's why."

"I would?"

"I don't want to depend on anyone that I can't trust, and I can't trust anyone who isn't with me of their own free will. I had thought that you were loyal, and my friend—I won't make that mistake twice."

"But why would I rather stay here?"

"How am I supposed to know? It was your decision, not mine."

"But I don't *like* it here, Princess."

"Well, you should have thought of that first."

"I did! That's why I don't want to stay."

"Then why did you decide to stay in the first place?"

"I never did! Why do I have to? I thought that you wanted me to help you?"

"Just a minute, Thud. You never told King Slagelse that you wanted to stay behind when I left?"

"Why would I tell him something like that?"

"I guess because you are a Kobold, like everyone else here."

"So?"

"So, aren't your real parents here? Your real mother and father?"

"I don't know."

"Well, haven't you tried to find out?"

"No one here knows who their parents are. They just have little Kobolds, and they get bigger, and that's all there is to it."

"Then you do want to go with me?"

"I never thought I wasn't."

"I think that we need to have another talk with the king."

King Slagelse, however, was not very pleased. "No," he told Bronwyn, when she and Thud returned to the throne room and told him of Thud's intention to leave with her, "that is impossible. Thud must remain here."

"Why? If he doesn't want to?"

"He is a Kobold. He has come home. The matter is settled."

"He's never lived here in his whole life—he didn't even know he *was* a Kobold until a few days ago."

"It makes no difference. This is his home. This is where he must stay."

"Even if he doesn't want to?"

"We find it hard to believe that a Kobold would not prefer to stay here, in the real world! Thud, tell us: what do you want to do? Do you want to stay with your people?"

"No."

"No?" A widening of the king's obsidian eyes denoted intense surprise. "And why not?"

"I don't know."

"You don't know . . . This is your home, Thud. You belong here."

"I've never been here before. My home is in Blavek: fifteen-oh-six Nixnixx Road. Room eight seventy-three, I think."

"Your Highness," Bronwyn interrupted, "how can you ask any loyalty from Thud? How can you ask him if he thinks this is home? Didn't you abandon him as a baby?"

"It was a great mission he was sent on."

"A mission? A little baby? He could have died or been killed! How can a baby know it is on a 'great mission'?"

"We will not force Thud to stay if he wishes not to. Perhaps it has been a mistake to send Kobolds into the outer world: Thud has been the first to ever return to us—now we can see what has happened to all of the others. They obviously have not been able to improve the blood of the outsiders, so that one day those might return to us; instead the outer world has destroyed our missionaries. I am saddened at the thought of the many hundreds of Kobold children we have condemned to Thud's terrible fate. Our only consolation is the thought of the equal number of surface children who have had the glorious advantage of being raised as Kobolds. Yes, you may go with the princess. You no longer belong here."

"Thank you," said Thud.

"Thank you," said Bronwyn.

"It pains us to insist upon this one final matter, however. We can only hope that the princess understands our position. We do not doubt the princess's good intentions for even one minute, but what guarantee do we have that she will abide by her bargain?"

"I've given you my word!" answered Bronwyn hotly.

"Yes, yes! Of course! It is not the princess whom we doubt. It is just that we have not had a great deal of experience with surface people—in the past it has almost always turned out badly for us. We know all too well that the farmers and woodsmen in the mountains above us leave their little offerings only because they fear us and in the hope that they might gain some gift in return. In the early days of our reign, our last guest from the surface abused our hospitality terribly. He was supposed to have kept our existence a secret yet, we are led to understand, he created images that reproduced everything he saw here and showed them to many thousands of his people. We've been waiting ever since for the invasion."

"Was his name Lach-Szyrma?"

"We have no idea. It has been a long time."

"I don't think you need worry—I don't believe that anyone took his pictures seriously. I mean, everyone thinks that he made them up. They think that they are pictures of the Weedking's kingdom."

"Oh, really? That's rather amusing. Nevertheless, we still feel we must have some sort of guarantee of your good faith. It is nothing personal."

Bronwyn felt a tug at her sleeve. She glanced down and Henda was pressing a folded scrap of paper into her hand. With an apologetic smile at the king, she opened and read the note. It was brief, and when she had finished it she favored the boy with another, sharper glance.

"prinses [the note read], tel the king that i wil stay as hostij. it dozint mater if yu do wat he wants or not. i *want* to stay here. pleese."

Henda nodded to her anxiously, his mouth grinning but his eyes filled with tears, pleading. She was neither so slow nor so sentimental not to realize that this was an opportunity.

"Your Highness," she said to the king, "I will leave this boy, who is like a brother to me, as hostage against carrying out my half of our bargain. Though it breaks my heart to do so."

"Agreed!" said the king, delightedly. "The princess is ready to leave, then?"

"Yes, your Highness, I believe so."

"Then our Thud will show the princess the way. Her visit has been a rare treat for us all. May Musrum go with her."

At a signal, the human Thud appeared. He was dressed as before; only a small satchel had been added, slung beneath one arm. Bronwyn sent her Thud back to their room to fetch the pack and the bag of letters. He returned after a few minutes carrying those items along with his big fur coat.

Bronwyn looked for Henda, but he had vanished somehow. She had a moment's pang of betrayal toward the boy—but it quickly passed. It had been his decision, after all.

There were a few more farewells, and an offer of food that Bronwyn declined as politely, but as forcibly, as she could. Still without having yet spoken a word, the king's Thud led Bronwyn and her Thud through a low door at the rear of the throne room. This opened into a broad passageway that sloped gently upwards. The going was easy and the three fell into line—new Thud, Bronwyn, old Thud—and walked silently. The princess, left with her thoughts, found them distracted by the figure ahead. The muscles beneath the white skin of the second Thud's back worked as though that broad expanse were being kneaded by invisible fingers. There was no fat to spare on the man's body and its muscles were revealed as bundles of writhing cords, a sack of boa constrictors, as sharply defined as though they had been engraved with a rake. His buttocks, nearly at Bronwyn's eye level as they ascended the slope, were as round and hard as a pair of ball bearings; they rolled alternately, as machinelike as a cow chewing her cud. When Bronwyn thought of the vacant face now turned away from her, she was sickened by the feelings she felt stirring in her.

The march, made without break, took nearly three hours. The air, blowing into their faces from ahead, had been steadily growing colder. The tunnel made two or three sharp bends and then suddenly they were outside. They had stepped from between a pair of giant boulders, whose tops leaned against one another, that lay on a grassless slope. The wind was strong and icy pellets of sleet stung their faces. Below, filling a grey meadow, lay the encampment of Baron Piers Monzon.

"By Musrum," muttered Bronwyn earnestly, "food at last!"

8

DISCUSSIONS

WHEN PAYNE ROELT FINALLY ARRIVED in Blavek and made his way to the palace, he found waiting there a situation far worse than that for which even his outstandingly unpleasant imagination had been able to prepare him. Even the news that the Princess Bronwyn was probably dead did not bring the roses back to his cheeks. He never did like the word *probably*. As long as the princess remained unaccounted for, she posed a threat. It was just two weeks until the ceremony of Ferenc's coronation, and a great deal of damage could be done in two weeks, as he knew very well. He meant to eliminate all possibilities of interference, however remote. It would mean considerable and numerous difficulties, but the magnitude of the rewards warranted the effort.

What angered him was that these efforts *needed* to be made. Had the prince been less of an idiot, Payne's schemes would never have been put into jeopardy. (Had the prince been less of an idiot, there might not have been any basis for Payne's schemes in the first place, but it would require a good deal more fairness than Payne possessed for him to realize that.) All that he asked was that the princess's powerlessness be maintained for only a few more weeks, and she would afterwards be forever harmless. And had the prince been able to accomplish this simple task? A task that had already been set into motion, and that he needed only oversee? No, the simple-minded peacock hadn't.

Payne had admitted himself unannounced into Ferenc's apartment, and when the prince saw the slight figure suddenly appear before him, as though it had materialized from the cigarette smoke that fogged the air, he suffered an almost religious ecstasy. He had been certain that there would be some warning of Payne's arrival, that he would be able to steel himself before facing him. He had spent that entire morning smoking cigarette after cigarette, pacing his rooms, rehearsing the excuses that he hoped would placate the chamberlain, laying the blame on other shoulders, *any* other shoulders. But when he turned and saw the figure that he wanted to see less than any other on the planet, all of the glib speeches slipped away from him like the cigarette that fell from his slack lips. Payne's arrival had been so silent that all that remained of Ferenc's resolve was a kind of supernatural awe.

The two men stared at one another for several speechless minutes: the tall one open-mouthed, bug-eyed, bloodless, perspiring; the small one cool and dark and motionless within the blue smoke. For one brief moment the hope began to flicker within the prince's mind that the apparition was only a figment of his own overwrought imagination, that he had had Payne on his mind so much that he was beginning to see things. But this wan hope was snuffed out at its first flicker when the apparition spoke.

"Been having fun?" it asked.

"Huh?" answered the prince. Payne crossed the room and flung himself into a chair. He helped himself to one of Ferenc's gold-banded cigarettes, kept in an onyx box on a table next to the chair. The sudden sputtering flame of a match illuminated his reptilian face briefly; then the match was flicked negligently across the room, leaving a thin, smoky parabola behind. Ferenc had jumped convulsively at the sound of the match being struck.

"Musrum! I'm tired," said Payne. "Do you know that I have been on the road nonstop for nearly a week? Couldn't take any of the main roads, not even the secondaries—the barons have all of them watched. I think that I have been on every lousy dirt track between here and the coast. A week to make a two-day trip! As to getting off the island itself . . . Well, I'm too tired to go into all of that now." He had been looking at the glowing end of his cigarette as he spoke, but now he turned his gaze toward the prince, who had not moved an inch since he first saw Payne. "And what have you been doing?"

Ferenc winced as though Payne's eyes had given him an electric shock, but managed to squeak an ineffective, "Me?"

"Yes . . . and how is your sister, by the way?"

"Bronwyn? Well, yes . . . I . . . ah, wanted to speak to you about her. Yes," Ferenc stammered, appreciating the chance to turn Payne's attention onto someone else.

"I, too, would like to talk about her."

"You would?"

"Yes, you pinheaded ass! Did you think that I was living in a vacuum while away from here? Did you think that I was not aware of what was happening in the capital? Almost as soon as I set foot on the road to Blavek I received news of what you had allowed Bronwyn to do . . ."

"Now, see here, Payne! I didn't . . ."

"Shut up when I'm speaking to you! You most certainly did allow her to do what she did! How was she able to steal those letters if you hadn't ignored my orders to destroy them? How was she able to have the run of the palace, to say nothing of your own apartments? You poor sap—maybe I must share the blame: for trusting you to do even the simplest thing."

"Now look here," answered Ferenc, wiping his beaded face with a silk handkerchief. "It's not as bad as you think. I don't know what you've been told, or who you've been talking to, but give me a minute and I'll set you straight."

"All right, I'll give you a minute. Tell me that things aren't as bad as I think they are."

"Well, now," the prince began, uncertainly, taking a chair hesitantly, as though *he* were seating himself before *his* sovereign. "Look, you're quite right: I am to blame for letting her take those letters. I was wrong there. I admit that. I should have listened to you. You're always right; I know that. It's just that . . . well, never mind. But as soon as I knew that the things were gone, I sicced the Guards on her—I knew right off who must have taken them."

"That was a bright deduction," Payne interrupted. "But how did she get out of the palace?"

"I don't know. And that's not my fault! You'll have to ask Praxx about that; it's not my fault if his men can't perform a simple thing like that!"

"And then she got out of the City?"

"Well, yes. You have to blame Praxx's men for that too; there's just no way that Bronwyn could have gotten away from them if they had been doing their duty!"

"Ferenc, you fool!" he stood and took a step toward the prince. He was small enough that even standing his eyes were not much above those of the seated Ferenc. "I could kill you this very minute!"

He turned from the blancmangelike Prince (white, quivering and speechless) and strode in a few quick, silent steps to the door. He flung it open and Praxx entered the room, stopping after only a few paces. It looked rehearsed and altogether too ominous to the prince, who hated being ganged upon.

"Praxx," said Payne, "tell me what has happened."

"Yes, sir. When I received the order to hunt for the Princess Bronwyn and recover the articles she had stolen from Prince Ferenc . . ."

"Just a moment. When did you get this order?"

"The day after the . . . articles . . . were taken."

"The next day. Ah. Go on."

"Yes, sir. The princess was discovered trying to enter the chambers of the Privy Council, but was prevented from doing so. She was pursued, but fled to the Transmoltus district where she was lost. We discovered later that she had enlisted the aid of a stoneworker with whose help she made her way across the City. Once again an attempt was made to apprehend her but, with the assistance of her accomplice, she again escaped. We discovered later that she eventually left the city with a company of gypsies."

"Gypsies," said Payne.

"I knew nothing of any of this . . ." began Ferenc.

"Shut up, I told you. Go on, Praxx."

"As soon as her route and means of escape were discovered, I dispatched a patrol of Guards, led by one of my most trusted captains, after her. There has been no report yet."

"Very good, Praxx. Now, Ferenc, where do you think the princess is going?"

"How am I supposed to know?"

"She can't get to the Privy Council. Who would she go to instead?"

"I don't know. One of the barons, I suppose."

"One of the barons, indeed. But which one? There are only thirty, and I have the approaches to their estates well watched as a matter of course. I have at least one man in the service of each, too. The princess would be easily stopped. But just any of these barons, formidable enemies though they may be, won't do.

It must be the one that they all would follow. The one they trust the most. Their leader."

"Piers Monzon!"

"Very good, my Prince. Now we know why she was so determined to travel north. Praxx, how long has it been since your men went in pursuit of the princess?"

"Just this morning, sir. I should have a report in no more than forty-eight hours."

"Excellent. Ferenc?"

"Yes, Payne?"

"You have more than an apology owed to me, and I mean to collect on that debt."

"Well, I . . . yes, Payne, of course," meekly answered the Crown Prince of Tamlaght.

Something more than forty-eight hours passed before news was received from the patrol that had been sent in pursuit of the princess, or, rather, from what remained of it. Only two Guards returned, the one who had been left with the horses on the bank of the Moltus and one who returned from the sinkhole.

The latter had found the body of the captain (not more than an hour after Bronwyn and Henda had left it, though he had no way of knowing that) and had also witnessed the destruction of the other three Guards in the landslide of the previous evening. He knew he was thus alone, and his search of the immediate area was therefore perfunctory; he was a city-bred boy and wildernesses made him nervous. They lacked symmetry and order; there was not a right angle within miles. Nor did he relish having to deal with someone who could squash the heads of older, experienced Guards like melons. Therefore he gave the surroundings a quick once-over and made his way out of the crater.

Rejoining his companion, he recited a story that he had had nearly two hours to perfect: how the princess had been rescued by a band of ferocious woodsmen, how his (the Guard's) party had been ambushed, how he had made his narrow escape, and his harrowing retreat through the strange forest (this latter part at least was true). As he and his companion made the long journey back to Blavek, the young Guard honed his tale to a simple perfection. When the pair finally arrived at the capital, after a sleepless three days' hard riding, exhausted to the point of death, they nevertheless went directly to Praxx and, to their surprise, Payne Roelt, to report. The young Guard told his story. Exhaustion lent it a verisimilitude it might not otherwise have possessed. As it came from cracked lips and a dusty face, it rang true.

"Who could they have been?" asked Payne of his general when the two patrollers had been taken away to their barracks.

"It can't possibly be anyone she met by prearrangement. There hasn't been time."

"True, if she took the letters on a whim," said Payne, forgetting himself: Praxx was not to have known the nature of the theft. "But what if she *planned* the theft? What if it were premeditated? If she had known of the papers from the first, she would have had weeks to create a plan."

"I don't think so, sir. So much of what she did was forced upon her, she couldn't have foreseen it all. Obviously she had intended to take the canal as far as its terminus; only the arrival of the patrol forced her to abandon it and head into the mountains. No, I believe that her 'rescuers' were as much a surprise to her as they were to the Guards."

"Who were they, then?"

"Could have been almost anyone. The mountains are wild. There are still people who live there in tribes: they are bandits, thieves, cutthroats and worse. You know that no one can travel through the deep mountains alone and unarmed—even large parties have been attacked, robbed and have even disappeared. I think that she has fallen in with such a band."

"What will they do with her?"

"Who knows? If they discover who she is, they might demand a ransom."

"In exchange for what? Her life? That'd be a joke on them!"

"I think that they'd learn who she was fast enough; the princess would not be slow in letting them know her identity. But what if she told them about your, ah, papers? What then?"

"What do you mean?"

"I think that she's smart enough to figure for herself what the chances of getting a ransom from the palace might be. What if she explained her position to the bandits, that she is worth nothing as a hostage? She could point to her pursuit as proof that something was amiss with her standing here."

"You mean that they might just go ahead and kill her, rather than be burdened? Or just keep her? Either would suit me equally well."

"Not exactly. What I mean is: what if she makes them a counteroffer of her own?"

"Such as?"

"She could show them your . . . um . . . property, explaining that it was the reason behind her flight. She could offer a reward of any amount she would care to name for her safe delivery to her cousin, Piers Monzon."

"What is to prevent these bandits from killing her and selling the goods to Monzon themselves?"

"Nothing, if she is unintelligent enough to tell them *why* the material is so important. Even if she did, the results for us . . . *you* would be the same, don't you see?"

"Yes, I do see. I don't think that there is any point in either of us pretending that you don't know what she stole, is there?"

"No, sir."

"I thought not. Well, it saves explanations. It's clear what we ought to do then, isn't it?"

"Yes, sir."

"We have to assume that Monzon will have the letters in his hands sometime in the near future—whoever he gets them from. If he gets them, say, anytime up to a week before the coronation, then he will have ample time to act on the information. If he gets them after that, it will be almost impossible to rally the other barons—most will be on the road to Blavek or already in the city; he won't know where. Once the coronation has taken place, he will be powerless; the letters will be so much scrap paper.

"We will need a force of men sufficient to take Monzon's encampment. It should not be difficult: he won't be expecting an attack from the south end, as it will be a force of his own countrymen, they should be able to ride directly into the camp without hindrance. It ought to be simple to eliminate the baron and merge the two armies. If the princess is there, she can be taken care of as well. If not, our own men will be there waiting when she does show up, if at all. After a week, the camp can be abandoned. It will make no difference then whether she is dead or alive, though I know which *I* would prefer."

"You would abandon the north border to Crotoy?"

"What difference does that make to me? A war is only a useless drain on the treasury. We will have the baron's own militia to contend with; they will remain loyal to him, but their resistance will be nominal."

"There is a way to eliminate any resistance whatsoever."

"How is that?"

"No soldier in the royal forces would dare to fire upon his own king. Or king-to-be."

"Ha! What a joke that will be! I understand! And it'll serve that idiot right, too. Do him good. I hope the dumb snot *does* get shot."

Which is how the unhappy prince found himself astride a horse, at the head of a small army, on a dusty, cold road heading toward the northern border.

The prince had been in fairly good spirits at the outset: the glamour of the occasion was an unexpected dividend and it cheered him immensely. He rode at the head of his small force, dressed in the navy blue and orange uniform of the 17th Bolassas Artillery, in which he was a major-general. And he did look fine: on his chestnut charger, a cuirass of elaborate silver frogging covering a chest decorated with glittering medals, a brazen helmet with its long orange plume whipping like a flame in the bitter wind, a heavy cape floating like a storm cloud below, boots as shiny and black as wet licorice, he looked every inch the soldier. He was followed by the neat ranks of cavalry that were under his command, in uniforms only slightly less resplendent than his own. Ferenc did indeed feel good, and when a few children and oldsters gave the departing parade a cheer, he felt that life could offer him little more.

It was a long march, some four days, and it took Ferenc only a few hours to decide that it might as well be forever, though truthfully there was nothing particularly rugged about it. They had the smooth roads that ran up the Zileheroum so the going was level and easy, and instead of bivouacking in the open air they had comfortable official barracks in the towns they stopped in when evening fell. If the food was not what Ferenc was accustomed to, and it wasn't, neither was it at all bad—and certainly better than the field rations Payne was without doubt thinking he was being fed. He would truly have hated those. In actual fact, he was probably eating far better food than he had consumed in years, no matter what the prince's opinion of it as a gourmand might be.

The men found the presence of their prince a constant source of amusement. They found his endless complaints, condescending airs and insults certainly far funnier than Ferenc intended them to be—which only added to his misery. Though the prince was a good enough horseman—not a week had ever gone by without his being in a steeplechase or hunt—the twelve hours or more of monotonous jogging in the saddle left him at the end of each day sore and blistered, which conditions worsened each day, like his temper.

He cursed Praxx, he cursed Praxx's men for being bungling fools: Really! They couldn't catch an eighteen-year-old girl! He cursed Baron Monzon for being so far away, he cursed his sister for being a meddling little bitch, he cursed himself for being stupid enough not to follow Payne's orders to the letter; if there ever was an example needed of his friend's wisdom, this was it. But he could not quite bring himself to curse Payne Roelt, though it was at Payne's direct order he found himself in this miserable position. He didn't have to like it, but if Payne thought it best, then it must be so.

Before dawn on the third day, they passed the lock where Praxx's patrol had caught up with the fugitive princess. From the sleepy lockkeeper Ferenc learned that there had been no further news of the girl. From a sealed letter left for the next official to arrive he learned that the gypsies had been escorted to the next town north, Biela-Slatina, by a squad from the garrison there, and were being held there until further orders.

They reached Biela-Slatina late that afternoon. Beyond, there were no other habitations before the border, only open tundra, cold, rock-strewn, and increasingly rugged as the high mountains of Crotoy were approached. Though the town was threadbare and rather seedy, the barracks were large and comfortable as they were the northernmost outpost of the Royal Army. The resident company was not happy at giving up their beds, but with the prince present, they were denied even the consolation of doing it gracelessly.

Ferenc and his little army arose well before dawn on the fourth day. Before the sun set, they would see the camp of Piers Monzon.

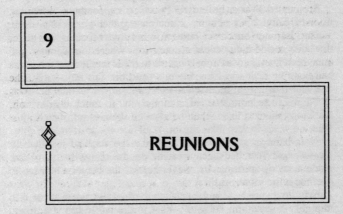

9

◈ REUNIONS

BRONWYN'S COUSIN, the Baron Piers Monzon, had never been more surprised than he was when the princess—whom he believed with all good reason to be in Blavek—suddenly appeared before him, as though she had just risen from the floor like a ghost, a magician's trick or a snake.

Though he of course recognized her immediately, he was taken aback by her dress. Never had he seen her, even at her most tomboyish, in such a costume; nor would he have ever expected to see the normally vain, fastidious princess thus. She looked like the most disreputable street urchin the alleys of the Transmoltus had ever spawned. If this disorienting sight were not enough, the poor baron was not unaware of Bronwyn's companions, who stood shyly just behind her. One was a shapeless giant whose head brushed the canvas roof of the tent. The other was like an alabaster sculpture of some perfect god, whose unnatural pallor the baron mistakenly ascribed to the man's being virtually nude in the subarctic weather. *Why* the man was nude, he daren't hazard a guess.

The trio had been intercepted by a perimeter Guard and had docilely allowed themselves to be taken to the commander's tent. By the time they had gotten there, after plowing through a sea of curious soldiers, they had a score of gaping men attached to them like barnacles. These were still milling outside the baron's tent, hoping for a glimpse of the queer strangers.

Bronwyn was as surprised at her cousin's appearance as he was by hers. Though it had been scarcely more than six months since she had last seen him, the alteration in his physical being was more than that period alone could account for. Where the tall man had once been lean, he was now gaunt. Where his intellectual forehead had been high, it was now balding—and the hair remaining was dull and faded from its original rich dark brown. Where he once stood erect, he now stooped, and she saw to much dismay that his hands shook a little when he allowed them to relax. Still, his aquiline nose looked like the prow of a torpedo ram, his grey eyes as hard as gunmetal, his lips like the slash of a saber. If the last half-year had been wearing on the man's body, it had made a strong spirit harder. Nevertheless, the harder a substance becomes, the more brittle it is.

"My dear girl!" exclaimed the startled baron, when he at last thought of something to say. "What in the world are you doing here? Who are these, um, men?" It is not strange that he thought little of the bizarre physical appearance of the Thuds: the mountainous one with a round, almost featureless head, the other almost supernaturally perfect. After more than forty years of military service, not much surprised him; there were some weirder specimens than these in his own army.

"I've brought you something, Cousin Piers," she answered, laying the battered leather case on a table.

"What is this?" Monzon asked, lifting the satchel in his hand. "Some sort of gift? I don't understand. But please, my dear Bronwyn! Sit down! You look terrible! When was the last time you ate?"

"I don't know," she answered bleakly. "It must be days."

"I can believe it! Orderly!" he shouted. When the servant appeared, the baron ordered hot food and drink. "And these, ah, gentlemen?" he asked the princess, gesturing toward the two big men.

"Thud?" she asked. "Will you and, um, Thud want to eat? Do you need anything?"

"I guess I could eat something," Thud answered. "Whatever they've got ready is all right with me."

"What about him?" The baron indicated the other.

"He'll eat whatever I do, I suppose." She thought that it would not do yet to suggest that the man might, for all she knew, prefer a bowl of steamed lichens.

"I think," offered the baron, sotto voce, "that we can also find the gentleman some clothing, can't we?"

"I should think so, sir," sniffed the orderly, eyeing the naked man with supercilious curiosity.

"Is there something wrong with that fellow?" the baron asked his cousin, indicating Thud number two.

"No, I don't think so. I'm not sure yet whether he even speaks our language."

"Where's he from, then? Odd-looking enough."

"I'm—ah—not sure."

"No? Easily ascertained. You there, without the clothes, do you speak our language?"

"Certainly," answered the second Thud.

"Well, there you go," the baron said to Bronwyn. "All you had to do was ask the man!"

"It hadn't occurred to me," she replied, looking at the second Thud with suspicion.

"Well, young man, follow this fellow here, he'll get you fixed up in no time. Orderly, take this man and get him whatever he needs. What *is* his name, Bronwyn?"

"Um? Pardon? Thud . . ."

"*His* name is Thud, too?"

"Oh, you mean *him*!" She thought quickly. "His name is, ah, Gyven." The first name that came to her mind was the name of a puppy she had had as a child.

"You seem a little distracted, my dear."

"I'm sorry, Cousin Piers; I'm just tired."

"Bronwyn, my dear child, wherever did you find that fellow?" he asked after the newly christened Gyven had left with the servant.

"That's not going to be an easy story to tell, Cousin Piers. First I have to tell you something much more important . . ."

"Ah! Well, it will have to wait just a bit longer. Here's our food." Piers interrupted as two servants entered the tent carrying trays while a third followed with a basket of bottles that nestled like eggs in a bedding of straw. At the smell of the food Bronwyn immediately rearranged her priorities. There was a deep pot full of thick, savory stew, pungent with pepper and onions; a slab of dark yellow, fragrant cheese; chunks of yeasty, crusty bread; butter, jams and preserves; pickled vegetables, boiled cabbage and a bowl of fruit. Her mouth began salivating like a starved dog's and she threw herself onto the food like one. As was her habit when anyone was not of immediate use, she forgot entirely about Thud's presence. However, the kindly baron did not overlook the big man and saw to it that he received his share of the meal.

Once the pangs of hunger had abated, and Bronwyn slowed down and actually began to taste her food, she started recounting to her cousin some of her adventures. When she got to the point of her rescue from the murderous Guard captain by Henda, she hesitated. What to tell the baron about the Kobolds? She scarcely believed the interlude herself and the longer she was removed from it, the more dreamlike it became. She decided, wisely, to forego that adventure, replacing it with a tale of meeting with a troupe of mountaineers—close enough, she reasoned (and coincidentally paralleling the almost simultaneous speculations Payne and Praxx were making).

"And this strange man, the one without the clothing," asked Piers. "He is one of these mountain people?"

"Yes!" she answered quickly. "He is, ah, an outcast. I think. He was exiled from his people. They stripped him of his belongings and left him to die. Thud and I found him and promised him sanctuary."

"But why did you call him Thud, like this man?"

"That's harder to explain. Sometimes I confuse them. But look at these letters first . . . that's what I've come all this way for, to give them to you."

"Yes," Piers replied, opening the packet, "I can't believe the treachery you've described—well, I *can* believe it of Payne Roelt; the man is a criminal of the first order—but that your own brother would conspire against you, that he would put you in mortal jeopardy, or that one of the Guards, even if in the service of Roelt, would raise a hand against his own princess . . . I don't know what to make of it. Other than, of course, that the evil influence of Roelt is spreading like a cancer and must be stopped!"

The baron carefully read the letters, every word of each one. When he finished he went through them once again, scanning them for their pertinencies. His gaunt face was pale with anger, his lips compressed to a bloodless slit. For a moment, he said not a word, but only sat at the camp table staring at a point just beyond Bronwyn's head, clenching his free hand. Bronwyn glanced to her side, toward Thud. The giant was sitting quietly, his button eyes vaguely unfocussed: a piece of furniture.

"The villain plots nothing less than the destruction of Tamlaght!" hissed Piers through tight lips. "He explains it all to your brother. I know that Ferenc is all but feebleminded, but is he so far gone that he would connive at the looting of his own country?"

"No," Bronwyn answered. "I don't think so. I think that he is just too simple to understand exactly what it is that Payne is planning. That's probably why Payne felt he could be so explicit in the letters—he knew that Ferenc wouldn't understand their implications. It was just his way of mocking my brother."

"Well, it's clear enough what we must do. The barons must know of this danger, they must see these letters; with them in our hands, Roelt has no defense. We are justified in taking any action against him necessary. And, believe me, my dearest Bronwyn, he will not escape with simple exile this time!

"I will leave a token force here—there will be no danger from Crotoy now that winter is beginning. The rest of the men I will take with me. If possible, we will be on our way south by morning's first light. There is little enough time to spare, Musrum knows, but I think that it will suffice. You are welcome to stay here, Bronwyn. You will be safe and I believe that you need the rest—you do look terrible, my dear! You can follow as soon as you are stronger; I'll see that you will have an escort. And your—ah—men?"

"I want them to stay with me."

"Fine. Look here, then; get some rest; I'll have a tent prepared for you. Anything you might need, just ask Lieutenant Proos, the orderly, and he'll see that you get it."

"Thank you, Piers. Just one thing: you must promise me that nothing will happen to Payne . . . until I get back to Blavek!"

Bronwyn was given a comfortable tent not far from her cousin's. It was like a small, canvas cottage with its square walls, wooden floor and furnishings. She found waiting for her the only new, clean clothes that the camp could provide for her: a uniform of the baron's own militia. She tried it on before a narrow metal mirror and was impressed with the effect. The fine, sturdy cloth was a deep indigo, with epaulets and piping of gold. A trapezoidal bib on the front of the short jacket was laced with elaborate frogging. The jacket had a high, stiff collar and was fastened at her waist by a wide black belt. The trousers were flared at the hips like riding breeches, but skin-tight at the knees where they were tucked into the tops of glossy black boots. The uniform came complete with a sleeved cloak, trimmed with black fur and matching frogs, and a peaked cap. She thought that she looked exceedingly smart, and the fact that it was the uniform of her beloved cousin pleased her.

The day was waning. The snow continued to fall, though in hard pellets that blew away before they could accumulate. Darkness came quickly. The princess undressed for bed, thankful for the long woolen underwear that had come with her uniform. She crawled into the cocoon of blankets and before she could even wonder whether or not she would dream, she was asleep, finding out.

She awoke before dawn the next morning, stirred by the noise of men, horses and their equipment. The baron was preparing to leave, bearing the incriminating letters. Bronwyn dressed quickly but carefully. Anxious to impress Piers with the effect of his cousin in uniform, and yet fearful that she would miss wishing him speed and success, she sprang from her tent only to stop in surprise before taking a second bound. Coming toward her was the handsomest man she had ever seen. Uniformed as an officer in her cousin's militia, he was a tall, lean figure; his chest a broad wedge balanced on narrow hips, long-legged and rugged of face. Bronwyn's disappointment was acute when she recognized the soldier as Gyven, ex-Thud.

He walked directly up to the girl and asked, "Princess Bronwyn?"

"Hm?" she answered.

"Princess Bronwyn?" he repeated, patiently.

"You *are* . . . ah, the person . . . from the caverns?"

"Yes."

"Well. You look good in uniform."

"Yes?"

"Those clothes, they're a uniform."

"Yes?"

Oh, my stars, she thought, *he's another Thud for sure. Worse!*

"These things?" he continued. "They feel awful. Why are they?"

"Why are they what?"

"Feeling awful."

"Well, you'll just have to get used to wearing them. They're clothes. It's a local custom."

"Oh."

Bronwyn was becoming glad that she had already been wise enough to decide not to burden herself with the man. It broke her heart that he was so beautiful and yet without a brain in his handsome head. Even his voice was beautiful. Such a pity.

"You've been taken care of? You've gotten some food?" she asked.

"I guess so. Strange stuff. I ate it anyway. Didn't like it much."

"I'm sure if we ask someone they'll be able to find you some nice lichens and moss."

"Oh, that'd be fine. Thank you."

"I suppose that you're anxious to get on with your mission?"

"Yes."

"Good. Well, the coast is only about a hundred and fifty miles or so east of here. I've no doubt that Cousin Piers will be able to spare a man to take you."

"I thought that you were supposed to take me."

"Well, I'm *arranging* things for you. It's the same thing."

"Oh. Yes."

A mounted soldier drew to a halt alongside the two, his horse stamping impatiently, puffing steam from its nostrils like an overcharged engine. "Princess Bronwyn?" he asked.

"Yes?"

"Your Highness," he continued, saluting, "the baron sends his compliments and asks if you will accompany me. He is anxious to depart and wishes to speak with you."

"Of course!"

The soldier dismounted and, leading his horse by its reins, walked with the princess. "The baron is just over this side of the camp, your Highness. There he is, on the big red horse."

The baron was at the head of his cavalry, which was arranging itself into orderly ranks and columns. The field was clouded with musky steam. She ran to her cousin, who turned to her when she called his name. "Well! Well!" he said, adding in all seriousness, and with evident pride, "If you aren't every inch a soldier!"

"I wish that I could go with you!"

"I do too, but it would be best if you follow."

"I understand," she lied.

"This is an ungracious goodbye, but . . . what's that?"

That was a lone rider charging into the midst of the ranked horsemen. He pulled his lathered horse up short before the baron. "Sir!" the rider cried, saluting.

"What is it, man?" asked Piers.

"It's an army, sir!"

"What's an army? Get a hold on yourself. Report!"

"Sir, sorry, sir. There's a column of armed horse soldiers approaching, not five miles distant."

"Crotoy? At this time?"

"No, sir, they're coming on the road from the south."

"The south? That's not possible. Who are they?"

"I couldn't tell, sir, it's still snowing in the pass."

"Could you tell how many?"

"It wasn't easy, sir, but I would guess perhaps two hundred."

"Could it be," the baron asked himself, "reinforcements? What for? And with no advance word? Who can they be?"

"I think I know, Cousin Piers," offered Bronwyn.

"What? Who do you think they are?"

"I think it must be Payne Roelt."

"Just a moment, Bronwyn. Soldier, take two men with you and return to the pass. I want word as soon as you can identify the force. I want to know how strong it is, and I want to know when they have approached within two miles. Bronwyn," he said as he dismounted from his animal, "come with me."

With his arm around her shoulders, the baron and Bronwyn retreated to a point a score of yards away from the cavalry. "Tell me, now," asked the baron, turning toward the girl, "what you think."

"I think that Payne is back in Blavek—we know he must be, from the letters. I think that he knows exactly where I was headed . . . he wouldn't believe me dead without seeing a body and he would never accept my merely being 'lost.' He would assume the worst and act on it. He has sent that army to either stop me from getting to you, or to stop you from taking the letters south."

"I believe you are right. But there is a full brigade here, more than three thousand men. There is no way that he would be able to send a comparable force to the border, certainly not on such short notice—he can't have had more than what? Three or four days? And at that, those men—only a few hundred?—must have been force-marched for more than four straight days. What can he be hoping to accomplish? I can smash anything he can send here."

"I wouldn't underestimate him, Piers."

"I don't."

Less than an hour passed before one of the scouts returned. The news he bore was disturbing: the small force approaching the camp carried at its head the quartered orange-and-white banner of

Tamlaght, with the scarlet double-headed eagle of the royal house superimposed on one white field. That indicated that a member of the royal family was present, and that could only be one person: Ferenc. Both Bronwyn and Piers were puzzled by the unexpected presence of the heir apparent. It was as though one of the moons had strayed from its orbit.

Ferenc's little army halted not more than a mile from Piers's camp and a courier was sent ahead. The message he bore was the expected one: a command for the baron to appear before the prince.

"Bronwyn," he asked his cousin, after showing her the order, "do you think that your brother has any reason to believe that you are here, or that I have the letters he seeks?"

"No—that is, he couldn't know for certain, anyway."

"Keep well out of sight, then. It's unlikely that you could be identified in this weather and in that uniform, but let's not take any chances. I'm keeping my cavalry mounted for the time being. He may simply be trying to block my return south."

"And if he is?"

"I'll have to force my way through."

"You can't do that! You'd have to raise arms against your own prince and the heir apparent—that'd·be treason! Your men would be justified in mutinying! Nor would the barons ever support doing that!"

"What you say is true. Well, I will just have to see what he wants before we decide what to do."

"You're going to meet him? Is that wise?"

"What would you suggest? He's your brother, after all; who should know him better?"

"I think that he would only be here if he were under the most severe duress, the kind of leverage only Payne could use on him. And Payne would not be using Ferenc if he didn't feel that he had good reason to: after all, he doesn't have any more faith in Ferenc's abilities than I do. What he *does* have in Ferenc is my brother's position, his rank. As I've just said, you cannot oppose him without becoming a traitor. If that happens, you'll be fair game for Payne. It may be just what he's trying to goad you into doing. Please be careful, Piers!"

"Don't worry. I'll give orders to keep the men at ready; this ought to be resolved one way or another in the next hour or so. But I won't meet him on his own ground. He must come here. Would he do that?"

"I think so, if his trip here has been the experience for him it must have been."

"All right then, I'll send the message. Until you hear otherwise from me, Bronwyn, keep well out of sight."

The reply to the baron's answer came quickly: the prince would be only too happy to meet him in the larger encampment, seeing as how the baron was kind enough to offer the camp's amenities to the royal visitor. Privately, Ferenc looked forward to hot water, decent food, and perhaps a comfortable, warm place to spend at least one night.

Ferenc rode into the camp alone, save for two Guard cavalrymen. These remained mounted while the prince climbed from his horse and entered the baron's tent. Piers rose from his desk to meet him, hand outstretched in greeting.

"Welcome, my Prince, Cousin Ferenc! Please be seated, you must be exhausted!" A little confused by the warmth of the welcome, the prince obeyed.

"I only wish that I had had some warning of your impending arrival," continued the baron. "You find us wholly unprepared for your visit. I must apologize!"

"No, no!" replied Ferenc. "My mission here, ah, was to be, that is, it is a secret. No one was to know!"

"What is it all about, then? May I offer you wine? Hot tea?"

"Yes, please, thank you, Cousin. Ah! It's good to be warm again! Mind if I move this chair closer to your stove?"

"Anything that you need, please. It is a pleasure to see you, I must say—even if unexpected. Seeing you here, of all places, is like"—he groped for an image—"like seeing the statue of Saint Wladimir walking down Pordka Avenue!" He laughed at the picture of the hundred tons of bronze on an afternoon stroll, but the prince's face darkened.

"Look here, Piers, I know that all of you think that I'm just a useless dandy, but I have depths you know, depths!"

"Well of course you do! Just look at you! Not many could have undertaken such a harrowing mission. Certainly not any heads of state that I can think of. What, then, is so important that it brings you here in person?"

"Perfidy, Cousin! Infamy and treason!"

"Yes? And in what form?"

"There are those who wish to destroy me! To prevent me from taking my rightful place on the throne! They wish to destroy the one person whom I can trust . . ."

"Payne Roelt?"

"Yes, Payne Roelt! The one person whom I can trust. They want to destroy him with their lies and manufactured evidence!"

"Evidence? Evidence of what?"

"It doesn't matter. I've come here directly, myself, so you can learn from my own lips what the truth is."

"The truth about what, Ferenc? I don't understand."

"There are people, traitors, who would like nothing better than to see me dethroned—that's blasphemy, you realize that, don't you? What has been ordained by Musrum cannot be defied without blasphemy! The throne is mine by Musrum's own dictation; it cannot be taken away from me! There are those who would want to see that happen, and to carry out their evil plans they will stop at nothing. We've learned, I've learned, that these people have planned to use you to their ends . . ."

"Me?"

"Through your influence with the baronage—they would use it as their tool for destroying us, me."

"How could they do that?"

"If they could make you believe that the nation was in peril, that either I or Payne constituted some threat to it—nonsense, of course!—then you would do everything in your power to raise the barons against me, to put someone else on the throne."

"They would be right. If I believed what they told me, if I thought it was true, it would be my duty. My allegiance is to Tamlaght, not the throne."

"They're the same thing!"

"Calm yourself! What is it exactly that you think I would have been told?"

"Well . . . I don't know. Anything, perhaps . . ."

"Something like this?" Piers asked, reaching beneath the desk and bringing into view the fat packet of letters.

"Where did you get those?" Ferenc squealed, leaping to his feet.

"Does it matter? You know what they are?"

"Of course . . . no, why should I? I take it that the, ah, traitors have already been in contact with you?"

"Who exactly are these traitors you are so afraid of?"

"Who? I, ah, don't know. Not exactly, that is. They're a secret band. Payne told me all about them. General Praxx uncovered their plans. He's searching for them right now. Why, I'll probably get back to Blavek and discover that they have all been arrested! May I see those?"

"Well, I don't think that would be necessary. You know what's in them."

"What do you mean? I just told you . . ."

"Yes, yes. But, you see, Ferenc, I believe what I've read here."

"They're all lies!"

"No, they are not."

"Is my sister here? Did she give you those? Is Bronwyn here?"

"It doesn't matter how I got these. What matters is that I believe what they say."

"I want you to give them to me!"

"No, Ferenc."

"You refuse me? I order you, as your prince, to hand that packet over!"

"No, I will not! Because, if it is within my power, you will no longer be my prince, and Musrum forbid that you shall be my king!"

"What? You dare to defy me? You traitor!"

"You had best go on back to Blavek and tell your master that his days in this kingdom are finished."

"My what? How dare you suggest! . . . I'll have your head for this, Piers! I swear that I will!" He pulled a revolver from his tunic and for a moment, Piers was afraid that he would be forced to shoot the young prince. Instead, Ferenc pointed the gun at the roof of the tent and fired it twice, its wicked cracks sounding like bones snapping, two tibia, *crack, crack,* filling the space with acrid blue smoke.

"You don't give me any other choice, Baron, but to take the letters from you!" The prince backed from the tent as a half-dozen soldiers hurried in, guns and swords drawn, attracted by the sound of the gunfire.

"If you attack this camp," shouted the baron after the retreating prince, "I'll defend it!"

"You do that, and you'll be hunted from one side of this island to the other, as will be any man that raises a finger to help you!" Then he was gone.

Another man entered as the prince disappeared, saluted and reported: "Baron, sir, cavalry have come over the ridge!"

The baron rushed to the doorway and turned to look to the southeast. Over the crest of a nearby hill was approaching a small force: orderly ranks of mounted, black-uniformed men. They halted on the far side of a small stream that separated the main camp from the surrounding tundra. Piers saw the prince join them.

The baron ran to the parade ground and threw himself upon the back of his waiting horse. His men had broken rank and they were milling about in some confusion, buzzing with consternation and speculation. Those who had not heard of the prince's presence in the camp could now see for themselves his distinctive figure, as well as the royal standard that floated brightly against the grey landscape. The baron ordered his troops back into position, anger making his voice harsh. His second-in-command, a stocky, swarthy man with a spade-shaped grey beard, a soldier who had been in the baron's militia since the baron himself had been a boy, pulled up his horse alongside Piers.

"The men," he said, "won't fight the prince."

"Yes they will, by Musrum!"

"The men of your personal troops, yes, I think they will. Their loyalty is to you, my lord, and they feel as you do about the prince and his cohorts. But they are not great in number. It is even possible that the remaining troops in the camp would side with the prince, treating us as the common enemy if we raise arms against him."

"Well, that may never have to come to pass. We will have to see what the prince does." And as he spoke he discovered exactly what the prince's intentions were. Aghast, disbelieving, he watched the vastly outnumbered force of Ferenc's army lower its lances and charge.

Bronwyn watched from the shelter of her tent as her brother fled from the camp and rejoined his small army on the far side of the stream. When she saw the charge, she ran to the tent that adjoined her own, snatched up the bandolier of cartridges that she had seen hanging within, as well as the brace of heavy, large-caliber revolvers that had been laying on the cot. These she jammed into her wide belt, the curved grips facing forward, like horns. By the time she had pulled her sword from its sheath, the first of the Guards had entered the camp.

There was at first nothing she could see but a mass of confused bodies. Then it became clear that the prince was trying to force his way, using the brute mass of his men as a wedge, to the baron's tent where he knew the damning letters were kept. The baron was doing all that he could to block the prince's progress, but there was little he could effectively do, reluctant as he was to order his men to use force—and unsure that they would obey him.

Back among the ranked tents as she was, and with the blustering flurries blurring the distant figures like a theatrical scrim, Bronwyn was unable to easily distinguish between the milling cavalries. Thus she was not able to tell who fired the first shot. Whichever side was responsible, at the sound of that report the two bodies parted momentarily. There was a figure on the ground, lying still. Bronwyn was for a terrible second afraid that it was the baron, but she recognized his tall figure still astride his horse. He had his sword drawn and was using it to rally his men around him.

She was uncertain what to do. Hiding in her tent, as her cousin had ordered her, was repugnant, however wise. To expose herself to her brother and the Guards promised terrible danger. Not just physical danger, a prospect she did not find particularly daunting, but the real possibility of capture. As a hostage she could be used to force Piers to do almost anything. She knew that his loyalty to her knew few bounds. His love for his young cousin was deep; beyond that, to him she represented the Crown, in effect Tamlaght itself. His hopes for the future of the nation rested upon her, and she realized that. There was no question in her mind that he would surrender to Ferenc if it was necessary to save her. Keeping herself out of harm's way would be the very best thing she could do to aid Piers.

But she couldn't remain a spectator, either. The hiatus in the parade ground activity was short-lived. The pistol shot acted as a kind of signal, a release, and the black-uniformed Guards attacked in earnest. They burst through the encompassing regular troops and entered the camp proper, the small, white tents collapsing under the horse's hooves. The small number of men loyal to the baron tried to prevent the Guards from reaching the headquarters tent, but they were being forced back easily. Bronwyn could scarcely follow what was happening in all of the confusion.

She heard her name called, and looked for the caller. It was her brother, some yards away, obviously torn between coming for her and remaining with the men who were fighting to get into the large pavilion. "It's Bronwyn!" he shrieked. "It's the princess! Get her! Get her!"

Fortunately for the princess, Ferenc had not addressed his orders to anyone in particular, so there was several moments' delay before it was settled who was to carry them out. During that time, Bronwyn ducked through the maze of tents, putting a half-dozen between her and the main body of Guards. As she did, she heard the first gunfire since the initial round had been fired. Now it came in ragged bursts, mingled with the rattle of clashing sabers. The fight was now in earnest, the baron apparently having fully decided where his loyalties lay. Bronwyn knew that the sounds she heard marked her cousin irrevocably as a traitor to his country. She turned at the sound of a crash behind her, and saw the tent she had just rounded collapse beneath the weight of a horse, its rider already swinging his saber back in preparation for a blow at her head.

She dodged beneath the flailing hooves, as the animal struggled to free itself from the entangling folds of canvas and cord. Coming up on the opposite side of the Guard, she slashed at him with her own sword, cutting diagonally down the side of one polished boot. She heard the man cry out. Others answered and she saw that additional pursuit was now on foot: two or three Guards had abandoned their mounts. They had not drawn their weapons; she guessed that they hoped to capture her alive.

She stood her ground, drawing one of her two revolvers, which seemed to surprise all of the men, not least the one she fired at. He was less than fifty yards away, and the bullet struck him in the hollow at the base of his throat. He clutched at his neck, blood fountaining from between his fingers as air from his lungs pumped through the wound. He pitched face first onto the frozen ground. The remaining men only picked up their pace in reaction to her self-defense. The three Guards spread out to prevent her from flanking them. Once more they were out of sight for a few seconds, as she threaded the narrow spaces between tents.

One of the Guards was surprised, then, to have the princess suddenly step out in front of him. He had thought her still a dozen yards ahead. He tried to stop, windmilling his arms against his momentum; the nearly point-blank explosion of the princess's revolver in his face threw him in a backward cartwheel. Her shot drew the remaining soldiers and she ran once more.

There was a soft, thumping explosion from somewhere behind her. She instinctively turned to look—one of the big tents near the parade ground had erupted into a tremendous column of fire—and was thrown to the ground by a heavy body. She felt her arms being twisted behind her back, and a knee pressed painfully into the base of her spine.

Suddenly the weight was lifted from her just at the moment she thought that her arms were going to snap, and she heard Thud's voice: "Hurry, Princess! You've got to run!" Leaping to her feet she saw that her friend, incongruous in his enormous fur coat, was holding two Guards beneath his arms. "Go on! Hurry, Princess!" he repeated, as he smashed the Guards' heads together with such force that they actually *merged*. Beyond him more Guards were coming. She turned and ran.

Men were everywhere. In the snow and smoke it was difficult to tell friend from foe. If what Piers had surmised had taken place—that most of the men would remain loyal to the prince, rather than raise arms against him and put themselves in mortal jeopardy—then she was relatively safe in assuming that *all* around her were her enemies. Sporadic shots banged in every direction—more than one bullet zinged past her head, buzzing like a live electric wire. But visibility was too bad to risk much shooting, and the sound that prevailed was the ringing clatter of sword upon sword.

She dodged from tent to tent, trying to locate the perimeter of the camp. She found herself on the tundra, beyond the garrison, quite suddenly. It looked as black as peat, with the round, bare, glacier-deposited rocks strewn upon it like grey mushrooms. The granular snow, blowing in clouds, had not yet been able to cover the ground. A voice shouted "Halt!" behind her. Without thinking she leaped away, like a startled cat. But whoever had given the order had been close and she felt a hand clench her arm. She was spun around and found herself facing a pair of Guards.

"It's her, all right," said the one holding her. "Get the prince."

"Hang onto her, Boskid. I think she'll be the making of our promotions!"

"Just hurry it up, will you? All right, Princess, behave yourself and I mean you no harm. Ho! What's this?"

Bronwyn had drawn her remaining pistol with her free hand, but the Guard named Boskid snatched it by the long barrel, twisting it from her grip so roughly that it wrenched her wrist painfully. He threw the gun into the darkening storm. Before the man could say another word, however, Bronwyn kicked him on his shin with all the force she could muster. As hard as her boots were, though, the boots worn by the Guard were equally tough. She did not cause him much pain, to her regret, but he did push her further away, retaining his grip on her forearm. She immediately swung her foot up in a straight-legged kick into his crotch. This time he gave an entirely satisfying shriek, doubling over with a gurgle. He released her arm and she drew her sword, backing several paces away from the man.

"You damned little bitch!" he wheezed. "Reward or no reward . . . !"

He stepped toward her, eyes red with fury in his sweat-streaked pale face, drawing his own revolver as he came closer. Bronwyn, without warning, swung her saber over her head in a downward-slicing chop as though she were splitting wood with an ax. Instead she split the Guard. The heavy blade grazed his cheek, slicing it off so that it hung flapping, exposing the teeth behind it. His ear flipped through the air like a poker chip. The saber tip just nicked his collarbone, entered the chest below, cut through cloth and nearly a foot of flesh. "Ah! Damn you!" he cried, as the sudden rush of blood spilled over his uniform. Bronwyn didn't wait to find out what he planned to do; instead she hacked at the man once again, using the weapon with both hands as though it were a club. This time the Guard unfolded like the blossoming of a wet red flower.

Saber in hand, Bronwyn ran away from the firelit camp. No one appeared to notice her flight, but the Guard who had gone to fetch her brother would soon return to his companion, she knew, and pursuit would be immediate. She hoped to lose herself in the confusion of low boulders and rocks that covered the surface of the tundra for miles around the camp. When she heard the sound of hoofbeats thudding behind her, she cursed the luck that had brought pursuit so quickly.

"Bronwyn! Stop!" called a familiar voice. She paused and turned. Silhouetted against the snow-diffused glow from the burning camp, she saw the tall, lean figure of her cousin bringing his horse to a halt. "Bronwyn?"

"Yes! Here, Piers!"

He dropped from the saddle quickly and Bronwyn ran to meet him. "There's not a minute to lose," he said. "Take the horse. It's the big red one—you know him—and there're a few provisions in the saddlebags; there's also a blanket and other things, you'll find them eventually. Now you must take the horse and run, get away. They must not get you!"

"But, Piers!"

"Never mind me. The barons will never allow Ferenc and Payne to destroy the throne, but their task will be almost impossible without you. If you fail to return to Blavek try, if you can, to get to Londeac, to your uncle Felix. You are the rallying point, the nucleus. And *you* must tell the story because you'll be believed. So go, and quickly!"

"What about Thud and Gyven?"

"Alive at last sight, but captured—so who knows? Most of my militia are in the same dilemma. If I go back now and surrender it will save many lives, and it will buy a lot of time for you."

"What can I do?"

"Do what you can."

"May Musrum go with you, Cousin," she said, climbing into the saddle. She bent down and the girl and the tall, weary man kissed.

"And may Musrum protect you," he replied, smacking the horse on its flank, sending it off into the swirling twilight. The sound of its hooves was quickly muffled by the dry, spongelike moss, absorbed by the insulating billows of snow. Bronwyn had vanished abruptly—there was nothing more to see. The old man turned his back to the darkness, and began walking to meet the horde of black figures that was approaching him.

10

LOST AND FOUND

BRONWYN STROKED the closely knotted cord, causing the cylindrical bell from which it hung to sing hollowly. The bell and the cord depended from the interior apex of one of the pyramidal shrines that could be found anywhere in the north country. She was doing something that she had not done seriously in years: preparing to pray. The business with the bell was simply to alert Musrum that a prayer was soon to be made; it was necessary to get His attention since sudden prayers made Musrum jump (*Musrum*, page 7, verse 11).

This was the beginning of Bronwyn's great trek, where she traveled the rough, uncertain territory between her old life and her new. She did not know this, of course, no more than she knew what lay ahead of her. She knew what she *wanted*, just as she always had done—her goals remained unchanged. What she was unaware of was the degree she was having to alter herself—and not only her actions—in order for those goals to become reality. Just as a key must be of a particular shape before it will open a door, so too must the princess be of a special order before she can enter her own future. And if the key does not quite work, then it must be altered so that it will. And no key has ever had any say as to what shape it must take; that is something that has forever been subordinate to the job it must do.

She had been traveling for three days since the disastrous attack on Piers's outpost. She had been heading east and a little south, as near as she could judge—the position of the sun was indicated only by a vague brightening in the overcast sky. She had crossed the divide that separated the watershed of the Moltus River from the rivers and streams that ran directly to the eastern sea. The camp had been high in the rugged western slopes in the first place, and the first hours of her headlong flight had carried her beyond the summits and into the range that bound the Zileheroum on the east.

Where the mountains that bound the Zileheroum in the west became higher and more precipitous the further one penetrated them, the mountains to the east sloped relatively gently from their summits to the coast, as though in some bygone epoch the land had been tilted up toward the center of the island (which is what in fact had happened). By following the slope or any stream that ran down it she would eventually reach the shore of the South Mostaza Sea; she could then merely turn to her right and follow the coast until it brought her to the plains that lay to the east of Blavek. By then the land would have flattened out and the going would be relatively easy. She would also be assured, by following the coast, of meeting sympathetic and helpful countrymen from whom she had every reason to believe she could expect succor.

However, the east coast of Guesclin is sawtoothed with deep fjords and embayments. To strictly follow this rambling coastline would add hundreds of miles and far too many days to her journey. It was now just over six days to the coronation. She had little enough hope of making it back to Blavek in time as things stood: alone and unsure of where she was, not at all certain whether or not she was being pursued, needing help but leery of the prospect of approaching anyone. The small amount of food that her cousin had left in his saddlebags had run out that morning—and only strict rationing had made it last that long.

An alternative plan to finding the coast and following it would be to try and determine the shortest line between where she was now, wherever that was, and Blavek, wherever it was, and to follow it. The sun was useless as an aid to direction-finding, and for the same reason the stars were of no help. It was just as well they were invisible: she wouldn't have known what to do with them otherwise. Therefore she was at least spared being both lost and feeling stupid.

Nevertheless, the flow of the streams she had been crossing told her which way the coast was: that is, the direction of east, more or less; upstream was therefore west, also more or less. Facing east, south was at her right hand. Heading immediately in that direction seemed at the time to be the best decision: she had felt as though she were actually heading home, as opposed to a journey of unknown length practically in the wrong direction just to reach the coast so *then* she could turn south.

So she had headed, finally, as directly south as she could.

Three days later she began to seriously doubt the wisdom of her decision. Her guiding streams had proven far more a hindrance than an assistance. The mountain slopes were more often steep than not and strewn with exposed boulders and rocks. The dozens of streams and rivulets that tumbled from the heights foamed over slippery, moss-covered rocks worn smooth on their faces but with edges as jagged as sawblades. Since she was trying to navigate a course perpendicular to the direction the water was naturally taking, Bronwyn was forced again and again to negotiate a hazardous crossing, consuming valuable time by the hours' worth, or to make frustrating detours up or downstream to find a safe ford. She found herself leading her horse as often as she was riding it.

The only thing she could feel grateful for was the virgin condition of the forest. The foliage of the towering trees grew together in an almost opaque green canopy far overhead. The shady cool earth between the trees was therefore blessedly free of undergrowth. Bronwyn was passing through a region of almost gothic perpendicularity, the floor of the forest broken only by the monster boles of trees so large in circumference that the surfaces of the nearest ones looked flat.

Nights, however, were worse. The princess had never in her life spent a night outdoors, if the night she collapsed exhausted in the cirque isn't counted. She had neither fire nor the means to start one. It became very cold when the sun disappeared behind the high ridges to her right. Brief flurries of hard, pelletlike snow accompanied the dusk. Wrapped into as small a sphere as possible within her woolen cape, she did her best to try and sleep, though she did little more than doze fitfully—worse than not sleeping at all. Hunger chewed at her; her stomach was a hard, painful knot. There had been little enough grazing for the horse, beyond the wiry, pale lichens it scraped from the rocks with its teeth.

She had not seen another living thing after crossing over onto the east slopes; all had already escaped or hidden from the coming winter. Yet at night the forest seemed alive with sound: the mournful groaning of the trees as their tall trunks ground against one another in the wind, like the wringing of skeletal hands; the muttering of that thin, hard wind that whispered conspiratorially in the darkness; the stirring of the horse in its discomfort and hunger, its occasional worrisome nicker startling her into an hour of wakeful apprehension; and innumerable scuttlings and cracklings that kept her high-strung imagination fully fueled. One night an owl had destroyed a squirrel or rabbit not more than a few yards from where she lay huddled against the base of a tree. The sudden soft hiss of the big wings, the shriek of the doomed animal, the beat of the departing bird, like a heavy blanket being shaken, had left the girl as terrified as though the Weedking himself had materialized before her. She had no idea what had been going on beyond her woolen cocoon, but it had sounded terrible.

Her brain would refuse to sleep, running like an ungoverned flywheel. Perhaps spurred by morbid imaginings about her own fate, she found herself uncharacteristically concerned about the part she had played in the fates of a large number of strangers. It was a problem that had never bothered her a great deal before. She was, after all, Princess of Tamlaght, and naturally accustomed to having a large number of people at her beck and call. She had never before given any thought to the trials and tribulations to which these less fortunate folk had been put to make her own life easier and more comfortable. And why should she have? Wasn't that what they were there for? Wasn't it their delight and purpose to serve her? There were even those, such as the Royal Palace Guard, whose duty it was to die, if need be, for her. And she knew that they would do it gladly, should the necessity present itself. Why, then, this odd and unprecedented sense of guilt—or if not guilt, unease?

It did seem that everyone who had attempted to help her in her quest had come to some unpleasant fate. The problem she was wrestling with was not why they had been willing to do so, but why it ought to concern her so strangely. Thud Mollockle had befriended her without question—in fact, she realized, long before he learned who she was, he had put himself at risk in her behalf. And now where was he? Dead, most likely. The strange being the Kobolds had entrusted to her, what of him? Probably dead, too. The family of gypsies that had helped her to escape from Blavek; what had they gained from helping the runaway princess? They could have easily asked for and received a substantial reward for turning her in to the Guards. Instead they earned, at the very least, arrest. Where were they now? Some horrible dungeon?

She had brought catastrophe to the lives of all who had tried to befriend her. And they *had* tried to befriend her, though she had made little enough effort to befriend *them*. She knew that there was a civic duty that required the protection of the person of a royal princess, just as any loyal citizen would not hesitate to defend the flag. What bothered her, even if she had not quite yet puzzled it out, was that these people had not been defending their princess, they had simply been helping a girl in trouble.

It was on the following morning that she was sending a prayer spinning toward the somnolent Musrum.

By the sixth day she realized that the horse was in distress. She knew that it had not been fed well. Was there more she could have been doing to relieve its discomfort? A better than fair horsewoman at home, she had of course left the care of the animals to the grooms. She could ride them well enough, but maintaining them was not a task for a princess. Had she neglected to do something necessary for her mount's well-being? She had no way of knowing, though it seemed so. Until this day she had given the horse little thought, though her plans, she realized too late, had depended upon the beast. Without it, afoot, she would be stranded in the middle of thousands of square miles of hostile wilderness, with winter only days away.

Urge, prod and cajole though she did, the horse refused to proceed more than a score of paces before slowing gradually to a halt, its head drooping sadly.

The next morning, when Bronwyn arose from another sleepless night, she saw that the horse lay on its side not far from her. She knew that horses did not lie down to sleep, and that all could not be well. It was true: this one had lain down to die.

Seldom had Bronwyn experienced despair; but now, hundreds of miles from a home that had become a hostile trap for her, without food, fire or the knowledge, skills and wherewithal for obtaining them, half lost and with her only friends and protectors either dead or prisoners—she felt a crushing hollowness, like an empty carton crumpled in a fist and tossed aside. Still curled within her cape, she sobbed tearlessly for a while, looking over the edge of black wool she clutched to her face at the poor, motionless brown heap that had done its best for her. As had so many. So far her hate for Payne Roelt and her brother had brought death and disaster to everyone to whom she had turned for help—even to this innocent animal.

Only three more days and the coronation of her brother would take place—and Payne Roelt would rule Tamlaght. It had been, to the present date, only eighteen days since she had stolen the letters from Ferenc's desk—two and a half weeks that might as well have been as many months. Decades seemed to separate the Princess Bronwyn of Tamlaght from the dreary, helpless creature that huddled, shivering and alone, more lost and vulnerable than even the smallest chipmunk, shrew, bird or frog. *They* were home already, *they* knew where they were, fat and well lardered for the winter.

So what to do, then? Obviously the plan to follow the direction of the ridge was no longer practical. She realized now that it had not been a very practical plan from the beginning. Cutting across the innumerable watercourses was slow, laborious and dangerous enough with the horse to carry her. Now it was simply impossible. The only thing for her to do now was to follow the next stream she struck until she found any habitation at all, where she could seek succor of the first people she would meet.

She took from the horse and its saddlebags what few things looked useful. There was the revolver, of course, one of those that she had purloined from the tent next to hers. At the bottom of one of the bags was a cardboard carton containing twenty-five rounds for the cannonlike 50mm Minch-Moappa. Unfortunately there was no holster for it and she had to carry the heavy gun wedged beneath the straps wound around her blanket. There was a smallish folding knife and a tin cup. There was neither extra clothing nor gloves.

She had a cavalry saber and knee-high riding boots, though she doubted the latter's efficiency in hiking. Other than a few lengths of twine and some leather straps, there was nothing else of use she could take with her.

For the first week of her sojourn rivers and streams had been an obstruction every quarter of a mile or so, but now that she was looking for one it was almost a full day before she stood at the brink of a foaming cascade. Turning to her left, she followed the tumbling water downstream.

Although she had had plenty of water—too much, in her opinion—the princess had not eaten any solid food in nearly half a week. At night her stomach felt like an angry fist, shaken rebelliously at an inattentive administration. During the day she had to rest too often, and even the slightest exertion left her weak and dizzy. She realized that she would have to find something to eat

or she might as well curl up and die right where she was. But
what was there to eat? She was well aware that a forest should be
literally alive with food; but how could she identify it? How would
she know what was safe? How could she find it? How could she
kill it? What did she have to do to it once it was dead, whatever it
was? How was she to cook it? Insurmountable questions.

She slept beside the stream, which was growing broader and less
swift as the land almost imperceptibly leveled. Upon awakening
one morning, she knelt beside a still pool in the bank to wash
the sleep from her face. Floating in the water was a mat of
bright green, circular leaves, each tiny pad smaller than her little
fingernail. On an impulse she scooped up a handful and sucked
them into her mouth. She chewed them cautiously; they had a
slightly bittersweet, grassy flavor that was not at all objectionable.
She ate another two handfuls and then sat back on her haunches
to reconsider the problem of food.

She began a systematic search of the area immediately surrounding her campsite. Right alongside the pool was a pale green reedy
plant. She gathered a half-dozen, breaking them off where their
stems joined a small bulb at the base. The green tubes immediately
began to leak a milky fluid that, she thought, looked nutritious
enough. She sucked on the broken ends, chewing at the stringy
stalk. Instantly her mouth began to burn. At first it was merely
mildly astringent, and no more distressing than strong pepper. But
the burning increased. She flung the stalks from her and began
scooping handfuls of water from the pool, trying to wash the acid
from her mouth. Waves of nausea began to churn at the back of
her throat. She vomited violently—mostly the water she had just
drunk. Then she vomited again, and then once more. She lay
prone at the edge of the pool, one cheek resting in the water,
a thread of mucus from the corner of her mouth tracing circular
patterns on the swirling surface. She was weak and her alimentary
canal felt as though it had just been stamped flat, but the burning
was virtually gone and the nausea had passed as quickly as it had
come.

The pale green stalks were unquestionably a plant to avoid.

There was no point in not looking any further. She had to eat.
Her next discovery was considerably more pleasant: a cache of
pine cones that had collected in a rocky hollow. From them she
was able to shake loose a double handful of small nuts that tasted
delicious. Emboldened, she looked around with a more critical
eye. She knew better than to attempt to eat any mushroom she

might find, but then she also knew that there was one variety so distinctive that it was impossible to confuse it with any other. She found two of them, half-buried beneath a blanket of leaves they nearly resembled in color. They were a pair of large morels that looked like bath sponges as much as anything else. Breaking off chunks of the cakelike fungus, she savored the nutty flavor.

For nearly a week the princess lived on what she found in the forest. She avoided most green plants (though she did find a patch of wild onions, which she identified by their odor), what few were remaining after the long frosts of autumn. While there were no berries or fruits, there was an abundance of nuts and she had no qualms about eating those. And once she found by accident what must have been some unlucky rodent's cache. She shamelessly looted the hard-won and painstakingly gathered harvest of nuts and dried berries. Once she discovered a half-dozen small mussels clinging to a rock in the stream. She ate them raw after prying them loose and cracking the shells open.

Still, it wasn't much. The princess was constantly hungry, the hunger an unending pain. She was growing weaker almost by the hour as her starved body fed upon itself.

As the stream led her into flatter countryside, the forest became abruptly thinner. Centuries of logging had replaced the massive towers she had grown accustomed to with second-growth trees that seemed almost insubstantial by comparison. Without the shade of large trees, the undergrowth, encouraged by the advent of sunlight, was becoming progressively thicker. To make any progress, Bronwyn was forced to stay close to the banks of the stream.

With trees now small enough for her to circle their trunks with one hand, and the space separating them filled with an almost impenetrable tangle of sere, leafless shrubbery and weeds, Bronwyn's source of nuts and morels quickly vanished. After a long day in which the undergrowth had crowded her into the icy water of the stream several times, in which she had covered scarcely a few miles, hot, tired, laced with scratches from thorns and needles, the princess found herself starving and once again without resources.

She turned to the stream once again, in the hope of discovering more mussels. Now that she had entered the relatively flat country that meant that the coast was not too many days' journey away, the stream had become a broad, relatively shallow river, its pebbly bottom visible all the way across. She searched but could not find any of the shellfish, the stones being far too small to support them.

Turning over a mossy rock, however, she discovered a family of crayfish. She plucked them from the water easily. When she had a dozen wriggling on the bank beside her, she settled down to eat.

When she had nearly finished, she idly tossed some of the remains into the stream, if for no other reason than to see how far they would go. When one of the tiny corpses struck the turbulent surface, she was surprised to be rewarded with a sudden splashing where the fragment landed. Why hadn't it occured to her before, she wondered, that there must be fish in the stream?

She had a considerable length of string to use as line, and she had already been given evidence of the efficacy of the crustaceans as bait. She only lacked a hook. After a short search she found a bush whose wood seemed fairly tough. With her knife she cut a few inches from a twig. Sitting on the ground she removed one of her boots and, again using the knife, prized out one of the nails that held the heel on. She split one end of the twig and inserted the nail, its pointed end angled toward the opposite end of the stick. With a piece of twine she tightly bound the split. She now had a piece of wood about two inches long, with a pointed piece of iron jutting from it, like an angular letter J. Splitting the opposite end, she inserted one end of the longest piece of string, once again binding the string into the split tightly. She now had a line and hook. She impaled a piece of crawfish onto the nail as bait.

She tossed the improvised tackle as far as she could into the stream, but the current swung the line so that the baited nail finally came to rest against the bank. She tried several times to throw the line further into the water, but no matter how far it would go, it still ended up in the shallow water on the shore. Hauling in her line in frustration, she left it coiled on the bank while she went in search of something that would help her to keep the hook well out into the stream.

After a few minutes she found a sapling an inch or two in diameter and almost fifteen feet tall. She whittled away at its base until she felled the young tree. Its few branches were easily stripped away. Dragging the resulting long pole back to her fishing site, she tied one end of her string to the top end of the sapling. She wedged the larger end into a crevice between some rocks, arranging it so that the pole was supported while leaning over the water at a shallow angle.

She tossed the baited hook back into the stream and was pleased to see the line stretch out parallel to the bank, some dozen feet from the shore. She found a comfortable place to rest and wait, confident that it would not take very long to hook a fish.

She was not wrong. After only a few minutes, the line began to jerk, the water frothing where the string entered the stream. At this point Bronwyn realized a minor error in her device: she had not made any arrangement by means of which a captured fish could be retrieved. Rather than go to all the tedium of taking in the long pole, with the strong possibility of losing the fish, she waded into the icy water. Following the line until it met the stream, she raised the struggling animal out of the water. It was a big trout, several pounds, and she felt extremely proud of her capture.

She let it flop to its death on the rocks while she rebaited and recast the line.

Bronwyn then came face to face—as it were—with having to eat the fish. She had been angling with her cousin Piers on the ponds and lakes that decorated the royal properties, and had been more or less a witness when he had cleaned the fish they had caught. But in those times they had grilled the fish over hot coals and accompanied the fragrant fillets with all sorts of delicious delicacies from the large hampers they had brought along, themselves prepared by the expert chefs of the palace. She had always looked upon these dreamy afternoons with Piers with fondness; but now she was faced with just a lone fish. There were no savory sauces prepared beforehand by the palace chef, no pungent herbs and spices, no yeasty breads, no cold soups made of fruit and thick cream, no golden, sweet wines, and to her infinite regret no fire. Just a poor dead cold fish.

Her knowledge of cleaning fish was strictly academic: she had watched her cousin do it a dozen times, though without any particular effort to impress it upon her memory. Her attempt on this present specimen was honest, but brutal. There was a great deal of unpleasant mess, but she was ultimately rewarded with two glistening fillets of translucent white meat. She fought back her gorge and gingerly bit into one of the pieces. It was not nearly so bad as she expected, but taste was not everything: imagination plays a great role in times like these. Nevertheless, she ate all of the fish and, most importantly, kept it all. In all of her adventures to follow, few things gave her more secret pride than the eating of this fish.

By the end of the afternoon she had caught three more trout. Stringing them on a piece of twine, she carried them away from the stream, looking for a sheltered place to spend the night. This she found nearby in the form of a great pile of broken boulders in the midst of which was a cavelike hollow perhaps twelve or fifteen feet deep.

She had just dropped the fish onto a tablelike slab of rock when a shadow rose over her. Startled, she gasped and whirled around, and found herself almost face to face with an enormous brown bear. The animal, undoubtedly attracted by the trout, blocked the entrance to the hollow with its shaggy body. Spying the girl, and alarmed by the noise she made and her sudden movement, the animal reared up on its short, bowed hind legs. Bronwyn backed further into the cave, but was brought up short against the rear wall after retreating only a few paces.

The bear ignored her. It dropped back onto all fours and began to snuffle noisily at the fish. Bronwyn, as slowly as she could, drew her big revolver from the blanket roll that was still slung from her back. Raising the massive weapon with both hands, she drew back its hammer with her thumbs. It made a click that sounded itself like a gun going off.

The bear turned at the sound, a low growl rumbling deep and speculatively within its throat. Bronwyn tried to freeze, but her hands shook with the weight of the revolver and sweat poured into her eyes, stinging them with the salt. She couldn't control her breath, which came in short gasps, a sound which seemed to annoy the bear. The animal turned away from the fish and took a few rolling steps toward the girl.

"Go away!" she whispered, feeling like an idiot, but after pausing only briefly, the bear came a few feet closer. "No!" she begged it, as the animal suddenly rose onto its hind legs again, its doglike head brushing the top of the shelter. Its black lips rolled back in a snarl, revealing yellow, wet tusks whose sharp points glinted like daggers.

The gun seemed to go off on its own accord. The recoil nearly threw the weapon from her grasp, and pain shot through her wrenched wrists. She saw a spray of red from behind the bear as the enormous projectile made its fearsome exit wound. The bear shrieked like a locomotive and instantly fell onto the princess, its hooked, black talons flailing in the blind frenzy of agony.

Bronwyn could feel her flesh parting like torn cloth, and with much the same sound. There was little or no pain—only a sort of reverie in which she seemed to be taking less and less part in the subjective action. As shock shut down her circulatory system, she found no will to resist her fate; even though she knew, as a kind of abstraction, that the bear was playing with her as a dog would a rag doll. She would now be a rag princess, she thought. There was a sudden, sharp explosion and everything went to red, then a black, dreamless oblivion.

11

 DREAMS AND SNOWDRIFTS

BRONWYN AWOKE to strange voices. She couldn't distinguish words at first, but the tones were friendly, muted and warm, which was something, anyway. She didn't open her eyes immediately. She was still too aware of her last remembered sensations: the suffocating weight of the bear, its sweetly rancid breath—and the moistness of it on her face—the black claws glistening with her own blood. She feared that perhaps she was in some shock-induced dream, that the first sight upon opening her eyes would be the glinting button-eyes of the huge animal. And she was afraid that she would see it eating.

The smells were all wrong, though. A fragrant combination of woodsmoke, pipe tobacco, bread, wool, pine tar, and—Musrum be blessed!—the heady odor of rich food. Her nostrils were successfully trying to convince her that some sort of meat was cooking nearby. She tried the mental exercise of sorting out the smells: meat and onions predominated, but there was also the earthiness of potatoes, the sweetness of carrots, licoricey fennel, the punctuation of peppers and other spices. A stew?

Her sense of touch was equally transformed. She was no longer cold, but was instead enveloped in some kind of soft cocoon that was deliciously warm and protecting.

187

"Has she wakened?" said one of the voices, a woman's, nearer now.

"I think perhaps so," came the answer, in a man's voice, also very close to her. She chanced opening one eye. Not far away hovered a pink globe of a face, not at all unlike a rising full moon. It beamed when it saw her open an eye, and grew immediately pinker and rounder, if that were possible. "Yes, yes!" the voice continued, and now she saw that the man's voice issued from the pink face. "I do believe that she is awake at last!"

Another face joined the first one, so much like it that Bronwyn wondered at first if her vision were playing her tricks. The second face spoke with the woman's voice.

"Oh, yes! She is awake! The poor dear; see to her, Burgos, while I fetch something for her to eat."

"Certainly, Mother," answered the other and, turning to Bronwyn, asked, "Are you awake?" Bronwyn nodded her head in answer—she tried to speak, but the words stuck in her throat.

"How are you feeling, then?" But all the girl could do was manage a kind of shrug.

"Can you sit up? Let me help you." The odor of wool and pipe smoke grew stronger, and powerful hands gently eased her up until she was propped into more or less of a slouch, her back supported by fat cushions. She looked around, carefully; she discovered that she felt incredibly lightheaded. As though she had not eaten in a week, rather than only a day or two, or so she thought.

She found that she was in a room—low-ceilinged, timbered, with plaster in the interstices, and crowded with details. Even in her confused condition, she was struck by the room's color and whimsy. Not a square inch was undecorated. The beams and timbers that framed and criss-crossed the walls and ceiling were intricately carved; the plastered areas had painted borders of flowery garlands, the centers filled with gaudy, framed chromos. The furniture, though simple in form, was as elaborately carved as the woodwork, and was painted in primary colors with decorations of vines and flowers in the most naïve style. At one end of the room an entire wall was occupied by a vast stone fireplace, its arched opening surrounded by a half-dozen smaller openings: ovens, probably. Within the main fireplace a fire flickered and crackled redly and friendlily, and within that was the bulbous black silhouette of a cooking-pot, puffing steam like an exasperated demon.

The only inhabitants of the cozy room, other than herself, were the chubby, red-cheeked man and woman. The former, his face still hovering over her like a ruddy eclipsed moon, was as kindly-looking an individual as she had ever seen. The latter, approaching from the side of the room that evidently served as kitchen, was virtually a female twin. In fact, the only pertinent differences she was able to discern at the time was that one was almost totally bald and possessed a small, grey moustache with upturned ends, and the other had long hair coiled into tight buns on either side of her head and possessed less moustache.

The woman placed a tray before Bronwyn on which there was a ceramic bowl—fancifully glazed, of course—filled with some sort of thick soup. The princess found her mouth suddenly awash with saliva. She snatched up the wooden spoon.

"Ho! Mother! Look at her!" laughed the man. "The poor thing's starved!"

"Don't let her wolf her food down like that, Burgos! She'll get sick!" She took the spoon from Bronwyn's fingers, which released it reluctantly.

"Finish what you have now, then I'll let you have another spoonful."

It took far longer than the hungry girl would have liked, but even in the rationed doses allotted by the woman the soupbowl seemed to empty magically fast. Her hunger seemed scarcely dented, though she acknowledged that a satisfying, warm fullness now occupied her abdomen.

"I feel like I haven't eaten in weeks!" she said, her first words.

"Well," said the man, "I don't know about that, but you haven't eaten in the week that you have been here."

"Week? I've been here a week?"

"Well, nearly so. Let's see, Mother. I found the poor thing when I went to pay Porsgrunn for the eggs, wasn't it?"

"No, it was when you took the charcoal to Wisbech."

"Ah! That'd be the day before, then. Otherwise, I wouldn't have had the gun with me. Lucky thing, too! Hardly ever go out with it anymore. Don't know why I did this time, come to think of it."

"I do: I told you to. It's getting dangerous to go any distance anymore."

"Yes, that's true enough. Old Wisbech was robbed only last month on his way to the Plibdols. Simple prudence. That's why I took the gun along."

"Lot of good it would have done you: you would probably have forgotten you had it with you."

"Well, I didn't forget it when I saw the bear, did I?"

"Oh, Musrum!" cried Bronwyn. "Yes! The bear!"

"I heard your cries, but it was terrible hard to find you, in that little grotto in the rocks. I never knew that hole was there. Can you believe that? There's always something new to discover in the forest, no matter how long you've lived here. Still, I got the beast in a single shot!"

"You probably could have talked it to death faster," added the woman, "but I wouldn't wish that fate even on a bear."

"Now, Mother!" chided the man.

"Well, I for one thank you!" said Bronwyn. "I thought that I was dead!"

"You're getting some revenge on the beast now, though."

"How's that?"

"We made soup from his bones."

Bronwyn glanced warily at the empty bowl, then laughed. When she did, a sharp pain lanced her ribs. "How much did the bear hurt me?" she asked. "I remember so much blood and pain."

"You were hurt some," answered the man, "but it was mostly blood." (*Small comfort*, Bronwyn thought.) "Those heavy clothes saved you, but I don't think that they will be of any use to you again."

"I've been working them into my braided rug," said the woman. "I didn't think that you would mind."

"There might be some scars, but I don't think that there will be any permanent injury."

"It still hurts."

"I'm sure that it will for a while yet."

"Where am I?"

"Oh, forgive us!" said the woman. "We've been rude! You've been with us so long, we've gotten quite used to you being here, but to you you've just arrived, so to speak."

"Yes, I guess so."

"You are in the house of Burgos the charcoal burner," answered the man. "I am Burgos and this is my wife, Melfi."

"I'm very pleased to meet you both!"

"And we are pleased to meet you . . ."

Bronwyn hesitated a moment before filling in that ellipsis. Should she identify herself? Would they believe her? And if they did, what would they do?

"My name is Bronwyn Tedeschiy . . ."

"Ah! The lost princess! I was right! Didn't I tell you, Burgos?"

"You know who I am?"

"We had some notion."

"*I* did . . . Burgos has been arguing just the opposite."

"They're looking for me, then. Is that how you found out?"

"Well, no, not exactly. Mother, do you have that newspaper?"

"I don't know, let me see . . . it hasn't been very long . . ."
She rummaged through a pile of old papers and magazines that
were heaped in a big box near the fireplace.

"Ah! Here it is! See?"

Bronwyn took the crumpled sheet from her. It was an edition
of the *Blavek Intelligencer* nearly two weeks old. There was a
column set apart by a heavy black border. Its headline somberly
announced the death of the Princess Bronwyn. It gave her a horribly chilly sense of unreality to read about the details of her own
demise, the unreality heightened by the almost wholly fictional
account.

She had died, she learned, after a prolonged decline following
an accident with a fish delivery van. News of the event had been
kept from the press at the family's wish. Unfortunately, the princess never recovered from her injuries and, on the morning of the
fourteenth, slipped from her earthly bonds and into the hands of
Musrum without ever regaining consciousness. The article con-
cluded with a few heartfelt words from her brother, expressing
the grief of the royal family . . . She crushed the brittle newsprint
before finishing the column.

"If you'd read this, why did you think I was the princess?" she
asked.

"Well," answered Melfi, "that's not too easy to explain."

"You see," continued Burgos, "Mother and I have been interested in our royal family for a very long time."

"We have albums full of things we've clipped from the magazines and papers."

"We even have the announcements of your birth somewhere."

"We were very proud that day, I can tell you."

"We've only been fortunate enough once to actually see one
of you in the flesh, so to speak. Not counting now, of course."

"We went all the way to Blavek to see your father's coronation."

"We couldn't actually see his face, but we could tell that it
was him."

"It was a great thrill, wasn't it, Burgos?"

"We must show you the postcards we collected."

"Wait a moment, please! I'll take it for granted that you recognized me, at least for the time being. But how long have I been here? What is the date?"

"Let's see," said Melfi. "You made your last charcoal delivery on the nineteenth?"

"Either that or the twentieth."

"Well, then, that was only four or five days ago."

"That'd make today, oh, somewhere around the twenty-fourth or twenty-fifth."

Bronwyn let her head fall back onto her pillow. The twenty-fourth or twenty-fifth! The coronation had been scheduled for the twenty-first: Ferenc had been king for half a week. The country was now in the hands of Payne Roelt and his looters. It was at least twelve days since she had left her uncle's emcampment.

"Oh! The poor thing!" cried Melfi. "Get the broth, Burgos . . . look how pale she's gotten!"

"I must get to Blavek," said Bronwyn.

"Blavek?" answered the man, incredulously. "That wouldn't be possible, I'm afraid."

"Why? How far away are we?"

"Well, that's not really the point."

"Where *am* I anyway, now that I'm thinking of it?"

"The nearest village is Hasselt-on-the-Dootlen, about fourteen miles down the river."

"Hasselt?"

"It's at the head of the fjord; mostly fishermen live there."

"Yes, I know where it is. Will you take me there?"

"I don't think that you are really up to doing any traveling yet . . ." said Melfi.

"But," added Burgos, "that isn't the point, anyway."

"Well, what *is* the point, then?"

Melfi went to one of the curtained windows and drew back the heavy drapery. There was nothing beyond the window but a featureless white. It took Bronwyn a long moment to interpret what she was seeing. "Snow!" she cried.

Snow, indeed. It had begun in earnest the day after Burgos had found the princess. Nor had it in any way abated in the week that had since passed. It had ceaselessly snowed until the little cottage in which the charcoal-maker and his wife lived was buried to its low-hanging eaves. Burgos had burrowed tunnels to the two or three outbuildings nearby—of course, needless to say, to the single most necessary of them. But those were only a dozen yards long—Hasselt was several miles away.

She could see her hosts' point, however. Three or four feet of snow, drifting to ten feet or more, in this country where roads were little better than dirt paths, when they existed at all, was an impediment of inarguable efficiency. But what to do? Spring was months away; even now she was probably too late to do anything about the villains in the capital—in three or four months they would be so well entrenched, their tentacles so well entwined around Society's neck, that they would be as impossible to extricate as an octopus from its den.

She explained her urgency to Burgos and Melfi, but they were not very helpful. They had never before had any need to leave their home once it was snowbound—they had no useful suggestions as to how Bronwyn could do so. Nor was what information they did have very encouraging. Hasselt-on-the-Dootlen was not far; even in the worst weather—provided it was not actually in the midst of a blizzard—it could be reached in just a few hours. It was only necessary to follow the river (which for the next several months would be frozen nearly solid and now was recognizable only as a broad meandering depression in the snow). But for a traveler on snowshoes and well bundled, it would provide a level and sure highway to the town. The fjord itself, she learned, was also frozen throughout the winter. Whether the town nevertheless maintained communication with the open sea beyond, her hosts were unable to say.

Bronwyn succeeded in convincing the elderly couple that she had to get at least as far as Hasselt. They felt that she ought to remain in bed for at least another week or two, and indoors even longer, but the girl was adamant. She compromised by agreeing to stay two more days. Burgos and Melfi had friends in the town, as they seemed to have friends everywhere. If the journey made her ill, Bronwyn promised, she could stay with one of the people there. Burgos insisted on accompanying the princess as far as the town—it would have been impossible for him to have let her go on her own.

She enjoyed the next two days, Bronwyn admitted to herself—she had not felt so much at home in weeks. She carefully did not admit to herself that much of this comfortable feeling came from having two kindly people eagerly waiting upon her. She liked them very much, far more so than she had any palace servant, and would have been very put out at the suggestion that she was simply allowing them to let her use them. But a lot of that anger would

have been created by the realization that it was true, and that someone had the tactlessness to agree aloud with her own conscience.

On the evening of the second day, Bronwyn noticed Melfi doing
something that puzzled her.

"What is the bowl of milk for?" she asked.

"Pardon?" Melfi replied, rising from the hearth, dusting ashes
from her knees. The princess pointed to the bowl of milk and
plate of small cakes that the woman had set on the stones.

"I've noticed that you've done that nearly every night. Do you
have a cat or something?"

"Oh, no," answered Melfi, pinking a little with embarrassment.
"I suppose the princess will think us silly."

"Of course not," said Bronwyn earnestly, prepared for something quaint.

"Well, it's for the Kobold . . ."

"Kobold?"

"Yes, Princess, a Kobold is a kind of fairy that lives in the
ground . . ."

"I know what a Kobold is, Melfi."

"You do?"

"Believe me."

"Well, it's just a kind of superstition, I suppose. Every house
has its Kobold, especially a house made of the earth, like this one
is. It's just a symbol, maybe, to remind us to thank the earth for
its gifts. But you get into the habit, you know? And, I will tell
you, there are nights and wet, misty mornings when you feel that
you just don't want to take any chances . . ."

"I know what you mean."

"I was afraid you'd laugh at an old woman's notions, Princess."

"Of course not. But what happens to the milk and cakes?"

"What do you mean?"

"What happens to them? What do you do with them in the morning?"

"Why, nothing. They're always gone."

Bronwyn had much to think about that night. She lay awake
as long as she could, listening. Her mind filtered out the familiar sounds, one by one: Burgos's rumbling snore and Melfi's
squeaking one, the faint hiss of the embers in the fireplace, the
muffled ticking of the clock's wooden gears, the murmur of her
own heart. Nothing else.

In the morning, the food was gone. She surprised, and pleased,
Burgos and Melfi by announcing that she would concede to their

arguments and stay for a few more days. That night, after the couple had gone to bed, Bronwyn lay awake until she was certain that they were soundly unconscious. Lighting her candle, shielding its light with the cup of her hand, she went to the fireplace. The bowl of milk and plate of cakes were in their usual place. Between two of the latter, she slipped a folded piece of paper she had surreptitiously prepared earlier. She crept back to her nook, extinguished the candle and tried to sleep. In spite of her efforts, she was soon dreaming, albeit fitfully and of terrible revenges.

In the morning, she was up even before the early-rising couple. The bowl and plate on the hearth were empty. Her note was not there.

That day and the following night were very long. She awakened when the clock softly chimed three times. She was puzzled for a moment, because that had never disturbed her before. Then she realized that the sound of the chime was just a coincidence—something else had roused her. Something standing over her bed. "Burgos?" she asked, for the round face, barely visible in the darkness, looked like his.

"Come with me," was the whispered reply, and Bronwyn knew that this was the answer to her message.

She rose from the bed silently. The big figure had retreated into the gloom, until it was only a darkness within the dark. It took only a moment for her to dress in the homespun garments Melfi had given her, high boots, gloves and fleece-lined leather coat and hat. She went toward the hearth, which looked like the black mouth of a tunnel. The word "Hurry!" appeared in her ear, though she couldn't see its source in the dark. She stepped onto the flat, broad stones of the hearth. She still could not see the back wall of the fireplace, even though a bed of embers glowed sullenly at her feet. She stepped over them, and kept on going. After two or three paces she stopped. She realized that she must, somehow, be beyond the fireplace; yet she also knew that the thing was built of massive stones several feet thick, and that beyond was the outside—or in the present instant, a deep snowdrift. Here was neither—only a blackness that seemed to press against her eyes, enveloping as though she were imbedded within black marble, like a fly in amber. And she was not about to take another step without knowing what was in front of her.

"Close your eyes," instructed the whisperer.

"Where am I?" There was no answer. She waited for a minute or so, then followed the instruction. No sooner had she done so than

the voice whispered, "Open your eyes." She did, and cried out
in alarm and pain. There was light, everywhere, and the surprise
and shock of it was frightening and hurtful. She squeezed her
eyes shut again, and tears were wrung from them. She opened
them again, after a moment, in a careful squint, shading them
with her fingers.

Gradually, like a photographic plate developing its image, the
enormous figure of a Kobold coalesced amid the pearly bright-
ness.

It was King Slagelse.

"We received the princess's message," he said, "and we are
not pleased."

"You must help me reach Blavek," Bronwyn pleaded.

"Why?"

"What do you mean?"

"Where is Thud?"

"Thud? You mean the man you sent with me?"

"Yes, the human the princess agreed to take to Londeac."

"I don't know."

"She doesn't know? What of our bargain?"

"It couldn't be helped! What was I supposed to do?"

"She was supposed to take him to Londeac!"

"Well, he's big enough to take care of himself! I had myself
to think of!"

"Then she can take care of herself now. There will be no further
help from us until she fulfills her part of our bargain."

"But you must help me!"

"Why?"

"My brother and Payne Roelt are going to destroy this country!"

"And what is that to us?"

"You won't help, then?"

"Fulfill the bargain."

"How?"

"When she has fulfilled the bargain, she can ask our help again.
Not before."

"No!" she cried, but the figure of the king was lost in a flood of
incandescent fluid that washed over her, blinding her, and when
it receded there was nothing around her but the darkness of her
bedroom.

The next morning her resolve to get to Hasselt by any means
was firmly established. All of Burgos's and Melfi's arguments
were to no avail: she would listen to them no longer.

"But you can't get to Hasselt yet," pleaded Burgos.

"Why not?" answered Bronwyn.

"It's fourteen miles from here!"

"So what? I can walk that in three hours; how much can the snow slow me?"

"You don't understand!" The poor man was close to tears.

"What's there to understand? The snow's stopped; it looks firm enough. Why can't I use snowshoes? And it's so close, I don't have to take anything with me. You know these people in the town; why don't you just write me a letter, asking for their help, and let me go?"

"But . . ."

"I'll go with or without your help or approval."

"Oh . . . Musrum help me! . . . All right, Princess, I'll go with you."

"Oh, Burgos!" wailed Melfi.

They packed in silence. Though the journey might be one of only fourteen miles, the charcoal-burner was taking no chances. In fact, the degree to which he was preparing began to engender disturbing thoughts in the princess—particularly thoughts casting doubts on the wisdom of her impatience. Perhaps in sixty-odd years Burgos had learned something from experience of the conditions that lay awaiting them.

While Melfi was busy stuffing a pair of bags with enough food for a polar expedition, snuffling back tears all the while, Burgos began preparing an exit. An open door exposed only a blank wall of snow. Digging away at this with a fireplace shovel and a bucket, he created a ramp leading to the surface.

Since she had not been in the outside air for weeks, Bronwyn scuttled up the slope. The sky was low and a featureless grey. All around her was a landscape of rolling white, punctuated only by pyramids of buried trees. Behind her the cottage was only one more hummock, distinguished solely by its smoking chimney. The air was intensely cold and the galelike wind sucked the warmth from her body . . . the sensation was vivid: she could actually feel her body heat passing through her skin. The wind seemed a supernatural force; it pierced her heavily layered clothing as though she were standing there naked.

Her breath was freezing on the outside of the scarf she had wound around her face. Her eyes were tearing in an effort to keep them warm and the overflow was icing her cheeks. Each inhalation filled her chest with pain as the metallic air tried to freeze her lungs. Too deep a breath and her glottis closed spasmodically, making her feel as though she were going to smother.

"This is impossible!" she thought. She would never have believed that such cold was possible.

She felt Burgos beside her.

"Come back in!" came his muffled voice.

She couldn't answer, but turned to go back down into the house. However, the perception of a strange sound stopped her. Were her ears ringing from the lacerating cold, or was she indeed hearing bells?

"Wait!" she managed to shout. She pulled the old man around to face her. All that was visible of him were two twinkling, worried eyes buried deeply within folds of wool and fur. She pointed to her ears with mittened hands.

"I hear something! Do you?"

"Of course!"

"What is it?"

"Basseliniden!"

"What?"

"Wait! You'll see!"

Wait? Fifteen more seconds and pieces of her would start snapping off like icicles. But the strange ringing sound was rapidly getting louder. Burgos took her by the shoulder and gestured to one side. Turning, she saw a dark object rushing over the snowfield. It was more than strange: it was uncanny. Until her senses of depth and proportion adjusted, all she was aware of was a tall, triangular shape rising and falling with the billows of ice and snow. It looked like a ship rising and falling with the waves, and it was with that perception that she realized what she was seeing. It was indeed a boat. A long, sleek hull with a mast supporting a bellying sail. It was held a foot or so above the snow by outrigger skis that made the craft look something like a waterstrider. The wind in its rigging sang like a mosquito. It approached rapidly and they waved. The iceboat's sail immediately furled and it coasted neatly to a stop only a few paces from Bronwyn and Burgos.

The latter shuffled across the intervening space on his clumsy snowshoes while a figure dropped from the boat. They embraced like a pair of friendly bears. Burgos and the figure from the boat returned to Bronwyn.

"Come on back in!" the old man shouted, and all three descended into the cottage.

Once back in the warmth, Bronwyn allowed Melfi to cluck over her. If anything, the heat from the fire made her feel colder at first as her gradual thaw tingled and stung.

"Look who's here!" said Burgos, as he and the other began the laborious process of deinsulation.

"Why, it's Basseliniden!" shouted Melfi, rushing to the stranger, who, his disrobing revealed, was a tall, thin man with a short beard and bulbous nose.

"What in the world were you doing outside, Burgos?" he asked, accepting a cup of tea from Melfi. "Thanks! No one's ever seen you before spring!"

"Well, we have a guest, Bassel . . ."

"So I see! I'm Basseliniden. It's a pleasure to meet you," he said, offering his hand to Bronwyn. In spite of his rather serious mien, there was a sarcastic sparkle to him that she liked.

"I'm Bronwyn Tedeschiy. It's a pleasure to meet you, too."

"Tedeschiy? Tedeschiy? Why does that sound so familiar?"

"She's the *Princess* Bronwyn, Basseliniden, that's why!" explained Burgos.

"What? What in the world are you talking about, Burgos?"

"It's true!"

"I read the papers, Burgos, and I think that your hobby has become an obsession. The princess is dead, Burgos."

"No," said Bronwyn. "It's true. I am the princess."

"Uh-huh," he answered, making Bronwyn angry.

"Look at this," she said, offering him her hand, displaying her signet ring.

"And this," added Melfi, holding out one of the albums that featured a full-page photograph of the princess cut from a magazine.

"But . . ." stammered the tall man. "How?"

The story was told, but neither quickly nor all that coherently since Bronwyn, Burgos and Melfi all insisted on sharing the chore. However, Basseliniden eventually got the gist of it.

"I believe you," he finally said.

"Thanks very much," replied Bronwyn with ill-concealed sarcasm, "but does that really do me any good?"

"Certainly," he answered, unabashed.

"How?"

"You want to get to Hasselt?"

"That's what you just heard me say."

"No problem. Are you ready to go now, or do you have something you have to do first? I really can't wait."

Her departure was sentimental but perfunctory. She genuinely liked the charcoal-burner and his wife, but was intensely impatient to be on her way. In spite of all the resolutions evolved from her recent self-revelations, she put her immediate goals ahead of any pain she might be causing the old couple. She realized what she was doing, but what could she do about it?

Basseliniden packed her away deeply within the hull of his snowboat. Protected from the wind, she was able to conserve her body heat and, except for her extremities, was not too uncomfortable. Her only serious complaint, and regret, was that she was unable to see the passing landscape.

The course must have been amazingly level; the snowboat felt as though it were flying. There were no bumps or sudden movements, just a sensation of great, smooth speed. The only sounds were those caused by the wind in the rigging: a combination of hums, low and high, that sounded like a sustained chord on an organ.

The trip was over before she had a chance to begin enjoying it. They had arrived in Hasselt-on-the-Dootlen.

There was very little to the town: it was simply a fishing village at the head of a large fjord. Other than a cannery, a few dozen houses and a handful of stores and shops, there was not much to it. Basseliniden had stopped in front of a tavern or inn. He handed the princess down to the people who came out of the building as though she were just one more item of cargo.

Inside, the inn was warm and crowded with people. There were both men and women of all ages, and even some children. The atmosphere was smoky and fragrant, noisy with laughter, talk and music. No one paid a lot of attention to their arrival at first. Following Basseliniden's example, Bronwyn began shedding her overcoats. Her companion kept a black cape on that made him look even taller and gaunter.

"Basseliniden!"

Bronwyn turned at the shout and saw a ruddy-faced, portly man pumping her companion's hand as though he expected water to start pouring from his mouth.

"Didn't expect you for days!"

"Trade's been off," Basseliniden answered. "Not much doing, so I thought I'd come on in."

"Well, glad to see you! Come on, seat yourself and I'll find something hot for you!"

The innkeeper (for so he seemed to be) plowed a path for them through the crowded room. Basseliniden was greeted from all sides by friendly shouts. They found seats together on a bench at the end of a trestle table already occupied by a dozen other people, all busily eating and drinking, or just drinking. "Well, hello, Basseliniden!" cried one of them. "Who's your pretty friend?"

"Just a traveler I gave a lift to," he answered.

"She wanted to come *here*? In the winter?"

The innkeeper returned with a tray bearing a pair of overflowing mugs, bread and bowls of soup. He set these before Basseliniden and Bronwyn. She buried her face in the food, grateful to be able to ignore her curious neighbors. Basseliniden caught the innkeeper by the sleeve, drawing his face down near his own.

"Say, Droomly, do you know of anyone going out soon?"

"To sea? In this weather?"

"Uh-huh."

"Well, I doubt it."

"Ask around, will you?"

"I'll let you know, but don't get your hopes up."

"How am I to get to Blavek?" Bronwyn asked as soon as the innkeeper left them.

"We'll see. There's always a way."

"It doesn't look like it to me."

"Just eat and don't worry about it. I'll be right back."

"Where are you going?" she asked, but got no answer as his long legs had already carried him well into the room. Sitting as she was in a corner with her back to two walls, Bronwyn had a moderately clear view of almost the entire interior of the inn. As small as the room was, there still must have been fifty or sixty people in it. She could see Basseliniden's balding head bobbing above all the others, like a fishing-net float. No one around her paid her any more attention, after the first, slight curiosity her arrival created.

The only clear memory that would remain with her about the few hours she would spend in the inn was that it smelled terribly bad: a heady combination of fish oil, tobacco smoke, wet wool, bodies that were unwashed and would remain that way until spring, spilled beer . . . that was rancid, stale and cloying at the same time.

Basseliniden returned presently with a short, stocky man in tow. "Miss Tedeschiy," he said, "this is Slivik Patooter."

"Pleased to meet you, ma'm," the smaller man said politely, scraping a shapeless hat from his shaggy head.

"I told Captain Patooter that you needed to get to Blavek."

"That's true, he did, ma'm. You're lucky that the fjord hasn't froze up yet, still too early in the year for much ice. Howsumever, ma'm, I really hadn't planned to go out again this season. In fact, I was just going to put my boat ashore when this gennelman approached me."

"I can pay you anything you want!" Bronwyn urged.

"Well, that may be so . . . and it may not. Begging your pardon, ma'm, but you don't give me much confidence in your solvency, if you'll forgive me for being so observant." He wrung the hat in his stained hands in embarrassment and the anxiety of incipient cupidity.

"Look," said Basseliniden, "sit down here with us for a few minutes, will you?"

"My pleasure, certainly. My, that ale looks good . . ."

While another mug was sent for, Bronwyn had a moment or two to assess the newcomer. Her impressions did not add up to a total that was either savory or encouraging. The small man was stocky, solidly built, with a froglike face laced with broken veins. His popeyes had a jellylike sheen to them.

"Listen to me," said Basseliniden, whispering conspiratorially. "There's more in this for you than you can possibly imagine. You do this right and you could have your own fleet next season, *Captain*."

"Exactly what do you want me to do?"

"I've got to get to Blavek," said Bronwyn, "as soon as I possibly can!"

"Blavek's a long way from here by sea," said Patooter. "I've not ever gone there, in fact."

"That's no matter," she said. "If you cannot sail to Blavek, then get me to the nearest coast town that has coach service to the city."

"Well, I didn't say that I couldn't take you to Blavek, ma'm, just that it's a long and difficult voyage."

"How long? How difficult?"

"That's not easy to say . . ."

"Is anything?"

"Well, ma'm, we'd have to go through the Straits—not easy this time of year—coast Thelot in the Gulf and finally up the Moltus . . . I'd say a good month, all told."

"A month! Impossible!"

"I don't make the weather or the winds, ma'm. And Musrum made the distance."

"Look here," interjected Basseliniden. "Why not just take her to the head of Stuckney Bay? She can get a coach at Glibner that will take her to Blavek; they aren't two hundred miles apart."

Bronwyn unfolded a map of Guesclin in her mind. Basseliniden was right: a boat could bypass the highlands that lay between her and Glibner, and all the severe snows that made normally rugged, twisting mountain tracks completely impassable. Between Glibner and Blavek lay only flat lowland whose roads would not yet be impeded. A fast coach could have her in the city in two or three days.

"How long would it take to get me to Glibner?"

"Oh, only two or three days; four maybe, depending on the winds."

She could be back in Blavek in less than two weeks!

"Basseliniden, can I trust this man?"

"Depends upon how much you want to trust him with. I wouldn't overburden him."

"One thing, Captain," she said. "There is no way that I can pay you now; in fact, I will probably have to send your money to Hasselt from Blavek, once I get there."

"If Basseliniden vouches for you, that's all right with me."

"I not only vouch for her," said Basseliniden, suddenly gaining a cutting edge to his voice, "I guarantee your trustworthiness."

"Yes, sir, I understand!" quavered Patooter, his pale face growing paler under a fresh coat of greasy sweat.

"When can we leave?" asked Bronwyn.

"Would dawn tomorrow suit you, ma'm?"

"That'd be fine," she answered.

"Then, if you would kindly pardon me, I had best make preparations. Good evening, ma'm, good evening, Mr. Basseliniden, sir." He scuttled off, slipping through the crowd like an avocado pit.

"Are you sure I can trust him?"

"No one can trust him, but you needn't worry because *he* trusts *me*." That had the same ominous ring to it that his voice had when speaking to Patooter a moment earlier. Bronwyn began to wonder exactly what Basseliniden did for a living.

"I've arranged for a room for you for tonight," he continued. "It's not much, but it'll be warm. I left word for you to be awakened just before dawn. I'll meet you here."

He started to rise, but Bronwyn caught his sleeve. There had not been many people whom she had thought to thank for their efforts on her behalf so far. She thought that perhaps she'd get at least one to her credit.

"I ought to thank you for all your help . . ." she began.

"There are people who'd never call me a patriot, maybe with good reason. They're wrong. *I* thank *you*." Raising her hand to his lips, he kissed it and, with a swirl of black cape, he vanished into the crowd. She heard the howl of wind as the outside door opened and shut.

12

HOMECOMING

BRONWYN KNEW that she would grow to hate the *Upsy Daisy* long before the wharves of Glibner were sighted. She hated the look, the smell and the feel of the little boat, and she hated the suggestiveness of its name. She clung to its bulwarks with knuckles white with desperation; her brain was betraying her. If she wouldn't allow it to think about the *Upsy Daisy*, then it insisted on dwelling upon how the ship *heaved* and *tossed*.

The *Upsy Daisy* was a round-bellied little lugger that scooted over the waves like a skipped stone. The wind was nearly gale force. It was from the north, as cold as steel, but it flung the ship before it like an autumn leaf, which was all that mattered to Bronwyn. Captain Patooter also was pleased and claimed that they'd reach their goal in less than three days, if the wind held. Bronwyn was pleased only because she now knew from experience that she could go that long without eating.

She had been awakened before dawn by Basseliniden and taken through the streets—in that claustrophobic silence peculiar to the hours before first light—to the docks, where she found the *Upsy Daisy* waiting. Although the shore was covered with a thin powdering of snow, and a thick scum of ice floated around the pilings and as far out as she could see, the fjord was yet still free of the pack ice that would impound it for the winter. With scarcely a word passed between anyone, the lugger departed immediately upon her arrival. When she had looked back, Basseliniden had disappeared.

The sea fluttered and rippled around the boat like a grey banner. Or like a woolen blanket, heavy and lusterless, except where the wind broke the crests, releasing thick bursts of mist and spume. The sky was dull and fishy—broken only by scraps of ragged sooty clouds that rushed overhead—and merged with the sea at the indistinct horizon. Occasional snowflakes fluttered past.

It was a little warmer and a little drier below deck, in the single small cabin the *Upsy Daisy* boasted, but Bronwyn refused to consider abandoning her place on deck unless necessity forced her to. Warmer and drier the cabin may be, but only in comparison to the open deck. In reality the clammy enclosure was not unlike the interior of a fish's stomach, redolent with a dank ripeness that Bronwyn knew she would not be able to endure while still possessing consciousness.

The *Upsy Daisy* was manned only by Captain Patooter and two other men, neither of whom had been introduced to her. In fact, she was barely aware of them other than as a pair of figures that lackadaisically attended to the ship's operation. They were repulsive-looking brutes in any case whose lack of interest in the princess was a social omission she was neither anxious nor encouraged to correct.

Nevertheless, even if she forewent eating, she would have to sleep at least once before reaching Glibner, which meant going into the cabin. The captain had a small alcove separated from the main cabin by a curtain, which he had promised to his passenger. Within was a hammock. Since she planned to sleep fully dressed, she had no fear about having to touch the repellent surface with her skin. It gave every indication of, when not in use for sleeping, being used in some capacity intimately concerned with fishing.

Bronwyn found herself thinking more and more about the mysterious Basseliniden—or Bassel, as he insisted she call him. He had entered into and departed from her life too quickly to be fully absorbed. Of everyone she had met during her adventure, especially those who had given her aid, he seemed to be the least motivated. Within minutes of being introduced he had accepted her as a passenger in his snowboat; he procured her passage on this boat and clearly bullied Patooter into taking her on a voyage that the captain obviously would never have otherwise considered. Any reward Patooter expected from her could scarcely repay the danger and difficulty he had taken upon himself. It was evident that the captain feared Basseliniden for some reason; fear and cupidity in fairly equal amounts had brought him and his ugly crew out into the winter sea.

Whatever power it was that Basseliniden possessed over Captain Patooter—and apparently the rest of Hasselt-on-the-Dootlen—she was grateful for it. If she ever met him again, there would be opportunity to discover his mystery.

The first day and a half went quickly enough, however boring the time might have been. They had rounded Cape Despair during the night, showing, whether Bronwyn was aware of it or not, exceptional seamanship on the part of Captain Patooter. The sea between that point of land and the Grand Bank that lay not far to the east was shallow and strewn with ragged reefs that had sawn the bottoms out of a hundred unlucky or careless ships. At night and in bad weather it took either iron nerves or brazen stupidity to enter those waters. After rounding the Cape they had turned to the south-southwest toward the entrance to Stuckney Bay.

Once again Patooter assured the princess that if the galelike wind held they would be at Glibner late the next day. In spite of that good news, the latter part of that day and that evening provided something new for Bronwyn to worry about.

Patooter's two crewmen were as repulsive examples of genetic black humor as she had ever seen. Individually they would have been repellent; together she found them a little frightening. All the more so since she continually discovered them leering at her, a habit that seemed to increase its incidents as the voyage progressed. She tried to avoid the men as much as possible, but there were few places in the small lugger where she could hope to be out of their way for more than a few minutes. In fact, she had no real way of knowing whether or not their presence near her was legitimate or invented. She didn't want to complain to the captain: he gave her little more confidence than his men did.

That night, when she finally forced herself to retire to the fetid alcove allotted to her, noises on the deck above her head kept her awake. It was an argument, and a violent one. Evidently Patooter didn't have the control over his men she thought he ought to have, or hoped he had. Through the thick planks and over the normal ship's noises, there were only a few words or phrases that came through distinctly: mostly curses. However, once she heard the captain's voice shout, "You'll have his wrath down upon you like the fist of Musrum!"

There was not much more said after that, but she remained awake the rest of the night.

The next morning she resumed her place at the bulwark. Through the mists to the north she could catch occasional glimpses of land. They appeared to be passing the mouth of a large river, which meant that they must be well within the bay. If so, then the captain was right and she would be in Glibner by nightfall, if not sooner.

Lunch came and went. She had gone below only long enough to fetch some salt fish and biscuits and returned to the deck to eat. No one else had been in the cabin. As she ate, watching the ghostly grey cliffs slip past, it occurred to her that she had not yet seen the captain. The two crewmen were as usual altogether too present—she glanced to one side and, sure enough, there they were, standard leer and all. But now she began to wonder: where was the captain? The lugger was a small craft; she knew that it possessed a hold (an empty one, she had heard him complain) and the small cabin below deck; above there was only a boothlike pilot house near the stern. The latter was glazed on four sides and it was clear the captain was not in it. In fact, the tiller was unattended; it had been lashed in place by a loop thrown over one of its handles. Unless Patooter was for some reason in the hold, where could he have gotten to?

The remainder of the afternoon went by without the captain's presence, and Bronwyn had become seriously concerned; little prickles of apprehension were beginning to coalesce into a knot of dread that found a place in the pit of her stomach to hide and quiver. She had not particularly wanted to consider the possibility, but it had been clear for a long time that the captain was no longer on his ship. Had she been less of a civilized creature, she would have listened to her instincts in the first place and later worked out whether they had been justified when she was someplace safe. Which was not a good thought to have had: it served to remind her that she had no place to run to.

Nevertheless, the crew left her scrupulously alone. She found that inexplicably sinister. In spite of the fact that they kept their distance, that deference was itself blatantly taunting.

The *Upsy Daisy*'s prow was driving into the lowering sun, following the golden path it laid. The bay was narrowing rapidly. Bronwyn could now see both sides: the cliffs of the north shore and the low plain of the south. Only an hour or two later she became aware of a patch of brown haze directly ahead, where the north and south shores met. Speckles of white and thin columns of smoke signalled a town—Glibner.

The *Upsy Daisy* was following the south shore closely. The reedy banks were only a quarter of a mile away, or less. Small cottages and huts appeared in increasing numbers; tall poles festooned with drying nets made them look like stranded boats. Perhaps half a dozen other sailing ships were in the bay, but none were closer than a mile. All seemed to be headed for Glibner as well, scurrying like scraps of confetti in the brisk gusts.

Bronwyn found herself looking forward to the wharves with an anxiety that almost made her nauseous. The premonitory feeling of peril was a palpable fist squeezing her stomach like a miserly artist working out the last daubs of oil from a tube of paint.

What she wanted more than anything was to turn her back to the *Upsy Daisy* and its foul crew; it was an immediate desire that had supplanted all other goals, present or future.

The two crewmen began taking in the sails, and the *Upsy Daisy* slowed to a crawl and then stopped dead in the water, bobbing and rolling like a cork in the deep swells. There was no reason for having done this and it was with almost a sense of relief that Bronwyn realized that her fears were no longer abstract.

The two men came toward her, one from the bow and one from the stern.

Bronwyn had but one thought: she dived through the hatch like a spooked prairie dog. In the rucksack which contained the few possessions remaining to her was the .50-caliber Minch-Moappa revolver. She was struggling to remove it from the clothing in which it was wrapped when a stinging blow made her spin around, the gun flying from her hand and landing with a clatter on the far side of the cabin.

Bronwyn was half reclining where she had fallen onto the deck; above her was the hulking figure of one of the men, his repulsiveness transmuted into horrendousness by the outré effects of the lantern that swung wildly from the ceiling. Shafts of chrome-yellow light swept up and down his face and figure, the swiftly changing angles of light and shadow making his countenance seem to writhe and twist, as if in an agony of indecision about what final shape would ultimately be ugly enough. His enormous shadow danced spasmodically around the room like some frantic audience.

"What do you want?" Bronwyn asked with as much bravado and indignation as she could muster, but the man did not answer.

"Ee'm kemmun doyn," said the sailor who had remained above, from the open hatch. His almost incomprehensible accent revealed his Fezzooan origin.

"You stay right there," ordered the one who had struck her.

"Ew, kem oon, min!"

"This was my idea, Shitsk, you get her next."

"Wooll, it layst lit moo vitch!"

"You just stay outa here and I don't give a damn what you do."

"Get out of here!" ordered Bronwyn, but the big man just laughed.

"Patooter was fool enough to take you on as supercargo for the *promise* of payment . . . well, I think that I'll take that payment *now*."

"Don't you dare touch me!" she growled unconvincingly, and the sailor grasped her by the shoulders in a grip that felt as though his fingers might meet through her flesh like iron pincers. She screamed in pain and kicked wildly, but the man simply ignored her, other than to give her a backhanded blow across the face that threw her to the deck again. Tears of pain and anger poured down her cheeks. There was the metallic taste of blood in her mouth, which she really hated. The man picked her up again, and again slapped her face so hard that she fell to the deck once more. His hands and knuckles were as rough as hemp. Ruby beads of blood seeped through the abrasions on her cheeks.

The sailor kneeled on the deck, straddling the princess across her thighs. With one huge hand pressed to her sternum, he pinned her to the planking.

"Hew! Hew! Dit's groyt!" cackled the man above them.

"You shut that hatch and just shut up!" shouted the other redundantly, without taking his eyes from his captive.

"Ew, doym oot, Smeen!" but despite the protest the heavy hatch slammed down.

With his free hand the man called Smeen clutched a fistful of Bronwyn's shirtfront and ripped it away, exposing one breast.

"Ahrr," he slobbered. "I thought you wore them baggy shirts for a good reason—yer hiding a pair o' nice pink titties!"

He grabbed at her breast as though it were an escaping fish and Bronwyn snarled with the pain.

"You pig!" she choked out. "You bastard! You fish-eyed son of a street-walker!"

He released her breast and reached lower. Bronwyn gasped in revulsion and indignation. He lowered his face toward hers. His eyes looked like cracked marbles; one was significantly larger than the other and neither looked quite in the same direction. His inflamed gums had drawn away from the teeth in advanced periodontosis. The crooked yellow tusks thus exposed made his mouth look like an ashtray full of wet cigarette butts. A sparse beard of pig bristles was flecked with dried snot and foamy spit.

He lowered this loathsome apparition toward Bronwyn's face, still pinning her with one hand while the other groped with the buttons on her trousers. Never again would she curse their inconvenience. The sailor weighed two hundred and thirty pounds, and his mass alone held her as helpless as though she were under a dead cow.

She felt warm, fetorous breath on her face and her gorge rose in response. He moved his face away from hers, a momentary relief only, for when she felt his moist, rubbery lips press against her exposed breast she vomited violently. This didn't seem to bother the sailor, who simply wiped her face with a rough swipe of his sleeve. He brought his plum-colored lips toward hers in a pucker that her mind perversely compared to a hemorrhoidal rectum.

In a blind panic she reached to push the face away. As before, he disdainfully ignored her defensive efforts. That is, until her thumb found one of his eyes; she pushed as hard as she could. The man howled in pain and grabbed her arm, but not before something gave and she felt her thumb plunge in to its joint; a warm glob of jelly rolled down the back of her hand. The man leaped to his feet with a high-pitched wail. He clutched his ruined face (a moot point that it could be ruined further), blood freely running between his fingers.

"Filthy, damned little bitch," he finally managed to cry. "You cunt! I'll kill you!"

But Bronwyn was already on her feet and scrambling for her gun. The man swung a foot into her ribs before she could rise with the weapon and she fell to the deck, but still holding the revolver. There was a big glass bottle in front of her face: five gallons of lantern oil. She struck at it with the gun and the jug burst, spraying her with the rancid contents. Ignoring the pain as she scrambled through the broken glass, she grasped the neck of the broken bottle and flung it over her shoulder into the sailor's face. He cursed and danced back a pace or two—leery now of anything approaching his face. Bronwyn jumped to her feet and ripped the swinging lantern free from its cord.

"What the hell are you going to do?" the man asked, sarcastically. Amazingly he seemed to have forgotten about his horribly wounded eye. Bronwyn could see the unattached muscles writhing within the wet, red socket.

"This!" Bronwyn hissed, throwing the lantern into the mess of oil that had spread across the deck. The glass globe exploded and instantly a blue flame danced across the film of fuel. A second later, tall yellow flames burst free amid thick black smoke, like some phosphorescent genie throwing aside its cloak.

"Damn it to hell!" cried the sailor, stepping through the flames as though they were merely a curtain. Bronwyn raised the big revolver and shot him in the mouth. As the heavy body fell backwards into the fire with a crash that shook the entire boat, the hatch slid back and the second sailor pushed his face into the cabin.

"Voot de hoyl's koyn oon dayn tare?"

His answer came in the form of an express message delivered by the princess's Minch-Moappa. The heavy bullet singed a part in his hair and the man leaped back into safety. Bronwyn scrambled up the short ladder and regained the deck. The other man was in the bows, brandishing a boat hook. A stream of blood trickling from his scalp wound bisected his face.

"Ztoy oovay vroom me!" he said to the figure that stood, bloody and disheveled, framed by the column of black smoke that welled from the hatch. A detached part of Bronwyn's mind realized how fearsome she must look: streaked with fresh blood, both hers and the dead man's, clothes half torn from her, her eyes as preternaturally green as that rare flash of emerald emitted by a setting sun, teeth bared in a feral grimace.

"Drop that hook!" she ordered, and when he didn't obey she sent a shot in his direction that excavated a crater in the planking between his feet. He threw the boat hook away as though he had suddenly discovered it had grown fangs.

"Koom en, latty," he pleaded. "E din't to neffinks do yoy!"

"Stay right there!"

Not taking her eyes from him for more than a second, she gave a quick glance toward the shore. The reed-covered bank was only a hundred yards away. Scattered weeds grew almost out to the boat, so she knew the water must be shallow. Turning back to the cowering man, she ordered, "Get over the side!"

"Voot?"

"I said, get over the side, the starboard side, away from the shore!"

"E'll vrooze oon dit fayter!"

"No, you *might* freeze, but if you stay here two more seconds you *will* be dead. Jump, damn it!"

The man jumped. Immediately, Bronwyn lowered herself over the port side, into the icy water. She gasped with the shock. She couldn't reach the bottom, so she lay on her back, keeping her rucksack out of the water as much as possible, and began a painfully slow backstroke.

From behind her came a muffled "Hilp! Hilp!"

Her body was being drained of its energy as though it were a sponge being wrung by the water's icy grip, or perhaps a colander through which her life's heat was pouring; her sodden clothing weighed her down as though she were encased in brick. Her abused joints were stiffening like supercooled taffy. She tried the bottom again. She could reach it—the water was now only four or five feet deep—but it was composed of a thin, nearly liquid mud that would not support her. She swam again, as best she could with joints becoming rigid and muscles cramping in an attempt to warm her with the energy of their spasmodic flexing. She was deep within the reeds and tried standing again. This time the water was shallower and the mud a little less viscous. The breeze made the freezing water seem warm by contrast. She staggered the remaining distance to the shore, shivering so violently that her whole body shuddered epileptically. The wind freshened and was lowering her surface temperature dangerously. Snow flurried around her, its hard pellets stinging her raw cheeks like salt. She was gasping for breath between chattering teeth and a thin rime of ice was starting to form on her. Goosebumps covered her as her follicles tried desperately to fluff up an insulating fur that her species had lost two hundred thousand years too early to do her any good.

She saw lanterns approaching and heard the sound of voices, though all as a kind of confused abstraction. The voices surrounded her and a bright light flashed in her face.

"Anyone else out there?"

"N-no," she managed to stutter. *Let the bastard fend for himself*, she thought, not so frozen that she couldn't manage to be vindictive.

"Get a blanket around her!" another voice said.

"Anybody got a blanket?"

"Here, get this around her!"

"Get her inside somewhere, she's freezing to death!"

There was a hiatus in her perception of time. She must have been operating automatically for some period, for when her brain finally thawed and took recognizance of reality, she was sitting in a chair, sipping something hot from a mug in the midst of telling a very personalized version of her story. She realized that she must be in one of the houses she had seen on the shore, because the burning *Upsy Daisy* was visible through a window. Enough time had passed that the boat had burnt nearly to its waterline.

"The dirty bastards!" said someone.

"I've known that Patooter and his rotten gang; good riddance, I say!" replied another.

Bronwyn glanced around. There were probably a dozen people in the small room, male and female. All had sturdy, honest-looking, peasants' faces.

"Look," said Bronwyn, "I can't explain why, but I've got to get to Blavek as soon as possible. Are there any coaches leaving soon?"

"Well, I don't know," answered one man. "I've never had to go to the City in my whole life, but I suppose we could find out for you."

"Would you, please?"

"I think," said one of the women, "that it would be best for the young lady to spend the night here."

"You're absolutely right; she must get her strength back."

"I know you're in a great hurry, my dear, for some reason, but there's nothing that can be done before morning, anyway."

She accepted the invitation as gracefully as her impatience allowed.

She spent a comfortable night wrapped in down in a room cozy with its own stove. In the morning, her hosts—a middle-aged fisherman and his wife—took her into Glibner, which turned out to be a sizable village since it was the capital of Guesclin's fishing industry; all of the riches of the fertile Grand Bank eventually made their way to the town's markets and canning plants.

The fisherman took the princess directly to the agency of the coach service where, with apologies, he left her. He had his own business to take care of.

Bronwyn entered the office, where she was faced with an unexpected obstacle.

The sole occupant of the agency was a rather prissy-looking young man seated behind a counter. After pointedly ignoring the girl for a full minute, he finally set his pen aside and, adjusting his pince-nez so he could more effectively look down his long nose, said with the greatest amount of doubt, "Is there something I can help you with?"

"Yes, I need to get to Blavek by the next coach."

He looked at the girl: her clothes filthy and torn, her face bruised, puffy and scratched, one eye blackened, her only baggage a single rucksack, and asked—not unreasonably, it must be admitted: "Have you the price of a ticket?"

"Pardon me?"

"The fare to Blavek is five crowns. Have you five crowns?" He leaned back in his chair and smirked—*got her on that one*!

"Well no, but I . . ."

"Please! A ticket is five crowns. That's that. If you haven't the money, would you please leave me to my work? Thank you very much!"

"I can pay when I get to Blavek!"

"Shall I call a policeman?"

"No, thank you. I'll be back with the money."

"Hmph."

Now what? she wondered. Five crowns isn't much. Once upon a time if she had dropped a five-crown coin she wouldn't have bothered to pick it up. But how to get one when you haven't got one? It was never a problem before: she just asked somebody and there it was. In fact, she couldn't recall ever having asked for anything as *small* as five crowns . . . though now it seemed like a fortune. Would someone give it to her? That smacked of begging, a nasty thought. She dare not start telling people who she was, either. She'd have to be a little more circumspect about that, this close to the capital. Could she *earn* it? Now there was a new idea. People did that, she knew, so why couldn't she? Thud did it, for Musrum's sake. All right, then, let's keep this thought going: to earn money one has to do something. What could she do? Well, she didn't know. She had never had to do anything, so she didn't know what she was capable of. Possibly most anything, so far as she knew. It actually sounded a little exciting.

While still emboldened, she crossed the street to a small public house and entered. She went to the bar and sat upon one of the stools. It was still early and the place was virtually empty, save for one or two old men who were probably always there—at least they looked like fixtures. Momentarily, a big, jolly-looking woman came from a back room that opened into the rear of the bar. She looked like she had been drawn entirely with a compass—

everything about her was round: eyes like robin's eggs, cheeks like apricots, a cascade of chins like a confection squeezed from a pastry-bag, soft round bosom like a down pillow and sleek, pink arms like fresh sausages. Altogether she looked like a giant marzipan lady who ought to be a decoration in some candy-shop window.

"Well, what can I do for you, honey?" she said, laughing. Even her voice was round. Bronwyn was to learn that everything the woman said, she said while laughing, even when discussing the most distressing subjects. "Though it looks like you've been pretty well done for already!" Hee hee.

"I was in a shipwreck last night," Bronwyn answered.

"Not the boat that burned?" She chuckled.

"Yes."

"Well, I just heard about that!" Titter, titter. "You're very lucky!"

"I guess so."

"You hungry?"

"Well, not really, not yet. I had a nice breakfast with the people who found me."

"The Rassendylls? Yes, they're very good people, I know them quite well! Something to drink, then? On the house?"

"A little ale?"

"Coming right up!" She set a small foamy glass of the dark beverage before the girl. "What are your plans, now, honey?"

"I've got to get to Blavek. It's literally a matter of life or death!"

"Truly, now?" She chuckled, but her eyes were serious.

"Oh, yes! Except I've no money: I've lost everything. But I can't get a coach ticket without money."

"How much do you need? It's been a long time since I've had to go to the city!"

"Five crowns."

The round lady whistled. "So much?"

"I was hoping to find a job. Just long enough to earn the fare."

"What can you do?"

"I don't know. I'm willing to try almost anything."

"Ever wash dishes?"

"Well, no."

"Where did you come from? Well, are you game to try?"

"Of course!"

"You wash dishes for me, say three days, and I'll buy your ticket! Fair enough?"

"Yes! Thank you very much!"

"What's your name, honey?"

"Bronwyn."

"Glad to meet you, Bronwyn! You can call me Mimsey!" Hee hee.

Which is how it came to pass that Bronwyn Tedeschiy, Princess of Tamlaght, found herself up to her elbows in hot water and dirty dishes. She liked Mimsey, who, after the few initial questions never asked another of her. But she didn't particularly like her work. She merely racked it up as one more debit against her brother and Payne Roelt.

Mimsey had provided a cot and linen for Bronwyn and allowed her to sleep in the kitchen, which was warmed by a big stove whose fire was never allowed to go out. She also kindly provided the girl with three good meals a day, above and beyond the money that was promised.

During business hours Mimsey tended the bar and a big brown man did the cooking. He was from Peigambar, which fascinated Bronwyn, though he was never heard to utter a word in any language she knew. Oddly enough, he seemed to understand the orders that Mimsey shouted back to him perfectly well.

Bronwyn wondered what he would think if he were to be told that she had once been a Peigambarese sultan for a few hours.

At the end of the three days, Bronwyn's bruises had faded to yellow stains, she had lost almost all the swelling and her scratched face had mostly healed. Mimsey had had her clothes cleaned and had repaired them herself, her chubby fingers surprisingly nimble with a needle. The princess looked cleaner and healthier than she had in a long time, if still not quite aristocratic.

"Here's your five crowns, dear," said Mimsey with a chortle. "And a little extra!"

"What's this for?" Bronwyn asked, fingering the additional coins.

"Tips!" giggled Mimsey. "Amkober and I always split the tips, and this time I split them three ways! It was his idea, really!"

"Thank you!" said the princess, turning to the Peigambarese.

"Omdurman ib bam Kuh-e-dinar! Efftah," he replied, ingenuously.

"Will you write and let me know you're all right?" asked Mimsey.

"Of course!"

"Well, good luck to you! You're a good, honest worker! Musrum knows I've had enough dishwashers who cost me more in broken dishes or thievery than I paid them! So many people think that it's a job beneath their dignity!"

"Uh, well, thanks."

"You'd best get along, honey! The coach leaves soon," giggled Mimsey, sniffling back a tear.

"You again?" said the prissy man at the coach agency, when he saw the familiar figure enter the office.

"I want a ticket to Blavek. One way."

"Do you have five crowns?"

"Yes, certainly."

"Well, may I see it?"

"Let me see the ticket."

"How do I know you have the money?"

"How do I know you have the ticket?"

"There are laws, you know, about loitering and fraud!"

"There are laws concerning your public obligations, too. Shall I go to your guild hall?"

The man sniffed, looking down his long, thin nose at the girl as though he were aiming some weapon at her, expecting her, evidently, to cringe before its deadly threat. Bronwyn merely stared back up at what she thought was an officious minor clerk who looked like a skinny bird. Perhaps it was because the girl's mien was something quite different from the impression her dress initially created, but the clerk held up a ticket where she could see it.

"Five crowns?" she asked.

"Yes!" he snapped.

She handed over the coins and watched while he deliberately counted them—one, two, three, four, five—before turning the pasteboard over to her.

"Thank you very much!" she said sweetly, turning to leave.

"The coaches leave from the rear!" the man said, smirking at having been able to catch her and get in the last word.

She left through a double door at the back of the lobby where there was a big coach waiting, already half-full of passengers. The driver was taking tickets and said, as he tore the receipt from hers, "Leaving in two or three minutes, miss. Take any seat."

"Thanks."

She found one remaining window seat, which she had hoped to find because she liked to lean against the wall and doze. She stowed her rucksack on the overhead rack and made herself comfortable.

The trip to Blavek was about two hundred miles, a slightly more than two-day journey including stops for meals and changes of horses. The coach made no provision for sleeping and, except for the brief stops just mentioned, otherwise ran nonstop day and night until it reached the city. There were no towns between Glibner and Blavek, just gently undulating and uninteresting farmland, now grey and umber, piebald with drifting snow-patches, all under a pewter sky.

Bronwyn's fellow travelers were a nondescript assortment of small businessmen, farmers and fishermen, going to the city for whatever reasons such people might have. They were all sullen, quiet, absorbed in their private thoughts and concerns, which suited the princess very well. The bland countryside was hypnotic, soporific and she spent most of the journey in a kind of reverie—half asleep, half awake. The few thoughts she had concerned themselves with the problem of just exactly what she intended to do once she got back to Blavek. Up to now she had been simply determined to get back, in order to wreak some sort of abstract, unspecified revenge on her two enemies. But now that she had to consider this revenge in concrete, specific terms she wasn't too certain how to implement it.

The only thing she could imagine was to try and locate one of the barons who had a residence in Blavek; there were three or four who maintained permanent homes in the City. She would have to pick one and hope that he would be able to help. At the moment she could not imagine what form that help would take.

Mimsey, Bronwyn discovered to her pleasure, had slipped food for the journey into the rucksack: some sandwiches wrapped in paper, some cakes and some fruit, and two bottles of ale. The sandwiches were enclosed in sheets of old newspaper, which she spread across her lap in the interest of neatness. She had taken only two or three bites before she became aware of the printed words. The two that caught her attention were *Piers Monzon*. She stopped eating and read the column of type. The news was more dreadful than she possibly could have imagined.

Piers was dead.

The baron had been taken back to the capital in chains, a prisoner. He had been labeled a traitor for the crime of raising arms against the prince and had been imprisoned in the Iron Tower for over a month before his trial . . . such as it was. Meanwhile, his army had been broken up with those even implicated in opposing the prince summarily executed there at the border camp. There had been no question of courts-martial.

The baron's personal army no longer existed.

Piers's trial had taken place barely two weeks ago. His execution was carried out the following day. Payne did not stop there, however; he was not satisfied. He was bound to wipe out the most remote possibility of any future opposition, however slight. That is when the great horror began. Bronwyn read the account with her face glistening with beads of cold sweat, with clammy, shaking hands rustling the paper so much that she attracted the annoyed attention of her fellow passengers, some of whom wondered if the pale, perspiring, quaking girl was somehow ill. If she is, most of them decided, it's to be hoped that she'll have the decency to wait until the next rest stop is reached.

Piers had been subjected to the execution traditionally reserved for traitors, but not carried out in fact for nearly a century: he had been broken on the wheel. Each of his limbs—arms and legs—had been broken by a man wielding an iron pipe. Broken systematically and thoroughly; so pulverized were the bones that Piers's arms and legs could be threaded in and out through the spokes of a giant wagon wheel like ribbons. He was left this way until he was on the verge of death from exposure—since the broken limbs were not intrinsically mortal, this took many days; he was then beheaded and quartered. The remains were burnt and the ashes scattered on unhallowed ground.

Piers's family were put to death as well. (Bronwyn began to have difficulty in comprehension: Aunt Sooky? Her cousins, nephews and nieces? Little Truro? Wigan's new baby? Her brain mercifully began shutting some doors.) So were the household staff and servants. The family of Monzon—like Piers's army—effectively no longer existed.

Payne was not yet satisfied.

Though this act of terrorism caused the barons' opposition to collapse, to assure himself of this, Payne caused the executions of any whom he had suspected of opposing him, or even of supporting or sympathizing with the opposition. It was the beginning of a reign of terror as whole families and retainers were included in the holocaust. It was a reign of terror that was ongoing as she read, though the newspaper had very carefully avoided that label.

It was clear that Ferenc had unopposed control of Tamlaght and that Payne had unopposed control of Ferenc.

Yet . . . for some reason the coronation—to her great surprise—had not yet taken place. Probably Payne considered it a mere formality, with the princess gone and most likely dead. The ceremony was scheduled for a month from now (she glanced at the top of the paper for the date: it was only yesterday's). It didn't really mean anything: Payne was right if he thought it an insignificant formality.

Bronwyn now had some concrete things to think about during the remainder of her journey back to Blavek.

13

REUNIONS AGAIN

BRONWYN FOUND Blavek to be greyer and bleaker than she had remembered. Of course, the city was always grey and bleak and certainly at its greyest and bleakest in the winter, when the colorless sun jealously drained any remaining fugitive hues from stone and pavement, until Blavek was as stark and cold as a linoleum-block print. But she had experienced seventeen or eighteen Blavekian winters, so the city's greyness and bleakness ought not to have been anything for her to remark upon. Perhaps she was now seeing it through a dense filter of experience and expectation; seeing it through an overlay of prejudicial knowledge in much the same way she might look at someone who she knew had a fatal disease.

If she learned anything in the past weeks, it might have been the lesson of caution. The last thing she ought to do, she realized, was to march up to the front gate of the palace and loudly announce herself, "This is the Princess Bronwyn and I want Payne Roelt's head and no nonsense!" No, that would probably be the unwise thing to do.

She needed to maintain a degree of anonymity. If she had any one advantage it was that not a living soul in the city was aware that she was alive. And there was probably no one outside Palace Island who would recognize her on sight. It was not much of an advantage, admittedly, but it was all that she had so it wouldn't do to use it unwisely.

She decided that what she needed to do was to assume a kind of protective coloration. Blending into the background, as it were, she could then learn what she could learn, and then act upon that knowledge. She would have to keep her inborn impatience under tight rein. Haste would not just make waste, haste would make a dead princess.

With her newfound employment experience—she now had a trade, it must be remembered—she had little difficulty in procuring a job. She became night dishwasher in the kitchen of a small hotel not far from the palace. It was an ideal situation for her: satisfactory meals and a small, but clean, cubbyhole for sleeping were provided in addition to her meager wages. Working nights left the bulk of the daylight hours available for espionage.

Little effort was really needed; most of what she learned during the first week she picked up from the newspaper, or from keeping her ears open on the street corners. In actual fact, the latter were by far the more accurate and unbiased source of news since it was clear that the *Intelligencer* was going out of its way to avoid outright criticism of the new regime. Yet it could scarcely flatly contradict what people could see with their own eyes. It took some effort for her to refine a nugget of genuine information from a dozen pages of closely set sycophantic raw ore.

What could not be hidden was that Tamlaght was on the verge of collapse. The market had fallen catastrophically in the past month, plummeting since the initiation of Payne's pogrom against the barons. A crown was worth only a fraction of the value it held when she left Blavek. When she began her job she was pleased at the seemingly large wage she was offered . . . until she first tried to buy something. She was given five times what Mimsey had paid, but prices were in turn ten times higher. Her money was worth only half what it had been. And prices were increasing almost daily. She was fortunate to have had room and board included with her job.

There had been major crop failures and, though it might not be entirely rational or fair, the blame for these was laid at the feet of the regime. To the simpler people of Tamlaght, to whom the royal family were next to Musrum Himself—and probably far more real, a successful harvest was as much due to clement weather and skillful farming as to the benevolent graces of the king. If he *wanted* the autumn markets to be overflowing with agricultural bounties, then they would be. It was obvious to the Tamlaghtan farmer that so far as the present king (the fact that Ferenc was not yet legally possessor of that title didn't matter) was concerned, the farms of Tamlaght could dry up and blow away.

The poor harvest was naturally reflected in the increased prices in the city, inflating the crown even further.

The weather had been terrible, even for this time of the year. Paradoxically, the temperatures had been slightly above normal which, one would think, would have been welcome. Anything that would delay the onslaught of the bitter Tamlaghtan winter would be ordinarily embraced enthusiastically; however, the above-freezing temperatures transformed the expected heavy snows to heavy rains. It had been a constant deluge since the day Bronwyn had returned. There was disastrous flooding all through the south plains and landslips all through the north.

This wouldn't have happened under the regime of the old king, either.

The rains contaminated water supplies and in a nation with primitive—if not actually nonexistent—sciences of medicine, hygiene and sanitation, plagues began to spread in the city and towns.

There was terror, famine, sickness and poverty and it was all the fault of a new king who had made Musrum turn His great back on Tamlaght and its people.

To make matters worse, Crotoy decided to ignore the rigors of mounting a campaign in the winter and invaded the northern border country in force. This was the most recent development among the catastrophes which were piling upon unfortunate Tamlaght, and Bronwyn followed its course as closely as the newspaper allowed. Much was made of Ferenc's immediate and vigorous defense . . . it was clear that her brother was trying to make the most of this chance to gain a little public esteem. An army was mounted and sent north with immense fanfare.

For a time it seemed as though the people were finally being roused from their sullen stupor, given a common, popular cause and an effective leader to rally round. Bronwyn found the change in temperament reflected in her work. For a week there had been very little for her to do, since people no longer had either the money or inclination to eat in a restaurant or to stay in a hotel— in fact, she had begun to fear for the future of her employment. Now, ever since the Crotoyan hostility and the departure of the

Grand Army of Tamlaghtan Defense, she was washing as many or more dishes than ever.

But the euphoria didn't last. The ragged remnant of the army staggered back to the capital with a tale of ignominious and total defeat. Ferenc had wildly underestimated the number of the enemy—in spite of accurate intelligence to the contrary—and had sent to the border scarcely half the force that would have been necessary to repel Crotoy's invasion. If the truth be known, Ferenc had been more afraid of being without the immediate presence of his army than he had been of any remote threat offered by Tamlaght's neighbor to the north. A truth Bronwyn knew and few others suspected.

The people reacted to this final disaster with typical Tamlaghtan fatalism, retreating into a sullen gloom like children whose parents have inexplicably and unfairly punished them.

This past fortnight had not by any means been the brightest in Tamlaght's history.

Bronwyn decided that she must finally do something active before her country literally collapsed around her, pinning her beneath its helplessness and inertia like a wounded elephant fallen upon some hapless pygmy. But what? She had neither friend nor ally in the city . . . at least not that she knew of. She began a systematic elimination of the barons: where were they? None were in the city—none, in fact, were within a hundred miles of Blavek. All had retreated to enclaves as far as possible from Payne Roelt's Guards. Any barons who remained in the city were there permanently in the grimmest sense of the word. Or so she thought.

It was only a casual notice in the *Intelligencer* (" . . . perhaps sharing a cell in the Iron Tower with the infamous Baron Drypol . . .") that made her aware of the proximity if not presence of Baron Sluys Drypol of Graustark. A search through the back numbers of the newspaper stacked in the hotel lobby enabled her to piece together the baron's recent history. Like half a dozen of his peers, Drypol had been arrested and summarily imprisoned. Unlike his fellows, Drypol had so far escaped execution. The reasons for this were unclear and Bronwyn could only speculate, basing her conclusions on the vaguenesses the *Intelligencer* permitted itself and what little factual knowledge she could remember concerning the baron.

Unlike the other barons, who were fairly solid landowners, as well rooted to their respective landscapes as any oak or ancient

castle keep, Drypol was an adventurer. Although he had many
fine homes, including one with his large stables on the outskirts
of the city, he was content to leave the running of his estates to
the more capable hands of his caretakers and tenants—in fact,
there were more than one of his people who had been born on
the Drypol land and had grown to adulthood without once having
seen his landlord.

Drypol was a rogue. He had seen the world; he had dab-
bled in every romantic and adventurous profession, from mer-
cenary to merchant, from slaver to pirate (so it was said). When
Bronwyn had been much younger there had even been a series
of poenig one-sheets, which could be folded twice and trimmed
to make an eight-page booklet, detailing in lurid prose the baron's incredible and improbable adventures. She had eventually—
with some regret—come to realize that these were almost wholly
fictitious (with a cynical part of her brain even hinting that the
baron himself had most likely reaped a healthy percentage from
their sale).

While he certainly was not the best baron—considered as either
landlord or member of the House—by any imaginable means, he
was probably the best known. (Piers Monzon, it must be pointed
out, for all the popularity and respect he had commanded, was
best known among his peers and not the general public.) He
was virtually a folk hero, on a par with such historical and
semimythical characters as the Iron Duck, the Headless Knight
of Grand Fenwick, Blue Rupert and the Sponge-cat, or Groonla
the Pirate Queen.

Which all went toward explaining why he had not yet suffered
the same fate as many of the other barons. Even Payne Roelt
would hesitate before ordering the execution of a man so dear to
the hearts of several million simple peasants. While the common
people certainly were horrified by the fact of the murders of many
of the barons and their families (after all, there *were* women and
children involved) it is also true that those murdered were of a
class figuratively, literally and legally above their own—a class
that in fact and for all practical purposes owned the lower one.
However, Baron Drypol, in spite of his title, represented exactly
that supralegal freedom that was the canvas that the dreams of the
lower and middle classes were painted upon.

It was also not beyond the realm of the possible that Payne
might be hoping to seduce the baron. There were indeed certain
qualities of temperament and philosophy they appeared to share,

even if the applications of those qualities differed. But perhaps that was a difference too subtle for Payne to appreciate: that it was the *application* that made the difference, not the similarities of material. Anyone could possess oil paints and brushes, but possession alone did not make a Ludek Lach-Szyrma.

Bronwyn was convinced that if anyone could help her, it would be the infamous Baron Drypol. But would he? An even larger and more pertinent question was: even if he would, how could he do it from the Iron Tower? She was quite familiar with that landmark, though perhaps not so intimately as those more luckless had been. It was highly regarded as escape-proof and its three hundred and fifty years of unviolated existence bore out that reputation. A few months earlier she would have dismissed the idea of the baron's escape, but the second thing her recent experiences had taught her was that not much was actually impossible—improbable or implausible, certainly; but for an event to possess odds of infinity to one against, that was, well, impossible.

She would have to see.

The first order of business would be to try to get a message to the baron. She wrung her brain like a sponge for even a drop of useful recollection about the arrangements of the Tower. All she could remember concerned the details of the intense security, which only kicked a brace or two from beneath her shakily propped-up spirits.

One afternoon, when the rain had abated to a mere freezing drizzle, she strolled to the Iron Tower.

It was located upstream from Pordka Park, above the falls of the Moltus River. Bronwyn had to cross the little footbridge spanning the canal cutting the isthmus connecting the city with the mainland, then make a long uphill hike along a path full of treacherously muddy switchbacks. She saw no one else once she reached the deserted park above the falls.

The weather really wasn't the reason for the desertion: that was more or less its normal condition. Nor was it the fault of the falls—they were certainly spectacular enough. The Tamlaghtan personality simply wasn't predisposed to admiring scenery—especially scenery that required some effort to appreciate. They could see no point to it. The only other reason for visiting the park was a rather bizarre statue of Shahalzin Pordka, that, too, failing to tempt curiosity.

A path led from the long-untended garden that surrounded the Pordka statue to the Iron Tower, the square top of which she could see looming above the treetops, blurred by the drifting mists.

The Fortress of Kaposvar, to give the Iron Tower (which wasn't even truly a tower) its proper name, is one of the most curious specimens of those formidable masses which arose in Tamlaght's violent past. It has a fine feudal aspect. It lacks only knights in its vaulted hall and ladies in long brocaded dresses at its arched windows, and archers and crossbowmen at its machicolations, its battlemented galleries, at the embrasures, mangonels, portcullis and drawbridge. Its massive stonework is still intact, but the warden in his modern uniform, the soldiers with their up-to-date weapons, the warders and turnkeys who no longer wear the particolored costume—half green, half orange—of the old days, strike a false note in the midst of all this ancient magnificence.

It was in this donjon that the Baron Sluys Drypol was being held. To consider his rescue was unreasonable, no doubt, for the princess did not even know in what part of the building the prisoner lay, nor had she given any thought as to how they would escape the country together.

Perhaps it was fortunate that her ignorance was complete in this matter. Had she known more she might have recoiled before the difficulties, to say nothing of the impossibilities, of the enterprise.

Any escape from the Tower had up to then been considered impossible.

The Iron Tower occupies one side of a terrace. When leaning over the parapet of this terrace, one's eye plunges into a large, deep gulf, whose rugged sides, covered with thick entanglements of creepers, are absolutely perpendicular. Nothing overhangs the wall; there is not a step to enable anyone to ascend or descend, not a prominence to seize hold upon in any part of it; nothing but the vertical lines, smooth, eroded and irregular, which mark the oblique clearage of the rocks. In a word, it is an abyss which attracts, fascinates and has never returned anything dropped into it.

Above the abyss rises one of the side walls of the Tower, pierced with a few windows giving light to the cells on the different floors. Were a prisoner to lean out of one of these openings (if he were not prevented from doing so by heavy iron bars) he would recoil with terror, seized with a vertigo that threatened to drag him into the void below. And if he fell? His body would be dashed to pieces on the rocks at the bottom, then swept away by the irresistible torrent of the Moltus.

The front of the Tower, the side opposite that which overlooks the gorge, possesses the single entrance, or exit, to the donjon: a massive iron door that is perpetually and heavily guarded. To leave the Tower by that door would—assuming one had gotten past whatever obstacles lay on its further side—entail avoiding the several Guards posted outside, at either end of the drawbridge, and passing through another locked and guarded gate, this one in the spike-topped wall surrounding both Tower and moat.

Bronwyn returned the way she had come when her observations began to draw the attention of one of the outside Guards. She was deep in thought, and walked with her chin sunk onto her chest and hands plunged deeply into her pockets, unmindful of the cold drizzle that was soaking her.

She lay awake a long time that night, wondering what she could do. She had to find which cell the baron was being kept in, she had to discover some way of releasing him from that cell, and then some way to arrange his escape. She had to do something the most desperate prisoners of the last three hundred years had been unable to accomplish.

The next morning, when she entered the kitchen to forage for her breakfast, she was greeted by the laughter of the cook and his assistant.

"What's so funny?" she asked.

"Oh, nothing much, I suppose," answered the fat cook.

"It's just a couple of guests that checked in yesterday, that's all," said the skinny assistant.

"Well?" Bronwyn prodded, ladling a helping of porridge into a bowl.

"Never have laid eyes on them," continued the cook. "Haven't come out of their room since yesterday."

"I think they're queer for each other!" said the assistant, a leer further disfiguring his pimply face.

"You're a pervert, Skeeter Pelfo! You haven't even seen them! No, what's so funny, Miss Brown, is that they've just sent down for some food."

"Yes?"

"Well, one of them asked if he could have a salad on the side."

"So what?"

"He wanted a *moss* salad!" The cook collapsed in laughter once again. "Do you think maybe he'd like a few twigs and dried leaves? Or should we send out to a florist for a banquet?"

This broke the assistant up and soon both of them were wiping away tears.

"Moss?" Bronwyn said, mostly to herself. She had met only one person in her life who liked to eat moss.

It was simple enough to discover the number of the strangers' room; the cook knew what it was. She tried as subtly as possible to get a description from the desk clerk, but the old man never noticed anything—only enough of his brain functioned to allow him to show guests the register and to hand out keys. He allowed Bronwyn to examine the book but the name scrawled on the line opposite the number 12 was indecipherable; in fact, it looked like little more than a random squiggle. The mark of someone whose handwriting was abysmally terrible, of someone who was trying to disguise his name, or of someone who had never before handled a pen . . . and possibly didn't know how to write in the first place?

Bronwyn tried not to get her hopes up. She knew full well who she hoped was in that room, but she didn't dare believe in it too much. How could they have gotten here? They had to be either dead or in prison. It just wasn't possible!

There was only one way to find out. She sneaked past the desk clerk—a wholly unnecessary maneuver, engendered by the demands of guilt, since the old man would not have noticed a locomotive passing through the lobby—and up the narrow stairs. The two men had registered in room 12, a room on the fourth floor back. Her heartbeat increased in proportion to her proximity to the door at the end of the passage. By the time she faced the number 12, she felt as though she had a snaredrummer trapped within her breast.

She raised her hand and rapped on the door with her fingertips.

There was no answer but there were sounds from within. She rapped again and this time the sounds stopped. She summoned all of her courage and, pressing her face close to the wooden panel, whispered, "Thud? Is that you?"

The door opened so suddenly she toppled into the room.

Looking up from the floor she saw looming above her like a menhir and an obelisk the amazing figures of Thud and Gyven.

"What are you doing here?" she cried.

"Well, to tell you the truth," replied Gyven, "we were trying to avoid being recognized by anyone."

Bronwyn was hoisted to her feet by Thud and she said, hugging as much of him as she could, "Thud! I'm so glad to see you!"

"Me too, Princess."

"I didn't know what had happened to you! I thought that you might be dead!"

"I was worried about you, too."

"We'd better get this door shut," said Gyven. "No one knows you're here, do they?"

"No, no!"

"How in the world did you find us?"

"I work here!"

"What?"

"I work here, in the kitchen; I wash dishes!" she said, a little defiantly, a little proudly, a little reluctantly.

"I don't believe it! You?"

"What do you mean by 'you'?"

"Is it a good job?" interjected Thud. "Do you think there's anything I can do?"

"Not now, Thud," said Bronwyn. "I can't believe the coincidence, that you'd stay at the same hotel I'm working at!"

"It was the name."

"What? Oh." The name of the hotel was The Stoneman House.

"It's so good to see both of you," she went on. "I was so afraid that I was just letting my hopes and imagination get away with me. Thud, you look wonderful!" Thud shuffled his feet in embarrassment at the first compliment his physique had ever earned. "And Gyven, well . . . you've certainly changed!"

He had, indeed. His hair had grown out thick and black, and he was several shades pinker than his original chalky white—though how he had managed that not only in the winter but in prison as well, she could not imagine. If it was possible—and Bronwyn, for one, never imagined it could be—the man was even handsomer than when she last saw him. But the difference was more than just physical.

"Gyven," she said, "you sound so different . . ."

"I'm a fast learner," he answered. *He must be*, she thought. *He speaks better than I do.*

"What happened to you?" asked Thud, and she told what had occurred since they parted at Piers's camp as succinctly as she could.

"What do you plan to do now?" asked Gyven.

"Well, just these last couple of days I've had the idea of trying to get Baron Drypol out of the Iron Tower. He would know a hundred ways out of the country."

"*Sluys* Drypol?" asked Thud. "*The* Sluys Drypol? I think I've read every one of his adventures!"

"I'm sure you have," said Gyven. "I've evidently been missing something."

"Oh yeah, they're great! If we can get the baron to help us . . ."

"You say that you want him to help you get out of Tamlaght?" interrupted Gyven.

"Yes, you see, I believe that if I can get to my uncle in Londeac, that he'll be able to give me the help I need."

"Your uncle?"

"My uncle Felix—he's king of Londeac."

"I see . . ."

"It's all very complicated and goes back for generations, but you see, Londeac was once a possession of Tamlaght. Even though they have been separate countries for a long time now, the throne is still held by a branch of our family. I've never met my uncle, but I know that he doesn't approve of either Payne or my brother."

"But what do you expect him to do?"

"He and I'd have to talk about that, but I'm sure he'd want to do something. But tell me, I'm anxious to know what the two of you have been doing!"

The two men were now sitting, one on the bed that bent under his weight like a swaybacked horse, the other on the room's only chair, and Bronwyn cross-legged on the floor facing them.

"The story's easily told," began Gyven. "We were made prisoner by the prince's troops and taken, along with a great many other men, to the town of Biela-Slatina."

"Biela-Slatina?" Bronwyn interrupted. "Were there any gypsies there?"

"Gypsies? No, not that I know of. Why?"

"You talking about Janos and . . ." began Thud.

"Never mind now. Go on with your story, Gyven."

"There we were put under guard in a large compound. We were soon separated from the others because it had become fairly apparent that we were not like them. In fact, there was eventually little difficulty in convincing those in charge that we were not members of your cousin's army. You will recall that my education was still rudimentary and, combined with Thud's misleading appearance, they considered us feebleminded. We would probably have been released except for the misfortune of someone realizing that Thud matched the description of the man who had helped you escape from Blavek . . . a description, you will admit, that would be hard to mistake."

"I'm unique," put in Thud.

"Since we were obviously together we were both put under heavy guard and sent back to the capital for questioning. We've been here ever since."

"But how did you escape? And what about this education of yours?"

"Oh, well . . . our captors did not reckon with the rather unusual vocational experience Thud and I possess. 'Stone walls do not a prison make' certainly holds true for a pair of Kobolds— or, rather, a Kobold and a demikobold." He smiled a little ruefully, a little secretively . . . the first time Bronwyn had seen him smile, and her heart gave a disturbing quiver, like a dreaming kitten.

Oh my, she thought. Gyven's face was no longer the soulless mask it had once been, his eyes no longer expressionless spheres of glass, with neither intelligence nor personality. His language was stilted and formal, and he spoke to her like a schoolmaster; he held himself rigidly and correctly erect . . . but there was *life* to him now. Where there had been merely movement before, there now was energy; where his eyes had once been distant, they now possessed depth. The features that once looked like a woodcut now looked like a steel engraving. It was difficult for Bronwyn to rationalize, though she thought much about it later. It was as though the Gyven she had first met had been shaped and animated by entirely external forces, like a puppet, where this new Gyven was self-animated, like an internal combustion engine.

"We decided," he continued, "not to attempt running from the City. We are, as you well know, rather conspicuous individuals. We had managed to find some money during our escape, so it seemed to be a clever idea to find a hotel to stay in . . . it would be, we thought, the last place the Guards would look. We chose this particular establishment because, as you now know, the name was peculiarly appealing."

"I chose it because it was close to the palace," added Bronwyn. "Another reason, I guess, why no one would look for you here."

"I suppose the princess would not object to our offer of help in releasing this baron?"

"Of course not!"

"It sounds like fun to me," added Thud. "It's been boring here."

"I must be forthright and explain that my offer of help is not entirely unselfish. I presume that the princess has not forgotten her obligation to take me to Londeac?"

"Oh! of course not!" she said, but it had never crossed her mind.

"If she is planning to have this man aid her, then it would only be to my own benefit to help in any way I can."

Bronwyn explained the situation of the Iron Tower to her friends, drawing a plan for them:

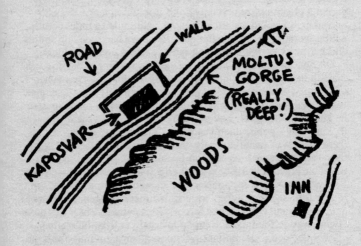

"It does seem formidable," commented Gyven. "I think the first order of business would be for you to determine which cell the baron is being held in. We can't make any plans until we know that."

"I have no idea how to do that," replied Bronwyn, "but I'll see what I can find out."

What she eventually discovered was that while security was excellent so far as the person of the baron was concerned, and so far as permitting the coming and going of visitors to the Tower, there were far fewer restrictions on inanimate objects. The administration of Kaposvar, after three centuries of escapelessness, had grown to believe that that was a quality inherent in the Tower itself. They had therefore gradually narrowed their responsibility to simply maintaining the impossibility of physical escape. That is: so long as windows were too small for egress, doors were made of iron and kept locked and barred at all times, lavish use made of Guards at all points, day and night, and anything large enough to contain a human being forbidden entry or exit . . . then nothing else need concern them.

All to the end that Bronwyn could, if she was clever enough, get a message to the baron.

She thought about how to do that for several days. She sought advice from Gyven, but he was at a loss. He was obviously clever enough and his spoken vocabulary was mysteriously excellent, but both of these qualities were neutralized by his lack of experience in the outside world.

In the meantime, there was terrible news. The coronation was finally going ahead. A firm date was set, only a fortnight hence, and preparations were set in motion (most of which had been only marking time since the last postponement).

What irked Bronwyn was that the event was to be held on Saint Wladimir's Day—what had once been her favorite holiday of the year. She had a collection of stuffed toy momraths in her room (which she wondered if and when she would ever see again), traditional Saint Wladimir's Day gifts accumulated since her birth. Wladimir, the patron saint of Blavek, had been a gentle hermit priest of some five hundred centuries earlier, lived in the bole of an enormous tree high in the Toth Molnar mountains, above the Zileheroum. His only friends were the momraths that roamed the dense forests—in much greater numbers than they do today. The orphaned ones the kindly old man took in, feeding and clothing them, selling a few on the side as fuel. One day the poor saint was mistaken for a momrath and martyred. It was just like Payne and Ferenc to use such a revered and festive holiday for their own purposes.

The coronation was to be the gala event of the century, and the palace's propaganda machine was going to make the best of it. Dozens of public works projects were announced and commenced, so the people would associate civic improvement with the new regime. Some of these were genuinely useful, while others were purely cosmetic, such as new parks, statues and murals, or ephemeral, such as banners, flags and posters. In the bleak, grey days of early winter and recent misfortune, the sudden and intense work added a badly needed gaiety to the city, a sense of purpose and hope. One could see and feel the morale of the citizens rising daily.

The propagandists made the most of this, and every number of the *Intelligencer* carried enthusiastic notices and editorials, underlining and applauding the palace's "firm commitment to roll up its sleeves and get to work creating a new and even better Tamlaght." Not mentioning, naturally, that outside the city limits things were as bad as ever and getting worse. The Church was recruited into the effort, and sermons were delivered whose texts left the impression that if Tamlaght was being shunned by Musrum, then it was only because the nation was, technically, without an ordained ruler. Once the coronation could be held and the prince be made king both legally and spiritually, Musrum would once again look benevolently upon the benighted country.

This was convincing to the lower and lower middle classes, but was only so much superstition to the business class. For them, the *Intelligencer* and the financial newsletters ran plausible analyses arguing that the national depression was mostly the fault of the prince's powerlessness. Uncrowned, he simply hadn't the authority to take the necessary strong measures required to restore Tamlaght's high standard of living.

All of the aristocracy had been invited and the hotels and inns were beginning to fill to capacity, and beyond. As a public token of accord, even the remaining barons were invited—a private thumbing of the royal nose, since none would dare refuse.

Fearful that the influx of members of her class would increase the chance of running across someone who knew her, Bronwyn quit her job and convinced her friends to join her in moving to a small roadside inn on the north side of the upper Moltus, between the northbound canal and the Iron Tower.

"The night of the coronation will be perfect for the baron's escape," she told her friends. "The confusion will be intense: it'll be a perfect diversion for us. The chances of getting away will be increased a hundredfold."

"I can see that," replied Gyven. "But we still need to know where Drypol is being held, before we can even consider how to get him out."

"Come on with me. I think we might find out this afternoon!"

The little inn lay at the edge of a woods that abutted the deep gorge above the falls. Directly opposite this point, on the other side of the river, was the Fortress of Kaposvar. Bronwyn, Gyven and Thud could safely observe it from the shelter of the heavy foliage that grew to the very brink of the abyss. The chasm was narrow here, only a little more than a hundred yards or so, but very deep, its precipitous black walls dropping without relief into the boiling water below. Anything falling into the river would be instantly swept away, to be carried over the Pordka Falls less than a quarter of a mile downstream. The roar of the river was tremendous and the air was wet with mist. Within the shaded gorge, the rock walls were glazed with ice and the limbs and branches surrounding the watchers were sheathed in transparent tubes, as complexly interconnected as some chemist's esoteric apparatus.

From their viewpoint the fortress presented a single, nearly featureless wall, continuous with the cliff below it, and pierced by a dozen small windows, looking terribly small in the vast smooth expanse of stone. The roof was steeply pitched and covered with heavy slate shingles. Two lightning rods stabbed skinny iron fingers into the sky. Cables ran from these down the face of the wall, eventually dropping into the chasm. To either side of the facade were two small wings where the surrounding wall joined the building. One wing had a semicircular opening at its base from which poured the overflow from the moat, creating a monstrous icicle a hundred feet tall.

"He may not even be in one of those cells," said Gyven. "Perhaps he's in one facing the other way."

"Just a moment," said Bronwyn. "I'm looking for something . . . Ah! There! See?" She pointed to a window near the left center of the wall. It was distinguished from the others by a small white patch. Gyven strained his eyes, trying to pierce the mist.

"There's something tied to one of the bars," he said, finally.

"That's what I thought," said Bronwyn, just a little smugly.

"What is it?"

"That's Drypol's cell," she replied.

"How do you know that?"

"I figured out how to get a message to him. You've seen all the religious tracts that have flooded the city? Most of them telling about how wonderful my brother's reign is going to be? I don't know why, but I was browsing through one—for laughs, I guess—when a passage caught my eye. It said, 'By a sign I shall know thee; by the symbol of thy purity shall I know thy place.' I don't know what it was supposed to mean; it was probably referring to my brother, Musrum forbid, but it gave me an idea. I marked that passage and sent it, along with a few others as camouflage, to the baron. I'm sure that his mail is severely censored, but I didn't think that they'd hold up anything of a religious nature. I was right."

"Well," said Gyven, "if that is his cell, now what?"

"I found out that much—I was hoping that you'd be able to think of something. You're the expert at jailbreaks."

"Let me give it some thought."

"Don't be too long about it."

That night, Gyven asked, "Do you think that you can get one more message to the baron?"

"I don't see why not. What?"

"I'd like him to put a candle in the window."

"A candle? What for?"

"I'd rather that you see when the time comes."

This annoyed the princess, who loathed mysteries, but Gyven refused to discuss it any further. Scowling, Bronwyn began to shuffle through the brochures and leaflets. It took her an hour to locate a passage in one of the tracts that she hoped would give the baron the right idea. It said, "Against My coming, make of your soul a lantern to guide My way." Not too bad, she hoped.

In the morning she sent it off by the first post. It would be at the fortress within a few hours. Gyven had vanished at first light, leaving the princess and Thud to entertain one another, an interesting task for both.

It was Saint Wladimir's Day, the day of the coronation. Before the sun set, her brother would be king. There would be no stuffed momrath for her this year.

The inn was deserted, as was most likely the case with every hostelry in the city. Most of the population would be crowded into the vast plaza in the center of Palace Island. The ceremonies and festivities would continue all day and well into the night. If there were to be any perfect time to effect an escape from Kaposvar, it would be now.

Gyven did not return until late afternoon. The sky had been growing more threatening all that day, thunder rumbled in the distance and the air was charged with electricity. Bronwyn's clothing and hair crackled with every movement; sparks popped from her fingertips every time they approached metal. A storm of extraordinary violence was clearly being promised. Gyven was carrying a pair of enormous bundles, which he deposited on the floor of the room with a heavy clatter.

"What's all this?" Bronwyn asked.

"You'll see," he answered. "There's not much time for explanations. Get your things together. We must be prepared to leave immediately."

Bronwyn wordlessly packed her few belongings into her rucksack. Neither Thud nor Gyven possessed anything to take, other than what the latter had just brought in.

They left the deserted inn unseen. In a few moments they had crossed the road, entered the woods, and were soon again within sight of the fortress. The trees surrounding them were swaying erratically in gusts of wind that blew from every direction. Between the roar of the river, the thunder that reverberated from the walls of the canyon and the rustling trees, Gyven had to shout to be heard.

"Look!"

In the dark mass of the fortress glimmered a single pale light. Gyven began unwrapping the bundle he'd been carrying. He revealed a crossbow of huge proportions.

"Where did you get that?" Bronwyn asked.

"Never mind!" he answered as he took in hand one of the heavy ten-inch steel quarrels. To its nether end he tied one end of a ball of string, then took several minutes to unwind several hundred feet of the twine.

"What are you going to do?"

"Watch!"

Placing a foot in the stirrup that terminated the wooden stock, he cranked a two-handed winch that pulled back the steel wire until the bow—as massive as a carriage spring—cocked. He inserted the quarrel with its trailing string, then, bracing the weapon atop the stump of a broken tree, took careful aim at the fortress.

"Wait a second!" cried Bronwyn, realizing what Gyven intended doing. "What if you hit the baron?"

"I don't think that I will! He must be expecting something like this!"

"How can you know that?"

But Gyven ignored her. He adjusted his aim microscopically, took a deep breath and pulled the trigger. The quarrel shot into the darkness with a wicked hum.

"Did you hit the window?"

"I think so! There! Look!" The candle made a circular motion, then disappeared. "Quick, Thud! Tie the rope to the end of the string! Hurry!"

Thud had already dumped a coil of heavy rope from the bag he was carrying. Without any wasted motion he tied its end to the remaining end of the string.

Gyven meanwhile had taken from a pocket a stub of candle and a box of matches. Hunching over to shelter it from the wind, he attempted to light the candle. Unfortunately, he had not counted on the storm and the erratic wind blew out his matches as fast as he struck them. Bronwyn, seeing what the point was, said, "Give me those!" and took the box from his hand. "All you want is a signal, right?"

"Yes!"

She took the box, opened it so that its contents were exposed, picked up a small rock and struck it across the match heads. The entire mass ignited at once with a flash and a flame a foot long. Bronwyn dropped it from her scorched hand with a cry.

But it seemed to have done the trick: the string began to move again, drawing off into the darkness of the abyss. When its end was reached the rope to which it was tied began to move, sliding across the wet grass and over the edge of the precipice like a suicidal anaconda.

"All right, Thud," Gyven shouted. "Get the rope secured!"

Thud tied their end of the cable in an elaborate if uncouth knot to the bole of a massive oak. A moment later the rope was taut—a nearly invisible, tenuous bridge linking the two sides of the gulf.

"I hope that the baron is as intelligent as you say," said Gyven. "Thud, are you ready?"

"Yes!"

"All right, then, *pull*!"

The two men grasped the rope and did just that.

"You've got to be mad!" cried the princess. "That won't work!" But they pulled just the same. Under the strain, Thud seemed to grow more compact and massive. His broad, flat feet dug six inches into the earth. Gyven, at the same time, was transformed into a kind of industrial machine, all steel and cables, pistons and drive rods.

The rope thrummed like an organ pipe and the princess could not imagine what kept it from snapping, even though it was nearly an inch thick.

She peered into the gloom. When the clouds of mist parted she could see the window clearly. By Musrum! There *were* cracks showing all around it; as she watched a large flake of masonry fell into the chasm. But that was all.

"It's not working!" she cried.

"I know what to do!" said Thud, suddenly.

"What?" said Bronwyn, desperately.

"What?" said Gyven, skeptically.

Thud untied the rope from the tree and took it to a huge boulder that stood at the brink of the cliff. The rock was as large as a small house, or so it seemed to the girl. It was, at least, several times larger than Thud. The Kobold took the rope in both hands, so that it made a vast loop, and tossed it over the boulder. He then tied it securely. The rope now came in from the darkness, made a turn around the tree, then ended at the boulder. Thud made a signal to the other man, who joined him behind the rock. Together they began to push against it. Under their combined masses, the rock, unbelievably, began to move.

"What are you doing?" cried Bronwyn, almost afraid to believe what she was seeing.

The rock began to oscillate like a ponderous metronome and the two men worked with its natural period. With each outward swing, it hung just a little further over the abyss. In the flashing lightning and swirling, misty rain Thud and Gyven looked like creatures from some primal, pagan mythology. Suddenly, with a grinding crash, the top of the boulder tipped past its center of gravity and plummeted into the chasm like an inverted rocket.

"Watch out!" screamed the princess. The rope snapped as taut as an iron rod with a sound that rivalled the lightning, as though Musrum Himself had just cracked a titanic whip over their heads. From across the gorge came a crackling burst that could be heard even above the thunder. The rope screamed as it wound around the big tree, nearly sawing it in half in a cloud of acrid smoke. An instant later something as large as an adult ox smashed into the tree like a meteorite, throwing splinters, rubble and dust in all directions. Bronwyn was thrown to the ground by a whipping branch and was only prevented from going over the edge of the cliff by the strong arm of Thud Mollockle.

"Are you all right?" he asked.

"I think so! Where's Gyven?"

"Here!" came his voice from the other side of the vast, grey mass that had nearly crushed them all.

"What is this?" she asked, then realized that she was looking at most of the outside wall of the Tower cell. "Holy Musrum!" she said to herself.

"Where's the baron?" she shouted to Gyven. "What's happened to him?"

"There he is!"

She looked across the gorge. In the lurid electrical illumination she could see that there was now a gaping black hole where the baron's window once was. A pale figure stood within it.

"It's the baron!" she cried. She waved to the figure, who waved back.

"We must hurry!" said Gyven. "What Thud accomplished won't go unnoticed!"

"How can we get him out?"

"I'm not sure! I think he needs to get to the roof! If he can get up there, then perhaps he could lower himself to the top of the wall there, where it meets the Tower." He pointed to the low wing with the outlet for the moat's overflow.

As he spoke, Gyven reloaded the crossbow. Once again he tied a string to the quarrel. This time, however, he aimed higher and the heavy projectile carried the line over the peak of the roof. "If he can get up there, he can pull over another rope to use!"

"But how can he climb up?"

"Look!"

The figure in the wall-less cell had swung out of the opening. Not more than a yard from the hole was the iron cable of the lightning conductor. By grasping the edge of the broken masonry with one hand, he was just able to reach the cable. Bronwyn gasped and shut her eyes when the baron swung from the cell, supported for the moment only by his grasp on the wet wire rope. Using the staples that attached the conductor to the wall, the baron began to climb the cable.

The wind had increased during the last quarter-hour—all the time that had passed, amazingly, since they first arrived at the cliff—and now howled down the confining chute of the gorge. Bronwyn had to hold onto the branch of a tree for security, and could only wonder at how the baron was able to withstand the buffeting gale that must be trying to pluck him from his precarious hold.

Lightning laced the low, smoky clouds and the thunder was almost a continuous roar.

The baron was only a yard or two from the eave when Bronwyn cried out, "Look!"

The twin spears of the lightning rods were glowing with an eerie, flickering aura of blue-violet light. The atmosphere was so heavily charged with electricity that Bronwyn could feel her skin prickling and the hairs on the back of her neck starting to rise. She had no idea what would happen to a man holding onto a lightning conductor when it was struck . . . her physics were not up to that. The baron's figure became radiant; pink and yellow rays shot from it and sparks flew from his fingertips, even from the ends of his every erect hair, so that his head was surrounded by a coruscating globe of fire. Bronwyn, certain that the baron had been fried like a moth in a candle flame, squeezed her eyes shut against the uncanny vision. However, when she opened them again, the baron was not only still there, but had managed to clamber over the projecting eave and was on the edge of the roof. The electrical effects were abating, though the lightning rods still flickered fitfully, gobbets of violet flame running up and down them like ghostly squirrels.

The baron quickly found the string and began reeling it in, eventually bringing a hundred feet of rope across the gorge; it now lay coiled at his feet. Carrying this to one of the lightning rods, he tied one end to the base and threw the other over the edge of the roof, where it dangled across the wall below.

"He's going to make it!" shouted Gyven. "Come on!"

Bronwyn, with Thud close behind, followed Gyven out of the woods. Running down the road, heedless of being seen—though that was unlikely on this night of all nights—they crossed the river by way of the scenic footbridge over the falls. Bronwyn, who never could run very far without cramping, had to stop. She was panting fitfully and the painful cramp in her side was bending her double. The road to the fortress was uphill from here and daunting. Gyven, with scarcely a pause, swept her into his arms and carried her. He seemed totally unaware of her weight. His arms felt to Bronwyn as though she were resting on a cradle of hard oak.

The vicinity of Kaposvar was reached in only a few minutes, and they slowed in order not to attract attention. Anyone not at the coronation would be instantly suspect. Gyven dropped the princess to her feet and the three left the road, cutting diagonally through a small woods toward the corner of the fortress wall that met the cliff. They were just in time to see a dark figure drop from the wall. Bronwyn gave a short, low whistle and the figure immediately turned toward them.

"Baron Drypol?" she asked.

"If you are my unknown friends, I am," was the reply.

"This is Gyven, and Thud Mollockle, and I am the Princess Bronwyn."

"Well, I'll be damned! What an interesting evening this is becoming."

"We'd best hurry," urged Gyven.

"Yes, indeed," agreed the baron. "I don't know how you people did it, but you've stirred up the whole fortress. They have no idea what happened, but they're searching the place and it won't be long before they discover that my cell no longer has a wall. Fortunately you chose a perfect night: the place is seriously understaffed."

"We'd better go," said Bronwyn.

The quartet found a shelter back down the road, erected for the sightseers who never came to the falls. The rain had finally begun in earnest, now that the preliminary electrical display was over. It was a deluge that quickly turned the narrow road into a river of mud. In the obscurity, Bronwyn was able to get her first real look at the baron. He resembled to a degree that surprised her the romanticized illustrations in the weeklies: the same tall, lean figure, gaunt face with eyes in a perpetually amused squint, long, erratic nose, upturned moustache and pointed goatee. His normally curly black hair was plastered to his head, revealing a normally hidden bald spot on his crown. However, instead of the flamboyantly fashionable clothing he normally affected, he was dressed in the flimsy pajamalike uniform issued by the prison. Gyven removed his own coat and draped it over the baron's shoulders.

"What a pleasure it is to see you, Princess," he said, with a bow. "I'm at your service!"

"That's what I had hoped you'd say," she replied.

The coronation, as it turned out, was a social disaster. Many of the old nobility had refused to attend, disdaining the anger of the king, protesting Payne's presence. Those who did attend were scandalized beyond expression when Payne was allowed to blasphemously carry the crown in the procession to the altar. More than one head turned nervously ceilingward, hoping that the wrath of Musrum would manifest itself in a carefully aimed fashion.

The arrangements for the coronation had been left entirely in Payne's hands and he botched them, well, royally. Schedules were either impossible to meet or were not met at all; nothing was on time and many sacred and traditional events were cancelled out of hand or performed out of their proper order. Ferenc was rude to everyone and Payne supercilious far above his birthright; the representatives of a score of ancient families—who had arrived willing to forgive and forget—went away insulted and offended.

Afterwards, the new king held a private party in the great lodge that dominated the Catstongue island, a celebration of victory that was going on well into the early hours of the following day. He and Payne surrounded themselves with their closest sycophants and toadies. The party was that sort of orgiastic revel that only Ferenc could organize or desire—especially now that he literally knew no restraints. There were several orchestras, trestles bending under the weight of more food than most Tamlaghtans were likely to be seeing over the entire winter, fountains of champagne and wine, glossily handsome men in full evening dress and fashionably beautiful women in spectacular evening undress—all of whom looked like they had been ordered from a catalog—and a gloating and bloated king looking down upon it all. To Ferenc, this was all that being king meant—he desired nothing more than an endless continuation of this night. To Payne there was only a herd of sheep and he was mentally flexing his shears.

Even the king was not so stupefied as to not be surprised when the enormous glass double doors at the head of the ballroom crashed open, showering his startled guests with a bright, tinkling hail. The music stopped, dying out raggedly as the individual musicians became aware of the disturbance. A monstrous black horse plunged through the open doors, looking as though a ragged piece of midnight had been ripped from the sky and flung into that little box of lurid, inimical illumination. It made the ballroom's brilliance look bleached and garish. Its vast hooves, each the size of half of Ferenc's head, sent pieces of parquet flying as they sunk inches into the floor. It looked around with rolling, wild eyes, its breath roaring and steaming like a supercharged engine. The woman riding it appeared almost diminutive compared to the shimmering monster. After only a moment's hesitation, the horse and rider, having found their bearings, approached the dais upon which sat the new king and his chamberlain. No one dared stop them.

Ferenc had turned a shade of blue-white that made his eyes
and nose almost luminously red in contrast and the tablecloth
he clutched split, spilling wine and food unnoticed into his lap.
Payne stared at the rider with an expression of mixed consternation, fury and frustration. Why had he ordered General Praxx
away from the island for the evening? (He did not know it, but
at that very moment the general was on his way to investigate the
mysterious disappearance of both a wall and a prisoner from the
Iron Tower.)

The slim figure, clad entirely in black leather, with a black
domino across the eyes, stared insolently at the two figures on
the dais.

"*Bronwyn!*" hissed Payne, who, as we have seen, was no
fool.

"What?" said Ferenc. "What?"

"I've got a message for you!" said the black rider.

"Someone stop her!" shouted Payne, a little shrilly, but not a
soul in the ballroom moved. One woman was weeping loudly;
the horse nickered impatiently.

"I've got a message for you, Payne Roelt!"

"What is it? Just what do you hope to accomplish?"

"Your defeat!" she answered. "I'm going to see you dead!"

"How? How are you going to do that? It's too late, Bronwyn,
can't you see that? How can you think of threatening me? You're
all alone; it's all just words, Bronwyn, just words. Do you know
how seriously I take this? I'll not even call the Guards, I'll not
have you pursued . . . You're harmless to me now, so threaten
all you like . . . you're only a minor nuisance. Someday I might
choose to slap you down, like an insect, if I decide to take
the trouble. So go ahead, do your worst . . . you simply don't
frighten me!"

"*I should!*"

She wheeled the midnight horse around and left the ballroom
with a sound that blended with the thunder of the storm outside.
The chamber shuddered with her passing.

Payne Roelt had just made the biggest mistake of his life.